IGNITION

LAUREN DANE

PRAISE FOR LAUREN DANE AND HER NOVELS

"*Inside Out* is tender, romantic, and unapologetically sexy...Lauren Dane writes with an emotional depth and authenticity that always leaves me breathless. Simply put, I love her books!"
—Lara Adrian, *New York Times* bestselling author

"Hot, hot, hot with the right mix of tenderness and depth! In other words, don't walk, run to read!"
—Carly Phillips, *New York Times* bestselling author on *The Best Kind of Trouble*

"*The Best Kind of Trouble* is a great example of what Lauren Dane is known for—strong family ties and confident characters with an extra touch os sexiness for good measure!"
—*Fresh Fiction*

"The perfect combination of sexy rock-star fantasy and emotionally tender romance."
—*Kirkus Reviews* on *The Best Kind of Trouble*

"Most remarkable is the fierce power of Dane's uniquely confident heroine, whose strength gives this story power... Dane's mastery of her characters and their emotional complexity shines, making it a book fans will savor."
—*RT Book Reviews* on *Broken Open*

"Sexy, pulse pounding adventure with a heart twist of emotion that'll leave you weak in the knees. Dane delivers!!"
—Jaci Burton, *New York Times* bestselling author on *Uncovered*

"Lauren Dane books have become a staple in my reading library. Her stories are character driven, emotional, and always a lot of fun to immerse yourself in for a few hours."
—*Romance Junkies*

"Lauren Dane is a highly talented writer who delivers emotionally charged, deeply sensual tales that are sexy, fun, and intimated."
—*Night Owl Reviews*

FOREWORD

Dear wonderful readers,

Ignition is the second in an expanded series universe that includes my Brown Family, Hurley Boys, Delicious and Whiskey Sharp books under the Ink and Chrome title.

Ignition is the story of Alexander, "Xander" Copeland Keenan, the son of Erin Brown, Todd Keenan and Ben Copeland (**Laid Bare**). He works at Written On the Body, a tattoo shop owned and run by his uncle, Brody Brown (**Coming Undone**) and Raven Warner (**Drawn Together**).

The other hero is Hamish Wilson, a singer songwriter we met in Ink and Chrome 3, **Coming Back**, as he's Jessi Franklin's brother.

And Pippa Hall, entirely new to these books, though she's close with the Franklin family and besties with Rennie Brown (Brody's daughter).

I hope you enjoy these three as much as I loved writing their story!

Lauren

CHAPTER
ONE

At the hail of his name, Xander set his sketchpad back on the shelf at his station, but when he walked to reception and saw Pippa Hall standing there, a shaft of pale, late-afternoon sunlight caressing her face, his fingers twitched. An urge sent from his brain to the part of him always ready to draw. The curves of her cheeks needed to be put to paper. The coppery tones in her eyelashes caught the light.

The outside was attractive enough, but something far more than looks called Xander's attention to her. She exuded an honesty and sweetness like perfume. What he'd considered curiosity had deepened into a craving in the two weeks since he'd first met her at a family party.

That night they'd chatted quickly about the tattoo she'd been scheduled to receive from his uncle Brody. After some fancy talk, Xander managed to convince her he had several great concepts already for the life cycle of a butterfly she wanted.

In the weeks since he'd texted her several times,

ostensibly to talk about the design she'd finally chosen after tweaks. He was a busy person, but he found himself turning toward her repeatedly. Even if for just a few lines and an emoji.

And when she turned and their gazes locked, his already very good life got better. All the noise and chaos seemed to fade away when she was near. Like every part of him focused its attention to her.

"Hi there, Xander," Pippa said, her mouth tipping up into a smile. "Ready for me?"

Was he? Hell if he knew. Normally he kept things mellow and casual, but there he was pulling her into his life.

The open, pleased tone in her voice stirred something deep in his belly. More than the chemistry that hung thick between them, there was a recognition there. Like he'd been waiting for her on some level. It was novel enough he couldn't wait to see what else was in store.

"Hey." He smiled at her before he leaned down to hug his cousin, Rennie, who also happened to be tight with Pippa. "Wasn't expecting to see your face. Though I'm not complaining. Are you here to keep Pippa company?"

If she didn't say no, Xander was putting coal in her stocking at Christmas.

"Not today. I've got a lunch date with my dad. I'll see you later, Pippa." Rennie hugged her and headed toward the back where Brody, the owner of Written On the Body, was working in his office.

"Again, I do appreciate you fitting me in today," Pippa told him as he led her to his station.

Deep-copper curls tumbled to her shoulders. Shiny silver clips caught it away from her face. Freckles danced over her cheeks and nose, peeking through the makeup she wore. She was under five and a half feet tall, petite but powerful in jeans, boots, and a light-purple sweater that hugged her curves.

There were moments around petite women where simply due to his size, he felt like a marauding Godzilla, or he was so worried about stepping on a toe or whatever that he kept a distance.

But she invited him closer. Didn't shrink away from the full force of him, and that was rather delicious.

Speaking of delicious. She smelled like sugar and something smoky and sexy. He desperately wanted to know what she tasted like.

Instead of giving in to the wild impulse to kiss her like some fuckin' weirdo, he led her to his station where he'd left the design they'd agreed upon a few days earlier. "I know we've spoken about these, but if you find you don't like it now that you're seeing it in person, I can adjust."

He'd created the butterfly as the center of the tattoo in blues and purples, with the green and brown of the chrysalis and the caterpillar as pops of color to draw the eye to the way they melded into the body of the butterfly in one instance and parts of the wing elsewhere.

"My plan is to focus on the purples, blues, and greens." He indicated the accompanying full-color sketch. "They'll last longer than yellows or orange would." He pointed out two other versions. "These are similar."

"I'd imagined it as a monarch, so with oranges and blacks, but this..." she held up the one that was his favorite, "...is better. It's delicate but not weak, if you know what I mean. I love the combination of all the colors and the way it's made up of individual parts, but when it's looked at as a big picture, it's one thing on a continuum. Different and yet the same thing all at once. I know it's the point. I still think it's magic."

"I'm glad you like it. That one was my top choice too." There was a warm, pleasant weight in his belly at her words. "Let me get this on a stencil. I want you in that chair, facing the back."

In an economic motion, she grabbed the hem of her sweater and pulled it off, leaving her in a halter bodysuit beneath.

He'd already noticed how she blushed. With her pale complexion, he bet he could clock every emotion on her skin.

Soon enough, he'd set up his inks, got the positioning of the stencil set according to her preference, and his hands were on her right arm as he adjusted the arm and headrest.

"What's the longest you've sat for a tattoo?" he asked her, putting thoughts of how sexy Pippa was away for the rest of the appointment.

She held out her other arm to show him a tattoo of a black-and-gray-shaded wrench. It was well done, all the dents and cracks as metal morphed into bone, the shading rendering it nearly three dimensional. A piece like that took a meticulous and patient hand and a great deal of experience. He recognized it without even being told who the artist was.

"That took two and a half hours," Pippa said.

"Raven is so damned good," he murmured as he took one last look before straightening.

"I love her work. I had just tossed out some ideas of

things I liked, and she created a few different sketches like you did. This one was it for me the instant I saw it. At some point I'm going to have her add some flowers for a pop of color. And the one Brody did is a blackbird on my hip. Simple. That was my first one, and it took less than an hour."

"Big jump between less than an hour up to over two. The positioning of this one won't be as painful as it might be in other places, but there'll be spots that hurt. If you need to take a break, let me know. There's no reason for this to be agony."

She smiled, and it sent a shiver over his skin. "It's okay if it hurts a little."

Christ. A blast of heat exploded through him. He coughed to cover the indrawn breath, and a dimple to the right of her mouth showed up for a moment.

He put gloves on and moved the light until he got it perfect. "Tip your head a little to the left." When she did what he asked and he was satisfied with the way the skin and muscle lay, he said, "Try to keep this arm relaxed."

The way she complied so easily flipped every switch he had. He *liked* being in charge, and not just when someone was in his chair.

She sighed softly as she settled in, and he picked up his tattoo machine, not missing the way her lips curved up as the hum filled the air.

Two weeks ago, Pippa had picked her friend Rennie up from a family party at her parents' house. When Pippa had gone inside to get her, she'd been enveloped by a wave of Rennie's loved ones. She'd been introduced to what felt like a hundred people, all of them colorful and charming and attractive. It had been no small amount overwhelming. Though she'd already known Rennie's parents and sister, the place busted at the seams with the genetically gifted.

And that had been before she'd been introduced to Xander. She'd sort of forgotten they were on their way out the door as he'd flirted and charmed her. Not a bit of artifice to it. He was smart and funny, and she hadn't been able to get him off her mind in the days since.

By the time she and Rennie had managed to get to the car, Pippa had found herself with an appointment in two weeks' time to get a tattoo from one of the country's next generation of ink superstars.

They'd texted and emailed back and forth to consult on the design, and she'd wondered if that arc of attraction they'd had at the party was a one-time thing. She got her answer when he'd come out to the waiting area and her senses had gone into overtime. Absolutely gorgeous.

More than tall, he was broad-shouldered. He was bigger than she'd remembered, even after looking—like fourteen times—at a recent magazine spread that featured multiple pictures and poses.

In person he also had...*substantial* energy. It drew her attention and held it. Magnetic. A lot of men his size made her uncomfortable. Their energy felt more like restless aggression. Xander took up space but not at her expense.

Sun-kissed skin, hazel eyes with lashes so thick and dark it looked like he'd lined his lids with black. He had a septum piercing which took the prettier parts of him and gave them an edge. It was mid-September, and it had dropped to the low fifties, and he wore a navy long-sleeved shirt that hugged his shoulders distractingly. His beard was perfectly trimmed, and when he smiled, her stomach and parts lower warmed and got a little fluttery.

His hair was short on the sides and back, but the top was thick and longer, a fetching bit of caramel brown he'd shoved back from his face with a very large hand at the party, but at work he had it caught away from his eyes.

Even as he jabbed ink into her skin with multiple needles, his touch was patient and gentle. The sound of the machine and the haze of pain that wasn't entirely negative seemed to lull her into a place where she floated as he spoke.

"We didn't get to talk much at Brody's birthday party," he said as he stood next to her, the heat of his body washing over her exposed arm and shoulder. "Not as much as I'd have liked. How'd you meet Rennie?"

He would have liked? All sorts of happy chemicals surged in her. "Twisted Steel is in a warehouse district. There are several other businesses and a few industrial art spaces like Rennie's in the same area, so multiple food trucks show up daily. My first week there, Rennie and I ended up in line together more than once. Friday morning, over a breakfast burrito, I asked her if she wanted to come to the film festival with me and another friend. We've hung out regularly since. Rennie was sort of a package deal, because when Martine moved back to Seattle six months ago, we became close. After I got to know Brody and Elise, I understand why their daughters are so wonderful."

"I can't believe I've never met you before that birthday party."

"I wager we're most likely not in the same social circles." He was in the super-gorgeous, inked-up-son-of-a-rock-star club, and she was in bed by nine thirty and took her slippers and an extra blanket when she traveled.

"My *cousins* are my social circle," he said, amused.

"You mean your cousin Miles, the international superstar? Or his fiancée, also a famous musician? Or do you mean Rennie, with her art shows and accolades?"

Rennie painted hyperrealistic works that were so detailed, the color so perfect, the application so precise, they looked like photographs. Miles was the lead singer of a band called Earthquakes, and they'd spent the last three years on back-to-back sold-out tours to support back-to-back hit albums. Handsome, talented, newly engaged, *and* he'd just wrapped his first major film role.

Xander spoke as he worked, his voice wrapping around the whine of the tattoo machine. "Okay, so we're not normal in the usual sense of the word. My family is huge, but super tight. A lot of us work together. We've never met an occasion we won't throw a party for. We've taken vacations together my whole life. There are chefs and caterers in the crew, so we're always well fed. Naturally there's fantastic music. We're like a small town really."

"Okay, I can see that." She tried to stay still when she laughed. That would be some magical small town. "I imagine being famous makes it even more important to have that safe and trusted circle of people. The outside world is sketchy enough without fans."

"That's totally true." He paused a moment. "My sister was killed by my mom's stalker. Back before I was born. But it changed everything. She withdrew from the spotlight. Stopped touring for several years until after my dads came along. And then me."

"I'm sorry I brought up a sad memory." She wanted to kick herself for not even thinking about that. The story of what had happened to Erin Brown and her young child had been the subject of more than one of those ripped-from-the-headlines-style shows the entertainment channels loved.

"Take it from me, you can't possibly run everything you think or say through an internal check. It's a thing that happened, and a million and one different triggers can pull it out of the blue. There's nothing for you to be sorry about. I'm just agreeing that having a tight circle of those you can trust is really important."

"Your family is special." There was a lull as he worked, and when he didn't add anything to the topic, she shifted it, not wanting him uncomfortable.

Which was...something she wasn't sure how to feel about. Pippa had spent her life until she was fifteen being taught all her focus should be on everything else but herself. Her parents, the phantom of the future husband that'd been the ultimate goal of any girl's life where she grew up. God. The church. Her younger siblings. The household. She wasn't on the first page of the list.

So she'd spent a lot of time unlearning. Finding a balance where she could care about and for the people in her closest circle without losing herself and what mattered to her. It brought up things both positive and negative that he evoked a protectiveness she rarely felt outside her very own closest circle.

"How long have you been tattooing?" she asked, giving them both space.

· · ·

The way she'd been paying such close attention was fucking delightful.

"Goes back to that small town I was talking about. My mother owns the café next door, so some of my earliest memories are of being there. At the back of the building there's a corridor running between the café and here. I spent so many hours of my life sliding back and forth, loving both worlds. One with food and my mom, and the other, ink and color. Brody would put me in a chair in the corner of his booth and let me watch him work. Raven gave me my first sketchbook when I was five and made a place in her station for me to keep them once I filled them up. I was eleven or twelve when Raven let me help *her* with some of her sketches. Fifteen when I did my first—very simple—tattoo. Once my uncle was satisfied I was serious about tattooing and being a tattooist, he let me apprentice. Which at the start is little more than sweeping and setting up stations between clients."

"Same in most repair shops," she murmured. "I've cleaned a lot of employee bathrooms. So disgusting. Swept up a lot of shop spills."

He liked that shared bit of history with her.

"I've cleaned the bathroom here plenty. Fortunately, Raven established some basic cleanliness rules before I was even born. Since everyone is afraid of her, it wasn't too bad." His mom's best friend and essentially his second mother was known for her larger-than-life personality, take-zero-bullshit attitude, and incredible talent.

"I was nineteen when I did my first solo tattoo that was more than a few lines. Got my own chair here all official like when I was twenty-one. I've had a client list pretty much since then. I've never wanted to be anything else. Oh, well, other than the year I tried to convince my parents I needed fencing lessons because I had plans to be in the next Olympics. Imagine my disappointment when I found out it took years of work and skill."

"Stop. You're going to make me laugh, and then I'll make you mess up the tattoo," she told him, amusement in her tone.

Her eyes were closed, and she looked utterly relaxed.

"You're obviously a natural," she said, sending warmth chasing through him. "The pieces included in that magazine article about you were all so good. Gave me some ideas for future work."

"Lucked out having two such close adults in my life who took the time to train me and trust me."

"Lucky for them too, I'd wager."

His mother would love hearing that.

"Well." He paused and then gave in to curiosity. "Which were your favorites? From the article I mean."

"The art nouveau woman's face with the purple flowers. I've seen that one in person, and I know it's even more stunning than the photos. When Rennie told me it had taken ten hours over two sessions, I could believe it. The detail work is evident."

"My family bravely allow me to tattoo them. Like I said, I'm fortunate," he told her, not wanting her to think he was a braggart.

"Or maybe it's that they're honored to have you tattoo them because you're so good. Food for thought."

·   ·   ·

Pippa rested her head and closed her eyes, letting the whine of the tattoo machine wash over her. A year and a half earlier, she'd gotten her very first tattoo. The experience had been hypnotic. It had hurt but in a good way. In a way she was certain she wasn't supposed to like but did just the same. Then, she told herself it had been the novelty of the experience.

A tattoo would have been impossible in the life she'd been born into. It had taken over a decade away from the group before she could even accept the growing desire to get one.

But then Raven had done the wrench on her inner arm, and over the few hours it had taken, Pippa had realized her reactions were far more than the rush of breaking a former taboo. There was something delicious about the sounds and vibrations of the machine humming through her, the sharp edge of pain and the tiny earthquakes of pleasure that soothed her agitation right down to her very soul.

Those two experiences had been pleasurable but *not* in a sexual or romantic way. She'd gone a little floaty. But this was different. The way his hands were on her, firm but gentle as he worked, not restraining exactly, but it got close enough that suddenly it was all her brain wanted to think about. Xander clasping her wrists, holding her down.

"How did you learn to fix cars?" he asked, head bent close to her skin. The vibration of his voice seemed to swirl around all the other sounds like a slow, firm stroke over her skin.

Pippa had to dig deep to find the control to answer his question before she had one of those phantom orgasms that wisped away right as you woke up from your dream.

"I grew up in the middle of nowhere. It was necessary to know how to fix the washing machine, the various lawn mowers, and other such things. One of my older brothers is really good with engines, and I watched and then pestered him until he gave in and started teaching me." It was best to skip the part where she'd been so good at fixing engines, her mother, and the aunts, stopped pushing to get her back in the house where she was supposed to be full-time. After she and her sisters had been forced to leave, Pippa'd had a marketable skill. One of the few she'd been given by her family or anyone within the group.

"Then when I moved to Washington with my sisters when I was fifteen, I registered for school midyear, and the principal put me in auto shop after I successfully argued her and my social worker out of another shop-based class. They agreed, but thought it was just a place to keep me until I could transfer into something else. But I loved it, and I was already good at it. I did some repair work regularly. Under the table of course. But it helped pay the bills. I kept at it, and then the school sent me off to a local technical college to take classes there once there wasn't anything left for me in high school. One of the teachers knew Hap, my old boss, was looking for someone for his shop. I did a work study thing there until I graduated, and I started full-time."

"Sweeping floors?" he teased.

"Yes. Dealing with all the worst jobs. I'm good with engines, but I was eighteen years old, and the shop was full of men in their forties. I had to bust my bottom for *years* to get them to take me seriously." It had been Hap, always on her side, always finding ways for her to gain more knowledge and experience while holding her out when she did a good job.

"Try being the nephew of the guy who owns the place," Xander muttered.

"Ah, I can see that." It was hard enough to prove oneself in the world; to have to overcome preconceptions that you only got your position because of who you were related to would be frustrating.

"Floor sweeping is a great equalizer for everyone," Brody teased as he approached. "Mind if I take a look?" he asked Pippa.

"Sure. Long as Xander is fine with that."

Xander shifted back from her body while his uncle turned a critical eye on his efforts.

"Boy's good at floor sweeping and tattooing," Brody murmured.

"I can also make a very good grilled cheese sandwich." The pleasure in Xander's voice was obvious. Pippa found herself liking him even more for it. He was a grown man with his own client list, but it was important his uncle respected him.

"Gonna be a stunner when you're finished," Brody told him.

Brody came and went over the next three hours. Checking on the work, but really it seemed to Pippa that he was pleased with his nephew's talent and genuinely wanted to watch the process. It made her like both men even more.

Finally, Xander sat back with a pleased sigh. "Take a look," he invited.

She paused in front of the mirror, holding another in her hand to reflect the back of her shoulder. He'd managed to create something that was big and strong but feminine and suited to her form and her personality. The blues and palest of greens bled into the browns and scattered bits of purple in exactly the way they did in real life.

"This is stunning." It made her feel beautiful. Like a piece of art.

"Yeah?" His smile as he stood and approached her had gone...different. A bit of that professional distance had fallen away. "I'm glad you like it."

He gave her instructions on aftercare, and he took her up front to pay. She disagreed with him briefly over the discount he gave her. "Friends and family. Don't argue. It's one of the benefits we provide. Helps make up for the fact we're noisy and in each other's business all day long." His grin lit up all sorts of things inside her, like a video game.

Once that had been taken care of, he put a hand on her arm to stay her movement as they neared the door. She looked up and then up some more. The intensity throbbed from him, leaving her a little breathless.

"Can I ask you a personal question?"

She nodded.

"Are you single? Now that you're not actively my client, I wanted to see if you were hungry and up for grabbing dinner with me. Or, even if you're with someone, I like you and I'd like to know you more. Honestly though, I'm hoping you're free."

"I'm dating people, but no one exclusively. And I'm starving."

CHAPTER
TWO

The restaurant was intimate. Nice and dim inside as candles cast romantic shadows against gleaming wood tables and railings. Music played but it was muted as they were led to a table by a server who was clearly happy to see them. Probably Xander most of all, and Pippa got why. She liked looking at him too.

Even better, it got them a great table off in a corner with a view of the rest of the room and a basket of bread with olive oil and balsamic vinegar before they'd even sat down.

Xander pulled out her chair and made sure she received a menu first. Oddly, she wasn't on guard because of it as she might have been back home. Where such behavior from a man often meant control. It nearly always came with ulterior motives.

Xander did seem to like taking charge. But he also appeared to have good manners, and she imagined—though it annoyed her to think of him with someone else—he was the same on any date. He gave off caregiver vibes, which she was fine with because she had her own tendencies toward such things.

It was nice to be taken care of in small ways. It meant someone else was thinking about her comfort. Her safety. Her pleasure.

The want to share that, to show those things to someone else, was strong. A pang echoed through her chest. A moment when she missed the only other person who called to her and her desire to spoil. Pippa wanted to comfort and take care of Hamish, but he got a little freaked out by it, so she'd reined those impulses in and accepted him for where he was in his life.

And it was time to stop thinking of anyone else when she was having the beginnings of what she hoped was a nice dinner with a guy she found herself really liking.

He scooted his chair closer to hers. Taking up space but not crowding her.

"You smell really good," she said without thinking.

"Thanks. One of the cousins makes perfume oils, and she made this one for me on my birthday last year. She says her goal is to create signature scents for everyone in the family. There are a lot of us, so good luck to her."

Without thinking, Pippa leaned in and took a long sniff at his neck. Embarrassed, she began to rear back and apologize, but he hummed in a very sexy way, putting a hand at the back of her chair. *He liked it*. Okay then.

She was terrible at this whole thing. Dating and trying to monitor her reactions so she didn't freak anyone out with her weirdness. But she hadn't scared him off. Not yet.

Emboldened, Pippa said, "A perfumer? Add that to the actors, dancers, painters, musicians, and tattoo artists." The whole family just seemed to burst with a need to create things.

"Right?"

Once they'd ordered, he poured them both a glass of wine.

"We've got a software developer, two social workers, a few ranchers, caterers, security types who work with my dads and my uncle, to balance everything out."

"Your dads who are married to your mom who is, well, let's be honest here, an icon. I feel like that bumps it up into artist territory on the cool scale."

He snickered. "Fair point. They like to think they're regular dudes, but yes. The fact that they run security for rock-and-roll tours and the like does bump them into the artsy category." He paused and then asked, "What about you and your family? Any funky jobs as cool as yours?"

"My sister, Rebecca, is an executive assistant to a high-profile attorney. She's got a gift for getting people to do whatever she wants them to and her boss benefits, so she gets paid really well and has excellent health care and a retirement plan. She and Vivi, that's her fiancée, live in Queen Anne. My other sister, Esther, lives in Fairbanks with my brother-in-law. He's a pilot for a small regional airline, and she's a corporate travel specialist. Essentially, she handles the travel for various businesses. It's a nifty job though because she gets to travel all over the place. Most everyone else I know is a grease monkey like me with some artists tossed into the mix."

"Are you close with your parents?"

"No."

There was a massive period at the end of that one-word sentence. So heavy he barely suppressed his wince. "Apologies." The last thing he wanted to do was hurt her feelings or make her uncomfortable.

She waved it away and kept eating her ziti. Finally, she said, "The sisters I told you about? The three of us are very close. They're more like aunts than siblings. They've raised me in a lot of ways."

"The ones you moved to Washington with?" He remembered the story she'd related while getting her ink.

"Yes. I was fifteen. They were twenty-two. Twins. Well, they're still twins." Her laugh was genuine and affectionate, but he thought about all she'd shared, and he had a moment of wonder at how easily she'd found some pleasure in the midst of it.

There was a lot to unpack with what she'd revealed. Questions he desperately wanted the answers to but knew he'd have to wait until she trusted him more. Why did she move to another state when she was just fifteen? Her sisters had been barely legal adults. Clearly it was about her parents she wasn't close with.

Protectiveness rose in him in a relentless wave. It took him aback. Rarely was that depth of feeling aroused by anyone outside his immediate circle.

"The funny thing is, Rebecca applied for an administrative position at the security company your dads run. We'd just moved here, and she didn't have much of a resume, so she didn't get it. But small world, huh? She said Todd recommended another place that was looking for people and was willing to train. He was kind. Which is not always as usual as it should be. Kindness when you need it most is the best sort."

"Small world indeed. That's wild. I'm glad—but not surprised—to hear he made a good impression. He's a solid dude, and I'm lucky to have had him and my dad raising me." He added, "I call one Pop, that's Todd, and Ben is Dad."

"Aw, I really like that. Plus, if they both have a different parent name, you can avoid a lot of pronoun confusion with all those *he* and *his* in any given conversation." She laughed, and he liked her so much for it.

He also liked that she didn't seem overly fascinated or in possession of any negative feelings about the shape of his parents' relationship, and he said so.

"Oh. Well, Jessi Roberts is one of my closest friends, and she's involved in a triad. I've spent a lot of time around her and Adam, and Mick is my boss, so I suppose it's not that unusual to me anymore. Your parents have been together decades by this point, so they must be doing something right."

Xander wouldn't have said it was a test really. But how people reacted to his parents and their relationship was nearly always an indicator of who they were inside. He'd learned that the hard way over the years, and it had left him even more protective than he already had been.

"I've heard a lot of ignorant bullshit, but that matters less when I've always had a close circle of loved ones who made the bad stuff not quite as bad."

She cocked her head and then smiled softly. Xander gave in to his desire to tuck an errant curl back from her face.

"You test my control," he said softly.

"Me?"

It had been a long time since he'd craved someone this badly. She called to every aspect of him. All he wanted was more.

He told her, "Somehow, I think I can manage this growing need to know you better. Maybe it'd be easier though if I knew you were feeling similarly."

Her expression brightened, and she said, "I am."

He nodded and took her hand, turning it to kiss the inside of her wrist. "Other than being a mechanic, what do you do for fun?"

"Rebecca and I have season tickets to the 5th Avenue Theater and the Pacific Northwest Ballet, so we regularly see shows. I love theater and live music." She paused. "I grew up in a family who looked upon such things as ungodly. We only had praise music during church services, and we didn't dance. I took a dance class at the community center near our apartment when we moved up here. I'm not that good, but I make up for it with my absolute love of movement. So now I watch incredibly talented people do it."

The curve of her lips into a different sort of smile chased arcs of chemistry between them.

"How about I make you dinner Friday night? You can come over and watch a movie." It wasn't so much that he felt an urgency in asking her out. But a yearning.

"Friday night my sister and I have tickets to the ballet. I'll be away this weekend. Rennie, me, and Jessi are all heading to an arts festival up in Port Townsend. I'll be back Sunday night."

"Tuesday night?" He had Wednesdays off. Also, he wasn't entirely used to being told no the first time he asked someone out. Huh.

"Depends on the movie," she told him, teasing. "Your family has a horror movie thing. I'm good with most horror, but I don't like excessively gory, rapey, or violent. Your aunt and uncle have good horror movie taste."

She'd even had movie night with them? "Seriously gonna have to talk to Rennie about hiding you from me for so long. It's...I don't know...I'm a little bummed you were right there, a step outside my vision the whole time." He ran a hand over his beard.

Pippa's intake of breath sent a blast of heat through him. Tangled him in the way she reacted. Left him utterly aware of her.

"I don't know if I'd have been ready for you even six months ago, much less a year."

Her quiet words were unsettling. But in a way he wanted to wallow in. Still, he let it go because he needed to think about it before commenting.

Instead, he replied, "I've got a pretty large collection of movies and access to streaming channels, so I'll come up with some options for you to choose from."

"All right. I'd like that."

After sharing a slice of chocolate torte, he drove them back to where her truck was parked. He really wanted to kiss her for hours, but first he needed to be sure she was right there with him in that.

He'd been chewing on what she'd said over dinner about not being ready, and though he should have left it alone, Xander found himself reaching out to touch her. The swell of her cheek called to his fingertips, and he gave in. Unable to stop his satisfied grunt when she leaned into him.

"Earlier you said you didn't know if you'd have been ready for me before, why is that?"

When she'd made the comment—blurted it more like—she'd been high on bravado. But right then it was harder. Pippa considered her words carefully. For both their sakes.

She decided on, "You're a lot. Big and tattooed and pierced. You fill a space effortlessly. You're very sexy and so confident in all those things. Not a surprise, but I find those traits attractive." She sucked in a breath as she thought, but it was full of him. "I've spent the last nearly fourteen years confronting, digging into, and then—mostly—throwing out the worst of the things I was raised to believe. That's taken up quite a bit of my time and effort. Between that, my sisters, and my job, someone like you expressing an interest in me would have overloaded all my circuits. Okay, scratch that, you specifically. Now?"

His expression had started intent, a little sweet, but by the end, his eyes had gone slumbrous, and one corner of his mouth canted up. Sexy AF. That's what he was.

Being with him in that moment wasn't scary. It was joyous and full of potential. It was time to open herself up to the possibility of a relationship with someone other than Hamish. Fate had put her and Xander in one another's path. Pippa liked him. Xander was compelling, and she wouldn't turn that away. She wasn't a coward.

"And now?" he prompted.

"Now, I'm still probably not ready for you," she admitted with a laugh. "But I want to be."

He hummed, and his fingertips were back to trace the curve of her cheek.

"I'm not sure I'm ready for you either," he said quietly.

She was entirely certain that had to be false. Who was she that he had to be ready for her? She was a regular-smegular person. Everything about him was unique and accomplished.

"I have every certainty you'll succeed," she said, and then realized how much innuendo she put into it. Giddiness rushed through her like bubbles in champagne.

He smiled. "How do you know I'm pierced?"

An unexpected question. "I can see your ears and your nose. And I...well I looked at the magazine spread. Congratulations, again. Some of the photos of you were shirtless. I'm not...congratulating you on your shirtless body, though, I mean. You should be proud. So, I...the nipples I meant." Her face was on fire, so she knew she blushed like mad.

"Ah."

"Are there piercings I can't see?" She nearly clapped her hand over her mouth but then decided not to be embarrassed at all.

"Do you *want* to see them?" he asked, his voice going lower.

Them? A flash of heat licked through her.

"Probably," she said.

He grinned, a flash in the dark between them in the front seat of his car. "Do you have any piercings?"

"Nowhere exciting." Her voice went up an octave.

"Everywhere on you is exciting," he said as he traced around the outer shell of her ear with his pinky.

"Why?" The question was out before she could call it back.

He cocked his head. "Why is everywhere on you exciting?"

Pippa licked her lips. "Why do you think so?"

"The first time I saw you, it was your eyes. The way you took everything in greedily. You were so open and friendly. You have this curl right here." He tugged it. "And it kept working itself free of the barrette. As if it declared itself independent of its brethren. I haven't gotten it out of my head since. I haven't gotten *you* out of my head since. Something about you calls to me. Speaks my language in a way that lures me away from the rock I like to hide under."

Envy and admiration filled her at equal turns that he could be so free to say such things.

"And that's exciting?" Surely his world was far more interesting than anything Pippa got up to.

"Very," he said, and then his lips were on hers. Gentle at first as he waited, listening to her reaction. Pippa knew to her toes if she'd indicated discomfort in any way he'd have backed right off.

Consent was so sexy. Especially from someone who could simply take what he wanted.

She ran her palm against the warm, taut skin of his neck and up into his hair, pulling him closer. An invitation.

Pippa loved kissing. It was delightful, but low stakes usually. Fun without being too much or worrisome. Different people kissed in vastly different ways. Hard, soft, in between.

Xander's kiss was a slow seduction. Little pecks. Nips of her bottom lip followed by a gentle suck. She leaned into his hold on a sigh, and his clever tongue swept into her mouth, sliding along hers. He tasted like the chocolate mint candy from the dish at the hostess stand.

She scored her nails along the back of his head, swallowing his growl in response.

The hand he'd had at her cheek tunneled through her hair. One of her barrettes flicked away, pinging off a seat, and it didn't matter. The heat of his other palm singed her as he caressed up her side, over the outer curve of her breast, and then rested against her throat as he held her. Not confined. Cradled. With an edge.

Xander was very much in charge of what was happening. Not in a way that robbed her of her own will. But oh, she wanted to give over to it, to that control and power.

Outside the car, people walked past on the sidewalk just beyond the low wall around the parking lot. For a time, none of it intruded on their world and those kisses, but ten minutes later a car alarm sounded in the spot next to where they sat.

Xander wrenched himself back with a groan. "It's Brody."

Pippa tried not to gulp at the sight of Xander backlit by the white glow of the security lighting. His face was rendered in shadows, so it was hard to see his expression, but what flowed from him in waves was barely reined desire.

It was so much she drowned in it for long moments, enjoying it, even if she wondered if she was up to the task with a person like Xander. Hamish was hiding from himself, but the man across from her seemed to know exactly what he wanted, how he wanted it. Without hesitation.

"Don't forget our place so we can get right back to it the

next time we're alone. Let me get your door," he said, proving her unspoken thoughts true.

Pippa thought she said something like *sure*, but it came out like a wheeze. Which seemed only fair given how sexy he was.

"Hey, Brody." Pippa waved after she got out.

Brody's gaze went to Xander, and Pippa wasn't certain, but she thought she caught a smile. "How was dinner? Elise and I had lunch there last week. I had the pesto with prawns. Now that I've just described it, I think I'm going to see if she wants to go tomorrow."

Pippa laughed. She liked Brody Brown and the way he'd made some room in his family for her. At first it had been for no other reason than she was Rennie's friend. But he and Elise had truly welcomed her, and as Pippa had gotten to know them better, she'd realized how lucky she was to have them in her life.

"It *was* excellent. I'm all carbed up and ready to change into pajama pants when I get home. My exciting life. I'll be in bed by ten thirty after I do my skincare regimen."

Xander bumped his hip against her playfully. "It's working for you though. Sleep is important."

Brody looked at his nephew again, this time with more scrutiny.

Finally, he tipped his chin. "I'll see you tomorrow, Xander. Have a good night, Pippa. Rennie says you two are headed to some sort of arts festival this weekend?"

"Sunday up in Port Townsend. One of the guys I work with at Twisted Steel has a vacation house not too far from town, so we'll spend Saturday night there and come back home after the festival on Sunday. Should be fun."

"I'm sure you'll all have a great time and be so safe no one's dad will worry."

Pippa laughed, truly liking Brody Brown. "We'll do our very best."

He got into his car and took off, leaving them alone again.

After unlocking her door, she tossed her bag into the truck. When she turned back to Xander, he was so close she ended up pressed against him. Not that she was complaining.

"Will you text me that you got home okay?"

No one other than her close friends and her sisters had ever asked such a thing. It made her fluttery inside.

"Okay. Thanks for dinner and the tattoo."

He bent to kiss her again, quickly but thoroughly. When he straightened though, he paused, reaching out to touch her seat belt briefly. "Talk to you soon. Take care of your tattoo."

Still, as she pulled her truck out of the lot and pointed herself toward home, her mouth tingled.

CHAPTER
THREE

Pippa woke up early on Sunday and took her mug of coffee out to the deck running along the back of the house. It faced Discovery Bay in the distance and was surrounded by trees. Jon Kingston, her friend, and co-worker at Twisted Steel, had offered up a weekend at his vacation home as an auction item for charity, and Pippa had snapped it up, along with lunch at one of the restaurants nearby.

The festival had been a great reason to bid and an opportunity to hang out with her girlfriends doing something fun away from home. She was often really busy, so any chance to be still and listen to the birds and the wind in the trees was one she tried to avail herself of.

The doorbell sounded, and she hurried back inside to see who it was.

"Delivery from Tastee Doughnuts for Pippa Hall." Pippa managed to locate a tip from the pocket of the jacket she'd worn the afternoon before.

The note read, "*I figured something sweet might hit the*

spot on a weekend getaway with your friends. See you Tuesday. Xander."

"This guy," the delivery person said. "Said all this stuff about you and how he wanted you to have a nice breakfast. Oh!" They held up a large, insulated tote. "Fruit variety, juice, and iced coffee."

"He's certainly working overtime with this stuff."

"What's going on?" Rennie asked as she shuffled into the kitchen where Pippa was unloading the food.

"Xander sent breakfast."

"My Xander? Wow." Rennie opened the doughnut box and chose a cinnamon twist. "He asked where we were. I guess this is why. Good luck resisting him. He's like this when he wants something." She waggled her brows.

"I'm not really trying to resist him," Pippa said, filling her own plate and settling in the sunny breakfast nook across from her friend. "I like Xander, and I can't lie, I also like that he's openly into me. I don't have to guess if he's interested."

"I have to say this whole song and dance where we're supposed to wait around to let the other person decide when and if we ever actually discuss feelings is stupid and I hate it. I'd set it on fire if I could," Rennie said as she topped off both their mugs of coffee.

"And if they're not being aloof, they're love-bombing you. Three minutes after you meet, they're telling you how perfect you are." Pippa groaned after a bite of the blueberry doughnut. "This is delicious. Anyway. It's nice. It's normal. It's brand new. Sending doughnuts instead of roses is a point in his favor."

Jessi came in shortly and joined them for doughnuts and coffee as they planned the rest of their morning. They'd take one last stroll through the festival. There'd be sales that day, and Pippa was already doing her holiday shopping. They'd grab lunch in Bainbridge and then catch the ferry back to Seattle.

When everyone headed to their rooms to gather their stuff, Pippa took a moment to text Xander.

"Thanks to you, our stomachs are full for the morning we'll be spending shopping. Very thoughtful."

It was lovely to know he'd been thinking of her.

Her phone pinged right after she'd zipped up her cosmetic bag and tucked it into her suitcase.

"I'm glad they were a hit. I tossed in the fruit in case you were feeling virtuous."

Pippa typed, *"I didn't expect you to be up yet."* No lie, it was nice imagining him still in bed, texting her. He seemed like the type to sleep naked when she was fantasizing about him.

"I'm at the shop already. My first tattoo is in about twenty minutes. Finishing up a half sleeve and then I'm doing two smaller tattoos before the day is done. I'm glad you reached out."

She was too, even if she had no idea what the heck she was doing. Dating was confusing enough. Dating multiple people at once was...not optimal. She was a person who wanted to be in a relationship. She'd dated someone for eighteen months, and it had been fine. Nothing more. Nothing less. Eventually, he broke things off and got married to his new girlfriend six months later. It hadn't been fraught at all. Pippa liked his wife and was the first to say they were suited for one another. They still sent her cards at Christmas and had two kids in elementary school.

And then the prior year, she'd met Hamish. Which had changed everything and nothing at the same time. That was a whole thing in and of itself.

Hamish with his hard outer shell and soft center. There'd been something between them from the start. Some spark that had ignited a fire between them.

He saw her in ways no one else did. He had unexpected depth in a variety of circumstances and topics. He was a poet whose heart had been so battered he'd stopped giving it out because he lived in fear of being left behind.

Which left Pippa in a no-man's-land of sorts where he couldn't let go of her entirely, but he seized up any time she got too close. All while she'd done what she could to be consistent and reliable in his life.

It was complicated. But she couldn't imagine her life without him.

Hamish adored Addie and James Franklin—his parents—with every part of himself. He hadn't been born to them, but that wasn't the important part. They'd given him a safe, permanent home with structure and rules. And so much love and support the street kid he'd been hadn't known how to process it for a long time.

No matter how wary he'd acted, how many buttons he pushed to test their commitment to him, their love and support had never wavered. Very few people in the universe knew the real Hamish Wilson. Even fewer knew the real him and loved him anyway.

Addie and James were his parents because they'd been

the ones who'd helped him understand he was worthy of the love and safety they offered as part of their family.

Currently, Hamish stood in the kitchen with his father, the main cook of the bunch, as his mother broke up a fight between a cat and a bird who remained out of reach while calling down insults at its furry sibling.

It was blessedly weird in a normal Franklin way. It settled him.

"Just leave the room and it'll stop," Addie muttered to the cat. Looking quite offended, the cat cast an angry glance up at the curtain rod where the bird had perched, and then with one last twitch of a very fluffy tail, sauntered away like it didn't matter anyway.

Addie spun and made a sound of warning toward the bird, pointing at it. "You will most assuredly *not* fly over that cat to harass her. Enough. Be nice or I'll put you out with the chickens."

James chuckled at that as he put a slice of garlic bread on Hamish's plate. "How have you been? Haven't seen you for a week or two."

"I had to run to Los Angeles—just a quick two days—to attend meetings and sign things. When I returned, I admit I holed up in my studio. I'm slowly starting to work on some new songs."

He'd been afraid he'd killed his creative mojo after his last tour. Nearly two years on the road had sucked the life out of him by the end. What he'd needed was to fly off somewhere sunny and tropical where he could be by himself in the quiet for a while. Naturally he'd ended up in London where it had been anything but quiet.

But only for a short time. Because while he'd been visiting his parents, he'd met Pippa. And two weeks into his London binge of excess, he'd tapped her phone number on his phone screen, and then pretended he'd done it on accident.

But when he'd heard Pippa's voice on the other end, he'd gotten his shite together and had finally headed to a cabin in the woods where he'd slept a lot, journaled and made lists for the next stage of his life and career, and let himself sit in the discomfort of kicking the sleeping pills he'd become accustomed to. And in those hours when he'd chosen to plow through his issues through writing, he realized he'd been using the chaos of that life to keep the door closed on anything truly intimate with anyone else.

He started to sketch out ideas for his next album and the next tour—and he made plenty of notes about how to structure live shows that wouldn't end up duplicating what he'd spent three months detoxing mentally and physically from.

He was grateful for the success he'd busted his ass for so long to earn. Even more so at the way his career and success continued to grow and mature with each new release. But there were aspects of celebrity he was wary of. Touring and fame were a theme park. Fun while it lasted but they weren't real. They weren't forever. And behind the curtain was where all the real stuff happened.

Real life was to be lived with people like Pippa. He just wasn't entirely sure if he could manage to give her what she deserved, what she needed. Love, yes. Could he stay faithful and be there whenever anything went wrong? The idea of failing her was more than he could wrap his head around. And until he got to a place where he could understand it, he couldn't get close enough that she was any more hurt than she'd been.

A kiss on the cheek from his mother as she passed where he'd been leaning against the counter brought him out of his head.

"Jessi said you've been hard at work. We're very glad to hear it. Your color is good too. You're no longer so thin I was worried you needed medical help. The dark shadows are gone from under your eyes."

There was a commotion at the front door, but no one paid it any mind. People constantly came and went from the Franklins'. Aside from Hamish, who'd come to live with them when he was thirteen, they had three adult children: Jessi, who was a costume designer, and the other two—Leif and Charlie—who worked at the veterinary clinic on the property along with their dad. Add all the various partners, children, and friends who made up their large circle of intentional family, and that meant there weren't always a lot of quiet moments in the main part of the house.

But then he heard her voice and everything inside him went taut.

Pippa bustled into the kitchen with Jessi at her side. Her hair was piled up into a bun, exposing her neck and the curves of her features including those big brown eyes that widened and filled with pleasure at the sight of him there.

"Pippa, love, what a pleasant surprise," he said, already on his feet and moving to her. The ease with which she slid into his embrace and the way she fit perfectly against him seemed to kick down the doors of his resistance.

Had him questioning why he'd thought he needed to

keep himself away from her when she clearly didn't want that, and for fuck's sake, neither did he.

"I thought you were still in work mode," she said, stepping back and then hugging James and Addie.

She wore a navy-blue sweater with white polka dots, and jeans. Simple and pretty. He wanted to bask in that even as the twin desire rose to dirty her up.

"I was just saying I've gotten a lot of work done this last ten days or so. When I got a text saying a certain someone had made garlic chicken and there were lemon bars for dessert, I knew what was good for me. I jumped in my car and came right over where I've been fed and loved up on. And then you." Hamish couldn't resist one last touch to her cheek before he took bags from Jessi, along with a quick hug.

"Are you hungry?" James asked them.

"Yes! We had lunch, but that was hours ago. We just dropped Rennie off at her apartment, and Pippa was kind enough to bring me over so I could grab my car. And lucky us, Hamish is here." Jessi sent him a sunny little-sister smile that was bright and full of affection but also had something sneaky going on.

More than his little sister; she was his dearest and most trusted friend and ally. So, she was a pest who barged into his home and his life regularly to nose around in whatever it was he got up to.

He'd moved to a house less than a mile from hers so she could do exactly that.

"There's a litter of puppies at the clinic," Addie said. "Someone dumped them in the ditch near the mailbox on the main road."

The house and the second building that held the veterinary practice sat on an acre and a half of land and were set back from the main road up on a gentle rise. Hamish could remember easily a dozen times various animals had been dumped somewhere on the property by their former owners.

"What is wrong with people? Are they okay?" Pippa clasped her hands in front of her chest, eyes wide, mouth turned down. So upset over puppies being mistreated.

Christ, he was mad for her.

He'd told himself over and over *she wasn't for him*. His life was too fast and rough for a being like her. She was soft. Kindhearted. He'd taken her on several dates, and they'd ended up in bed repeatedly. She was anything but soft in bed. Christ, he'd never experienced the type of chemistry and attraction he had with her. But it had been those hours he'd stolen away with her that had changed him fundamentally. Quietly tucked up in her little townhouse watching movies as she crocheted the whole time had created a craving for more.

And for the first time ever, he found himself thinking about love and a future with someone. Someone who knew him on levels very few did.

Which terrified him. *She* terrified him. There were no masks with Pippa. It lightened his heart even as he'd thrown distance between them, telling her he was working through too much shit to be in a serious romantic relationship.

He'd noted the brief flash of hurt in her eyes when he'd said it, but she'd respected what she saw as a boundary.

Like a fool, he'd thought prioritizing the friendship over commitment would be a way to have her in his life without the eventual hurt he'd bring if he tried to be a boyfriend. He wasn't a good bet. He couldn't bear to be a disappointment in her life.

But all it had done was allow him to get to know her better and on a deeper level when both their defenses were down. She was unlike most everyone he'd known, and there was no one else he wanted. No one else fit him the way she did. He treasured it. Craved it. In the late hours when he'd been unable to sleep, he'd written about her instead. Let his lyrics speak when his heart really wanted him to stop fucking around and give himself permission to love her.

The feral part of him, the remainder of that street kid, couldn't take the risk. But the man he'd grown into yearned for what she brought to his life.

"Go on out and give them a snuggle. Charlie's over there now, so you can give her a cuddle too," James said. Charlie was the oldest of the Franklin siblings, and though she'd been in college when he'd come to live there, she'd bossed him around like she bossed Jessi and Leif around. Like he was her brother. The first time she yelled at him for using her special hair conditioner something in Hamish that had been waiting to be rejected eased up.

Which he supposed was a good thing because both his sisters were incredibly bossy and nosy. It ran in the family full of intelligent, successful, brilliant women.

"I'm going to unload all these veggies first and join you in a bit," Jessi said to Pippa.

"I'll come along. Can't refuse puppy cuddling," Hamish teased, laughing as he sidled close.

They walked outside and across the wide yard bordered by gardens of various types. "When I lived here, one of my chores was to help weed the vegetable and herb gardens," he told her, holding an arm out for her to take.

It was mid-September, so at seven the sun was still up but beginning to float toward the horizon. There'd been a misty rain for a few hours, but it had cleared up, leaving beads of water on the leaves and grass. He loved the garden decked out in brilliant raindrops with the leaves changing as a backdrop.

"Addie's gardens never cease to amaze me. It's always so lovely out here. No matter the season, she's got something to show off. Still, between you and me, weeding was one of my most hated chores. I did it anyway because I got out of the house," she confessed.

He forgot sometimes that she'd grown up in what he privately thought of as a religious cult. Complete with a multifamily compound. But he never forgot how it made him feel when she trusted him with the details of her life.

Yard work was easier than being on the street. But he didn't want to say that and make her feel bad. He shrugged. "It killed my back and left me with sore hands. It also was time for me to be with Addie. Being useful." He'd wanted to prove his worth. The early years he'd still worried they might find him wanting and send him away. "I refused to go to school, so she and James put together a home school program and had various people stop in to do my lessons. We'd be out here, and she'd tell me all sorts of stories. Only they were actually history lectures. Then we read books together about those events and would talk about them while we weeded or planted. You know, all the work that's so monotonous but has to be done. I still come out to help her winterize things if I'm in town." It was their thing together.

Pippa leaned in closer to him for a moment, acknowledging what he'd shared. "Of course you do. She's your mom."

He had a biological mother who'd been in and out of his life since he was nine years old. The only thing he shared with her was a penchant for addiction and very poor life choices.

Pippa said, "The monotony of repetitive tasks is one of my favorite things. I realized years later in therapy." She paused to chuckle, but it wasn't all amusement in her tone. "I'd used that time for meditation. In the house supervision was far more intense. My mother or other siblings were always there. My aunts would stop over all the time with their kids. There was no time or opportunity to meditate or even simply to think deeply on anything. But the vegetable garden was huge, and I could be out there with five other people, and no one was going to notice if I was having deep thoughts as long as I knew how to twist a tomato just right when I picked it, and I did it at a decent speed."

"I hate that young Pippa had to grow up that way."

"I hate that too. And I hate that you were a street kid. But I love that you and the Franklins found one another and became family."

"What are you doing tomorrow?" he asked.

She paused, and they stood in the evening gone purple and orange. "Why?" There was no calculation there. Pippa tipped her face up, looking at him directly. Always so forthright.

"Because I'd like to see you. Catch up. I haven't spent much time with you in the last few weeks. I missed you."

"We texted all the time."

"It's not the same as being with you." Not the same as smelling her on the air or being able to touch her.

"This is dangerously close to romantic, Hamish," she said with a smile.

"Will you come to my house?" he asked. "I'll make us brunch."

"Tomorrow is Monday. We're closing in on the deadline for three builds at once at work, so I'll be there until seven or so. Even if your scrambled eggs are a powerful motivator to accept your invitation, I can't."

He winced a little. "Sorry. I've been in the studio at all hours. Honestly, I don't know what day it is. How about Tuesday night?"

She opened her mouth and then shut it again, hesitating before finally saying, "I have plans that night."

He realized what she meant. "Ah. A date? Who's the lucky guy then?"

Her features fell a moment, and she stepped back, away from him. He stepped forward, closing the gap he'd created.

"I'm sorry. I was trying to sound cavalier and modern, but I'm jealous. It's not a good look."

"I don't know how to do this," she said. "I'm not sophisticated like other people."

He shook his head and cupped her face, swamped by tenderness. "It's not about sophistication at all. You just don't know how not to be truthful."

She frowned, frustration flowing from her. "Don't fool yourself. I can lie perfectly fine."

He leaned in and kissed her forehead, closing his eyes as he did, drinking her in. "How about you tell me what day coming up works best for you, and that's the day we'll catch up?"

Her breath hitched a moment, and then she nodded.

"Let's go play with puppies," he said, getting them headed toward the vet clinic.

CHAPTER
FOUR

I n the locker room at Twisted Steel Tuesday night, Pippa had given up trying to appear nonchalant.

Naturally that's when PJ showed up.

"Nervous?" PJ asked as Pippa grabbed her things from her locker.

PJ Coleman-Barrons wasn't just a co-worker and wife of one of the owners, she was a good friend. Pippa met her before she'd even begun working at Twisted Steel. Being women in a male-dominated industry meant they'd been thrown together at events like auctions and the like, and before too very long, PJ had invited her to the racetrack. Which had turned out to be a regular part of Pippa's life in the years since.

Three years later when Pippa's boss decided to move to Montana, Pippa had wavered on whether to accept Hap's offer and relocate with him to work at his new shop. Washington had become her home, and though she loved her job, she didn't like the idea of being hours away from both her sisters.

Turned out she didn't have to waver too long because a few days after that, Mick, one of the owners of Twisted Steel, called asking her to come in for an interview. An interview she never even got to finish because they offered her the job halfway through. They'd known of her work and her reputation and chose her to be one of them.

Twisted Steel, like Hap's before them, had given her the tools to make her own living. Only with TS, she'd come on as a professional instead of the high school kid who'd grown up on the job. She felt like an equal, though she certainly had more to learn and was always doing so.

"Not in any scary sort of way. Xander is out of my league. And I don't mean he's too good for me or whatever." She pointed a finger at PJ. "He's so sure of himself. Confident. Ridiculously sexy. But like, I'm a…what's the baby belt? Baby duckling yellow? Whatever it is, I'm that. And he's probably a black belt. A titanium belt. With piercings. Damn."

PJ's face brightened, and her grin made Pippa blush.

"I'm just going to say piercings are not overrated." PJ's tone was dry.

It took Pippa a second, and then she got what her friend was referring to. "I don't know if he's got a piercing anywhere, um, genital related," she whispered. "I just meant." Pippa paused and pulled the magazine from her backpack. She flipped it open and held it out. "Look at this!"

She took another peek herself and then had to fan her face. Shirtless, straddling a tattoo chair, suspenders hanging at his sides. All his ink, all his skin and piercings and muscles and the look on his face sent little shocks through her.

"He's very *mmmmm*. Like, there are words I'm sure

would do him justice. Maybe. I just sort of short circuit. When I look at that, words fall away, and all I can hear is that sound. But like low in my belly where a lot of my sex feelings live. Plus, he loves his family. How the flip am I supposed to resist that?"

PJ snorted. "Lady ma'am, I think the better question is why would you *want* to resist that? You're old enough to know how rare it is to not only think *mmmmm*, but to feel it. Ride it out. The feeling and whatever parts you might want to climb aboard. Take it from a person who was in your place five years ago when Asa came along. Not that this is necessarily some big forever moment," she added quickly. "Just why not see? Man like that can keep you warm at night. Do you know I never get jostled in a crowd because he walks ahead of me like one of those icebreaker things. The crowd bounces off him, and he plows me a path. It's fucking delightful, I tell you what."

Pippa started to giggle.

It wasn't as if she was a virgin. She'd been with Hamish, who certainly wasn't a baby lamb in the sexy department. She could do this! *Okay, stop thinking of Hamish.*

Xander wasn't a brute. Everything would be fine. Even if nothing more than some dinner came out of it.

"I'm off. I'll see you tomorrow."

Somehow when he'd said he lived in an apartment, Pippa had imagined something distinctly smaller than the huge penthouse he'd invited her into.

"I know," he said with an infectious smile. "It's the place I grew up in until I was in middle school. Then we moved into a house so I could attend the same performing arts school Miles and Rennie had attended. My family rented this place out for years, but right after I turned twenty-two, it was empty, and my parents offered it to me. I could never afford it on my own, but my dads talked me into it. They didn't have to try all that hard. I love this apartment."

He blushed, and she didn't want him to think she'd judge him negatively. He'd clearly made the explanation before.

"It's beautiful," she said, moving to the floor-to-ceiling windows showcasing west-facing views of Puget Sound with the Olympic Mountain Range in the distance.

"Sunsets are my favorite time of day," he said. "When we lived here, we'd have snack time and watch the sky change colors. A few times a month my mom comes by, and we have a glass of wine and do the same."

That was lovely. Pippa hoped to be the kind of mother whose adult children still liked being with her. "I like your relationship with your mom a lot."

"Yeah? Me too." He took her things. "Pizza is on the way. I was planning to cook. I even bought the ingredients, but then I had a tattoo go over the time I'd thought I needed; the client was...a challenge. By the point I got home I didn't want to cook."

"I'm so glad I'm not the only one who orders pizza when they're too tired to cook. Or who has challenging clients. Sometimes I'll have cereal by the time I slink home. Pizza sounds great."

He paused, his hand coming to rest at her hip. Heart racing, Pippa remained still as he leaned down to brush a kiss over her lips. "I like it that you're easy with things like that. Makes things less stressful."

"Don't think I'm free of my hot buttons. I have many of them." She sent him a smile.

"How about a glass of red and tour while we wait for food?"

"Yes, please."

In the kitchen, he pointed her toward the cabinet for glasses, which she grabbed and then filled once he'd opened the bottle.

"Red okay? This is a pretty basic one, perfect for pizza. There's white too if you'd prefer."

"I don't know a lot about wine. Not more than if I like something or don't like it. I know there are rules I'm breaking."

The way she'd just served him sent a shiver up his spine. He believed women were intelligent, brilliant people who often did the work of three with a tenth of the recognition. He believed in equal pay and equal rights, but he really got off on small submissive acts like that. When they were *chosen*.

It made him want to take care of her in return. A feedback loop. Something he rarely felt this deeply and never this early.

"The only rules are if you like it or not." He shrugged. "My dad—Ben—is a wine guy. A couple of years ago we got him a wine class done at a friend's restaurant, so I went too. Learned a lot. Forgot most of it except for the parts where I figured out what sorts of things I liked."

Even he heard the innuendo in that.

He began to lead her through the apartment. At the base of the staircase, he pointed upward. "Guest rooms. The old master is up there, but I prefer down here." Around the corner, he pushed open the double doors. "This is my room."

A wall of windows looked out over the terrace that wrapped around the entire penthouse. His bed dominated the room, positioned so he could lay and see the northern end of downtown including the Space Needle and parts of Seattle Center.

A massive bed. Substantial. He liked a great deal of room to sleep and to fuck. It was a bed made for a hedonist. He looked forward to seeing her bare skin against the pale blue of his sheets. To her scent on his pillows.

There were shelves on the far wall that led to the ceiling. Pippa paused there to take a closer look at their contents, her fingers stretching to touch but not quite making contact.

"Those are all my pads and sketchbooks."

"All these are yours?" After a glance back over her shoulder at him, she turned back to take in row after row. "Wonderful."

He breathed in her pleasure for a moment. "Raven gave me the first when I was five or so. Then two more because she told me she didn't want me to hesitate in filling up all the pages with my drawings. I've kept them all since. It's a great way to see how far I've come."

"This is a special sort of memory book. May I look?"

He moved to the row with his most recent work and slid one free, handing it her way. Trying to pretend he wasn't dying to know what she thought as she slowly paged through it.

Finally, she closed it with a happy sigh and gave it back. "Thank you. You're quite a talented artist. I hope you're proud of yourself."

"Every night when I go to sleep, I see them and I know I'm supposed to be doing exactly what I'm doing." Spines of years' worth of his work filled him with confidence and purpose.

She nodded. "I like that. A good way to view it. I hope I'll get to see more at some point."

"I'll make you a deal. Every time you visit me here, you can choose a book to look at," he told her, getting close.

She looked up into his face, her eyes wide before she smiled. "Okay. I'd like that."

"I got the idea from Raven. She's got all her books too. From her early teens. When I'd stay over at her house, we'd look through them." He'd been so excited that she'd shared her art with him. And later she'd started giving him his own art supplies and encouraged his love of drawing.

He led her out onto the terrace and then back into the kitchen.

"If I lived here, I'd never want to leave," she murmured. "Of course, you accepted your parents' very fine offer."

Pippa had noticed he was sensitive on the topic of the benefits he'd received from his family. Who didn't want to be taken seriously on their own merit after all? His parents had made the offer because they had the place to offer up. And no, most people wouldn't have that opportunity. But one day she hoped to be able to help her kids in whatever way she could, and if Xander kept his head and remembered his good fortune, it wouldn't reflect negatively on him at all.

She'd seen him at his job. She knew he'd built a reputation that was based on his talent. He didn't cover himself in designer logos, and though the bathrooms were beyond luxurious, they weren't gold-toilet-level ostentation.

Every one of his family she'd met had been genuine and down to earth. Including Xander.

It just made her like them all even more.

The pizza arrived shortly after that. "Screening room is right through here."

He indicated a two-seater couch. "There's a blanket on the back if you like to get tucked up while you're watching movies."

"I have a freakish metabolism. My feet get cold." She blushed.

"Freakishly adorable," he muttered before kissing her forehead, leaving her pleased.

He grabbed the fleecy throw, and once she got herself seated, he placed it over her legs and paid attention to be sure her toes were safely wrapped and toasty.

Then he made it absolutely perfect by handing her a plate with multiple slices of pizza and gave her three movies to choose from ranging from thriller-level scares to full-on hiding behind your hands and sleeping with the lights on.

"I only watch ones that scary if I'm sleeping over at Rebecca's," Pippa admitted of a recent haunted house flick. "She and I saw it at the theater, and she showed up at my place three hours later because she was afraid to sleep alone and Vivi—her partner—was out of town. Thank goodness she chickened out first or I'd have shown up on her doorstep."

"Remind me to give you the building code so you can come on up to my door should you need company in the middle of the night. I also have guest rooms if you'd prefer." He winked. "Should we go with vampires then?"

"Let's go with vampires," she said, pleased he wouldn't judge her for her movie choice.

There she was in his place, relaxed and open with him. As if she'd been there dozens of times before. That was the level of comfort he had around her. Like they'd known one another for years.

She watched the movie, laughing at moments, pulling her hood down over her eyes at others. A steady stream of happiness flowed from her and all around him.

Every once in a while, she made sure he had enough to drink—just a quick check in—and passed over some of the red licorice he'd picked up on a whim.

Xander really liked the way it felt having her in his house.

After the movie ended, he coaxed her into the living room so they could sit on his couch and look at the city beyond.

"I know you're close with two of your sisters, the ones you came here to Washington with," Xander said as they relaxed on the couch. "The rest of your family is still in Arizona?"

"My parents and eight of my siblings live there still. Four are married with kids of their own." Five if she counted Esther, but they didn't.

"How many siblings are there in total then?"

"Eleven including me. I was never very close with any of the others, though some of the littlest ones were so sweet. I do miss that." She shrugged. "Even though Esther and Danny live in Fairbanks, they come to Seattle to visit all the time. They have their own room at Rebecca's, so they don't have to always bring clothes back and forth or pay for a hotel. When they're here, I stay over too, so we do wild and crazy things like put together jigsaw puzzles and play board games."

"That sounds fun. I love jigsaw puzzles." He took her hand. "So you're not in contact with any of your family back in Arizona?"

"My parents forbid them any contact with me, Rebecca, and Esther." She paused while sipping her cocoa. "Maybe someday when they grow up. If they leave." The sadness in her voice was a punch.

"Religious stuff?" he hazarded a guess.

"Pretty much, yes."

"What happened? Don't feel like you need to answer," he added quickly, though he was dying of curiosity.

"I was cast out, to be more accurate. I was keeping a secret for Rebecca. My oldest brother found out and he ran to tattle, not once thinking about the outcome other than the points he would get for it. Our father is a bishop, a church elder. There was a trial. Sort of. The three of us were told to go or submit to some *behavior adjustment*." A fine shiver ran through her, and he wished he hadn't asked even as the desire to punch someone's face rose.

"I want to know you, but not to hurt," he said. "Let's change the subject."

Pippa smiled at him. "No, it's okay. There's nothing to apologize for. It took me time and a lot of therapy, but I didn't do anything wrong. Rebecca and Esther had done nothing wrong. Esther had met Danny about eight months before that. He came with us, thank goodness. He'd grown up in the real world. Knew how to live in it. He made sure we got an education. I went to high school, my sisters got their GED and worked part time while Danny was the main breadwinner. He and Esther moved to Alaska two years ago for his job. I miss them both, but like I said, we see each other regularly, and I'm with Rebecca and Vivi multiple times every week."

She sucked in a breath.

"Thank you for sharing all that."

He couldn't fathom parents just tossing their kids away. He'd never doubted for a moment just how loved and valued he was. He had a sneaking suspicion the secret she'd been keeping had to do with Rebecca being gay. And that made him even angrier, but also his admiration of these three sisters who fled everything and made themselves a whole life deepened.

It wasn't that she was embarrassed about what her family had done to her. There was shame for all sorts of reasons. Some of them were wrong. She knew it. Accepted it. In her brain. But sometimes her heart wasn't sure. The parts of her that had been built before she'd had much chance to develop her own set of values and beliefs sometimes took over.

In those moments it was her sin to simply be a woman. A woman who wanted things she was not told it was acceptable to want. A voice. Freedom to live where she pleased. To love who she pleased. To have an opinion she developed on her own instead of repeating what she'd been told to say.

The child she'd been had been taught from the cradle that it was her place to serve first her parents and then her husband. There was no need for an education beyond how to keep a home. The only acceptable ambition was to have a husband and children. The only acceptable emotion was submission.

Even having been away from it since the age of fifteen, unlearning all that, clearing out the toxic waste of self-loathing and fear, took time and effort. And sometimes she stumbled. As long as there were two steps forward, one step back still meant positive movement.

"I think we should cuddle and make out for a while before you have to leave," he said, breaking the tension.

"I can get on board with that plan."

In one easy movement, he lifted her onto his lap, and she straddled his waist, facing him. He was still big this way, but not overwhelmingly so.

"I hate that people who should know better don't seem to understand your worth."

"I hate it a lot more for my sisters who are still there. It was hard to make the decision to go, knowing the little ones would grow up there without me to protect them." Rebecca had hidden her sexual identity for so long because she'd felt the same. But in the end, there was no other choice. Behavioral adjustment would have broken her spirit, and she'd have been useless except as the wrong sort of message. *This is what happens when you disobey.*

"Do you think they'd have let you continue to be around them after that? If you'd stayed, I mean."

She shook her head. "We'd have been sent to Montana. That's where rulebreakers go for behavioral adjustment. Very rarely they came back. Sometimes they're sent to other families, married into them to anchor them to their new community. I'd never have been allowed to speak to them again. In the end, I chose to be selfish instead of broken."

She thought often of those girls who'd been sent away sunny and full of life and had returned...deflated. That thread of joy gone. Pippa used those memories to remind herself she was better off.

He wrapped his arms around her and held on. Snug. Surrounded her with his strength.

He didn't tell her it would be okay. Didn't say it was for the best or anything like that. Pippa was fairly certain she'd never felt so safe and seen as she did right there in Xander's arms.

It seemed like a movie plot that such things still happened. He held her firmly, the weight of her in his lap, against his chest, perfect enough to make his pulse thunder.

She relaxed against him, warm and right. He kissed her temple, and she turned her face to meet his lips with her own.

Her taste didn't rush into his veins like it had a few days before. This time it was a slow and steady recognition.

In an easy movement, he eased her to the side slightly, so she rested her sweet ass on his lap, and leaned her back against the arm of the couch to his left. This way she was spread out for him like a gift. His mouth left hers and took a slow meander across the line of her jaw and down her throat. She made a low sound of approval when he used the edge of his teeth.

That sound...tore something loose. Whatever it was that had been holding him back was gone, and everything rushed forward to greet her. To taste and tease.

Her fingers dug into his shoulders and released. Only to tighten again a few seconds later. Xander couldn't stop the curve of his lips as he paused at the hollow of her throat. A swirl of his tongue and then a nibble. Sharp. Followed by a lick to ease the sting.

The nibble brought another low sound and the tightening of her hold.

She liked that.

That worked well as he liked bringing that edge of pain.

She tipped slightly, arching her back. His dick was so hard each beat of his pulse echoed through his body. A deep, rather delightful ache.

A line of her belly showed as her sweater rode up, and that creamy expanse of skin called to his touch. So soft. Warm. Responsive as gooseflesh rose in the wake of his fingertips.

"You're delicious," he said against her cheek.

"Me?" she said faintly, like she couldn't possibly have heard him right. Like he wasn't there, utterly immersed in her.

"You."

Xander shifted her and paused at the sight of her. Pupils wide, eyes glossy. A blush had pinked her cheeks.

Fuck. He wanted to spoon her up and take a bite.

They could continue and end up naked. He really wanted that. Wanted to watch her features as orgasm stole through her. Wanted to learn all the things that caused those moans and growls she'd made so he could do them again and again.

She smiled up at him, reaching up to brush the pads of her fingers over his bottom lip.

He wanted it so badly he forced himself to slow. To savor the woman in his lap. Keep her so well satisfied she never had a moment to doubt him. There was a shyness to her that flipped every fucking switch he had. That, too, would take slowing down. To draw her along instead of shoving her into the deep end.

Because all the things he wanted to do to Pippa Hall were worth doing right.

When he gave her everything he was, darkness included, he wanted her to be ready for it. And what it would mean for her to accept it. He'd never wanted another person to be *his* the way the woman in his lap made him yearn for.

He kissed her again, easing back from the edge they'd been poised on. With a soft sigh, she sat upright again on his lap and wrapped her arms around him.

He hummed his pleasure at the way it felt. "The rest of this week is slammed with clients. What are you doing this weekend?" He worked Saturday and Sunday, but he'd be off by six each day. Opening his world up to her and including her in it would be a big part of learning her.

She dropped kisses down his neck and then across his jaw. "Working Saturday until three or so. Sunday, I have a bunch of errands to run. Books to return to the library. Laundry to do, and then I promised the Franklins I'd be there for dinner."

The Franklins. He'd met them a time or two, as the world of the Browns/Keenans/Copelands often brushed up against the similar-sized intentional family the Franklins had created. Knew Jessi, their youngest daughter, and Hamish. Well, Xander knew Hamish in a different way.

None of that mattered.

"I'm working Friday until nine or so. A group of us usually go out to a place not too far from the shop. Pinball. Pool. Dozens of beers on tap. What do you say?"

"I've never played pinball!" Her eyes lit, and all he wanted in his life was to make her look that happy every single day. "There are pool tables at our regular bar but no pinball."

"What's your regular bar?"

"The Ditch. It's sort of the official Twisted Steel place."

"I've seen live music there more than once. It's so weird to me that you were in some of the same places I've been, know several members of my closest family, and we never met until Brody's party." Like this was one of those things, right place, right time, right person. Magic.

"I'm sure I'd have noticed you if we'd been there at the same time though," she said.

Flattered, he grinned. "Same. That pretty red hair would have caught my attention immediately."

She raised an eyebrow at him. "Or, you would have been surrounded by stylish, gorgeous people you were paying attention to instead."

He didn't have an entourage or anything like that, and he said so.

"I don't mean a group of sycophants. I mean you're you. Look at you. I'm me."

"I don't follow."

"You're trendy and handsome, and you pump out a

steady stream of chemistry and confidence. You feature on magazine covers. People are drawn to you. People like you. I'm a girl, who as my sister reminded me last week, wasn't allowed to wear skirts shorter than my lower calves or cut my hair until we'd left. I was sixteen the first time I went to a hair salon and found out first-hand what short hair looks like on someone with big red curls. I could have been Annie on Broadway if I had any musical talent. I still can't wing my liner at all."

"Oh." He set her to the side. "I wish I'd known that before we got started on this thing. I don't think I can kiss someone who can't wing their liner."

She blushed furiously and then burst out laughing.

"Maybe," he told her as he leaned her back, "we can keep kissing while you keep working on the liner? Perseverance. That's the key to success."

Laughing, she pulled him down into another kiss.

CHAPTER
FIVE

amish paused a moment before he opened the door to find her standing on his porch that Wednesday night. It was as if the breeze had blown the clouds away and the sun shone bright and warm.

"Hi." She grinned, and he stepped back, allowing her entry.

"When you smile at me the way you do, it fills me up with so much joy I can't quite contain it all." He said it, not entirely having meant to.

She turned then, the light from the chandelier suspended in the entry sending a shower of jewels across her skin.

The smile she wore was even better. Open and full of affection. "That's a very nice thing to say. Thank you. I'm genuinely happy to see you."

He kicked the door closed, and she winced.

"That's such a beautiful piece of woodwork. I was thinking you might put one of those strike-plate type things right where you kick it closed. That way you won't harm the craftsmanship." She bent to slide her fingertips over the place he habitually used as a hands-free spot to shut the front door.

Hamish wrapped an arm around her waist and hauled her to his side. "Hello, my beautiful Pippa. I'm going to need a taste."

Her expression smoothed as that smile of hers returned, sending his senses into overdrive. As he lowered his head to take her mouth, he drew a deep breath, filling his lungs with caramelized sugar and heady flowers.

In those moments when it was this…simple, gorgeous, intense connection between them, there was absolutely no doubt within him. She was it. She was *it,* and he was happy to snap her up and fill her life with pleasure.

His self-doubt fell away, and he let himself trust this true thing.

She moaned low in her throat, and in two steps he'd backed her against the nearby wall and had bent his legs enough to have better access to the kiss that built between them like wildfire. Christ. He wanted more and more. All.

He might have taken her right then if the bleeding timer on the stove hadn't gone off.

"I'm going to blow that oven up," he muttered as he broke away from that kiss, leaving her giggles in his wake. "Come through to the kitchen. I need to check on dinner."

"You were made for candlelight," he told her as they dug in. He'd lit every candle he had, as well as about thirty flameless ones.

"You're full of compliments tonight," she said, spreading

butter on a slice of bread for each of them. Always taking care.

"I'm…" He broke off, and she let him, keeping a close eye while she ate. "I guess I just wanted you to know what I was feeling."

She nodded. "Okay. Tell me about what you've been up to for the last two weeks."

If he'd said the same thing a month earlier, she'd have pursued it. He felt that distance—distance he'd put there—more than ever.

"I wasn't entirely ready to start on a new album, but it happened anyway. I've got two new songs completed and a few more in the incubation stage."

Her pleasure seemed to build and fill the space. "That's amazing! I'm so happy for you. I can't wait until you're at the stage where you want to share."

Before her he *never* shared. He made his music, recorded it fourteen times until it was perfect, and then he sent it to his management who got the music to the label.

His lyrics were very personal, and it was one thing when it was out in the wider world because for whatever reason, it felt more anonymous. But letting someone else see or hear before he finished was to lay himself bare.

Of all the people he knew, Pippa deserved that intimacy. No. *He* wanted to share that intimacy with her. Show her parts of himself she would protect. Knew, too, on some level he needed to get over his bullshit fear or it truly would be the end of any chance they had to be together as more than close friends who had sex and kissed a lot.

He'd fantasized about sharing that depth of connection

between them. All the while she'd been there, waiting for him to get his head right.

Decision made, Hamish stood and held a hand to her. Her eyes widened, but she placed her fingers against his, and he helped her to her feet and then downstairs to the home studio he'd had built.

He pushed open the door into the main room. "I do most of my writing in here." Suddenly shy, he looked down, but her laugh was so full of wonder his gaze was drawn back to her.

She'd wandered to the rack of guitars but kept her hands at her back, fingers laced tightly. "These are yours? That's a stupid question. Obviously, they are."

"I write with the acoustic, but once I start laying down tracks, I'll use the others too." He pulled one free. "You can touch it. Do you play?" She loved music, he knew. They listened to it together frequently.

"I don't. I just love it when other people do." Her gaze dropped to the instrument in his hands. "Looks well loved."

"I bought this when I was twenty. It's been with me ever since." The bridge was smooth from years of use; touching it always made him feel welcome. The Martin had been at his side for every song he'd ever recorded and a hundred more he never had.

"Addie and James wanted to give it to me for my birthday, but it was, I don't know how to explain it. I just needed to earn it." It had meant everything to him that they'd listened and respected what he'd wanted to do. And had been so proud of him when he'd done it and managed to save enough.

They wanted to do for him. To make him happy and fill

his life with all the things he'd never had. Love and attention chief among them. "Once I showed a real interest in music, they were behind me all the way. Drove me to gigs. Helped with gear loadout more than once. They paid for a pressing of what later became my first EP."

"They're really just the best. The kind of parents I wish I'd grown up with. No wonder you, Jessi, Leif, and Charlie are all so fantastic." Pippa paused in front of what Addie called his awards wall. He'd tried to pretend it was no big deal. But she'd known, as real moms did, how much it meant that he could see the product of all his hard work when he was down there. It helped him keep going on the days when it felt like he'd never write a good song ever again.

"Is this where you do all your recording? Does this mean you're rooted here in Seattle now? At least for the next while?"

"Would that make you happy?"

That slipped out, but once he said the words, they both knew he was hoping the answer was yes.

"It nearly always makes me happy to see you." She turned and lifted a hand to his cheek, and he covered it with his own.

"Nearly always?"

"When you push me away it doesn't make me happy. I respect it, because everyone should have the right to set those boundaries."

"I'm a mess," he told her quietly.

"No, you aren't." She shook her head.

"I'm terrified of hurting you so much you leave me forever."

Her features softened. "I can't do any of this for you. I wish I could. But I'm *always* your friend. I know your heart. But eventually, if you keep pushing, I'll give you all the distance you claim to want. If you don't want it, be a big boy and act like it."

That gave him pause. Sometimes she was so soft and sweet it was hard to remember she also had a spine of steel when necessary.

"I don't want you out of my life."

But that wasn't what she meant. One of her brows rose. "Okay."

"I can't imagine my life without you in it," he amended. "This distance is never about you."

"In the end, it is. But you need to do what's best for yourself. I will too. But I'm not out to break your heart. Or disappear."

He brushed a kiss against her temple as he pulled her into a hug.

After they both seemed to feel better, Hamish led her to one of the chairs before he settled in the recliner he composed in most often. She seemed to know he needed her not to speak. Which moved him so deeply the ground at his feet felt like it crumbled to dust.

All his life he'd been a stranger. Everywhere he went. Everyone he was around. Over the years there'd been a handful of people who'd ever made him feel seen and understood. Through it all it was music he'd felt recognized and welcomed by.

He drew fingertips over the strings before he grabbed a pick, and without thinking it over too hard began to play. He'd started writing it months back. It had been tender, like a toothache, but he put it aside over and over until finally getting it all in place just a few days before.

Pippa knew, of course, that he was a musician. She'd seen him on stage more than once before she'd met him in person. Even when he was cooking or driving a car, he was otherworldly. He'd sung her little snippets. Always other people's songs.

And though she'd been in his home on multiple occasions, he'd never brought her down to his studio.

The moment was so precious to her she was afraid to breathe too heavily, afraid to move and shatter this magic that had developed between them. With this man she'd wanted to know so much.

And that he'd do this after their whatever it had been. Not a fight. But she'd laid down some of her own boundaries too. And now he was opening to her in a way he never had before. Which was wonderful but also...made it harder to continue to see both Xander and Hamish at the same time.

He sang conversationally, his accent rising as he did. *"Don't tell me you miss me when I've been here all along."* Nearly a plea.

Tears in her eyes, hands clasped tight, she listened and opened the door to her heart a crack more because he was Hamish. Unique and perfect in his own way. But so very soft. Wounded beneath a mask of sarcasm. Beautiful. So beautiful.

Eyes nearly as dark as his hair, currently in a messy tousle around his gorgeous face. A nose slightly crooked from being broken twice. He'd told her the story of the second time, being caught up in a brawl before a show. A show he'd performed anyway. His beard had gotten long over the summer but currently it was closer trimmed. A septril piercing in his nose currently held a titanium hoop she'd given him. It only made him more handsome.

He looked a little rough and dark. Broody. Sometimes on stage he leaned hard into that Scottish rock-and-roll star persona, playing up the accent and the swagger. But it was a mask. His lyrics were a glimpse into the heart of the songwriter. He felt things deeply and seriously.

But every time she'd tried to hold him closer, to know him on a deeper level, he'd dissolved like smoke.

She might have walked away a dozen times, but he'd never rejected her. He'd just gotten terrified of opening up. She could watch it on his features, and though it had made her sad, hurt her feelings even, mainly she wanted to get that look off his face. She didn't want to back him into a corner like a rabid animal, but she couldn't walk away either. Something unfurled and blossomed every time she was with him.

He took up a place inside her, and she wasn't sure how or when or even why. But he was there.

When he finished, she wanted to clap. Instead, she said, "That's astonishing. Hamish, I'm so honored you shared that."

His smile in response made her so glad she'd said what she had.

"It's called 'Ghost'. It came during the sad, slow death of a close friendship," he told her. "It was a low point on several levels in my life. Things had gotten very dark, and I felt so fucking alone. Judged by everyone. Betrayed by those who'd just wandered off when I needed them most. Stung. Humiliated."

"It takes so much courage to be that honest with your art."

He said, "Ah, but they don't know, you see? They think I'm a hard-living slag, aye?"

"You want them to see that. But music is a language all its own. People hear your songs, and they know who you are. Here." She pressed the heel of her hand against her chest, over her heart.

He set his guitar aside, leaning it against the chair, and moved to her, crouching. The look on his face wrenched something deep inside.

"I'm not nearly as good as you make me out to be," he whispered.

"Or. You're so much better than you let yourself believe."

He rested his forehead against hers before he stood and brought her along with him. "Come through. I'll show you the recording booth and the soundboards. I'll even let you peek at my platinum records."

CHAPTER
SIX

Churchkey was set back at an angle, so the entrance was down a small alley, across from a pho shop currently filling the air with spicy goodness that made Pippa's stomach growl.

At nearly ten on a Friday, the place was already full. Tables to the left, the bar lined with stools. The games were all off to the rear. Pool, darts, and pinball machines. More tables, as well as a window where it appeared food was being served.

It definitely had the same vibe as the Ditch, and she let go of her worry that the place would be too cool and would make her awkward and uncomfortable. Though it was wall-to-wall beautiful people, most of them smiled at her as she walked through, and a few waved or tipped a chin in welcome.

Rennie had come with her, and at Pippa's side, her friend was just as beautiful as the patrons saying hello. Not a small number did a double take at the sight of Irene Brown looking absolutely breathtaking in nothing more exciting than jeans and a cute shirt.

Pippa was about to tease Rennie about it when she saw Xander at the bar, the wide expanse of his shoulders and back to the room.

The physical sight of him seemed to ricochet through her, stealing her breath for a moment. Naturally there was a woman standing at his side, looking up at him with *hi, let's touch our tingly bits* in her gaze.

Several things happened then. First, she got mad at herself because wasn't she just kissing Hamish a few nights earlier? Then she thought, well, she hadn't been on a date with Xander at the time. And on the heels of that, she didn't really care how hypocritical she was because it was in her head, and she could be as irrationally jealous as she wanted to be.

Naturally that's when he turned, and like he'd known she was there, his gaze locked on hers immediately. Even across the dim room she saw his smile as he handed money to the bartender, and with a nod toward the woman sending him sex vibes, he headed Pippa's way.

With a tip of his chin, he directed her toward the table where several others sat. As he had his hands full of multiple drinks, she pulled herself out of her stupor and got moving toward him.

Rennie had already reached the table and helped pass around various drinks, so Xander stepped to Pippa and pulled her into a hug. "You look fantastic."

"Hi," she said, her voice muffled as she snuggled into his hold, her face pressed into his neck so she could breathe him in.

"I need to know something." A hand at her elbow, he drew her away a little.

"What?" Her heart pounded.

"Is that lipstick kiss-proof?" One corner of his mouth slid up, and she wanted to lick it.

Totally at the expert level, this one.

"It said transfer-proof on the packaging. It can withstand pizza. Anything else, well, I think we might need scientific testing."

Delighted and charmed, she sighed as he pulled her close. "I'm glad to see you," he said, before laying a kiss on her right there in the bar in front of dozens of people. Not a long, lascivious smooch. But thorough enough to leave her flushed with rubbery knees at the end.

"I feel very welcomed," she managed to say around a tongue that felt twice the normal size.

With a grin, he pressed his lips to her forehead and then slid an arm around her shoulders, propelling them back to the table.

The possessive part of her soul preened. He'd made a public declaration of sorts. Bold enough that even she knew what it was.

Introductions were made. Pippa recognized most everyone except for the guy from Written On the Body, Ca, who seemed friendly as he tipped his chin in greeting.

Xander told them all, "They had to change out a keg, so two pitchers should arrive at the table shortly. Pippa and I are going to play pinball. Don't drink all the beer."

She dropped off her jacket, draping it over the back of a chair next to his, and he took her hand, leading her to an open slot.

"I've had my quarter on this one, so it's our turn," he said, and took that coin, handing it her way. "Drop it there."

She did, and the lights and music, the theme of one of her favorite 70s detective shows she used to watch on cable when she was home sick, sounded and flashed. It reminded her of those first heady years of freedom.

He kissed the tip of her nose. "You're smart. This is simple but takes some finesse and strategy along with luck. Remember, there's always another quarter, so when you lose, it's not a thing."

That was sort of the way Danny had explained dealing with the world outside the group, so Pippa took his meaning, pulled back the silver plunger, and let it go, sending the ball up the chute and into the heart of the game.

She figured out the buttons on the side after the first ball sailed between the flippers. By the second game, Pippa had gotten over how sad she was to have missed this her whole life and instead celebrated how much fun it really was.

Xander stood at her side and watched. Her, not the game. Took in the pleasure as she began to figure out what to do, the happiness in her grin and the shimmy of her hips when she'd managed to escape losing the next ball a few times.

The curves of her features called to him over and over. The swell of her bottom lip and the apples of her cheeks caught the light from the machines. Splashes of orange, red, and white made her look like a painting. Or a cartoon, given the angle. He was going to need to sketch her that way.

One of his favorite things about Pippa was how she found joy in the smallest things. Her eyes lit with interest as she learned new techniques and tricks. When she lost a ball, she laughed it off and moved on.

In all the chaos of the world around them, just being with her soothed his nerves. Pleased him.

When the last ball—after she'd earned a bonus one—was gone, he spun her and took her back to the table.

"That was really good for a first time," he said.

Her eyes shone, and she grinned. "It was even more fun than I imagined it would be! One of my sisters worked at a pizza restaurant, and they had three video game machines. *Ms. Pacman*, *Centipede*, and *Frogger*."

"Whoa, old school," Rennie said.

"The whole place was a time capsule to the early 1980s. The *Centipede* game broke, and I was there in the back doing my homework during Esther's shift. I fixed it because it was way more fun than chemistry. The owner let me play for free whenever Esther had a shift. Sandy, one of the owners, told me her husband imprinted on 1983. Those were games he'd wanted to play as a kid, but he lived in farm country and never had the chance until they bought the place when he was already an adult. He refused to get rid of the machines from sentiment."

"We're big game people. As with most of our traditions, it's because Adrian, my mother, and Brody created them. They're all hypercompetitive, so everything from cards and video games to three-legged races and flag football are made into marathon events with teams and prizes."

Poppy, Xander's younger cousin, Miles Brown's little sister, and the daughter of Adrian and Gillian Brown said, "When my dad would tour, we had a family bus and Erin had one too. At the venue while they were off at soundcheck or performing, all the tour kids would gather to play games and watch movies. My mom was sort of the unofficial tour mom to everyone."

Xander shrugged. "There were tours where Sweetwater Ranch shared the bill, and all of the Hurleys are family too. Poppy's aunt, Mary, runs the catering company that went out on tour with us. So there were all these giant feasts backstage. People expected it to be a bacchanal, but really it was a bunch of kids watching cartoons and playing board games. From the outside I know it seemed glamorous or whatever. But to us, it was just what we did on summer breaks with our cousins and extended family."

"I like that you're all so close with each other," Pippa said.

"Rennie and Miles sort of managed us," Martine said.

"Like sheepdogs," Rennie said with a wink at her sister.

"And not all the family has been supportive. Fortunately, by the time we were old enough to see who was missing, it didn't matter as much as who was there," Fox added with a glance at Xander.

Xander, Ashley, and Fox's paternal grandfather was a man none of them had met because of how he acted after Xander's parents had all gotten together. He'd made a scene at the hospital when Erin had been in labor with Xander. In the aftermath, their grandma Annalee had divorced her husband of thirty-five years because of it. And according to Xander's Dad, their grandfather hadn't spoken another word to *any* of the siblings who still had a relationship with Erin, Todd, and Ben or their child. That included Xander's uncle Andrew and another one of their aunts who'd moved to Massachusetts just to get away from it.

Sadly, two of his dad's siblings had sided with their father, closing out their own mother and the rest of their siblings, nieces, and nephews.

Fucking stupid. Least of all because it wasn't any of their business if the loving household Xander grew up in had three parents. But truth and logic were strangers to bigotry and his life had never been hindered by the lack of his grandfather.

Pippa nodded. "It's always about the people who choose to be there, in the end."

She had her own family baggage. Far worse than theirs. For a moment he felt the weight of that—of his close-knit family and friend circle—against the fact that of eleven siblings she only spoke with two and the rest, along with her parents, had chosen to shun them instead of love them.

Pippa, though, continued to exude light and pleasure. He'd bring her more people to care about her. Another large harbor in a storm.

"Music?" Rennie stood. "There's a jukebox, and I have a bunch of ones."

"If Dad was here, he'd start talking about how songs were three for a quarter back in his day," Marti teased as she joined the group at Pippa's side.

They made a pretty picture as they moved across the bar, heads bent toward one another as they talked. Xander found a deep sense of satisfaction at the way Pippa fit in like there'd always been a spot for her.

A group of dudes who'd been in the bar a few times when Xander had been in the past was seated at a table nearest the jukebox, and when the women started perusing the list of songs, a few got up and headed over.

Xander watched closely. Were they just choosing a song like Pippa and his cousins, or did they have an eye on the knot of beautiful women and thought to shoot their shot? Who could blame them really?

Rennie ignored them, but they managed to get Pippa's attention. She smiled but shook her head and turned back to the others.

That's when one of them touched her. Xander shot to his feet and stalked over before he'd even registered the thought.

"Time to get moving," he said, annoyance and possession roaring through his system. She'd said no. He'd seen it from across the bar, so these dicks needed to get stepping.

The enormity of emotion surprised him for a long moment. Certainly Pippa and the others were capable of shooing these dudes away, but he couldn't remain seated and watch yet another dude not take no for a fucking answer the first time. Especially when it was Pippa who'd already said it.

Pippa looked up—at him and no one else—placing her hand on the one he'd had crossed over his chest. "Hi. We just spent about thirty dollars on eighties music."

Duran Duran's "Rio" started playing, and she grinned.

Laughing, he bent enough to kiss her fingertips and tuck her arm through his before he gave the retreating guys one last look.

"They weren't being scary," Rennie said quietly to him as he held the chair for Pippa. "Martine and Poppy were blunter. Pippa is nice to everyone. He wanted her to be nicer, and he tried it a second time, but she knows how to flick a dude off. She'd have been more forceful about it, and the rest of us would have intervened otherwise."

Fox just stared at him for long moments, wearing a

smirk. Yeah, yeah, he hadn't done shit like that before, but he apparently did now.

Pippa's laugh caught his attention, and he settled beside her.

"After this, you want to hang out at your place a while?" he asked, lips against her ear.

Pippa knew everything would change if she had him over. She also knew she'd allowed herself to get in a rut with Hamish. Caring for him so deeply she'd closed herself off to anyone else. The ember of hope in her chest had begun to burn again when he'd taken her down to his studio and shared that part of himself. It had made her ache with how much she loved him.

But he hadn't followed up. And she was tired of loving him and waiting for him to wake the heck up and be worthy.

Going back to her townhouse with Xander didn't mean she'd stop caring for Hamish. But maybe it would help her step out of that rut and into a better place. One where she was able to let go of that ember of hope but never his friendship. One where she could let herself love someone else.

A place alone with Xander. Mmmmm.

That moment at the bar when she got hit on had been... thrilling. He hadn't threatened anyone or anything like that. It had been protective. Anyone else and she had no doubt it would have felt different.

· · ·

Two hours later they snuggled on the comfortable couch in her cozy living room.

"Did you have a good time tonight?" he asked.

"I did. I like your cousins a lot."

"You already knew half of them anyway."

It was weird trying to balance her growing attraction to Xander with her friendship with Rennie. But she'd had a friendship with Jessi while she had whatever it was with Hamish, so the learning curve wasn't as severe.

Xander murmured, "Come a little closer. I want you."

Pippa leaned in, meeting his mouth in a kiss. He groaned, the sound laced with so much desire it flattered her to her toes currently curled in delight.

She'd been about to reply when the hand sliding up her ribs continued up to cover and then take the weight of her breast. Then nothing else mattered but the heat of his palm against her nipple.

He paused until she arched further into his touch, opened her eyes, and then said, "Yes."

He muttered something she thought was *thank god.*

But she couldn't be sure, and it didn't matter, because his mouth was back on hers, and the heat of his skin burned a path from her belly, up under her shirt to the cup of her bra he pulled down so slowly the rasp of fabric and then the pinch of her nipple sent a ripples of pleasure storming through her.

"Tell me something, Pippa," he said as his mouth skated down her throat to the keyhole in the fabric. He breathed over the bare skin and then licked, dragging a surprised moan from her lips.

"Yes?" she answered around a brain muddled by desire.

He pinched her nipple again, this time harder. Hard enough to make her hiss. But the pain bloomed into something else. Something darker and bigger. Rich and velvet and lush and so good she lost herself in it.

He hummed, and it sent warmth caressing over skin already hypersensitive. He bent, replacing his fingers with his mouth, dragging his teeth against her nipple through her shirt and bra before blowing over it. And again, leaving her with a sharp nip and the sweet balm of a rush of cool air.

"There's my answer." He slid her blouse up, rearing back to make room. To stare down at her like he saw straight to her soul. "You like it when it hurts. Not too much," he assured her. "Enough to make the pleasure all the sweeter."

Oh.

She blinked up at him, blushing, slightly uncomfortable with such a truth being spoken out loud.

He watched her features as he pinched once more, this time adding a twist.

The discomfort at having her desires voiced faded away as he continued to look at her like she was amazing.

He bent his head and captured her bare nipple between his teeth, the bristles of his beard scratching over tender skin.

A shuddering breath exploded from her as light flashed against her closed eyelids. Everything ached. It was too much and not enough.

He licked, swirling his tongue, teasing until she writhed, her fingers digging into his upper arms, holding him close. Touching him was her anchor in the storm of pleasure he created. New sensations that should have scared or embarrassed her but instead, because it was him, she could revel in.

"You taste like every choice I want to make from now on," he murmured, lips a whisper on her skin, making her so wet she probably should be trying to hide. Wet because he gave her the freedom to love it.

She gasped as he twisted, getting to his knees in front of the couch, settling between her thighs.

He rose slightly, his hands at the button of her pants. "I want to eat your pussy," he said in a growl that had gooseflesh rising on her arms.

"Yes, please!"

It was a good thing she was sitting and that he had the muscle coordination necessary to take her pants off, because her body seemed to go tingly and superhot, her coordination jerky as all sorts of different signals crossed in her brain.

He ran his palms down her thighs and calves and then back up once he'd gotten rid of her pants.

All she could see was him. His hands, so large, on her, his hair had fallen over his forehead. He hooked the strings to each side of her panties and tugged, leaving her bare. He drew in a breath as if steadying himself.

Pippa would have moved to close her thighs, but he was there, looking his fill. Naked greed on his features so blatantly a small wave of pleasure burst from low in her gut. A whisper of an orgasm.

He traced a fingertip over her labia, slick and swollen with desire, and then while she watched, he sucked that finger in between his lips, his eyelids going half-mast as he hummed. "You taste even better than you smell."

"I..." She didn't even know how to respond to that. Thank you seemed paltry.

He saved her by leaning in, using his thumbs to spread her pussy open, and taking a long lick. No words were possible after that. All she could manage was to feel as he devastated her with flicks, laves, sucks, and nips before shoving her so hard into climax she probably left permanent divots in her couch cushions where she'd been holding on.

As he rested his head on her thigh, Xander realized he'd never forget her taste or the way she sounded as she came all over his face.

His emotions skittered in his belly. He hadn't set out to get in this deep with this woman. Certainly not as fast as it had hit. Anticipated or not, he found himself unwilling to back away.

She sighed, a pleased, smug sound, sifting his hair through her fingers until he straightened to get a look at her.

Her sweater was still rucked up, one cup of her bra down, exposing her right breast. Her gaze was glossy, and her features had gone soft and relaxed.

He'd never in his life seen anything more beautiful.

"Up," she said, her voice slightly rough.

He stood, but she stayed him with her hand at his belt and slowly unbuckled it, her gaze returning to his repeatedly as she did.

He watched as she eased his zipper down, noted the coral-toned polish on her short nails. When she pulled his cock out—with a delighted indrawn breath—her attention moved to his face again. What he saw there did something to him. Deep inside things shifted, and a rush of desire hit him so hard his hands shook.

He fisted them briefly to ease the tremors and then gave in, snapping her barrettes free and sliding his fingers through those big, bouncy curls. Cradling the back of her head, he guided her toward his dick, and she moaned. Low and a little hungry.

He locked his knees before he fell over when she flicked her tongue across the head, smearing pre-come and sending tiny zings of sensation over his skin.

Lost. He was lost in her as she took him into her mouth, surrounding his cock with hot and wet. Xander wanted to close his eyes, but right as he was, he saw their reflection in the glass of the pantry door.

Unbelievably erotic. He stood between her bare legs. By contrast he was fully dressed. He'd follow up on that particular button with her the next time they were together.

On and on, her right hand tangled in the waist of his pants, holding him close, her left encircling his dick at the root.

He wanted it to last forever.

He needed it to end before he went up in a flash and was only ashes. As climax approached, he attempted to pull back, not knowing if she was cool with him coming in her mouth, but she held on with an annoyed little grunt.

From the balls of his feet and the top of his head, climax rushed through him in a scalding wave while she continued to suck and lick until he had to collapse on the couch to catch his breath.

Once he could sit up again and tucked his dick away, he pulled her into his lap.

"This was the best date I've had," she said sleepily.

He laughed. "Ever? Or today?"

She lifted her head, which had been resting on his shoulder. "In the last few hours, I guess. You want some hot cocoa?"

He really liked the feel of her there, mostly naked, on his lap. But it was after two, and even though he wanted to stay, take things into her bedroom, and spend hours on her, he didn't have hours. He had a tattoo scheduled at ten, and he'd heard her say earlier that evening that she had work in the morning hours too.

"Cocoa would be nice. I promise to clear out of here before too much later."

She sat, frowning. "No one is kicking you out. But I am going to go put on pajamas. Be right back." She dashed off while he admired the sight of her bare ass.

CHAPTER
SEVEN

"Hold that right there," she told Xander of the beam from the flashlight. They were at his apartment, and she was currently trying to fix a dishwasher.

"We can call a repair person. You're supposed to be here for sunset watching, wine, snacks, and subtle interrogation," Erin said.

When Pippa had shown up at his door, it had been his mother the rock star who'd answered. After hauling her inside and hugging her, Erin had stepped back to give her the once-over and announce they'd brought food and were staying to hang out for a bit with her and Xander.

"You can interrogate me now while I'm moderately defenseless and distracted by the guts of this dishwasher," she said truthfully.

Xander laughed.

"What are your intentions with our son?" Erin asked.

Xander's laugh choked off.

If she just concentrated on taking the motor apart

instead of the fact that her boyfriend's mother was asking her questions, it made her less nervous. "I like being with him. He's good at making grilled cheese sandwiches."

"Ben taught him that because one Mother's Day I said I wanted one with a cup of tomato soup," Erin confessed.

Xander was a very big man. In charge. Confident and bossy. But when he was around his parents, those instincts softened. It did something to her insides watching the way he cared for them. He'd done the same for her, Pippa had realized.

It wasn't just the door opening and the carrying of heavy things. He focused on her when she spoke. He listened. And remembered what things were important to her. Like bringing her potted plants instead of cut flowers because she'd created a lush oasis of green on her tiny front porch.

He'd said, "I want you to think of me every time you come home and see them."

"How is it you know how to fix a dishwasher?" Erin asked, bringing Pippa back from the memory.

"I've always been good at mechanical things. Engines mainly. I fixed the washing machine a lot when I was growing up. There were eleven kids, so as you might imagine, that washer got a lot of use. Later when the dishwasher in our apartment broke, my sister and I didn't have the money for repairs, so I added them to the list of things I can fix. So far, I can dismantle and rebuild car and motorcycle engines, dishwashers, washers, dryers, and small appliances like blenders. Keeps my hands busy and pays the bills."

Pippa twisted to stand and then rinsed the parts that had gotten food residue on them and did the same for two internal filters before reinstalling them and the casings she'd removed.

"Try it now," she said, washing her hands.

The grinding sound was gone, and everything seemed to work once again, so the four of them moved to the couches facing the west.

Xander really liked the sight of her there at his side as they drank wine and watched the sky go orange and red. Liked her in his space, talking to the people he loved and trusted.

"We've never met any of Xander's girlfriends or boyfriends before," his mom said to Pippa.

Xander's Pop choked out a laugh disguised as a cough and put a hand on Erin's knee. "My love."

"I just meant it was nice to be able to hang out with her doing this stuff. You're acting like I asked if they use protection. You do, right?"

Xander sighed. She was the most extra of people. It was simply who his mother had been all of his life.

"I should probably explain that none of them—my family I mean—have filters and boundaries when it comes to being nosy about one another's private lives. And of them, my mother is queen. But she wouldn't want to freak you out and scare you away," he said, giving his mother a look.

"This woman is made of sterner stuff than to be freaked out by a few questions. And I think she'd tell me to mind my own business if she wanted to. Probably in nicer terms."

Pippa laughed.

"We didn't get a chance to do more than say hello when you came to Brody's birthday party to pick Rennie up," Erin said to Pippa. "So I've had to ask around. Check my sources, so to speak. My brother and Elise speak really highly of you. Rennie and Marti as well. But I was convinced when Raven said she liked you."

His mother's best friend had been pretty close to a second mom in his life. She scared off plenty of people—and rightfully so, she didn't show her soft side to very many—but she'd always made a Xander-shaped space, no matter what.

She'd had a hard life and didn't trust easily or often. Her stamp of approval would have indeed swayed Erin.

Still, Xander sent a look that he hoped conveyed *back off now*.

"I didn't stop being your mother when you turned eighteen. Nor can I turn into a different mom. I'm genuine! Moms want to know this stuff."

Xander closed his eyes a moment, reaching out to take Pippa's hand and give it squeeze. "I didn't say anything about it. It's your story to tell or not," he murmured to her.

"Oh no. What did I do?" his mother asked.

"Not everyone is close to their mom," he said.

Pippa patted Erin's arm hoping to reassure her she wasn't upset. "I don't have a relationship with my parents. But I'm close with two of my sisters, and they ask me about condoms all the time."

Erin's mouth turned down into a frown. "I'm sorry. I know the pain of being estranged from family."

"Please don't apologize. Truly. It was nearly fourteen years ago now. I've been without them nearly as long as I had them. My life is better. It was the right choice."

They shifted topics as his dads shared the story of how Ben and Todd ended up married to Erin and having a family with her. Pippa and his mother seemed easy with one another, which was a relief.

But he wasn't sorry to hear them say their good nights so he could have some time alone with her.

"I'm sorry about that bit with my mother," he told her once they were on their own once again.

Her back was to him as she looked out over the lights of the city. "My mother's existence was consumed by keeping the household going, making sure everyone was fed, clothed and clean. So much so the older kids ended up doing a lot of the emotional parenting. Big families across the world have their own rules. Big families mandated and governed by the bishops of our church? Dozens more. With changes and additions all the time so you were always thinking about every little choice you made. Anxious. Keeps you tired."

He forced himself to remain still rather than go to her. Knowing she'd freeze up otherwise.

"Of the eleven kids, there were small groups with an older sibling who talked them through nightmares and the like. In some—though not all—that older sibling was the one who dried your tears and gave you a hug when you needed it. Rebecca and Esther are still the ones who I turn to when I need a pep talk and some love. I have another brother, he's the next oldest up from me. I was close to him. He protected me and the twins more than once from various things. He also looked me in the face and repudiated me. My mother did the same, and it didn't hurt nearly as much."

She shifted to face him with a reassuring look. "What I'm saying is, she's just fine," Pippa told him of his mother.

"She's interested in your life. She's invested in your emotional health. Absolutely not a bad thing. There are those moms who are overbearing and awful. She's not one of those either."

She didn't often talk about her childhood or the so-called group she grew up as part of. He'd done some research on them and the larger religious organization they were connected to. The guy at the head of it sounded like an abusive asshole, and Xander was relieved Pippa was far away from those assholes.

But he loved it that she'd given him those details. Trusted him enough to be vulnerable with those tender parts of herself.

"Thank you for sharing with me. I just want you to understand I hadn't told them those private details. She'll never bring it up again." In fact, she'd go out of her way to protect Pippa.

"It's not a secret, really. The group exists openly and brazenly. One of these days someone is going to cross the line, and it won't be one of their cronies on the police force or in the mayor's office protecting them. Power always reaches too far and too high eventually."

"Are there multiple wives? I mean, look, I come from a family with multiple husbands, so on its face I don't judge."

She shook her head. "What your family has is consensual and based on all three of them being adults and capable of choosing the lives they wanted to build. They're true partners and equals. There's no polygamy in the group. But there are *a lot* of very young wives and mothers trapped there by weaponized ignorance. The kids have been removed from public school and are taught at home, but not to any real standards. There are people my age still there who can barely read. We had no concept of what the world was like. I was fifteen years old, and I'd never been on the internet. I'd never been in a public library. When they told me I could check out as many books as I wanted…" She shook her head, a look of wonder on her features. "For so long I believed everything I'd been told, and then after we left it was hard to believe anything. The outside world wasn't on fire and full of pain. Or, it was in parts, but it was so much more than that. I had to learn to see and understand complexity because it wasn't a skill I'd ever been taught or could model. Out here there are women running corporations and sports teams, women inventing products and conducting lifesaving research. My uncle, who is a church leader too, said once in a church service that women were like farm animals. Not abusing them—too much—was simply good husbandry of resources. After all, if you mistreat your chickens, they lay less."

He blew out a breath instead of calling the guy a fucker.

"Keeping the women pregnant and in households full of very young children means they're too busy to want anything. Too busy to want equal rights. Too busy to even think about it. He said this in a room full of women. In a room full of people who claimed to love women all while telling stories about how to keep us shackled by exhaustion, so we never figured out we're worthy of so much more in life."

Xander said, "I don't know how to react because I don't want to make you responsible for how I feel. It's so far away from my reality. I know groups like yours exist but from reality television and the like."

"When we settled up here, Danny talked to my sisters about getting me, and them both as well, into therapy. So much change was happening, and I'd lost most everything I'd ever known. I didn't know how to be around other people. Information within the group—gossip, to be blunt—was currency. And a weapon. The older church women were always looking for something to pick at. Something to use to manipulate. So, at first, I said nothing. Shared nothing. CPS was involved at the start because when I finally went to the doctor and got registered for school, they were alarmed at how messed up my teeth were. And my wrist had been broken but not reset correctly, and they interviewed me to see how it happened."

"How did it happen?"

She'd been looking out the window, off to some distant memory, but her gaze swung to him then. "My oldest brother pushed me off the roof for not moving fast enough to suit him when they were fixing a leak."

"And the hospital did nothing? Aren't they mandatory reporters?"

"Yes. Which is why they didn't take me to the hospital. One of my aunts on my mom's side is the closest thing to a nurse we had. She did her best. I can still write and pick things up and fix cars because of her. There were other injuries she treated less successfully. They healed poorly enough to raise more red flags. So I had to tell the authorities here everything and then do it a few more times with some watchdog organizations keeping an eye on fringe groups like theirs. When they can, they help those who want to leave. One organization did trainings for law enforcement. Taught them ways to get inside compounds in cases of reported and suspected abuse. These groups help put together cases that'll result in convictions. Otherwise when these leaders get away with stuff and return to their congregations, it emboldens them and endangers everyone."

He gave in and took her hand, weaving their fingers together. "So, you're afraid to say too much, but also not enough."

She nodded. "It's something I still work on. All my life I yearned to be able to use my voice however I wanted, and then I got out and realized how much responsibility comes with that. Ever since I've been trying to find a middle path between too much and not enough."

"I want you to feel safe. Like you can tell me anything."

Her smile was a little wobbly at the edges. "I'm not normal. I grew up in a cult. I still go to therapy once every six weeks. I don't know if I'll ever be okay. I don't want to be dead weight, you know?"

Sometimes she broke his heart. She staggered him because he'd never imagined this was what it could feel like to be with someone. To care this much.

He slid a little closer and pulled her up and into his lap where she snuggled into his body, and he held her tight.

"Getting what you need makes you strong." He kissed the top of her head. "I don't even know what normal is. I do know you're beautiful and smart and a survivor. And that I value your voice. I want you to use it with me."

"You say that now. But I have a lot to say. I just *seem* quiet, but really that's a lie. I'm full of facts I need you to know."

He twisted to see her face better, grinning. "Promise?"

Her laughter seemed to dance over his skin.

No wonder people in love were so fucking insufferable. It felt amazing. Like nothing he'd ever experienced. Hell, like nothing he had the vocabulary to describe before Pippa came into his life.

"So go on then. Tell me a fact I need to know."

She managed to spin so she straddled his lap, facing him. "You sure? Once I pop that cork, goodness only knows what will come out."

"I can hardly wait," he teased.

"Crows can remember faces. If they like you, they bring you things. But if they don't, they totally hold grudges. They're super smart. Oh! And they have caws that are different by region. So, like a southern accent, or what have you."

"I heard they were smart. I didn't know about the regional differences. I'll make a note to always be nice to them," Xander said.

"Good. Now this next part is also facts, but feelings type facts about me and you. Ready?

Damn she was fun to be around.

"I think so. Hit me."

"I have *so much* romantic feeling for you. Desire for your attention. For your respect and your kindness. For the sound of your voice. Especially when you say my name." She blushed. "The way you make me feel is wondrous and beautiful, and there's no way I believe it's anything other than a gift."

Thank the heavens for her. He'd have been miserable for the last twenty-seven years if he'd known *this* was possible. Yet somehow it felt more miraculous when it burst into his life with sound and color and so much fucking feeling it was like a full symphony.

He stood, managing to keep her in his arms as he took them to his bedroom.

She kept herself wrapped around him as she trailed kisses up his neck and then nibbled the outer shell of his ear until goose bumps pebbled his skin.

That she wanted him so openly—all of him—was unbelievably sexy. He dropped his shoulder to get them both to the bed, and the sound of her laughter floated in the air between them.

He owed Rennie big time for bringing Pippa into his life.

Now that she was in it, he had every intention of doing all he could to keep her.

He wanted her at his side by choice, not out of obligation or fear. He knew she was dating someone else, but he'd let it play out as they'd gotten to know one another. She'd been with Xander so often, whoever it was wasn't getting much of her. And if whoever it was couldn't do the work to keep a woman like Pippa satisfied, Xander wasn't going to feel bad when he brought up being exclusive.

CHAPTER
EIGHT

Pippa lay there, content to do nothing more than watch as he went to his knees and pulled his sweater free, tossing it on the nearby chair.

He was unabashedly beautiful. Ink spreading across his chest and upper arms. Taking up much of his right shoulder and chest was a massive black-and-gray-scale snake twining around roses. The length of it wrapped around his pectoral muscles and then under his arm and up his back. The tip of the tail nestled against his neck, just below his ear. On his left inner biceps was a traditional black cat. On his left side, a Tank Girl tattoo Raven had done with a glamor design. Beauty with a snarl. Smaller ones marked his body here and there, like the Nordic-themed hare at the inside of his elbow.

Both his nipples beaded, small platinum rings in each as he lazily drew his fingertips up the wall of his very wide chest and then reversed. Her gaze seemed locked to the movement as he slid his hands down to the waist of his pants.

Clever fingers undid the buckle of his belt, before the

muffled *pop* sounded as the button won free. The click-click-click of the descending zipper was a finger down her spine. The smirk he wore told her he knew exactly what he was doing to her.

Shivers ran riot at the sound of his belt sliding through the loops as he pulled it free. One of his brows rose as he took her in. He rolled the leather, tucking the buckle around the tail to hold it, and then he laid it on her belly.

Anticipation burned through her at the weight of it there. At all the *what ifs* in her head.

"The look on your face is unbelievably sexy," he said as he got rid of his clothes.

Fully naked, lit by a bedside lamp, Alexander Copeland Keenan was absolutely breathtaking. She let out a shaky breath as she took him in. "I can't quite believe you're real. Here. Naked."

"It's about to get even better," he said in a desire-thick voice that sent her senses into overdrive. She couldn't stop the little shiver and writhe in response.

He set the belt on the bed next to her, and she turned her head a moment, taking it in with a dark slice of desire as she thought about what he might do with it.

She'd worn a wrap dress, and he pulled the tie free of the bow before unbuttoning it. He made a sound—an aching, yearning sort of groan—that sent a rush of pleasure through her, as if she was the sexiest person alive.

It was unexpectedly powerful to be wanted like that. But, like the belt, she drank it in. It was safe to feel this way, so surrounded by pleasure she floated, because it was him.

.   .   .

Sliding the soft material apart, Xander hummed at the sight. Delight and desire chased through his gut. On the outside the dress was pretty; the pale-blue material had called to his fingertips all night long.

Beneath? Soft pink lace covered her tits, serving them higher. Presenting them to him like the gift they were. Underpants of the same color in the bikini style she favored. He traced his fingers from her lips down, over her chin, pausing to dip into the hollow of her throat, across her collarbone.

Her breath went ragged, and a deep-pink flush kissed her chest and neck.

The scent of her, so wet and responsive, rose as he cupped her pussy, the heat of her slick against his palm.

Pippa rolled her hips, shifting her legs restlessly. Easing that need a little, he helped her out of her bra and pulled her dress free. Last, he drew her panties off, and she lay there smiling up at him in a way that managed to incite and soothe at the same time.

He dropped a kiss on the blackbird on her hip and then across her belly to the other hip. Her skin was warm and soft as he slid his lips up her ribs and neck, back to her mouth.

Her flavor was addictive, so he gave in and fed his craving, kissing her as he reached for the belt, letting the leather fall from the roll he'd put it in, listening to changes in her body as she heard the sound, felt the light tap as it fell across her arm and side.

The gasp of surprised pleasure she gave sent a full body tremor through his muscles. He got to his knees, straddling her, deliberately dragging his cock along her labia.

"I've been thinking about this for a few weeks now," he

told her, taking her wrists and wrapping his belt around them. Xander secured it enough that she was bound, but not so tight she couldn't get free if she pulled her wrists apart hard enough.

They'd slowly wade into deeper waters. He wanted her to understand she could trust him, and he wanted to learn what she liked. And didn't like.

"Just because you like some edge, doesn't mean you'll like everything we try." He kissed her and then stretched her arms above her head. Her pupils were huge, her lips parted. "If we do something you're uncomfortable with or you don't like, say so. It's not fun for either of us that way. We can slow down too."

She nodded. "Can we speed it up?"

Laughing, he bent to kiss her again. "Greedy. I like it. Do you know what else I like?"

He scooted up so he straddled her chest, his knees just under her arms. When she made an O with her mouth, he tapped her lips with the head of his cock and groaned when she licked across it.

"Yes," he nearly crooned. Reeling at her easy submission. "You can hold on to your headboard if it helps."

She stretched her fingers out, wrapping them loosely around one of the slats, and took a deep breath. He waited until they'd connected again, their gazes meeting before he brushed his cock against her mouth once more, and she opened up.

Xander eased his hips forward, insistent, his desire clear, and she swallowed first the head and then the shaft. She made low, needy sounds he used to gauge how far to thrust, listening for that point when pleasure became anxiety. Then he eased back.

Learning her. Hell, learning himself because sex with her was different, and that meant he was different. They were making something unique.

Those little sounds worked on him though. Really well. So much so he pulled back because he wanted to fuck her.

She gave an annoyed huff when he moved, her eyes snapping open.

"I have plans," he told her before she could say anything. "Stay as you are." When she obeyed, he leaned to her ear and whispered, "Good girl."

She whimpered, and his cock responded.

He licked and bit her nipples until they were dark and stiff. He left a lazy trail of kisses down her belly, past her pussy entirely. Starting upward again when he reached her ankle.

The back of her knee seemed very sensitive, as was the seam where her leg met her body.

"Your cunt is so fucking pretty," he said, and then spread it open, blowing over all those juicy folds.

There was another of those sounds at that, so he did it again and then kissed her deep and slow, his tongue making firm, steady circles until her thighs trembled and he worried he was going to come before he even got inside her. His fingers stretched her, their thrusts in time with those circles.

Her sounds changed to incoherent nonsense words until she said, "If you stop, I will kick you in the face."

So he didn't; instead he increased the speed and pressure, turning his wrist just so until she arched, her thighs clamping against his shoulders as she tried to move away, but he built a second orgasm right on the heels of the first. When it hit, she tensed for long moments before finally relaxing to the mattress with a sated sigh.

"I'm glad I didn't have to kick you in the face," she said lazily, making him laugh. That tease! He kept taking her right to the point of climax and then stopping, only to do it all over again. She couldn't deny the end product was pretty damned spectacular, and she told him so.

"On your belly," he said, and she managed to turn over without her hands coming loose. Later Pippa would maybe examine why that was so pleasing, but for that moment she wanted to weep with joy when she heard the sound of the condom wrapper being opened.

He pulled her hips up after bending her right leg slightly. Then, thank the heavens, she felt the press of the head of him against her and then the first sweet burn of entry. That burn wisped away as he continued to stroke deeper each time until he was finally all the way in.

He stilled, waiting until she settled a little. Which was comforting and also totally hot.

Pippa sighed, drunk with pleasure as she gave herself over to his control. Xander's weight was just right, pressing her into the mattress but not oppressively so. It added to that delicious ache he created with the belt wrapped around her wrists. It wasn't so much the thing restraining her as his very clear desire to take over. Letting go and trusting him left her exposed. Vulnerable.

And for the first time in her life, being vulnerable wasn't a curse or a problem to overcome. It was a gift because she knew on some level she was safe in his keeping.

He fucked her slow but deep. Over and over and over again until she wasn't sure of anything but that bed with the two of them in it. It was almost too much, but in a good way. Every time she held on past that little bit of fear it felt even better.

His grip at her hip dug in sharply, and she knew he was drawing closer because his pace sped slightly. He arranged her again, getting impossibly deeper, harder until her aching nipples stroked over the blankets, sending ribbons of pleasure to join the rest until he went deep one last time with a grunt of her name and what sounded like *fuck yes*.

"Will you stay?" he asked her a few minutes later after she'd turned to back into him.

"I have to be at Twisted Steel first thing and my work bag is at home." Which sucked because he was warm, and she was totally relaxed and sleepy.

"Damn."

She smiled there in the dark. Utterly happy.

"Do you work on Saturday?"

"Not this week."

"Stay here Friday night. We'll go out, hear music, hang out with our friends, and end up here. I've got to work, but my first client isn't until nine thirty, and you're welcome to sleep in as long as you like."

"I'll make you pancakes first, and then I'll head out with you. There's a garden show Rebecca wants to go to, so I'll just drive directly to her place." She kissed his arm and then rolled from bed, getting dressed.

"I'll walk you down to your car."

CHAPTER
NINE

Pippa saw Hamish's name on her screen and smiled before answering the call. "Hi there."

"Hello yourself, Pippa. Since we had to cancel our last date, I was thinking we could reschedule. I want to hear what you've been up to in person. I miss you."

"I miss you too." Pippa'd been working to fill her life with other things. And people. She loved Hamish. Had for a while. Though she knew he liked her, cared about her deeply, she also knew he fought himself and his feelings for her. For a while she'd tried to find a way to meet him where he was. Hamish was afraid to trust, be truly vulnerable. And to love someone truly—and goodness help her, she loved him—you had to let them close enough to see your softest parts.

Though she knew he wasn't in a place to love her in return, she honestly couldn't imagine a life without him in it. And she didn't want to.

The wake up call moment occurred to her just a few days earlier. Xander readily gave her what Hamish resisted so hard. She didn't need to guess, or tiptoe. He paid attention and he didn't hesitate. It didn't make it hurt less that she and Hamish weren't going to have what she'd wanted for so long. But it was easier to accept.

That, and things had gotten more serious between her and Xander over the last week or so. It was still early, but they'd taken another step toward a relationship after they'd finally slept together several nights prior. An exclusive relationship. Soon enough the conversation would be had, though it was already understood.

She had to tell Xander about Hamish. After she told Hamish about Xander. She needed Hamish to understand that just because there'd be no sex between them, she would still be there for him. Still his friend—always his friend.

"What are you doing tonight?"

"I...I have a date," she said. It was best to be honest, and she was a terrible liar anyway. "How about tomorrow? I'm busy in the morning and early afternoon. Rebecca and I are doing the garden expo. But I'll be free after two or so."

"Shall I come round at two? I'll bring snacks."

"That sounds great. I'll see you then."

He put the phone on his nightstand. The problem with not being high all the time was it left him without anything to hide from reality. He was in love with Pippa Hall.

Worse. It might be too late. He'd taken her presence for granted as he'd fumbled around, trying to pretend he didn't really need a long-term romantic commitment.

Now he was alone. Knowing he wanted to make promises like that. Not with anyone else but Pippa. Pippa who he'd pushed away. Thinking she'd be there when he was ready. What an ass he'd been.

Over the last few weeks since he'd made her dinner at his place, he'd seen her less and less. They'd connected regularly via text, and they'd had a date scheduled for the week prior, but he'd had to make a quick trip to Los Angeles to deal with some label stuff and he'd needed to cancel. Though he had asked if she wanted to come along, thinking a few days by the beach might have been lovely. But she had work and it wasn't so easy for her to leave.

Normally, she'd follow up when he returned from a trip. Suggest another day to meet. But though they'd been in contact since, she hadn't brought it up.

So, he'd tried a few times. Had even shown up at her townhouse a few days before so they could talk. She'd been gone and out of contact until late that same night when she'd texted that she'd been out for the day and was sad to have missed him.

Out with Xander, he figured. Hamish knew she'd started seeing him some weeks prior, but his pride had left him with a blind spot.

He'd created the distance between himself and Pippa. And in that distance, someone else had come along and filled that need Hamish hadn't. Like a fool.

He created the problem, and he was the one who had to fix it. Or lose everything.

He'd spent much of his life alone. Had told himself he was not only used to it, but that he liked it.

Which was true to a certain point. He did like being on his own. But he had a circle. A small, tight, trusted group. He *needed* that connection and understanding. And she'd given it to him.

He'd acted like a rabid animal, but she hadn't run. Everything he'd ever wanted was right there in the form of a redheaded grease monkey and he'd just...screwed it up. Like he'd been terrified of all along, but what a fucked-up self-fulfilling prophecy that was.

With a groan, he swung his legs from bed and went to get himself showered. Doing nothing got him into this mess, so it was time to do something. Before it was too late. Even if it *was* too late.

Not wanting to obsess on it any further, Hamish got in his car and headed east across the bridge. Driving until there were less houses and more trees. More space between lots. Out at the Franklins' you could still see the stars at night. It smelled green and clean, and the birds were louder than traffic.

The house wasn't fancy. Though Hamish and the other three Franklin children now adults had helped here and there with improvements. James could make a far higher profit with his vet practice if he didn't take in every stray and hard case he came upon.

But if he hadn't, Hamish wouldn't be using his key to let himself inside the main house. "Mom?"

He heard the creak of her chair and headed to her sewing room where she'd just snipped a thread and was making her way to the door.

"Thought I heard you come in." She turned her cheek for the kiss he delivered, and then he was engulfed in an Addie hug. One he'd needed.

"I had some free time, and you mentioned your garden

was overgrown and was wanting some clean up, so I'm here to volunteer my hands and my back."

She grinned as she patted his cheek. "How about this? Your dad made eggplant parm last night. Let's have some for lunch, and you can tell me why there are shadows in your gaze." Addie tucked her arm through his, and they sauntered to the kitchen.

Hamish had a gourmet chef's dream of a kitchen. One designed for him by his elegant and very well-paid interior designer. It had all the bells and whistles with high-end finishes that made him feel successful every time he came into the room. But this was what he would forever think of as perfect.

The floor near the table had been replaced more than once. It was the direct line of traffic to the back doors that led out to the deck and the passage to the gardens and the clinic, so the wood was smoothest there.

The table was huge. Even bigger when it had all the leaves in it. During the holidays and for anyone's birthday it would hold so much food Hamish would be certain he'd never be hungry again in his life.

He'd studied for his driver's license exam at that table. Had done homework supervised by various Franklins depending on the subject. He'd written songs there. Wrapped presents at Christmastime on the huge surface.

Every bit of that house carried a special memory for him. Which lauas, he supposed, what home meant.

She bustled around as he grabbed plates and filled glasses with ice and tea.

"I'm in love with Pippa Hall, but I've mucked it up so

badly I think I might have lost her," he blurted out before he could convince himself not to.

She sat across from him and pushed a plate of cookies in his direction. "For the wait for the eggplant to reheat. And also, because there's no wrong time for a chocolate chip cookie. Before we go any further, let me start by saying it's rarely as close to *too late* as it seems. Tell me why you think you might have lost her."

"We started seeing one another a year ago. You all threw me that big welcome home party after the tour ended, remember? Anyway. She was there, and I'd met her before because she and Jessi were tight, but that night we ended up in a twenty-four-hour diner eating pancakes and talking about...nothing. And everything. It was so intense at the start I kept waiting for it to wear off. But it didn't. And then I got scared. Because I mess everything up. She's...well she's good and compassionate and kind, and I am nowhere near good enough for her. So, I pushed her away. Said I needed space to get myself together. That I couldn't commit to a relationship."

Addie sucked in a breath but said nothing.

"I know. It was stupid and cowardly. I panicked."

She patted his hand. "It was *human*. You've been left by people you loved. It marks you forever."

His ma had abandoned him when he'd been nine years old. He'd lived on the streets and in and out of the system until he got good enough to duck authority whenever he could. Plenty of adults failed him. Until the Franklins had met him one night and changed the trajectory of his entire life.

Proved that it was possible to trust someone who wasn't

going to walk away. Proved there were people who deserved to be called parents.

"Don't make excuses for me," he said.

She waved a lazy hand. "I don't make excuses for anyone's behavior. You're a grown man, responsible for yourself. Understanding why you might do something is important. Helps you avoid mistakes in the future. So, what happened to bring you here?"

"I know I broke her heart. I could see how much I hurt her in her eyes. But she gave me space. I continued to see her regularly around my work and travel. We got closer. She's dated other people, but none of them mattered. None of them changed her focus. None of them got in between us. Until now. Until Xander."

The words actually hurt to say, but it felt necessary to name him rather than let Xander be some nameless ghost.

Then again, he knew more than most just how flesh and blood Xander was. How alluring and intense. The Xander he'd experienced had been so focused on Hamish it had left him a little lightheaded. The whiskey had helped, he imagined. Still, one needn't be drunk to give over to just how sexy and in charge Xander had been. But that Xander had been of a temporary sort. It had been years since anything sexual had happened between them.

Apparently, he'd been waiting for Pippa. Hamish's someone, damn it.

"I heard they were getting close. Have you spoken to her about this? What is it you want here?" his mother asked without a bit of judgment. Whatever it was, she'd love him as much after the saying of it.

He sucked in a breath like he was going to dive into the

ocean. "I'm seeing her tomorrow, and I think she's going to tell me she's with him now and we can't be together."

"But you don't know for sure?"

"She didn't say it to me directly. But I know her. I can hear the distance she's making. But I can also hear she still cares about me. I need the chance to tell her how I feel. I don't think it'll miraculously fix things, I just know nothing can be fixed until I'm honest."

His mom paused, thinking carefully before saying anything else, and Hamish wanted to kick himself for not coming to her sooner.

"There's much to love about Pippa." She smiled and then shook her head. "The first time I met her I made her cry because I asked her what her full name was. I didn't mean to. Of course, I don't have to tell you that. You know my heart as well as I know yours."

"Oh no." Hamish knew his mom would have been wrecked to make anyone cry, much less someone she really cared about.

"Her given name is beautiful. A very big name for a wee sprite. Epiphany. I repeated it back because it's such a lovely word. And she burst into tears. A great storm of emotion. After it had passed, she told me she'd cried because she'd never heard anyone say it with love like that before."

"Good god," he said, heart breaking for her.

"Pippa is the name she chose for herself when she started her life outside the group. Epiphany was left behind, you know, in that compound down in Arizona. But there are parts of her still, that little girl who *should* have been treated like one of one, and instead was one of dozens. Interchangeable uteruses. They made her feel like any deviation from the norm they set was a defect. So much that she analyzed and overanalyzed every single thing she did or felt. Or thought."

Her gaze met his. "Every time someone says your name you should hear you're loved. But you didn't have that, and she didn't even know it wasn't normal until she was fifteen. You didn't believe you deserved it until you were even older than she was. You two are soul mates."

The truth of it should have been lowering but instead... instead it offered him a glimpse of what life could be if he loved her out loud, the way she deserved. If he got the chance. "That's what I'm afraid of. I'm afraid I've left it too long."

She got up, circling the table to kneel next to him, putting an arm around his shoulders. "I've seen how she looks at you. I've seen how you are with her. I don't know if you can continue a romance with her. I hope so because I'd love that for you. But you're soul mates regardless. The connection is the connection. You and she are the same where it counts. If she has moved on, you will be in her life in a different way. But in it. Pippa keeps people she cares about."

She stood and then kissed the top of his head in a way that made him feel young and vulnerable but totally safe at the same time, and he thanked fate for the thousandth time he'd been found by James and Addie and showed what real love was.

"What I want you to understand and admit—first and foremost you deserve a soul connection with other people. You deserve love and kindness, and you deserve to work for them like everyone else. You're handsome and talented and so very smart, and a few layers beneath that devil-may-care mask you wear is a sweet, softhearted boy who has a hand with poetry."

He blinked back tears. "You'll go swelling my head."

"Impossible for it to be any worse than it is already. Ah, and look, lunch is ready now. My shoulder is acting up. Can you bring it to the table, please?"

He stood and pulled her into a hug. "I love you, Mom."

Never ma. He called the woman who birthed him that. He'd spent years unpacking that one, and he was still working on it.

"I love you too, sweetheart."

CHAPTER
TEN

"Sourdough pancakes and bacon after a night of sex so spectacular I have a little bit of a limp today. I think I need to keep you."

Xander looked at Pippa, backlit by the rainy October morning beyond the windows. In a bit they'd head in opposite directions, him to the shop and her to Rebecca's so he wanted to savor these last minutes.

"*I think* I'd be okay with that," she teased.

"Yeah? And would you be okay keeping me?"

Her smile softened and then got serious as she nodded. "I imagine the care and keeping of a Xander is pretty complicated and vigorous."

He said, "I think it's time we step up and take this into an exclusive situation. I don't want to fuck around. I want you."

She nodded, a pretty pink flush on her cheeks and neck. "I want you too."

He'd been trying to get that shade of pink right since they'd met. Each time she blushed he got a little closer on the next drawing.

Damn she filled him up with good shit. He leaned close enough to kiss her. "Okay then. That's that. I'm at work until ten or so. Are you free after?"

"I am. You can come to me, or text me and I'll meet you here."

"I'll come to you." He locked his focus on her. "I will always come for you."

"I need to tell you something. Mainly because I don't want to hide things. Being lied to is a big deal for me. After I go out with Rebecca, I'm seeing the person I've been sort of dating. It's my plan to tell him we can only be friends. I knew this was coming. I *hoped* it was. Nothing has happened with him since before you and I…just so you know."

God, she was so fucking adorable.

"I haven't been with anyone else since our second date," he confessed, though he honestly didn't care who came before him, and all who came before her were pale comparisons. She was his now.

"Oh. Well. Good."

Since she was being so honest, he figured he should probably do the same. "I know it's Hamish Wilson."

"I…I thought you might hear if you asked Rennie."

He nodded. "I did ask Rennie. And she told me to talk to you about it."

Her laugh broke the tension and had him taking her hand. "So, you went to…" she pursed her lips as she thought, "…Brody."

That had him laughing. "You know us both pretty well, huh?" Brody had confirmed Hamish's identity and had said Pippa and the musician seemed to have a fairly deep connection.

Her pleased blush was just as enchanting as her embarrassed one. "He's my friend," she repeated. "Nothing more."

Xander accepted it as the truth. Challenges would come their way, but she wasn't going to betray him.

"I got you." He kissed her forehead.

On their way out, he gave her a keycard for the elevators up to the apartment along with a controller for the parking gate. "You already know the spot to park. This way you can come in directly without having to wait for me to buzz you in."

"You're determined to make me cry this morning. Thank you."

They headed the same direction for a little while until she peeled off toward her sister's place and he kept north to get to Written On the Body.

She went over what she was going to say to Hamish a dozen times. Because no matter how happy she was with Xander and the way their relationship was deepening and getting more serious, she loved Hamish. She couldn't switch it off. Didn't want to. He was part of her. Someone she turned to all the time. The core being of who she was just knew he was supposed to be in her life.

Pippa needed to firmly put him out of all sweaty, naked activities. Unfortunately. He was *very good* at sweaty, naked things.

Before she could make herself any more anxious, Hamish was standing on her porch. "I brought hand pies."

"You're my favorite," she teased, motioning him inside, neatly sidestepping a mouth kiss but happily taking the hug.

Several minutes later, they ended up in her living room with food and drinks.

"I need to talk to you about something important," she said. "I've been dating other people. Generally, I did to keep busy. It was okay. I can admit the only person I had sex with during the last year has been you. Not a difficult choice. It's important you understand it wasn't because I felt I couldn't. I didn't...desire the depth of intimacy and connection from anyone but you. Early last month I started seeing someone, and it's gotten serious. I'd planned to talk to you about it before now, but you had to travel. I should have rescheduled sooner, I know. I was a coward. I don't want to hurt you. I don't want to lose you, but some aspects of our friendship need to change."

He blurted out, "*I panicked.* I told you a bunch of bullshit to keep you around but not let you get closer. It was desperate and petty, but I couldn't let you go. I told myself I didn't have it in me to be in a monogamous romance. When I came off tour, right before we met, I had a problem with sleeping pills. And staying-awake pills. Pills of all kinds really. And so, I had to get myself right and thinking straight again. Being very honest with you, there were times when being around you was so soothing and relaxing it felt a lot like addiction."

"Why didn't you tell me this earlier?" Before she'd let herself love someone else. "I could have reacted differently. We could have addressed it." They could have fixed it!

"It was bullshit. I'm a bad bet. I eventually fuck everything up and people walk away. And I know on an instinctual level I can't take you walking away like we never had this connection."

She blinked back tears. "I would *never* walk away from you. I cherish this connection we share. It's important to me. *You're* important to me. You tried to push me away for months. Did I desert you?"

"I'd rather press my face to the window of your life than not have you at all because I fucked up somehow and drove you off. Look at what I've done as it is. I had you. You wanted me. I wanted you, and I complicated it and messed it up so severely I've lost you to someone else who can love you better."

"You haven't lost me. Like the lyric you played me, I've been here all along. You are part of me. Forever. Always my dear friend. I don't want you out of my life. God. I'd be lost without you."

"Xander can't be happy about me being around."

She gave him a look. Pippa hadn't said names to either of them, and yet they'd both known. She'd been clueless.

"I told him I was speaking to you today about everything. I won't betray him or the promise I made when we took our relationship exclusive. And I don't think you'd ask that of me. I want to be clear though. I'm not hiding you. Lies are opportunities to lose the people you care about. I care about him. A lot. But it doesn't mean I don't care about you."

"I'm in love with you, Pippa," he said, knocking the wind from her chest. She went hot and cold as her heart pounded so hard, she wondered if she was going to pass out.

. . .

"Do you know how long I waited to hear that?" she asked him quietly, her voice full of emotion. "How many times I told myself if I was patient and showed you I was worthy of trust, you'd finally see me and what I felt?"

He rose, but she shook her head and pointed him back to the couch, but he went to her, got to his knees in front of where she sat. "Tell me it's not too late. Tell me we can make it work."

"I don't know what to say." She dashed away her tears with the back of her hand.

"I'm sorry. I'm sorry I pushed you away. I'm sorry I ran. I'm sorry I took you for granted. I'm sorry I didn't tell you how I felt before now because you deserved to know. I haven't been with anyone since the first time I kissed you. *There is no one else but you.*

"It was never that you weren't worthy of me. It's the opposite. You deserve better than me, but I'm too selfish to let that keep me from speaking at long last. I should have long before now. Let me make it up to you. Give me the opportunity to love you better than I have."

Her gaze roved over his face, and he hated that he'd made her so wary of his motives.

"Just tell me this. Do you love me?"

She swallowed and then chewed her bottom lip a moment before she said, "I'm in love with you."

He started to speak, but she put her fingers against his lips.

"I'm falling in love with Xander, and I like that. You and I spend time together and it's wonderful, but after someone tells you they can't commit to you, it's hard to not second-guess everything you do. I'm always anticipating you finally moving on."

He had to breathe through the pain of that one.

"I used to ration you," he said. "Tell myself I could only see you a certain number of times a month because I didn't want to send you the wrong message. But I was lying to myself because here you are, getting the message, only it's not true. I want to love you the way you deserve to be loved."

She touched his cheek and then clasped her hands in her lap again.

"It's not that simple. I'm with Xander and…he makes me happy. He gets me. I'm not worried he's going to walk away. He holds my hand in public. He introduced me as his girlfriend a few days ago."

"So what? We've got a year worth of experiences."

Her eyes widened, and her head tilted in a way that sent the primal part of his brain cowering. He'd meant it didn't compare, but he should have kept his mouth shut.

"*So what*? So what? The last time we were out on a date, and we saw someone you knew, you introduced me as your *friend*. That's what. It's unfair of you to pretend that's meaningless."

He admitted, "You're right. It was unfair. I'm jealous. I was a dick. I wanted to keep you far enough away I didn't get too attached but not so far you weren't attached to *me* and that's fucked. I'm sorry. Give me a chance to be better. To introduce you as my girlfriend. To shout it from the rooftops."

She shook her head, but he spoke before she could because he needed her to understand why he waited so long to open up to her fully.

"I met the Franklins because I lived on the streets. They're part of a faith-based group that delivers supplies and support to unhoused people, at risk youth, that sort of thing. Over months they would find me and bring me food, warm clothing. A better sleeping bag. Eventually I let them convince me to come to their home for dinner. A few visits later, they convinced me to wash clothes there. Take showers. But I always made them bring me back out. Even after I'd been at their table dozens of times."

He hadn't really told her all the details of his life before he ended up with the Franklin family. She sensed it was a difficult story and never pushed. But it left him with a few scars.

If he was going to win Pippa back, he had to lay himself bare to her.

"I was absolutely terrified they were using me, and I just couldn't see it. That's the life I was living. Everything was transactional. But my mom never gave up. Like a dog with a bone, that one." He smiled. "I slept in their tool shed at first. Three, maybe four months. They kept sneaking in furniture. Blankets. Clean clothes. They put a fridge in the garage so I could eat whenever I wanted to. By the time I slept inside the house, it had taken about eighteen months since I'd first met them. Then they were able to get me in the system and be my foster parents in a long-term placement. They tried to adopt me, but my biological mother would resurface, cause trouble, and fuck off again when she got bored. The upheaval and constant anxiety she brought with her would mess everything up. I'd have nightmares I'd end up on the street again, alone. My mom—Addie—saw how it changed my behavior." And the way it had broken his heart a little more each time Carol Hall had abandoned him anew. "It was easiest and most secure to keep the situation we had as a permanent placement. Once they stopped talking adoption my ma lost interest. No trouble to stir, I guess. Anyway, since she left me alone, we were able to move on with our lives and our family. The Franklins gave me a safe, stable life full of love. And then they taught me what it meant to build a real home and family."

"How old were you?"

"I was eleven when they first came around. I lived with them from just before thirteen until nineteen when I started touring and working on my music career. They couldn't adopt me when I was a minor, but right before I turned twenty, they were finally able to." It shouldn't have meant so much. He knew they loved him and thought of him as their son. But that official paperwork, even as he was an adult— especially because he was of age and had a choice—had enabled him to close that door to his past and face his future knowing he was loved.

He shook himself from that memory. "I still have a room at the house. It's my *home*. But the years before that? They made me into a person who finds it very hard to trust other people fully. I make shitty, reckless choices that push people away. Mostly it's for the best because they're not good people. But sometimes they're life-altering connections. I was scared absolutely witless by the way you move me. Honestly? I'm afraid right now I'm not good enough for you, but I want to try anyway."

He took a deep breath, surprised at how light he felt after saying all that. Knowing on a visceral level Pippa was his safe place too.

"I wanted to explain a little. So you understood why I did what I did. You don't need to answer me now. Take some time to think it over. Just don't reject it out of hand. *Give me a chance*," he repeated.

She opened her mouth, but the doorbell rang, followed by a knock.

Frowning, she got up and Hamish followed. "I can get my own door," she muttered.

"I know you can," Hamish said. "Think of me as backup in case you need it."

"Backup? To save me from some kids selling band candy or cookies? Ooh, or that popcorn. I like the popcorn. Did you know popcorn is different from other types of corn in that the hull is thicker? It's what allows the steam to build and make it pop."

"I love your facts." Hamish bet she was a sucker for every single earnest little face she opened the door to.

She stretched to look through the peephole and then sighed. "Don't start anything," she told him and then opened up.

CHAPTER
ELEVEN

Xander looked down at her, noting the red eyes. He stepped into her place and pulled her close. A great deal of his annoyance at what he'd overheard melted away at her response.

"What's going on?" she asked him as she leaned back. "I thought you were working until later?"

He flicked his attention to Hamish. "I was finishing up some ink for King. We chatted about you and how awesome you are. Hamish came up. Don't be mad, baby, he wasn't gossiping. He was telling a story about a Twisted Steel party that Hamish was at. With you."

More accurately, Xander had sort of engineered the subject to come up because he was nosy. King had said Hamish looked at Pippa like she was integral to his existence when he thought no one was paying attention. No need to share that part though.

Her expression softened a little, and he bent to drop a kiss on that mouth he thought of night and day. She went to her toes to meet him, easing the rising need to punch

Hamish for trying to convince her to choose him over Xander.

"And so, you trotted right over to mark your territory?" Hamish said, and Pippa growled.

"I don't need to mark her. She's not a thing. She's mine here." Xander rubbed his fist over his heart. Early days or not, Xander knew what he knew. Pippa was meant to be in his life. He also knew when King had told him that, it had combined with what he'd already known and experienced with Hamish. He was compelling and charming and incredibly intelligent. He certainly wasn't going to miss what a fantastic catch Pippa Hall was.

He'd finished up with King and moved his next client to his day off the following week. He needed to speak with her.

That morning between the two of them had sealed something. A promise that made her his. And once he'd accepted that, everything was clear. Hamish was a storm of a different type, and Xander wasn't going to let him blow up their relationship.

"Stop this. I'm in the middle of eating a very delicious thyme and mushroom hand pie, so you two can brood at each other in the hall or join me so we can deal with this whole whatever." Clearly done with them, she turned and headed toward the living room.

"I can't be sorry. I know you dig her too, but, mate, I'm in love with her," Hamish said quietly.

"So am I," Xander told him as he trailed after Pippa.

She'd tucked herself in the recliner near the window, and Xander realized that's where she'd been sitting when he'd overheard their conversation. A chair, not the couch where Hamish could have snuggled up on her.

"Now that we're all seated and I'm not choking on testosterone," Pippa began, "let's just deal with this. Obviously, I don't need to make introductions. Though what I sense is that your prior connection isn't *merely* social, which wasn't mentioned earlier today."

Xander looked over to Hamish before he decided to be honest. "We met six, maybe seven years ago. We've hung out many times in large groups. And a handful of times we had sex of some type."

Hamish interrupted, "My friend Harlow is engaged to his cousin Miles, so we were both at the engagement party in June."

"This sex of some type, when was that?" Pippa asked Hamish directly. That had something to do with the two of them obviously, so Xander stayed out of it.

"I said I hadn't been with anyone since you and I was being truthful. The last time was a drunken fist fuck in the dark after a Showbox gig. Four years ago," Hamish answered.

Pippa nodded. "Thank you."

"He knows me well enough to understand I'm not just going to stand by while he swoops in and attempts to steal you," Xander told her, getting back to the subject. Though undeniable heat had flashed through him at the memory of those stolen moments, his hand shoved down the front of Hamish's jeans, both of them jerking the other's cock.

"There's a great deal of *she's mine* sort of language going on here," she said, though not necessarily in complaint. More like a question.

Knowing dug in with sharp claws.

Xander said, "I'm going to be blunt. You know who I am

and what I am. And you like it. Which is one of the main reasons I do it. Because, my beautiful Pippa, you want to be possessed."

She let out a slow breath, but her pupils got wider, and she licked her lips. Goddamn, she was sexy as fuck.

In the background, he registered Hamish's groan. "I will never put you in a cage. I know what you lived with. I will never stifle your will and independence." Xander took her hand and squeezed. "I'll hold you down in the best way. I'll keep you safe. I'll spoil you and take care of you the way you deserve to be. You're mine and I am most assuredly yours. You take care of me too, don't you? Don't you bring extra food in your lunch these days because I might show up for a visit and you want to be sure I've got a snack? When I was in the shower last night, you put my pajama bottoms in the dryer, so they were warm when I got out. You fixed my dishwasher and let my mother get away with asking if we use protection. If that's not the care and keeping of a Xander, what is then, baby? Hm?"

She laughed a little at that. *Definitely his.*

Xander had always liked being in charge. Of everything. He'd wanted to do it himself. Wanted to do it better than anyone else. Wanted to take care of the people he loved.

Later with lovers it had shifted into something a little harder. A little sharper. Rougher. But with Pippa it was more. She brought out those darker urges but also to cosset and pet. That she *liked* the edge of his teeth and to be bound at his whims made it even hotter.

That's why he was so certain she was *it*. That what they had was worth defending. All those parts of him turned themselves toward her. She saw them and accepted them. It left him deeply satisfied.

He pulled her chair over to the couch where he and Hamish sat. Needing to be able to touch her.

She shook her head, amused at him. Indulgent. Another one of those things she did that made his cock hard as hell.

Pippa waved a hand between him and Hamish. "As you already know one another, that part is done. Hamish and I saw one another casually for the last year or so. On and off. We were always friends, and that's what we'll continue to be." Her voice broke at the end.

"He's in love with you." Xander looked over to Hamish briefly. Hamish met his gaze directly, and there was a *click.* Something flared between them. Something unexpected because they saw the other through Pippa, but also knew things like what the other sounded like when they came.

Potential. Dark and sexy and not necessarily shaped like most other relationships.

"I love you too," Xander said to Pippa.

"You do?" Surprised pleasure brought a blush to her cheeks.

He couldn't help his grin her way. "Yep."

The blush paled, and she burst into tears. "I love you."

"Why are you crying? Pippa. Don't cry." He looked to Hamish, who appeared to be as clueless as Xander.

She covered her face with her hands and kept crying. "I love him too. I love you both and I don't want to choose. I'm selfish. A terrible, awful person."

Xander handed over the box of tissues. "Here now. Seeing you cry makes me want to punch him all over again. I'd just gotten past it."

That brought a surprised laugh from her and from Hamish as well.

Xander tucked one of her curls back. "You're as far from terrible-awful as anyone I can think of. Tell me this, why aren't you with Hamish now? Exclusively, like we are?" He wasn't trying to be a dick. He needed to understand.

"That's down to me. I'll give you the bullet points." Hamish confessed his fear of fucking up and losing her forever. Told of the way he'd pushed her away to try to protect himself and of the fear, no matter how irrational in hindsight, that his feelings for her were echoes of what addiction felt like. In the telling, Xander began to understand what Pippa saw in him.

And it began to grow roots in that chemical attraction they already shared.

At the end Hamish said, "I woke up and knew if I didn't move immediately, it would be too late. It might still be too late."

"You say you don't want to choose," Xander told Pippa. "But you've already admitted you're mine." He needed to underline that so she understood, no matter how the next bit worked out. "So, let's approach this from a different perspective. What if you choose us both?"

Her eyes widened a bit, and Hamish hummed. A question and a declaration at the same time.

"Why?" she asked.

"I'm sitting here and I'm with you, this person who fits me in a way that seems to multiply my potential. You don't take from me, Pippa. You add to me. You see where I might be lacking, and you compensate. I do the same. It's how I've been waiting to feel about someone for a long time, and I didn't know it until you.

"And I know you love me as surely as I know if you can't have Hamish in your life, it would break you and I apart. You and he have a bond. I can see it."

"Which makes you feel what?" Hamish demanded.

"At first I wasn't threatened because I knew where she was spending more and more of her time. Then, she told me she was going to speak to you and in that I heard..." he paused, "...I heard the depth of feeling she had. For me, don't get it twisted."

Xander needed Hamish to accept for this to work.

He continued, "Then I heard you make your case to her. And I remembered what it felt to be with you. I like you, Hamish. We're part of the same extended community, so we're already in a relationship in that sense. If it turns out that you're interested in having a sexual relationship with Pippa only, I think we can work it so we're all together and no one feels left out."

"But?" Hamish asked.

"But I'm attracted to you. I know we've got that compatibility."

Xander knew triads could work. He'd not only seen his parents, but later in his life there'd been family friends, and then he'd met Jessi, Adam, and Mick. All in long-term, successful threesomes. Each a little different given who those who made up the group were. Which made sense.

He'd honestly never imagined it for himself, though he'd never completely ruled it out either. He'd had a few one-time threesomes. They'd been hot enough, but it hadn't made him yearn for anything more. Then again, until her, he'd never felt the need to only be with one person.

But right then what he realized was they could create something special. Because of Pippa, yes. But because he and Hamish had a connection and a spark as well. One they could nurture and grow as each of them continued to nurture and grow their relationship with Pippa.

"The three of us could build something. For us. Uniquely us. What do you think, Pippa? Do you see potential?" Xander asked. "Each of us has to be on board or it will fail before we even get started. If it's not what you want, that's okay too. We'll work through it. Regardless, I'm right here."

Her attention moved back and forth between the two men for a bit until she nodded. "I do. But...it seems very complicated. I don't want anyone hurt, darn it." She tried to wring her hands, but Xander took them and kissed them gently, unfisting them.

"It *is* complicated. But lots of complicated things are worth doing." Xander continued, "I have a proposal."

Hamish's skin went clammy.

"I don't want to share with anyone else. And I don't want Pippa to either. But. You're not anyone else, Hamish. You're not Trevor in accounting," Xander told him.

"Don't make me regret telling you about his crush," Pippa warned.

Xander grinned, and the heaviness of the moment lightened a bit. "I feel bad for the guy."

Pippa explained to Hamish, "Trevor is a coworker at Twisted Steel. He asked me on a date one time. Two years ago. I said no, and that was it. He's a work acquaintance. Nothing more."

Xander hummed before getting back to the point. "So, my bottom line is I'm only interested in a committed relationship between the three of us. What do you want from this, Hamish? Because your answer is integral in how we move forward. I don't want you doing something you don't feel."

Hamish's heart pounded, and he got himself together. This was too important to panic through or play at half-arsed. He took a chance, reaching out to tangle his fingers with hers. Her mouth curving up into a smile just for him felt right. So right he white-knuckled the next part. Hoping to fuck he wasn't going to walk away disappointed.

"Pippa." He looked to her. That day had been a roller coaster of emotion. At some points he'd been sure it was over. But hope had begun to make itself at home in him. "Love, I've made mistakes. Big ones. I'm going to try really hard not to make those same ones again. I'll make new ones because I'm a fuckup. But I'd like the chance to love you like you deserve."

Pippa's eyes had gotten wider, but she kept his hand.

He looked over to Xander, who held her other hand. "I'd be a liar if I denied he didn't make my pulse jump."

Pippa giggled. "You're both ridiculous."

"We're all three ridiculous." Hamish squeezed her fingers. "There are times when I look at Jessi, Mick, and Adam, and I envy them. One of them is always there to catch the others. To notice a bad day or a moment worth celebrating. What I see is three people doing the work and making a safe place for one another."

Coming home at the end of the day to have Pippa waiting? Pippa and Xander? A shiver worked through him. She'd never want for looking after with the two of them as a team keeping her spoiled and loved.

He and Xander didn't need to love each other. Eventually they'd develop what he hoped was love. But they could build a relationship that kept them all happy. And he could be with her at last.

"What do *you* want, then?" Hamish asked her, hoping this whole situation worked out. "We know what Xander and I feel. How about you?"

Everyone was shaped by how they grew up, Pippa included. He was overwhelmed at that moment, so he imagined it was difficult for her as well.

She sat straighter, looked at both men, and then sucked in a breath. "I know there are lots of different ways to do this, and I'm not judging whatever other consenting adults do. But between the three of us I expect fidelity."

He blew out a slow breath. Hamish liked the rush of sex. It allowed him to shove all his emotion into that and avoid feeling anything more than geniality toward his partners. He kept the sex on the other side of the moat he dug around his emotions.

The first time he'd pressed his cock into her body, and she'd looked up into his face, so open it was a gift, there was no moat left when it came to Pippa Hall. No amount of running was going to cure him. And that was a fucking miracle for a loser like him.

"I can agree to that. And you?" Hamish asked Xander.

Xander nodded. "The three of us. Together. We talk

things over before they blow up. This won't work if we aren't all honest."

Hamish's heart leapt into his throat.

Pippa blushed but didn't argue, and she didn't let go of Hamish's hand.

"You're a public figure," Xander said. "This might be a story. I do tattoos and my parents are in a three-person relationship. Pippa's boss is himself in a triad. She and I are fine. You might want to think on how to deal with it."

"It'd sell more units," Hamish said with total honesty. He already had a reputation as a bad boy. He wasn't as famous as Xander's mom, or his uncle. He was more concerned for Pippa's privacy than anything else. Hamish had top-of-the-line security at his home, but Pippa's little townhouse was far easier for anyone to approach.

He didn't want to scare her, but he'd think on ways to keep her safe. Speak with Xander about it as well. His fathers ran a business that should easily address the problem.

"So? You, Pippa, and me," Xander said, satisfaction in his tone.

Hamish told them, "Look, I'm gonna be honest wit'cha. Most of the times in the relationship it's gonna be me who fucks things sideways. I can be a terrible vexation, I hear."

Xander snorted a laugh, but Pippa shook her head. "You're very hard on yourself. If you don't give yourself a break, how can anyone else?"

He dragged in a breath, always so awed by the way she spoke to him. "I don't know that I could do this one-on-one. I don't know if I have enough to make another person who matters to me as happy as they need to be. But I can damned well do my part."

"I can see this will be one of my tasks," Pippa said. "You don't think you can make me happy? Or Xander?" She touched his cheek and then yanked on his beard sharply until he yelped.

"She only looks soft and sweet. Our Pippa is made of far sterner stuff than people assume." Xander winked at her.

"I *want* to make you happy," Hamish admitted. "I just don't know if I can do it. I don't know if I have what it takes."

"What does it take, then?" she asked.

"I don't know. That's the problem."

She smiled. "Okay. I don't know either. I only know I want to try. Seems to me, beating yourself up over not knowing how to do something most people don't know how to do isn't very fair."

Xander shrugged as if to say, *Are you listening to her making sense?*

"I don't know if I'll feel jealous," Pippa added. "I do of the people who constantly throw themselves in Xander's path. He's always so nice, but I want to punch their throats."

Xander burst out laughing. "You do? That's so ridiculously sexy. But what's important is that none of them is a threat to us. You're who I want."

She gave him such a pretty smile.

"Oh, I know. If they were, I'd punch *your* throat instead. You two are around attractive people who want to fuck you on a regular basis. It's going to take me some time and practice to not let myself imagine worst-case scenarios. I haven't even been around Hamish backstage yet. I'll probably have to take a Xanax first for that. But I'm willing to keep at it."

Hamish hated that she felt that way. Even though she was right. Being with someone in the entertainment industry would be a challenge. Hamish had zero desire to be with another performer because of the toxicity. A world rife with temptation. Temptation he'd given in to countless times.

"I will do my fucking best not to ever make you worry. Not going to lie, backstage is pretty wild sometimes. But a lot can be avoided." He'd already been in the process of revamping what being on the road would look like, so he'd ask for advice on how to make things easier. Miles and Harlow were a resource. "I've been trying to distance myself from most of that stuff for the last two years anyway. It's fun for a while, but then it becomes normal. Usual, I guess is a better way to put it. But it's not real. It's got a short shelf life, and it'll tear you down eventually if you're not careful. And then you miss out on wonderful, true things like tiny redheads with smiles to make a man feel like everything in the world is better." He paused a moment. "Are you bothered Xander and I have a history?" Hamish asked, trying for teasing, but threads of truth ran through the question.

She shook her head. "No. I think it's a good thing you two are attracted to one another. Also unbelievably sexy."

Xander grinned at her and then pulled her into his lap, wrapping his arms around her body. "How lucky am I to have two such beautiful people who want me?"

"Pretty lucky, Alexander. I'm just saying," Pippa said, her voice muffled as she pressed her face into Xander's neck.

That made Hamish laugh too.

And he realized, yes, this could work. Truly.

CHAPTER
TWELVE

"In the future, I'm not going to be bothered if two of us are together without the third one. But right now?" Hamish caught his lip between his teeth as Pippa looked at him, eyes snagged on his mouth. "I don't want to wait another day."

"And how do you feel about that, Pippa?" Xander asked as he shifted her on his lap, so she faced outward, her legs to either side of his. One of his hands splayed across her belly to hold her in place.

"Don't you have work right now?" she asked, her voice faint.

"I moved that client to Wednesday. It was a five-hour slot. I'm fairly certain Hamish and I can keep you busy for five hours."

"Oh." She blushed. "I don't know if I mind you two being together without me. I guess we'll find out."

Hamish went to his knees before them, his hands resting lightly on her thighs. Inside, the storm of need quieted. Focused on her. On her flesh beneath his hands.

Anticipation hung heavy in the air.

Hamish said softly, "Look at you, love, avoiding the real question. I believe Xander wants to know if you're okay with the three of us being together right now."

"Um. Okay. But not in me at the same time. I just think that's way more than I want to be stuffed with. It sounds uncomfortable. Like a sausage that splits through the casing. No thank you."

Xander guffawed and then kissed her neck, his gaze locked on Hamish's.

"I can accept those terms," Hamish told her around a laugh.

"I can as well," Xander agreed.

"Then can we please take that top off because I want what's underneath," Hamish asked as he reached toward her.

"Shut the windows or the whole complex will start showing up to borrow sugar every time you two come over."

Chuckling, Hamish obeyed quickly and returned to her as she rocked forward slightly to slip free of the blouse.

With a gentle fingertip, he traced over her shoulder and the sweet little clusters of freckles there. Then he cupped her cheeks and looked at her for long moments before kissing her.

Slow, until she relaxed against him with a sigh. It hadn't been so very long since he'd kissed her, but what felt like forever since he'd allowed himself to fully enjoy it. To accept what she offered him so freely.

The difference was a revolution.

When they broke the kiss, Hamish stretched up to capture Xander's mouth. Yes, Pippa was a driving need in his veins, but Xander affected him too. He'd just offered a doorway into something Hamish hadn't dared even dream of.

If nothing else, he considered Xander a friend. The base of that, the foundation of this relationship, was strong. A good start that gave him hope they could make it, even when times got rough. And they would eventually. Pippa was too sweet, and they'd push her too far. Then she'd push back.

He couldn't wait. A pissed-off Pippa when it was just silly shite was absurdly alluring. He never wanted to hurt her heart again, but he did so love the way her nose wrinkled up just a little when she was annoyed.

God knew Hamish was moody and prone to dark periods. Used to making decisions without seeking permission. Xander was bossy. Really bossy. A beautiful prince accustomed to everyone in his orbit obeying him. Hamish liked to think he was in charge, but truthfully, it was pretty clear Xander was born to be.

They'd all have to find ways to let one another be who they were while also accommodating everyone else's stuff and toning down the bullshit.

His thoughts scattered when Xander bit his bottom lip as he surged forward, Pippa between them. She made a surprised sound and then threw her arms around Hamish, even as Xander kept a hold around her waist to keep her from falling.

Hamish soaked in the embrace the three of them made until Pippa squirmed a little, and he stepped back.

"Come on then." Pippa grabbed each of their hands. "For future reference, my tiny queen-sized bed isn't going to be up to the task of the three of us on a regular basis."

"Noted," Xander said as they got to her bedroom.

As much as he'd enjoyed snuggling in her bed, she was right. Hamish made a mental note to order a new one for her. In the meantime, they'd be inventive and make do.

Xander's shirt was up and off within moments, and he was at Pippa's body, unsnapping her bra.

Hamish was there, kissing the red marks from the underwire before he'd given it a thought, and any worry that he'd feel like a guest instead of an equal fell away as she said his name so softly it tugged at things low in his belly.

Reality crashed through the filter he'd had on his memories of her. Her taste, the soft, insistent sounds she made, the scent of her pussy dragged its nails down his spine. There was no turning back. No unknowing this was what she brought him alongside his name on her lips and the way her tone laced it with welcome and pleasure. Without reservation *he'd* put there. She wanted him and not just his dick. And she was going to be there tomorrow and the day after that.

When he reached for her, it was so much more than that moment. It was as if some sort of magic snapped into place, and she was *everything*.

Hamish rolled her to the bed, settling with her atop his body, his hands only moving from her ass long enough to help Xander get her pants and panties off, leaving her gloriously naked. Writhing, her eyes glossy, lips swollen.

He'd seen a lot. Done a lot. But this, even with two people he'd been with before, was devastatingly sexy. Alluring in ways he had no defenses against.

Xander joined them on the bed, naked as he dropped kisses up Pippa's spine.

She propped her chin on her fist resting on Hamish's chest and smiled. "Look here. Xander and I are naked. You aren't. I don't think that's a good example to set, do you?"

"But I'd have to let you go to do so." It was a tease, but the truth of those words hung between them.

"I'm not going anywhere," she said, and then scooted up a little to kiss him. "I'll be right here. I promise."

He rolled so she was on her back, and he loomed over her. "I'll hold you to that," he said, his own promise before dropping a kiss on her lips and then Xander's as he stepped away to get rid of his clothes.

Pippa watched him, still not quite trusting reality. Clothed, Hamish seemed to give off an effortless cool. Dark brown hair and eyes, tall but an inch or two shy of six feet. Even if it was just jeans and a T-shirt, he looked broody and sexy and dirty enough that it was a good thing, without being so dirty it was a bad one.

Unclothed there was an unleashed sort of feral sexuality to him. Where Xander was tall, broad-shouldered, and muscular, Hamish was long and lean. In public he hid the way his muscles were coiled, ready to bolt at any moment. He played at being laid-back and carefree, but it was a costume.

Pippa saw through that to the softness below, and it rendered him irresistible.

His ink was mainly of the traditional and neo-traditional style, about half done in color, including the bleeding heart on the back of his right hand. There were mermaids and pumas, sharks, a few female faces. Dates she wasn't sure of the meaning for.

Beneath all that colorful skin he had the soul of a poet. And the way he looked at her now that he'd finally told her how he felt filled her with joy.

Just a few hours before she wasn't certain she'd be able to find a way to keep him in her life without it backfiring on them all. Now she was in bed with two of the most incredible beings on the planet. Together.

"See? I'm right here," she told him as he got on the mattress.

The energy he gave off softened her heart further. Nervous. Anxious.

"Still here. Still naked. Lucky me." He kissed her again, and that nervous energy flowed into something else. Determination perhaps. Whatever it was, she was glad he'd relaxed and hopefully allowed himself to believe she'd be there like she said she would.

"This feels like a dream," he murmured against her lips.

She pushed his shoulder until he lay flat on the bed, and straddled his body, staring down at him. Moved that he exposed his fears the way he did. That he trusted her left her a little dizzy.

Xander went to his knees next to her, first kissing her long and slow, and then resting his head on her shoulder as they both stared down at Hamish.

"Not a dream," he said to Hamish. Xander took one of Hamish's hands and placed it over Pippa's nipple. She drew a breath at the way it looked. Blatantly carnal. "She's right here. So pretty it makes my chest hurt sometimes. But she's ours."

Hamish's eyelids slid down for long moments, but when he opened them again, his gaze was clear and full of purpose, and it met Xander's in a way that sent a shiver of anticipation up her spine.

"Love?" Hamish purred at her, and a flash of molten fire shot through her straight to her pussy. "Well," he said after she ground herself against his cock.

She managed to unstick her lips and restart her brain enough to respond. "Y-yes?"

At her side, Xander's sharply indrawn breath made her lightheaded.

Hamish said in a low, thick burr, "What I think, to break the ice, is that you should sit on my face."

Xander cursed low, and there was a slight tremble when he put a hand at her elbow. "Mmm. I agree. But if I might make a suggestion?"

Pippa had never in her life been more excited to hear a suggestion.

Xander got off the bed, and went to the pegs, hooks, and little drawers where she kept all her accessories. "The last time I was here you put laundry away while I was lazy and watched you." He pulled something free and returned to them. With a movement of his wrist, deep-blue fabric rolled free.

"You asked me about that scarf," she said in a voice thick with desire. He'd taken it from her hands and had caressed her neck and shoulders with it.

"Metal cuffs or restraints aren't what I think our Pippa's skin needs. But this is silk. It can pad between her skin and my belt. I picked up a little something a few days ago, but it's at my place. Quilted and padded cuffs. She can struggle all she likes, but it won't hurt, and they won't break. But for the present, this will suit our purposes just fine."

Her skin from head to toe heated and then prickled. Every single nerve ending sparked.

He'd used his belt, and that had been wonderful. But this was more. So much more her head spun.

"Keep her hands front," Hamish murmured, and she squirmed against his cock. "That way she can grab my hair for balance."

Not quite withholding her whimper at the image that evoked, Pippa held her arms out, and he expertly wrapped the wrist and then did the same for the other before he used his belt. Tightening and securing it until shivers ran riot over her skin, leaving her slightly faint. Once he'd finished, he looked her over carefully.

Xander said, "If it's too much and you want to stop, say so. If it's too much and you want to hold on to see if it gets even better, that's okay too. We've got you."

Hamish knew she was utterly in support of that when her pussy got even hotter and wetter. Her nipples had tightened further and darkened. Her lips parted, pupils huge.

She'd been uninhibited. Openly sensual in their time together. Before. The sex had been stunningly memorable. It had been vigorous. He'd left fingerprint bruises on her ass after he held on so tight while fucking her. He'd jerked off to that memory dozens of times since.

This was another step. Deeper. A little darker. But still full of the light she brought. It seemed unimaginable to allow himself to accept that he could have this with her. Tomorrow and the day after.

But she had it with Xander. It had been impossible to miss just how she softened when Xander gave her direction of one sort or another. Could he have that too? He'd have to earn it. If he was willing to.

Xander helped her move up Hamish's body, and the scent of her, the heat and slick, salty sweet of her taste as her pussy met his lips, sent a full-body shiver through him.

He groaned when she gripped his hair and then tugged to get his attention back to her clit.

He filled his hands, splaying them at her hips, holding her steady.

The tremble in her thighs seemed tied to his dick. He was so hard it hurt, but the center of his universe was the center of this woman. The soft, insistent sounds. Urging him.

Xander's thigh rested against his side, just below hers. The wiry hairs tickled and yet provided some sort of balancing sensation, so he didn't get totally lost in Pippa's cunt as he devoured her.

She hurtled toward climax. He knew her body well enough by that point to taste the change in her. The fingers she had tangled in his hair tightened incrementally.

This first time he wasn't going to tease. He needed her orgasm all over his face, and when he sucked her clit between his lips softly, over and over, her back bowed as she gasped.

Her thighs clamped tight at his ears as all he tasted, felt, breathed was her. Her pussy. Her pleasure.

When she slumped forward, he was up rolling so she

flipped to her back, wrists still bound, and he came to his knees between her thighs.

Xander leaned and Hamish met him halfway in a kiss that was a gnash of lips, teeth, and tongue.

"Fuck," Xander snarled as he pulled away. "You taste like her pussy."

He did. And it spoiled him forever. Nothing else could possibly be this good. This right.

Hamish bent and caught one of her nipples between his teeth, giving a sharp bite that brought a near squeal from her. A sound caught between surprise and arousal.

He moved to the other nipple, and then Xander followed. Pippa arched into them, her bound wrists limiting her range of movement.

"Condom?" he croaked.

Xander was back within seconds, thrusting one into his hand.

He tore it open, rolled it on, and slid his cock through her pussy a few times. Teasing them both.

Her gaze was slightly blurry from orgasm, and a smile flirted on her mouth, so alluring he paused to kiss it before settling back, shifting to nudge his cock into her pussy slow and deep where he had to pause, breathing slowly to keep himself under control instead of coming like he'd needed to before he'd even gotten the damned condom on.

Home. Sweet fuck, she was home.

He bit hard enough to leave a mark on the side of her breast. The way she'd closed her eyes and shivered, arching into his mouth for more, incited him. Spurred him on as he sped his pace. He knew the fingers he gripped her with would leave marks. Gripped that hard on purpose. Needing to mark her as deeply as she'd marked him. Knowing, too, she loved it as much as he did.

That freedom to push, go a little rougher because *she* got off on it as well, left him nearly giddy.

Over and over, so fucking deep, Hamish fucked into her body, sending her tits bouncing quite delightfully until he came on a strangled cry, burying his face in the crook of her neck until he got his breath back and could move to shift his weight off her and get rid of the condom.

Hamish returned to bed quickly, and she backed herself into his body, Xander bracketing her other side, all three of them tangling their legs.

He'd never been more terrified and satisfied in the entirety of his life. Hamish closed his eyes and breathed her in.

She opened her eyes and stared right into his heart. "Xander," she said.

What was it about her that the way she said his name sent his senses racing? Toward her. As if all the cells making up the whole of him simply turned every bit of their focus to her.

There was a question in her gaze. Was he upset by what he'd just seen? By what they'd done?

Not wanting her to worry another second, he cupped her cheek and kissed her. She tasted slightly different now. As if Hamish had been another spice to add to their recipe.

It was...unbelievably fucking hot to watch them. Beautiful. Sexy.

He was strung tight, needing to come desperately. He

didn't want to overwhelm her, so he watched her closely, making sure she wasn't upset or truly in pain.

She squirmed to get closer, and he obliged, his arms wrapping around her to haul her to his body, but also taking Hamish's hand as he did. Just because Xander had a thing for watching his girlfriend get her pussy eaten by their boyfriend didn't mean Hamish had the same switch to get flipped.

Wouldn't it be fun though? To find out what they all liked? Together.

"Can you take me?" he asked softly, rolling his hips.

"Yes. Yes, please," she said.

It was Hamish who handed him a condom that time. He needed no foreplay other than watching the real-life dirty movie that was Hamish and Pippa.

Hamish settled at the top of the bed, just above Pippa's head. Xander stretched her arms up to him, and Hamish ran the edge of his nails down the inside of her arms and back up again.

Xander propped a pillow beneath the small of her back and her ass, so she was at a perfect angle for his thrusts.

Once he'd buried himself to the root, he had to get his breath and yank himself back from the edge. She was hot and slick, her inner walls tightening in little waves that felt so good sweat broke out down his spine.

Soon enough, he'd settled in with a rhythm that kept him deep where he liked it best. Where *she* liked it best too. He knew it wouldn't be a long, drawn-out fuck. There'd already been too much emotion. Too much sex and desire. Too much nervousness overcome. It made them all drunk as Hamish held her wrists and Xander stroked into her.

As he drew close, he worked a hand between them and squeezed her clit in time with those thrusts sliding all the way in.

Hotter and wetter, Pippa writhed as she begged and finally, he let her tip over, her cunt gripping his cock until he had no strength left to hold back and came, lights flashing against his closed eyelids.

Hamish freed her wrists, kissing them as he handed the belt back to Xander.

"I think if we rest up now, there's time for another round before I have to go back to the shop," Xander said.

CHAPTER
THIRTEEN

Pippa had just pulled a starter from a '65 Impala when Jessi sidled over. "Hi!"

"Yes, all three of us," Pippa said, anticipating the question while she kept working. She knew what her friend was poking around over.

Jessi laughed. "Am I so transparent?"

"Frankly, I'm surprised you waited until Wednesday. At breakfast this morning, Hamish mentioned he saw you Sunday. You're his sister, sure, but the most important part here is that you're his best friend. Of course, he told you. It was the day after the first time the three of us had been together. Plus, he asked if I was okay with going public. I am, but no one cares what a mechanic gets up to with other consenting adults. Now Hamish? He says it's going to be a good thing for him, so I'm choosing to believe that instead of thinking he's just saying so to mollify me."

"He's a bad boy musician." Jessi snorted. "They'll eat this up. Aside from you and all that redheaded, petite, and beautiful thing you have going on, look at Xander. Who's going to kick that out of bed for eating crackers?"

"Sure as heck isn't me. But he doesn't eat anything but me in bed anyway."

Pippa couldn't believe what she'd just said out loud, but the way Jessi guffawed made her feel better.

"A couple of things. First, he and our mom will be seeing one another today after his board meeting."

Hamish sat on the board of an organization that served foster kids both in the system and beyond, either after permanent placement or aging out. It pleased Pippa greatly that he was involved. It fed the kid he'd been, but also gave the adult he'd become something positive to do with his voice.

"That means he'll be seeing Raven too." Xander's second mom had a close friendship with Hamish. They'd connected because she'd also spent years as a child in and out of the foster care system, though with less eventual success than Hamish. As an adult who'd found real, lasting love and commitment while also doing a job she enjoyed and was very good at, Raven had been able to turn those successes into action as she helped run the organization's biggest fundraising events alongside her society matron mother-in-law.

"Xander probably told her already anyway. I swear they both ran out to tell people like little kids with a secret." Grinning, Pippa examined the starter closely. She was going to have to take it apart to see why it wasn't turning over.

She put it at her workbench and wiped her hands off. "I need caffeine. I haven't taken a break in hours and my back is killing me."

Once she'd washed up better, she joined Jessi in their break room where her friend had already put a steaming mug of coffee out, along with a plate of cookies.

"Thank you."

"Small price to pay for getting the good gossip." Jessi winked. "Don't you think it's sort of sweet though?" Jessi asked. "That Xander and Hamish seem so excited to tell everyone you're all together?"

Was it? Pippa shrugged. "Maybe? I'm not offended, if that's the real question. If they were hiding me, that would be upsetting. But they aren't. If they want to share hot gossip when it's about their own lives, they should do it." And it was insanely flattering they wanted to tell everyone about her.

"Have you told your sisters yet?" Jessi asked.

"I'm having dinner with Rebecca tonight. I'll tell her then." It wasn't over the phone or text type of news. "We'll probably call Esther together. That's how we usually do this stuff. Otherwise? You already know. For sure Rennie knows. She and Xander are tight. Otherwise, aside from Hamish's fans, who is going to pay any attention?" Not likely anyone living in Arizona had a subscription to Entertainment News Monthly, or that they'd be scrolling through social media to see any photos or blind items.

It had been a few years—two years and seven months to be exact—since anyone from the group had contacted her, and she wanted to keep it that way. She remained in her top left corner of the country, and they had souls to save down in the southwest.

Jessi snickered. "I showed up at his house the day after it all happened. Sunday, like you said. In my defense, I was bringing him cinnamon rolls. Anyway, he told me then. He was so sweet about it. Proud you'd chosen him. Full of your praises and for Xander too."

"I wish he could see himself the way I do. He's so much more than he gives himself credit for."

Jessi reached across the table and squeezed Pippa's arm. "Thank you. He deserves it. Going to guess Xander's family reacts just fine. I like him a lot."

"I do too." Pippa snickered. "Xander must have told them by now. He's been at work this whole week, and if he told Brody or Raven before he told his parents, there'd be hell to pay." Pippa tried not to panic at what people must be thinking of her. "I hope your parents will be all right with it. I can't lie, it's a relief you already broke them in on the threesome, throuple, triad, whatever-you-call-it thing."

"We call it a triad. I thought threesome sounded too sex based, and Adam wasn't a fan of throuple. As for my mom and dad? I'm one hundred percent certain they're pleased."

"I can't imagine them not being lovely to someone," Pippa said. "But I'd hate to disappoint them in some way."

"Mostly they are. But she's got four kids, a houseful of animals, and her husband can't say no to a stray. I've seen her angry loads of times." Jessi laughed, and Pippa ached a little. Pippa's mother's anger had been a deep-rooted bitter taste in the air. Frustrated. Overworked and overwhelmed. Unappreciated.

Jessi continued, "Even so, the only times when either of them got truly angry in a way that made me a little awestruck and slightly afraid were concerning Mick's father's treatment of Mick and me, and Hamish's birth mother. That woman is truly awful. My parents tried to adopt him more than once. It's a process. They have to notify the birth parents during the adoption proceedings, and rightfully so. Carol would never respond to anything regarding Hamish's life. She blew off other hearings, which is how he ended up in foster care and how he ended up with us. But once the official adoption started moving, she showed up. Contested something, which took the process back to the beginning. Which meant Hamish had to be interviewed again by social workers. His grades plummeted. He got in trouble. Then Carol, the birth mom, just wandered off halfway through. So they waited another ten months and started again. Carol did the same thing. After that time, our parents consulted with his counselors, doctors, and with him. They didn't want him to suffer, especially if nothing happened in the end and he was abandoned by her yet again. They put a permanent guardianship in place instead. It gave him stability, and she couldn't show up randomly to mess with him. On that. There've been other times over the years. But she always got pissed when he did interviews and said kind things about our family. After we adopted him. He spoke about it in an interview, and of course that's what she —Carol—got in contact about. Showed up at the clinic to confront my dad. But Mom was there too. There was a physical confrontation, and Leif had to pull her back and hold her in another room while my dad made Carol leave. Believe me when I assure you Addie Franklin has no problem letting it be known when she thinks you're bad news for one of her kids."

It was so hard to imagine Addie getting into a fistfight with someone Pippa was certain this Carol was a real piece of work.

"Hamish has been searching for as long as I've known him. He pretends to be hard. Pretends he doesn't care. But he does. He's got a bottomless well of compassion. He just wants a place to belong and people to belong to. He's less... frantic with you."

Interestingly enough, it had been his relaxing and accepting what he'd felt for her that had allowed Pippa to be vulnerable enough to accept it.

"Xander is...he's the calm at the center of the storm, you know? He's the one who forges ahead, so certain." Pippa thought it was one of the most sexy things about him.

"Brody has done some of my ink," Jessi said. "Xander reminds me a lot of him and that steady sort of competence and self-confidence. Also, and don't tell Rennie or Elise I said this, Xander is big and gorgeous like Brody. It's nice to see what he'll look like in middle age."

That made Pippa snicker. "His dads are like that too. Big, powerful men who move through life, taking care of the people they love most. No lie, being loved by Xander is pretty wonderful. And it doesn't take away from Hamish. Not from how he feels about me or for how I feel about him. I don't know why it works that way, but it does."

"That's absolutely what counts most."

CHAPTER
FOURTEEN

Xander came home to find Pippa in his kitchen chopping vegetables while wearing an apron emblazoned with pizza slices of all types. This woman, fuck, he loved her.

"This is eerily close to what a porn movie would look like if I had it made just for me," he told her, kissing her neck.

"Eggplant curry is on the stove. Rice is nearly done. King brought hot honey to work last week, and there were sweet potatoes in my produce box, so I made this salad I saw in a magazine with a quick red onion pickle and some toasted walnuts. I confess I may have eaten more than strictly necessary to taste for seasoning. It's really good. Did you know honey has historically been used on wounds to keep them from getting infected? Hamish ran to the market to get wine and some sort of dessert."

"My life is so much better with you in it. I do love your facts. Keep them coming." He kissed her nose. "Missed you." It had started out as a tease, but he realized how true it was.

Everything was better with her in it. Smelled better. Tasted better. Looked better.

"It's only been a few days. You're very spoiled."

"I'm totally spoiled, and I can't see getting less so where you're concerned. Enough that a gap from Monday to Thursday is not acceptable to me."

"You had clients late every night this week. I understand. Plus, we had lunch together twice and texted the whole time. It's not like you fell off the planet."

"In my defense, I came home at nearly midnight, headed to bed, and essentially passed out. But I still missed you. You're so nice to come home to at the end of a long day. Soft and snuggly. Warm in my bed. I got a lot of work done, but it sucked being without you."

"You're very fortunate," she said primly.

"I really am. I know I am."

Her teasing expression softened as she turned to face him. "I'm certain you've already told everyone. What does your family think?"

It was the first direct question she'd asked about it, and he caught the nervousness in her tone.

"They're all fine with it. I knew they would be."

He'd gone to his parents' place after he'd gotten off work Monday night. He'd had to say nothing to Brody or Raven, but he'd been slammed, so it hadn't been as difficult as he'd anticipated. They'd been pleased he was with Pippa, and after he'd answered the question they'd asked him about whether he was with them both because he didn't think he could be with Pippa any other way—the answer had been no —they'd given their support to his three-person romance.

Xander filled Pippa in on Thanksgiving and birthday

plans the following month—both to be held at Adrian and Gillian's place on Bainbridge Island—and told her he'd show her a few little nooks where she could hide out when the noise got to be too much.

"Miles and Harlow will be there. I haven't seen him in four months or so since the engagement party. He wrapped a movie and then went into the studio with his band to work on their next release." Xander's cousin was very much an older-brother presence in his life. "I've also got him in my chair for a few days to finish up a thigh piece he and I have been working on for the last year or so. It'll be good to catch up. You're going to like them both."

"Hamish only has positive things to say about her and her work ethic. I'd have been jealous if I hadn't seen three dozen paparazzi shots of Miles and Harlow looking at one another like they were the best thing to walk the earth." Pippa laughed as she pulled out the griddle portion of his stovetop to get it heated.

"Hamish is a wild flirt, but I've seen the way he looks at you. Heard the way his voice changes when he speaks to or about you. He's ours, baby." Xander cupped her cheeks, and she went to her toes to kiss him.

Pippa said, "Plus, Miles is a big guy and probably would punch him in the nose if he tried anything. After I kicked his balls, that is."

Hamish strolled into the kitchen and tossed the totes full of groceries to the counter.

"Whose bollocks are you kicking, love?" he asked with a grin before he danced between Xander and Pippa and pulled her into his arms.

"The alternate universe Hamish who tries to romance Harlow."

Hamish kissed her forehead and turned, delivering a kiss to Xander as well. "Why would *any* version of Hamish want to romance anyone but Pippa Hall and Xander Copeland Keenan? Harlow is a delight. Certainly not hard to look at. She's very talented too. And ass over teakettle in love with Miles. I used to think it was quite annoying and overmuch."

Hamish gave Pippa a teasing glance.

"Now what do you think?" Xander asked as he got them all wineglasses from the nearby cabinet.

"Now *I'm* ass over teakettle in love. Perspective changes everything. I'm far more stylish at it obviously." Hamish gave a theatrical sniff as he rooted through a drawer and found the wine opener.

"Obviously," Pippa said.

Xander and Hamish set the table and ferried food over as she joined them.

"Raven sends a hello," Hamish told her as they began to eat. He'd seen his friend the day before at a board meeting. "My mom as well."

"How is auction planning going?" Pippa asked.

Their organization had a spring gala with a silent auction to benefit children of all ages within the foster care system. Hamish's life had been altered forever when the Franklins had become his foster parents, and he wanted other young people to have that sense of belonging and love.

"I don't have the best experience with the system in

general," he said. "Created Families does truly excellent work. Fills a lot of gaps these kids fall through. This event is going to be the best yet. There's so much variety in donations. Something for everyone. We've got some fantastic rarer and higher ticket things. Raven already got to Adrian and Miles, *and* Harlow too. Backstage VIP concert experiences have been offered." Hamish sniffed his annoyance that Raven had gotten to them first. "I'm doing the same. Rennie donated a painting that's going to be hotly fought over. Raven said she'd have taken credit for it, but Pippa asked Rennie first. So now *I* get to take credit for it." Hamish winked at her, pleased she'd reached out to her friend. More pleased she'd thought of it because she wanted to help in a cause he held very dear.

"Raven and her mother-in-law have been able to get all the catering donated, along with the event space. The printing of the invitations and programs. The linens. Liesl, Raven's mother-in-law and quite frankly the scariest person I've ever met, has managed to get an orchestra as well. It's rather impressive. Such low costs mean we can plow the most possible back into the organization."

"Scarier than Raven?" Pippa asked.

"Liesl Warner is an archetype. Society matron. Elegant. Perfect manners. I've never seen her anything less than fully made up, hair done, and in some delightfully unique designer gear. But she's a bear when it comes to this cause. She sits on multiple boards across the state, but it's this one she's given her heart to. I admire her greatly and do my utmost best to never make her frown or cause her to be disappointed and/or angry with me or my actions. Raven is a version, but I'd say Liesl is the OG."

"Now I'm slightly terrified of meeting her at this gala,"

Pippa said with a laugh. "I've been scanning the list of auction items and I'd circled several until a certain person…" she looked up from her plate, directly at Xander, "…saw one of the things I'd marked was a three-hour tattoo from Raven."

"Your skin is mine. We've already had this discussion." Xander crossed his arms over his chest rather arrestingly. "What if you make one of those sexy sounds but it's not me in the chair? Those sounds belong to me."

"Sounds?" Hamish asked.

"She likes it when it hurts a little," Xander murmured, never taking his attention from Pippa, who blushed furiously. "You know that intimately."

"I don't make those sounds when someone else is tattooing me. For goodness' sake. Your uncle tattooed me! I would never." Pippa's voice was breathy.

"Ah." Xander made a sound so full of desire the skin on Hamish's forearms pebbled in response.

"Ah?" Pippa asked. "I mean, obviously it feels, um, nice sometimes. But there's context. With you? I guess it felt okay to make a sound or two. Just between us. With anyone else? No. I'll do my breathing."

"*That's* the ah. You have enough control to not let go when it's anyone else doing it. But you trusted me enough, even then, before we knew one another really, to make some of those little Pippa sex squeaks. Fucking sat there working on you, hoping you didn't look down to see how hard I was. Wishing you had anyway."

Hamish laughed at that very accurate descriptor. "You do make the sexiest sounds when it hurts just right. Like when I bite you right here." He trailed his fingertips against the side of her breast and watched as her lips parted on a shaky sigh.

"So, bid on something else," Xander said.

"Your father—Todd—told Rennie he was going to buy the motorcycle rebuild consult for your other dad. I guess Ben has wanted a custom bike for years. I thought that was romantic. You might also tell him if they don't win the item at the auction, they can come in for a consult anyway. There's a waitlist, but we can bump him up when we get cancellations and finish other projects early."

"What a lucky man I am," Xander said in a slow drawl, his gaze locked on to Pippa's. Hamish tried to remember not to hold his breath as he watched their interplay.

"You let me jump to the head of the line for my tattoo. I figure I can repay the favor. I'll bid on your tattoo services instead of Raven's and save my sounds for your ears. And Hamish's."

"I told my parents about us," Hamish said. "After the board meeting, my dad met us at my house and the three of us had lunch."

"What…how did they react?"

How could she not know how absolutely thrilled they'd be? He'd said her name, and they'd actually beamed at him. Because it was her. "Love, they already have Jessi, Adam, and Mick in their lives. They're not easily shocked. You're like family to them at this point anyway. They want us to bring Xander around more so they can get to know him. Starting with Thanksgiving brunch."

"My family doesn't eat until seven or so. We used to go earlier when I was younger, but the last decade or so as all of us have met other people and combined their lives with ours, we've shifted to accommodate the best we can. By the way, please thank your sisters for moving their dinner to Friday so Hamish and I could be there too." Xander took a bite of potato and hummed. "I was a little concerned as you described the salad, but damn, this is fire."

Because Xander's birthday was always right around Thanksgiving, it had spilled into the whole celebration of the holiday and had morphed—like everything else the Browns tended to do—into a mega event lasting multiple days.

"Xander has told his family and I've told mine. What about you?" Hamish asked her.

"I saw Rebecca and Vivi last night, and we divvied up the menu for Thanksgiving dinner. Told them about us. Then we called Esther and Danny and told them. That was a little more complicated because it was over the phone, and I had to explain it twice because I think they thought they missed something the first time." Pippa's laugh settled something deep inside. "Danny wanted to know if either of you play console games. He's bringing some stuff with him when they come down next month."

Hamish knew how important her sisters were to her. It would have been trouble if they hadn't backed her choice. It definitely would have made Pippa sad, and her unhappiness wasn't something he planned to tolerate. Especially now that they'd worked through their issues, and she was with him. *Truly with him.* He'd nearly fucked it all up and lost her. He'd gotten a second chance, and he wasn't going to mess it up by not protecting her.

"I've spent more than a few hours gaming in the tour bus or in some green room somewhere while waiting to go on stage," Hamish told her, making a mental note that it would be a good way to get to know Danny—whose approval Hamish knew was important.

"You'll like him. He's nerdy and goofy and has a very big heart. He's going to be a great father."

"Can't wait," Xander said, leaning close enough to kiss her.

"find myself in need of assistance," Hamish told Pippa.

They were currently sprawled in Xander's big bed.

The sun was beginning to rise, and Pippa needed to get up and moving to go to work. But they were so warm, and everyone was naked and in that place between sleep and fully awake, so she let herself drift.

"I'm your gal," she told him, smiling when he leaned in to kiss her and then tug on one of her curls.

"You are. What's your schedule like tonight?"

"I'm off at six thirty. What do you need?"

"And do you need me too?" Xander's sleepy rumble came at her back.

"Always," Hamish said, pleasing Pippa very much.

Over the weeks, Hamish and Xander had gotten closer. Easier with one another. They liked to team up on her, which she had no real complaints about when they were sex related.

"I was told yesterday by the lady from across my street that our neighborhood will be expecting a lot of trick-ortreaters this year. This is the first year since I've owned that house that I'll be home on Halloween. I need candy, I suppose. And just between us, I've never been responsible for answering the door. Does one stand there waiting? Do you hover and watch television, pausing every time there's a door knock? I'm feeling slightly out of my depth. Any help you can lend would be appreciated."

Addie and James lived in a more rural part of the county. The houses sat on large plots of land and were far enough apart Pippa bet a lot of kids opted to go to other neighborhoods or parties instead.

"If you come to Twisted Steel at lunchtime, we can go to the store to get candy. I'm not sure what the selection will be, but we'll find something. Then when I get off, I'll come straight to your house and we can do the door together," Pippa said. "I find watching TV and pausing the show when the doorbell rings is the best way. Especially during the thick of it."

"I don't have to be at work until nine this morning," Xander explained sleepily. "I'll go with you to get candy. That way Pippa can eat on her lunch hour instead."

"Good idea," Hamish agreed, pleasure in his voice. He'd definitely liked it that Xander had offered to help. "Come over after you're off work too. Spend the night."

"I'll be done by seven tonight. I'll bring some dinner and an overnight bag." Xander gave his arm a quick squeeze.

Hamish was absolutely fucking delighted by each little witch and teenaged zombie that showed up on his doorstep.

He currently sat on his haunches to get a better look into

the face of a wee superhero who simply shouted, "Treat! Treat!"

"I'm on it." He held out a basket with the candy and MegaCutie's little eyes widened. "What's your choice then?" He pointed at the full-sized bars Xander had managed to talk his way into the back of a local box store to produce, like Hamish's Halloween coach. After the tot chose one, Hamish tossed another in her sack. "Need to keep your strength up for all that superhero business."

"You! You!" His tiny visitor toddled off the porch with the help of a parent.

"This is fun," he told Pippa.

She pulled him into a hug on a laugh that brightened and lightened everything inside him. After dropping kisses all over his face, she told him, "You're so adorable I can't stand it."

"It's this type of thing that calls into stark relief the life I was blessed with when the Franklins opened their family to me. I thought myself too mature for such baby activities as trick-or-treat. But Jessi would drag me to parties with her friends, so I dressed up, drank suspiciously altered fruit punch, got drunk, snogged indiscriminately in dark corners."

"Always the best kind of Halloween parties. Rennie and Miles took me to more than one of those," Xander said as he brought more candy to refill the basket near the door.

After the next round of monsters, race car drivers, and astronauts, Hamish settled back in the nearby living room where she told them, "I love Halloween. *Now* anyway. I give out candy and decorate my porch. This year I left my cauldron out front full of candy with a sign wishing them all a spooktacular night. Sometimes I dress up at work because I can."

The doorbell rang, and Hamish dashed off to deal with it, so happy there were kids who got tucked in at night, whose adults stood out on the walk proudly waiting for their mini progeny costumed in all their glory to go demand candy from strangers.

When he came back to the living room, Pippa asked what his nephews were up to that night. "Charlie and her man took them to a party at their school. She dressed them as little milk cartons." He showed them both the pictures his sister had texted him.

Like their mom, they were rough-and-tumble. Forever jumping off things, climbing, and all manner of absolute heart-stopping mayhem. Hamish lived in terror of them getting hurt when he was in charge.

Charlie sensed this and structured Hamish's time with her sons so she was there too. Wanting him to have an active part of their lives without his fear or anxiety in the way. She was an excellent big sister as well as mother.

"They're so sweet. They're how old? Three and five?"

"Just turned three and soon to be five, yes. My mother, Jessi, and Charlie are planning the five-year-old shindig now. There are to be hard hats with everyone's name on them."

"Oh! I want a hard hat."

He laughed. "Love, you have a welding mask. That's even better."

Her smile was so sunny. "Well yeah, but that's not a *party* welding mask. Duh."

"I'll be sure to tell Charlie. There'll be a family gathering as well. Given Jessi's involvement, it's a safe assumption we'll *all* have personalized hard hats," Hamish teased, loving the picture in his head of them at Franklin parties.

She deserved it, and god knew his parents and siblings loved her to death. Hamish couldn't give her everything, even though he wanted to. But he could give her a family who always had a space at the table for her.

She had so much light and music and chatter with her endless facts. Imagining her in a world where all of that was stripped from her never failed to set Xander's head spinning.

It wasn't even that she'd said, *Hey, we weren't allowed to have Halloween growing up.* It was the way she'd spoken around it.

"Those babies are the most adorable milk cartons in the world." Pippa's grin lightened his heart. "I saw them at Jessi's studio a few weeks back. What a cool thing it is to have an aunt who creates theatrical costumes. They're always going to have the best things to wear to parties."

Hamish said, "Even before Jessi opened her studio, she used to make us all the most amazing costumes. She still creates my stage stuff."

Pippa waved a hand between Xander and Hamish. "Truly, being connected to all your super-talented relatives is a big plus. As if the gorgeous looks and excellent moves in bed weren't enough to turn my head." Pausing, she cocked her head and took Xander in.

He knew she saw straight to the heart of him. Especially when she said, "It's okay. If I spent all my time thinking about all the things I missed, I'd still be trapped by them and their ideology. I'm free now. They can't control my mind or my body. Not anymore."

Xander asked, "They've left you alone though, right? Since you escaped?" He reined it in. Sort of. As much as he could. It was impossible when it came to her. "Apologies. Only if you feel up to talking about it."

"It's been two years and seven months since the last voicemail from my father. Intermittently since I left they've called. Or sent letters ordering me to repent and come home. Tracts have shown up on Gretchen's windshield over the years. The same as the group uses in the nearby towns surrounding the compound. Twice they sent my oldest brother here in person." She shivered and lost color in her face.

Xander and Hamish shared a look.

"What happened?" Xander made a superhuman effort to keep his voice calm.

She swallowed hard and then took a deep breath. Violence coursed through him.

"He showed up on my doorstep. Said it was time to come home. Take my place. Our family was leadership and others looked to our example, and my continued disobedience hurt our father. They didn't want the twins, he said. Esther was damaged goods because she'd gone and married an outsider. Rebecca's gay. But me and my uterus were still salvageable. I declined his invitation, said not to contact me again and to leave. That's when he grabbed my upper arm and started to pull me toward the parking lot telling me I was going to do what I was told or else. Danny and Esther drove up right then, thank goodness, and intervened. Timothy, that's my brother, he had to let me go to use both hands to defend himself. He finally ran off when we all three turned on him. Danny wanted to call the cops but…" Pippa looked up from her glass. "Honestly, I felt like if we got the authorities involved, we'd be prolonging having my brother in the same state. And I didn't know what he could have done with more time and thought. Sending him running away was more effective. It was three more years before he came back."

The doorbell rang, and Hamish went to deal with it, saying he'd be right back and kissing the top of Pippa's head.

"You're so much more than they think you are," Xander told her.

They cleared up the dinner dishes, and when Hamish returned, they settled on his couch in the living room so she could continue.

Xander stroked over her hair, and she leaned into him like a cat. Needing that contact.

She'd held on to this story for a long time. It was…freeing to tell it to them right then.

"When Timothy came again, Danny and Esther had moved into a place of their own. They married when we left Arizona. They did it that young so they could have custody of me. Anyway. Rebecca and I ended up in the same complex right across the walk. Same place I live now. Even then I went to work early most days because I could get a lot more done in those quiet hours before most everyone rolled in. Rebecca and I often left the house at the same time, but that morning she was behind me by a few minutes. He was at my car, waiting for me. It was

January, so at six in the morning it was dark and cold. At first, I thought he was a neighbor, but then I recognized him."

She paused because even then, six years after that day, it still had the power to shake her foundations. Because he'd made her *afraid*.

"He wanted me to go back. He'd said that before. And my parents had said the same in the letters they sent."

"We argued. I tried to get in my car and leave, but he got in between me and the door." She'd run to the other side, but when she used the fob, it unlocked both doors and Timothy had gotten in on the driver's side.

"It was more of the same stuff about how coming back and breeding for the cause was my calling. There was a political play going on, and our father felt he could use my return to the fold as a sign of leadership. It's honestly so stupid to say out loud at this point."

Pippa had been twenty-three years old at the time, and it had been ridiculous even as she'd been scared at the way his violence and aggression had ramped up the longer she didn't comply with his demands to get in his car and come back to Arizona with him.

Xander bristled. He wanted to fix things, she knew. But some things couldn't be fixed.

"He said many ugly and hateful things, and then he kicked out the driver's side window. It wasn't Gretchen then, that car had an alarm though, so I hit the button and started yelling about a fire and to call 911. Rebecca came tearing down the path toward us. She had a baseball bat, and she was screaming—like, horror movie screaming—at him."

She laughed at the memory of how fierce Rebecca had

been as she ran at their brother, bat raised, screeching, intent on protecting Pippa.

"He swaggered to his car and drove off. We had the same debate about calling the cops. But we didn't have to because several of my neighbors, including Danny and Esther who'd been woken up by the racket, had contacted the authorities. They came out and saw the broken window. Timothy got a ticket after pleading no contest to a misdemeanor charge. I haven't seen him since the court date. They issued an order of protection too." She shrugged. "That was six years ago, and *he* hasn't said boo directly to me since."

In the hallway outside the court, Timothy had called her a harlot. Said she, Rebecca, and Esther were killing their parents by being ungrateful and spiteful. Said she deserved to burn in hell for eternity. Their attorney had been there. The permanent order was issued about ten minutes later.

Xander's expression had darkened as he'd continued to pet her while she spoke.

"I'm sorry that happened to you," he said, voice low and full of emotion.

"At the time it was a lot. But the thing is, I got past it. Because I resisted. And again, it was me, Rebecca, and Esther standing shoulder-to-shoulder to defend ourselves. It made me stronger. And it made me a bigger threat because I had stood up to their authority on multiple occasions and I'd gotten the courts involved. I was a kid then, but I'm not now. So yes, it was terrible, and it made me really mad and sad and scared, which only made me more resolved to continue to live a life where I choose to decorate my porch and give out candy to munchkins hopped up on sugar and the excitement of dressing up."

"You said they put tracts on your car and call you still?" Hamish asked, not willing to let go just yet. Sweet man.

"No tracts for two years or so. My mother calls and writes usually around Easter and Christmas. I used to open the envelopes hoping for a real letter, but it was always bible verses about obedience. Now I put them straight into the shredder. It's been a while since she's sent anything. I have a real life. Full of love." She wanted them to understand she wasn't hindered by her past. She loved her present too much.

Xander said, "They sure as hell won't get at you through me."

"Or me," Hamish added.

"I'm nearing thirty. Positively ancient in terms of being married off to another family in some sort of attempt to consolidate power. The little ones? I can't protect them. I hate that. We talked to attorneys over the years about trying to get them out. We all offered ourselves up as guardians. But the way the law is, it's next to impossible outside heavy claims. We could make them, but proof is harder. And we end up making it worse for people still there."

But the guilt got to her.

"This isn't your fault," Hamish said.

"It isn't. But it's something I feel responsible for anyway. So, I never give up entirely. We keep informed as we can about what's happening. If there's ever an opportunity for us to step in and help, we will. Esther works closely with a program that assists people who live within closed religious communities like the group. They create escape plans and find housing. They're the ones we went through to get all the things we needed, including the guardianship stuff."

She wished it was more but since they'd left, things had

tightened up. Only a handful managed to get out in the years to follow. And of that handful, three had been minors.

"What can I do to make you feel better, love?" Hamish asked, and she heard it, the thread of helplessness.

"If you feel up to it, I think hearing something new you're working on might help." She fluttered her lashes.

She had no idea what it did to him when she asked to hear his music. That she so genuinely was interested what he was working on seemed to soothe all his jagged edges. And, he could also admit, it was a huge ego boost. He loved his fans. Thanked the heavens for them. But he *loved* Pippa, and that she truly liked his music made him feel like a king.

"As it happens, my sweet, I do have something." A song he'd been polishing. "I'm meeting with two producers in Los Angeles the week after Thanksgiving. I want to keep evolving as an artist. Both have a direction that's different than my last few releases, and even better, a really good sense of what sort of departure is right for what artist they're producing." He knew his strengths, knew what he wouldn't pursue versus the directions that intrigued him.

"Really? How exciting!"

Her story had been shaken off. Their Pippa had returned, bright and full of joy. Part of him ached for the little girl who had to hide that, even as he was grateful the woman was at his side.

"Would you like to come with me?" He hadn't considered asking, and yet there he'd gone and done it and he was glad.

Because she brightened further. "Yes! That week is a

quiet one for us before things kick into high gear to get as much done as we can before the year end."

"Xander, what about you?"

Pippa made a happy sound, and both men relaxed, turning their attention to her for a moment. "What?" she asked. "I'm just so very happy that you two like being with one another. I don't think it would be nearly as lovely or sexy if you two were only in this for me."

"It makes me happy too." Xander kissed her and then Hamish. "Yeah, I'd love that. I need the times to check my calendar. If you're interested, my parents have a condo in Westwood. They stay there when Adrian and my mom are doing studio work in Southern California, so it's close to where you need to go. They'd be happy to let us use it while we're there. More private than a hotel. Walking distance to a bunch of great places to eat."

Licking his lips to get that last taste, Hamish looked at his phone and gave them the dates.

And just like that, they planned their first trip together.

CHAPTER
SIXTEEN

"I can't believe you bought me an entire bed," Pippa said to Hamish. She locked her front door and they walked toward the small parking lot. She had to be at work in forty minutes, and he was headed off home.

They were bound for L.A. soon, and he'd poured himself into his songs. Tinkering and editing to create material as perfect as could be. Though he tried to hide it, he was stressed out. He'd decided to take a bold new step with this career. He had so much talent. So much passion it was blatantly obvious he was going to achieve exactly what he wanted to achieve.

"Xander's feet hung off the old one." Hamish laughed as he said it. "We fit much better now. Though it does take up considerably more space in your bedroom."

The bed Hamish had given her was a supersized king. She'd had to take out a dresser to make it all fit so she could still walk in there. But then when she'd put the dresser in the spare room and she'd pointed out that she'd emptied the drawers so he could use them, he'd pulled her into a hug so tight she'd nearly burst into tears at the emotion in it.

On her lunch break she had a plan to grab some things to put in her kitchen and bathroom that would be his. Pippa knew what it felt like to belong somewhere. And to *someone*. It was a wonderful thing when it was genuine. Hamish needed more of it. Even Xander, with his bright, busy life full of people who adored him, needed to feel like he belonged. And he did. To her. And Hamish too.

She'd make them both keys to her place when she was grabbing supplies.

"After Thanksgiving, you promised you'd finally consider moving in together. Don't think I've forgotten," Hamish said.

It wasn't that she thought things wouldn't work out with the three of them. Each challenge that came up was dealt with eventually. They all tried in their own way, and that's really what the most important thing was.

Her lease was up in several months, and she'd decided when she signed up last time that she'd finally make good on her dreams of leaving her little townhouse behind and upgrading to something bigger. Safer. Closer to work.

Like fate had known even then.

But moving in together with Xander and Hamish was huge. It took their relationship to a totally new level. Far more serious. She'd no longer have her own place to retreat. Which was scary.

She was absolutely going to say yes. Pippa had gotten spoiled by Xander's regular presence in her life and her bed, and Hamish being around with no more hesitation or holding back.

Buying a new place was unnecessary when they both

already had really lovely houses more than perfect to serve their particular needs—Xander's penthouse also had a mini studio that could be customized for Hamish. He got a lot of work done in his home, and not having to travel was less pressure on his continued health and emotional well-being. It meant he had an easier time choosing not to be out at three in the morning with a gut full of pills and booze. Instead, he could be a few doors away from people who'd be sure he got sleep and ate something.

"Obviously that's where we're all headed. I promise." She scoffed. "Like I'd let you two get away."

After Halloween, there'd been a flurry of breathless gossip items about the three of them. Hamish had been at his local wine shop when someone cornered him and asked him questions. Being Hamish, he'd happily answered. Yes, the neighbors who'd reported there was a man and a woman who appeared to be in a romantic relationship with Hamish —as rumors had hinted at over the last few weeks—were telling the truth. He was head over arse in love with his sweet, redheaded mechanic, and their boyfriend was a badass tattoo artist Hamish was now lucky enough to always get his ink done by.

Then the paps had shown up at Written On the Body where Xander had menaced at them but then got all sweet when he talked about Pippa and Hamish before going broody and dangerous again and ordered them to leave.

They might have felt at ease, but there'd been days since where she'd felt like a rabbit. Poking her head out of her hole and dashing off to the next safe place. She'd learned early on —after her first regrettable foray into the comments section —to *never ever never times infinity* read the comments.

Mainly, over the last weeks, Pippa had simply been someone in love. She'd spent time with her sister and friends, with the Franklins and various members of Xander's family. But every once in a while, in the middle of the night or while she was doing her laundry, some of those early comments barged into her brain with balled-up fists, ready to cause some pain. She was only human. Reading comments about her looks or her job or that she was some super slutty, slutbag clout chaser out to steal all the rich men made her self-conscious in a way she hadn't been since she left Arizona.

She was working on it. And part of that was she had to find a way to process it all without it poisoning her life or her relationship.

He took her hand, tugging her close to kiss her. "We're going to hold you to that promise. We're impatient for you."

"Thanksgiving and Xander's birthday party are in just a few days. Then your meetings. Once that's all handled and you've taken your pick of hotshot producers, then we'll decide which one of your houses to live in. That sounds ridiculous, but as you both live in absolute palaces, it's a win for me either way."

"Xander and I will do our best to be patient. Patient adjacent really for Xander because he's very used to getting his way in most things." Hamish winked and stole a kiss.

There was something stuck to her windshield, tucked beneath one of her wipers. At first, she thought she'd gotten some sort of traffic-related ticket, but when she got closer, she saw what it was.

A religious tract. A chill slid down her spine.

"Pippa?" Hamish asked. "What is it?"

Pippa looked at the tract, uneasiness creeping through her. It felt like her telling Xander and Hamish about them on Halloween had somehow invoked the group and they had bled back into her life.

She wasn't willing to let that happen again, but it was best not to get worked up over every shadow and sound. There was no use giving in to fear and letting it paralyze her. That would be allowing them to win.

"Remember how I told you at Halloween about some of the ways my family has harassed me over the years?"

He stepped closer and examined the tract still in her hand. "This is from them?"

She examined it one last time. "They're popular enough. It's the same type as what we handed out and what they've left on my cars in the past, but you buy them in bulk. It's probably not connected."

He turned her and kissed her softly. "Should we call the police?"

"Even if it is the group, what have they done that's illegal?" She knew he was trying to help, so she softened her tone. "They want me to second-guess everything. I'm not going to. Not at this stage." She walked the tract over to the garbage and recycling bins and got rid of it.

"Okay. I hate that answer, but I understand it. As for those assholes back in Arizona? That world is so far from you now you can't even see it in the rearview anymore, aye? You're here with me. Where you're loved and valued and free. Remember that. Xander and I won't let anything happen to you but a great deal of orgasms from sitting on my face."

That was what she needed to hear—even the sitting on

his face comment—and she told him so. Glad she had when his features shifted into a pleased smile. "Good. That's what I'm here for. I'll see you tonight at Xander's, right?"

"Yep. I'm working until seven or so though. We're trying to keep on deadline for two big projects."

"Keep my love safe," he told her before he opened her door for her.

"I'll do my best. I put some of those snack pack things in the fridge down in your studio, and also some pistachios and dried fruit, the apricots you like so much. Eat them. Three or four of them count as one of your fruit servings. I looked it up. They're high in vitamin A."

Otherwise, he'd reach for empty junk, if he ate at all. It was nice he no longer seemed anxious by her being in his studio. She generally only went down if he was with her, or if she had some snacks to put in the fridge so he'd have them.

He told her once that his first drafts were like a messy house. He didn't want anyone seeing them until he could clean it up. As if she'd judge harshly? But lately when she asked to hear things, he'd been pleased. Eager to share. It felt like she'd won some very important prize.

He kissed her again. "I love it when you take care of me. I'll check in with you later on if I don't see you at Xander's first. You're my everything. I love you."

Oh, how she loved hearing that from him. The words and sentiment helped chase away her unease.

"I love you too." She kissed his chin and then headed off to work, where she quickly got involved with a touchy exhaust in the '77 Cadillac Eldorado they were restoring and put the group out of her head.

A few hours later, she finally took a break and headed in search of more caffeine and to stretch her legs and back.

"You've got a call," Carmella said as Pippa passed by her desk.

She settled at the empty spot, a nearby workstation, and picked up. "This is Pippa."

"My name is Carl Brush. I'm doing a story about Hamish Wilson. I know you're his…*girlfriend.*"

Oh god. That. There'd been a few calls at work from people asking about Hamish and her connection to him. She'd even gotten emails and a text about it. Generally, she forwarded things like that to Hamish's management. Pippa knew if she'd said anything directly to Hamish about it all, he'd feel guilty she was being hounded.

Hamish had enough guilt in his life, and she wasn't going to add a bit more if she didn't have to. So she just went around him for stuff like this.

"I am," was all Pippa said in response. It was public information. There'd been more than one breathless piece about the Scot rocker in a threesome with the latest batch just after Halloween.

Hamish and his team managed to make their responses to it charming and flirty instead of gross. And it had worked to keep the stories on the positive end. Some were a little lurid, but that came with the territory, she was learning.

"How long have you known one another? Are you a fan of his music?"

"I have excellent taste, so I'm a big fan, yes. Fortunately, I'm certainly not alone. He's got many fans who love his work." And he was working on a new album. But that was

PR Hamish controlled. What he was up to business-wise was his to share or not.

"And do you all live together? Since you can't get married legally to two people, I mean. They don't do that back home where you're from. What made you decide to flout convention and have two boyfriends? Is it a message to your family? Is it because of Alexander Copeland Keenan's family history?"

The comments about *back home* and messages to her family sent alarm bells ringing so loud her heart pounded. Still, she impressed herself when she managed to sound nearly bored. "I'm at work now, so I need to get back to it." Hamish was famous. She wasn't, and she had no plans to engage in that part of his world unless she had to or to protect him.

Brush kept on like she hadn't spoken at all. "You come from a deeply religious background. How do your parents feel? They can't be pleased you're part of this threesome situation."

Pippa curled her lip. "Mr. Brush, again, let me stop you right here. I can give you the contact information for Hamish's reps, as I said. But I have nothing else to tell you other than Hamish is wildly talented and I'm very fortunate to be loved by him. Have a good day." She disconnected.

"Is everything okay?" Carmella asked in the silence after the call had ended.

"It's just the media nosing around." Though none of them had asked about her family before. And now that they had come into the conversation, Pippa's anxiety about what might be next began to rise.

"Oh no! I'll be more careful about calls in the future.

There's no reason for you to be bothered over something like that." Carmella looked so upset Pippa immediately felt bad.

"Please don't make extra work for yourself," Pippa said, blushing wildly. "But his name is Carl Brush, and if he calls again, please send him to voicemail. I don't expect you to interrogate everyone. Especially when he'd already procured the internal number to make the call."

"I hadn't thought of that," Carmella said, frowning. Twisted Steel had a receptionist who handled visitors to their showroom and all the public calls in to the various parts of the business from the paint stalls to the body shop. "The call came directly to my line, but that happens, so I didn't think twice."

Trevor had come out to the printer and paused, listening to them a moment before saying, "He's a reporter. They're good at finding information. It's not a secret. Anyone who's done business with us would have your line, Carmella."

Pippa nodded. It had to be that. From the crankiest mechanic to the prettiest custom painter, everyone at Twisted Steel protected the rest. It was just how they were.

Carmella smiled at Pippa, shaking her head. "Honey, if this asshole calls again, I'll handle it."

"Thanks."

"I guess it comes with the territory when you're with a celebrity like you say," Trevor said. "These men should protect you better. They're the reason all this attention is on you."

"From a phone call? How can they protect her from that?" Carmella waved a hand at that.

"It's ridiculous either way." Carmella sipped her tea. "Did he threaten you?" Her gaze narrowed.

"No. Not really. Some of his questions were nosy." And about things he had no business knowing.

Trevor sighed his relief at that, and she felt the same.

"Someone threatened Pippa?" Mick asked, joining them. Carmella's kingdom was also where the best coffee in the shop was located, so her area wasn't often empty of people. Plus, it was right down the hall from the break room and where Mick, Asa, and Duke's—the three who owned Twisted Steel—offices were.

"No one threatened me," Pippa said quickly. If these giant, nearly feral men thought anyone in their employ— also considered their family—was being harassed, they'd spring into action, and it could very likely end in flying fists.

She wasn't worried about Duke, Asa, or Mick being hurt, but she didn't want them getting into trouble with the authorities over something so silly.

Pippa gave him a quick update about the call. She omitted the stuff about her family because she didn't want to get into it. It made her feel paranoid. Always jumping at shadows like prey.

"Sounds like it's just a stupid gossip columnist, or whatever they're called these days." Trevor grabbed a stack of invoices. "Gotta get back to work. You're safe here with us. Don't sweat it," he said to her with a smile.

Pippa smiled his way and then over to Mick and Carmella. "Me too." She held up her mug. "Caffeine obtained. Don't want the boss to see me slacking." She winked at Mick, who snorted.

CHAPTER
SEVENTEEN

Xander grinned as his cousin Miles came through the shop to his station. He stood and got a big hug.

"I wasn't expecting to see you until later this week," Xander said. Miles and Harlow had been traveling all over the place for various work events. She and her band had shows in London, Edinburgh, and Dublin while Miles had done some postproduction stuff in London for the movie he'd finished.

Miles told him, "We just got back after midnight last night and pretty much passed out. Harlow is off with Maddie and Nora doing some shopping for your party, as it happens, so I caught a ride over here."

Maddie Hurley was in Earthquakes, Miles's band, and Nora was Harlow's best friend and the drummer for her band Above Me.

"*My* party? Why? What do they need?"

"Presents. And some clothes I'm told. Harlow has a way about her. She can find the most amazing secondhand and vintage stuff in thrift stores, so they're mainly doing that. Makes my girl happy, so I'm all about it. How are you?"

Xander tipped his head toward his station. "My next client isn't for an hour and a half. Want to grab some lunch and catch up?"

"Fuck yeah, I do."

Ten minutes later they'd settled in the back room of the café with panini and drinks.

"We settled on a date for the wedding," Miles said. "It was a whole thing between not just Harlow and me, but her dad and stepmom's schedule, my parents' schedule, a thousand other Browns and Hurleys and all that. It took months just to get straight." Miles laughed, but it was a sound full of contentedness.

"Congratulations! When did you decide?" Xander could only imagine the absolute chaos of planning a wedding that would involve so many people. It was going to be a great party though.

"Clear your calendar for September sixteenth and the eighteenth because I really need you to be my best man in both ceremonies."

Surprised pleasure hit. "Fuck yeah. I'd be honored. I already love Harlow. Speaking of loving Harlow, she's got a huge fan in my dad."

When Xander's dad, Ben, first met Harlow two and a half years before, there'd been a misunderstanding that had been rapidly addressed and fixed. But an uncle bond had formed between Ben and Harlow during that time, and they'd remained tight ever since.

Miles said, "It's mutual. Plus, it helped humanize your

mom. When you watch movies and eat sandwiches with someone a few times, it's not so much like staring into the sun anymore. Still gotta wear sunglasses because she'll always be Erin Brown."

They both laughed at that. Xander's mom never did anything halfway, and that included loving her people.

"To keep the size of the wedding party down—god knows there are so many of us we'd need twenty attendants —and to avoid hurt feelings by those who don't get chosen, it's just going to be you and Nora. We're doing two ceremonies in Southern California. I know, it's got excess written all over it. Believe me, I did consider how it looked." Miles held his hands up a moment.

Xander shrugged. "Even if it *was* dripping with excess, I'd support you. But that's not who either of you are. I figure you have a reason, like you're doing it to have an intimate ceremony and one that's for a bigger group, and you'll tell me."

"That's it pretty much. We want to do one that's just the family. Which is huge enough. But that's the important one to the two of us," Miles told him. "We'll have a dinner afterward and party our asses off. Then two days later we'll have a swanky ceremony and reception that will include friends and business associates as well as the family at The Shoreline in their ballroom. They deal with high-profile events frequently and have an excellent reputation for keeping the press out. Plus, the hotel is owned by the family of one of Harlow's closest friends. That's actually how we ended up choosing them. Ginger, Har's friend, put the woman who runs security for the property in contact with your Pop. They're putting together a plan for the event with CKS."

Copeland Keenan Security was the longer name, but they'd chosen CKS to stay simple and low key. His fathers and uncle ran it, and Fox had taken over their IT a few years back, so it continued to be a family business.

Which meant his cousin and Harlow were dealing with some privacy and safety issues. "The two-ceremony thing makes sense. What's going on with the red alert type planning?" Xander asked.

"My profile right now is pretty high, and according to my agency, will probably only get more intense over the next year as we do a mini tour in the winter and early spring, then the movie comes out. A few months after that I'm getting married. The same friend whose family owns the Shoreline, Ginger Miller, went to the arts school Harlow and Nora went to. Anyway, Ginger creates custom rock-and-roll outfits. For events and for tours, and she's doing a capsule collection with some Italian fashion line. Which is cool on its own, but even better, Harlow was just offered an advertising campaign for it. It's a great career move for them both. Harlow starts shooting the first wave in December for print. It'll mean even more attention. We had to put a gate up at the house and add more fencing and lights at the back because people would come right up to the front door to attempt to interview me or take my picture. Fans wanted to camp on the front yard. The dog got out so many times we had to rehome him with Harlow's aunt."

"That sucks. I know how much she loved that little mutt."

Miles said, "Yeah, thanks. She can still go visit, which

also gives her an opportunity to see her aunt. But it's not the same. Anyway, we just want everyone to be safe and to have a good time without worrying about photographers in helicopters or staff selling photos. I want your mom to feel safe. It means a lot to me, but also to my dad, that she doesn't for even a second have to worry."

Xander blew out a breath. That sort of intense fan behavior drove his mother from the stage for a decade after her stalker killed Xander's big sister, Adele. His mother had nearly died as well. Decades later and his mom's PTSD had been treated and mostly abated, but there were times that something would happen, and it would bring back the horror of what she lived through.

It was one of the reasons they were all very much aware of what it meant to be a celebrity and did all they could to protect their circle. They were a big group of weirdos. But they were all tight. Loyal. Protective.

"Okay. Congratulations to you both for doing so well. I'm fucking thrilled for you." He didn't thank his cousin for protecting Erin. It was what they did. But it also sounded like it would protect them as well, and that was absolutely all right with him.

"We chose California for the ceremonies because that's where Harlow is from. She's got a lot of friends and her dad, stepmom, and sister live there. We'll probably do something up here later that year. At the winter holidays most likely. The first ceremony is at a tiny hotel on a bluff in La Jolla. We're renting the whole place for three days. There's a pool and bikes to ride down to the beach. A restaurant on site we'll have meals in for the group. Harlow loves the water and La Jolla, and at this point, our family and close friends alone will be over a hundred people. We can all fit. And there's another hotel not too far away if we need overflow."

"It all sounds amazing and very much like you both."

"Tell me about Pippa and Hamish. I know Hamish, I've met him a few times because he's worked with Harlow. I can see the appeal. And Pippa? Well. I've seen pictures of the two of you and not only is she gorgeous, but the way you look at her tells me everything I need to know. I mean, I'm demanding you tell me way more and all, but you love this woman. It's written all over you."

Xander nodded. "I do. She's fucking *it*. Before she walked into that party, I was just great, you know? My career is heating up. I'm booked up nearly a year in advance. I saw men and women here and there. Nothing deep. And it was fine. But then there she was, standing with Rennie, and it was like no one else was in the room except the two of us."

Even at the time it had felt like magic.

"And Hamish? Where does he come in?"

"He was with her on and off for a year before I came along. He's like a lot of artists, wildly talented and full of self-doubt. He worries he's not good enough. She loves him. I could see it. Yes, she would have chosen me. She *did* choose me." He paused, wiping a hand over his face before he admitted, "I knew she was telling her ex that she'd become serious with me. Knew the ex was Hamish, who I've got some history with. I was fine at work for a few hours. Then? Well, I was concerned because there's something magnetic about Hamish. I pushed my client to another time and then rushed over to her townhouse like a seventeen-year-old. And I walked into the conversation as he was telling her he loved her and wanted a second chance."

He talked awhile about that with Miles. Explaining the situation.

"In the end? I stood there looking at this person who is, I don't even have the words but it's like she's that key to the door to the rest of my life. And I looked at Hamish and there was definitely affection and attraction and I thought, hey, maybe this might work if we all try together. Then she'll never look at me and wish she'd made a different choice. He'll be able to know he's absolutely worth love and a relationship. And me? I have the woman I adore and this man I'm growing more attached to by the day." And a deep understanding that all the protectiveness he'd felt for his family was nothing compared to how he felt when it came to Pippa.

"You don't feel pushed out or less than?" Miles's question was without judgment.

"I really don't. Maybe that's because I grew up with an example of what it looked like to make a threesome work? I don't know. I just don't feel like sharing her means less for me." He was learning how to be a good partner to her and to Hamish as well. "The two of us have this unspoken thing when it comes to her. We unite to protect her. Always. He sees little things I miss, and I do the same." Xander raised his shoulders because it was hard to explain.

"I'll be seeing them both Thursday, right?" Miles asked.

"Yep. Then again on Saturday for my birthday. Her sisters are coming to that."

Xander gave his cousin an overview of the whole "group" thing and the very close relationship the three sisters who'd escaped had.

"The one thing I do get a little jealous over is how close

she is with the Franklins. I'll get over it as she gets to know us, but it's hard."

"We're a big, colorful, noisy bunch. Even someone like Harlow got a little overwhelmed at first. She'll get used to us. We won't allow anything else." Miles laughed at that, and so did Xander because yes, that was how they were.

"The Franklins are too. They're Hamish's family. Because of Jessi's connection to Mick and Twisted Steel, their parties now are full of as much ink as ours. They have more animals than musicians. Two of the kids are vets like the dad. The clinic is on the same property, so there are chickens and goats and dogs and cats and birds all over the place. Not in an annoying way, which I would have thought hearing someone else describe it all. I don't know. It's happy and jolly and free with all the hugs and kisses you can imagine. The Franklins will fit in with us just fine once everyone has gotten used to one another."

He'd relax more once that happened. He wanted to be sure her safe places were myriad as possible. He knew without a doubt that every one of his family members would protect and defend her and Hamish both if for no other reason than they were his.

Miles left a while later with a promise to see Xander the following day for the holiday, but before Xander got back to work, he checked in with Pippa, making sure she was still planning to come over and spend the night.

She agreed quickly, which settled his soul. Being obeyed was something he enjoyed a great deal. Hamish would join them if he finished work early enough.

It wasn't until he'd gotten home and was drying off after a shower that he realized her energy when he'd invited her over that night was unusual. Yes, she was pleased to come over, and knowing where she was satisfied him. He could take care of her in his place. And it was a delight to have her fingerprints all over the place via a throw blanket she always used on the couch across from the fireplace. She'd folded it over the nearest arm, and the bright blue popped against the dark-gray fabric of the cushion.

Sort of like how she was in any room. A bright pop of color and joyful energy.

At first her speech had been faster than usual. Maybe there'd been…relief in it as well as affection.

Frowning, he resolved to talk to her about it when she arrived.

Pippa watched Xander move through the kitchen with effortless grace for someone so big. He had on low-slung lounge pants that left pretty much nothing to the imagination with the way they clung to his dick.

She gulped and did not fan herself, but it was a close thing.

"I hadn't tried this place yet," he told her as they brought their food over to the table.

"I had lunch there a few weeks back with Rennie, and she says it's a pretty good copy of mixed plates in Hawaii. I didn't know which one you'd prefer, so I got the shrimp, chicken, and the fish too."

The entire time she'd been waiting for their food, the nervousness from earlier in the day slowly returned. Filling her until her hands shook slightly and her heart pounded.

Once she'd driven into the garage downstairs and the

gate had closed behind her, she'd begun to feel better. Now, twenty minutes later, her heart had stopped racing, and it no longer felt like someone was watching her.

"What's wrong?" Xander demanded, snapping her out of her head. She might not feel like she was under a microscope anymore, but he'd been watching her closely, and the clarity in his gaze told Pippa it was useless to even consider minimizing or lying about her mood. Xander was mellow until he wasn't. And when anyone he felt was his to protect was threatened, the mellow fell away, replaced with a fierce determination.

"Nothing big, More like a bunch of little things. I started the day off coming out to my car to find a religious tract on my windshield." Pippa hadn't thought about it at the time, but later in the day she realized hers had been the only car with a tract. Which had left her even more certain it had been for her specifically. Which meant it had been the group.

"I mentioned they do that from time to time. Just to remind me, I guess. Then I got a weird phone call at work." Pippa waved a hand. "That's all."

"That is a lot in one day." He firmed his lips. "First issue, the tract. What do we do about it? How do we handle it?"

"We don't." She shrugged. "Maybe there's a city or local ordinance about leafleting or littering that might be applicable. But for what? A ticket? And what happens is that I jump to their call. I don't want to give them that. They don't deserve my attention." She sniffed, feeling rather indignant.

He smiled, leaning close to kiss her quick. "It's so sexy when you get a fire in your belly over something. I'd rather you mad and saucy than sad. I get the point about not doing anything about it. But what I think is that you should just be extra aware, and if for even half a second you get worried, you contact me or Hamish or the cops. If you see anyone from your family, I want to know about it. Don't engage."

The idea of Timothy on her porch freaked her out for a moment, but she got past it. They'd known where she lived for years, and for the last six, he'd stayed away from her like he was supposed to.

"Second bit of business. You mentioned a weird call. Related to the tract?"

Her snort was totally undignified, but she didn't care. "Not related. This was a reporter." She explained what had been said and what Carmella and the main receptionist would do should Brush call back and also what Trevor had brought up about how easy it would be to get those direct phone numbers. "I offered to give him the contact information for Hamish's management, but I don't think..." Pippa shook her head, trying to word just what bothered her.

Xander took her hand, tangling their fingers together. "What?"

"Ever since Halloween and all the gossip about the three of us, a few calls have gotten through to me at work. I have the email address for Hamish's people memorized at this point. Those calls had a basic script and this one did too. But none of them have ever made a reference to my family in Arizona and my upbringing. I worry."

She chewed her lip, and he waited patiently for her to be ready. Even though she knew inside he wanted to rush out to punch people.

"I worry if he makes some connection to the group, others will, and then it becomes a regular part of these breathless little stories. It's not a secret I grew up where I did. Or that we left. I'm certain Rebecca and Esther have told many people, and Esther works with the groups she does, which is public knowledge. I don't want to be a curiosity in any more ways than I already am. And as I said, every time they remember I exist, there's trouble. And Esther is pregnant. She doesn't need any hassle from reporters or anyone in Arizona."

"What does Rebecca think?"

"They leave her alone for the most part. She's so in your face and angry about the group and our family that the times they've come at her, she comes right back at them five times harder. She finds satisfaction in that, and I think it's a healthy response. *For Rebecca.* I find dealing with them emotionally exhausting."

Xander nodded. "I can see that. Both for Rebecca, and for you too. It's not about me, but I want to punch the people who make you flinch, even all these years later," he said, low and mean. But the hand he held hers with was gentle. As he always was with her.

"That's a lot of noses. You'd hurt your hand. And you make your living with your hands so let's be satisfied with them all being fifteen hundred miles away. Usually." The group had multiple businesses that connected the various compounds across the west. Group members passed through Washington, Oregon, California, Montana, and Arizona regularly but generally left her be. "At this point it's just a few coincidences, so I'll be extra wary, but there's not much else to be done."

Xander didn't look convinced. "Give me the contact info on the reporter. I'll have someone at CKS look into it. You should stay with me or Hamish for the next while. Your townhouse is the least secure, and they know where you are. No one is getting up to my apartment without permission, and Hamish's system was put in place by our company, so it's top-of-the-line too."

Pippa frowned. She liked spending time in Xander's place. High above the street, it felt safe and comfortable. The windows could be open all day, and no one was going to see. Hamish's place similarly felt like home. Moreso since they'd officially started their relationship. If she was in his bed, he slept. And if she tempted him with bits and bobs of things he liked to snack on, he ate.

What Pippa didn't like was feeling unsafe in the home she'd built for herself. Staying with Xander or Hamish felt like running away. She hated that.

Even if it was the best choice, at least for the time being.

"I'm probably overreacting," she said. "I don't want to make a fuss."

"Stop that. I trust your judgment, and you should too. You being with us is safer on multiple levels. You said you'd be more wary," he reminded her.

Hamish arrived, sleepy and late, but Xander realized as he came into the apartment they needed to work together to get Pippa to move in with one or the other of them. Period.

She was exposed—too exposed—in her townhouse. Even if those assholes in her family weren't involved, the ability to get at her, the person dating a celebrity, was far too easy.

"Hallo, my loves," he said after dropping his bag and coat off and coming to sit on Pippa's other side. He kissed her. "I'm so glad I broke away. This is exactly what I needed."

Xander leaned over her to receive his own kiss. "I'm glad you did too. Now Pippa can tell you about the call from the reporter."

Pippa sat up, back stiff as she glared at Xander. "You should have let me tell him tomorrow. After he got some rest. There was no reason to do that tonight."

Goddamn she was hot when she was pissed off.

Still. "There's every reason," Xander said.

"Why don't you tell me what is going on and then we can talk afterward about the whens and whys of the telling?" Hamish interrupted.

Pippa huffed a breath and then told Hamish about the call.

"And so, I suggested she stay here or with you for the next while because she's safer that way," Xander said once she'd finished.

"I think he's right, love," Hamish said to Pippa, taking her hand and kissing her wrist. "You have keys to both our places. You can come and go as you want. Have people over. Be at home and also safe. That whatsits on your windscreen has had me rather cross all day. I'd been planning on proposing the same thing Xander did."

"I'm not helpless." She remained very stiff.

"We don't think you are. But they know exactly where you live." Hamish wanted to say more, Xander could see it on his face, but he didn't.

Xander told them about some of the things Miles had said earlier about expecting more media attention. "I know from experience whenever any of us gets a lot of publicity for one reason or another, it spills over to the rest. We have to kick people out of the shop regularly because of the connection to my mom and uncle. Any gossip news that floats in always makes it worse for a while until it dies back."

"Has it been worse since Halloween?" Hamish asked.

Xander said, "Yes. But I don't want you to feel guilty, so get that look off your face. It was already getting out that the three of us were a thing. My point is we need to be real here. Pippa, you and I are with a famous person. I'm the son of famous people. I'm related to multiple other famous people. We need to think about how exposed we are, and how secure our homes and jobs are. That comes with the territory, and as you've admitted you love us both, it's not like we aren't having this relationship. So."

Hamish said, "Twisted Steel is safe because access to the shop floor is limited. But maybe talk to them about being extra vigilant about who comes in."

"Mick already did. He was there right after I got the call, so he got all protective and tightened up security." Pippa sucked in a breath and looked like she was counting to ten in her head.

Her voice was so clipped Xander finally gave in and demanded to know what was going on. "Why are you angry at me? This isn't some silly overreaction. They've tried to hurt you before. Tried to *kidnap* you. I know what happens when some fucking bananapants asshole decides to put his plans into action. I will not stand by while you are unsafe."

.   .   .

Pippa blew out a breath. *Oh.* There it was. She'd wondered exactly what it was other than her being threatened that'd sent his protectiveness into overdrive.

She turned to face him better and took his hands in hers. "I'm sorry. I was in my feelings about the whole thing. Feeling hemmed in, watching all my choices drifting away. It's one of my buttons, you understand? But, I missed your worries and how they connected with *your* buttons."

"Do I like bossing you around? Yes, I really do." Xander sent her one of those smoldering looks of his. "But that's sex. That's private romantic life stuff. I do not want to take your freedom away. I don't want to strip you of your choices. I just want you safe. And if you're here or with Hamish, I'll know you are. Please. Do this for us."

That was it. How could she say no when she wanted to be safe too? When she liked being with them both? She never wanted to be a burden. It was important that she be able to take care of herself. But this moment was bigger than that. And truth was, making a choice to be safer was taking care of herself.

"All right. I'll stay here. Then Hamish can come to us whenever he wants to get away from work, but he's got the space to do whatever he needs whenever he needs to. Thank you for offering. But I can't do a back and forth forever." She didn't want to! She couldn't go back to her townhouse. Now that they'd talked about it more, she knew she was too exposed there. She'd never feel comfortable or safe again. Which meant she'd need to speed up her plans to move.

"Exactly," Xander said, snapping up her assent quickly before she could change her mind. "We're past the staying over for a few days here and there part of the relationship.

So, I say we consider this a trial run for living together. We can revisit the exact location when Hamish finishes this project." All tied up with a bow.

He really was good at getting what he wanted.

"This is a fine idea. I think this place is the safer of the two. I love my house, but no one can camp on the lawn when the backyard is all the way up here." Hamish looked at her with a smile. "I know the attention is uncomfortable for you."

"It's just." She opened and closed her mouth twice. In the end, the need for him to understand rather than get his feelings hurt pushed her that last bit to share. "I'm super proud of you. And it *is* fun to go out and do things with you. Things we get invited to because you're a celebrity. It's not that."

When his features relaxed, it made her extra glad she'd decided to clarify.

"What is it then?" Hamish asked.

"For a long time, going unnoticed was the way to stay safest. Especially after we left. Anyway." She blew out a breath. "It's ingrained I suppose. Trying to avoid calling attention to myself. That was one of my biggest sins."

"You're living your life. Not calling attention to yourself." Hamish leaned close to kiss her temple.

"Having red, curly hair was *unseemly*. My mother, or more often, one of my older sisters, would wet it down and braid it tightly every single day. So, that's what I'm working with. I still wore it braided for another eight months or so after we left. Old habits. That's really my point. The way I react isn't about you or your success at all," she told Hamish. "It's my own stuff rattling around."

"I would very much like to punch every one of these motherfuckers in your family square in the face," Hamish said, echoing Xander's earlier statements.

"If you see one of them and they're trying to shove me in a car to forcibly take me to another state, please feel free. Otherwise, we should pretend to ignore it. In the meantime, we should have sex. Just a suggestion."

CHAPTER
EIGHTEEN

Hamish let himself free to take her. Reveled in the fact that this fine, beautiful sprite of a being was *his*.

Wanted to be. That she braved her memories to share with him and Xander, to trust them to be that vulnerable, had lit a fire in his belly.

He stood as she did, and he turned, clasping her upper arms, hauling her closer, dipping to claim her mouth.

Need throbbed like a toothache, driving him to pick her up as she laughed. In Xander's bedroom, he set to pulling her clothes free before loosing her glory of curls from the tail she'd drawn them up into. From then on, Hamish would always think on that story she'd just told about having to remain unnoticed, keeping her hair bound. As if the beauty of her hair was sinful when it was the opposite.

He buried his face in it, breathing deep as he maneuvered them both to the bed.

He traced over her collarbone with his mouth and the pads of his fingers, tasting, teasing. At his back, the rustle of clothes coming off as Xander got himself naked and then settled on the bed, rolling her from Hamish's hold into his own.

A game, not a competition.

Hamish went to his knees and kissed up the back of Xander's calf and then over to Pippa's knee and her thigh. The skin there was so soft, so sensitive, that when he blew over it, right below the spot her leg met her body, gooseflesh rose.

A shuddering breath went through him as the scent of her pussy hit him.

Xander had one of her nipples, biting down just shy of too hard as he looked down her body where Hamish muscled himself fully between her thighs after tossing his clothes off. He dragged the edge of his teeth over her skin, letting himself fall into that haze of desire.

When her fingertips slid against his shoulder and then tunneled into his hair, he groaned and let go completely, teasing his lips over her belly and then down to her pussy, diving in with circles around and around her clit.

He cupped her ass, tipping her hips to accommodate himself. Make deeper sweeps of his tongue inside her cunt.

Sweetly helpless sounds vibrated through her, and when Hamish opened his eyes, he locked his gaze with Xander's and felt that perfect *snap* of their connection falling into place.

Hamish drove her up hard and fast, devouring her as she came all over his face.

"Pippa," Xander said softly, but with enough authority Pippa and Hamish both looked up. Xander's mouth curved into a smile so full of wicked promise she swallowed hard in response.

Hamish crawled up her body, and she stretched to meet his kiss before Xander joined with nips of Hamish's neck and Pippa's earlobes.

"I'm going to fuck you," Xander said, sending a shiver through everyone. "And you're going to suck Hamish's cock while I do."

"Oh!" Her pupils swallowed most of the color of her eyes as she nodded slowly.

Xander kept himself under ruthless control as he rolled a condom on. It got increasingly difficult as he sat, his back against the headboard, and she looked to him, eyes huge, skin flushed. Her hair a tousle of curls around her face.

"See that mirror there?" He pointed at the stand-up mirror in the corner. She turned and then she understood. Where he'd sat himself was angled so that their reflection was perfect in all its carnal glory.

Hamish helped her straddle Xander's lap, her back to Xander's front. Xander slid his palms from her hips up to cup her tits, pinching and tugging on her nipples until he got her worked up all over again.

"Hamish. On your knees so she can bend." Xander put a hand at the center of her back and pushed gently. Then he angled her hips just right and thrust, sinking into her pussy in one movement that surrounded his cock with scorching heat.

In the mirror, Xander watched as Pippa braced her hands on Hamish's thighs and lowered her mouth, taking the head of his cock between her lips and then deeper before pulling back and doing it again.

Xander was torn between watching that and the look on Hamish's face as he stared down at Pippa.

This was what it should be. In unison. Working together. Not two people dating the same woman. This was connection. This was three.

"Yes, baby. Does it feel good?" Xander asked Hamish as he flexed his hips and slid in impossibly deeper.

At Pippa's startled moan, Hamish shuddered and dragged his gaze upward to meet Xander's. He'd seen Hamish's expression during some sort of sexual activity on multiple occasions, but when it was the three of them like this, all the tension was gone. He looked pleased and young. Happy.

"So good. Nothing finer in all of my life than this with you two." Hamish traced a fingertip over the bite mark he'd left on her right hip and then reached out to caress Pippa's back, but on the way back up, he scored his nails over her skin roughly.

She jerked back with a cry.

Xander cursed as her cunt superheated around his cock. "She liked that a whole lot," he snarled as he added a circular thrust, grinding himself against her clit.

Hamish's whimper and the way her pussy clamped around his cock told Xander they were all getting close.

First, their girl needed to come again.

Xander pushed down just above her tailbone as he thrust upward, grinding. She began to make soft, demanding sounds around a mouthful of Hamish's dick.

And then she was coming, her inner walls hugging him so tight he was nearly senseless at how good it was.

Hamish snarled her name, his fingers tightening around Xander's at her hip.

Not many breaths after that, Pippa's body still fluttering around his cock, Xander's orgasm hit in a wave, pulling him deep as he was lost to everything else but that moment between the three of them.

Xander managed to get himself untangled from them to clean up and then join them again, pausing to kiss Hamish as they met halfway.

"The benefits of living together are already presenting themselves, Pippa," Xander said as he settled in bed and pulled her close.

"Mmmm," she said by way of assent, her eyes barely open. "We'll see how you feel once we're back from our trip to L.A. and I have to get up for work at five thirty."

"You're wrong if you think I'm in any way bothered by that. I can get lots of things done if I get up with you. Or I can go back to sleep when you leave for work. It's all good."

"The best part for us both is that we know you're safer," Hamish added as he snuggled up on Pippa's other side.

CHAPTER
NINETEEN

Pippa had been to enough Thanksgiving dinners during her childhood where multiple families with all their children were in attendance that brunch with the Franklins and followed by dinner with Xander's crew wasn't as overwhelming as it might have been. Since they'd arrived at Gillian and Adrian's absolute stunner of a home on Bainbridge Island for dinner, Pippa had been introduced to about forty-seven thousand people whose names she'd already half forgotten. Though she'd known several of them by sight, like the members of Sweet Hollow Ranch.

The food had been fantastic, as had the company.

The sun had gone down, so they kept close to one of the stand-up heaters in the yard. Xander's arm was around her shoulders as they chatted with the cousins, as she'd come to think of them all as. And as Xander had predicted, Pippa adored Miles and Harlow both.

Hamish came out with a mug of warm cider for her, which he handed over and then kissed the tip of her nose.

"Hello, my love. Your nose is cold. Drink that then. It'll get you toasty. There's a little bit of whiskey in there."

When she sipped and nearly choked, Pippa looked his way with a wheeze. "*Little bit* must mean something different to you." Then again, there were so many people there and she *was* chilly.

Rennie had been inside with her sister but came out to where they stood. "Hi there." She hugged Xander, Hamish, and then Pippa. "You haven't run away, so things must be going well."

The weed probably helped, but whatever the reason, it had been fine as long as she kept to the smaller groups instead of the boisterous crowd in the living room where Hamish had been hanging out doing karaoke. Though he'd come to find her every little while, which she thought was rather sweet.

Xander, on the other hand, had been at her side the whole time. Introducing her around. Showing her various places in the house and yard, including a few she'd been invited to take refuge in if she needed to.

And she had a time or two, but Xander had found that the perfect opportunity to kiss her senseless or cop a feel like a horny college student.

"The food was ridiculously good. This place is stunning. What's to run away from? Thanks for checking in though." Rennie was a good friend, and the more time Pippa spent around their family, the more she realized those traits she so valued—compassion, loyalty, humor, creativity, and a sense of purpose—seemed to be widely held among Xander's friends and family.

It made being with them so much easier.

"I'm so glad. I'm very selfish, but I'm pleased that means you'll be around us all more. Things are always fun when you're at a party. Oh, have you met Carrie yet?" Rennie asked her as she waved at someone inside.

"If that's Carrie, then no."

"Carrie is Raven's stepdaughter. That guy talking to my dad? That's Mal, he's Carrie's uncle. Jonah's brother. You'll like her."

Carrie came over, tall with glossy dark-brown hair she'd caught back at the nape of her neck. Pippa had met Raven's husband Jonah a few times, and she definitely saw the resemblance. Carrie was elegant and poised in ways Pippa used to look at in magazine spreads, wishing she could carry off.

Rennie pointed. "Carrie, this is Pippa. She's Xander's girlfriend."

"Raven thinks really highly of you. I was hoping to meet you today or this weekend at Xander's birthday." Carrie's gaze went to Hamish, and then she blushed. "Hamish has told me a lot about you too."

It took all Pippa's control not to look at Hamish. She'd blushed like that about someone a time or two. Instead, she said, "He's very sweet that way. It's nice to meet you."

Pippa was utterly certain he wouldn't cheat now that they were all together, which was the only thing it was fair to be concerned about. There was nothing she could do about what he did before she came into his life and no reason to make Carrie—who seemed very nice as well as gorgeous—uncomfortable.

Hamish left Pippa's side a moment to give Carrie a hug

before stepping back to his spot. "You're looking well, darlin'."

Darlin'? Well, *that* felt sort of icky.

Then Xander squeezed her to his side a little tighter. No one else would have noticed. It was enough to get her head back on straight. If she was going to get worked up every time some former lover of either of her men came into her path, Pippa would need to stay inside all the time. True, she wasn't expecting it there at the first big all-family event when she was already amped up and nervous. But it was how things had played out, and it was unfair of her to be mad at anyone, least of all herself for being human.

Time to apply grace to everyone and move on.

Rennie's attention shifted as she realized what was happening, which only made Pippa feel worse. At her side, Hamish blathered on, being totally charming and not inappropriate in any way.

Pippa wanted to punch him in the throat. For just a moment and then it passed.

She chugged the rest of the cider as the absolutely delightful Carrie—with the very interesting job doing fine arts restoration at a prestigious firm based in Portland—told them about the project that had landed her in Seattle for the next several months.

God. She found herself liking Carrie a lot. Though for whatever reason—probably the pet name—Pippa was still annoyed with Hamish. *Who had done nothing wrong.*

Pippa's phone began to buzz. She had it on do-not-disturb except for her sisters, so she answered after excusing herself to walk a few feet away.

·　·　·

"Oh my god, I'm so sorry. Why didn't you say something earlier, Hamish?" Rennie said after Carrie had been called inside by her father.

Xander's attention was on Pippa, who'd been managing the awkwardness just fine before she'd stepped away. Her back had gone ramrod straight, and she held one arm around her middle. It had to be one of her sisters because he knew she'd turned her phone off to all calls but theirs.

Hamish sounded amused when he said, "I wasn't paying attention when you invited her over, and then I didn't even see it was her until she was nearly to us. I didn't want to spring it on Pippa with only a millisecond to respond and get herself composed. It wasn't...I met her through Created Families, through Raven. It was just twice. Four years ago? Maybe even five. I've seen her at meetings and events in the years since, and there's never been a repeat. Pippa knows who she is to me. Let's not make a problem when there's none."

Xander wasn't so sure Pippa hadn't been at least a little shaken. Especially when Hamish had gone in for the hug and the *darlin'*. It didn't mean anything. Hamish wasn't being a predator. It wasn't romantic or sexual at all. He was simply a charming flirt.

But her back got stiff when she was upset. And as his arm had been around her at the time, that's exactly what had happened, though she'd been nothing but friendly toward Carrie. Their Pippa stored her feelings in her muscles. He'd have to give her a workout when they got back to his place. Help her exorcise her emotions.

All thoughts of sex fled when Pippa turned a little more

into the lights from the porch and he saw her expression more clearly. Concerned, he was moving toward her, needing to fix whatever it was that had her looking that way.

In the background he heard Hamish excuse them both to Rennie as he joined Xander at Pippa's side.

"No. No I understand," Pippa said into her phone. "Thank you. *I said no.* I'm going to leave right now and go check it out myself."

Xander and Hamish glanced at one another. She rarely spoke in that tone to her sisters. Something was very wrong.

"It's not that I don't think you can handle a police report. I'm not coming back to talk to the cops. I have to see it for myself. Thank goodness they don't know where you live. Well of course it's them. Who else? Random Christians in the mood to vandalize my house for reasons?"

She finally looked up from her shoes and registered they were standing in front of her. She waved a hand, telling them she was okay and to go away. They remained there because it was absolutely clear she was nowhere near fine.

Pippa said to whoever was on the other end of the call, obviously Rebecca, "Don't wait for me there. Go home. Lock your doors. I'll see you in the morning. I promise I won't go over there alone even though I'd be just fine if I did." Always thinking about everyone else.

"She sure won't," Xander said loud enough that his voice would carry. He didn't know exactly what was going on, but she wasn't going to face it by herself.

She got that cute little wrinkle at the bridge of her nose, and then she narrowed her gaze at him a moment.

"Yes. I'll text you. I love you too."

She tucked her phone away, and Xander watched her pull herself back together.

"What's going on?" Hamish asked her, voice gentle in a way it only ever was with Pippa.

"My townhouse was vandalized. I need to get back. I'm sorry," she said. "I'll need a ride because I didn't drive on my own."

Both men scoffed at any need to apologize.

"I'm going to go get our things and tell my parents. Then they'll handle the exit as far as keeping everyone out of our way as we go." Xander kissed her and then gave her a hug. "We'll get through this."

He handed her off to Hamish, who tucked her neatly into his side. "Come on. Let's make our way out."

Pippa was grateful for her neighbors who'd clearly helped clean up the front of her townhouse. *Harlot* had been painted in all caps across the front wall and door, Rebecca had said. But the word had been obliterated with a few coats of primer that stood stark against the bright blue.

The vandals had kicked out all the spindles on her porch railing and had knocked her planters down, breaking them on the ground below. Her front windows had been destroyed and had been boarded up.

Xander had insisted on going inside first, but she was relieved there wasn't irreparable damage in there. The glass and other debris from the large terra cotta pot that had been thrown through the window had been cleaned up. The carpet and her secondhand couch had been stained.

She packed up a few more boxes. Things she couldn't

bear to lose. They made the drive back to Xander's in relative silence, though Hamish held her hand the entire time.

Xander carried the boxes up and then placed them carefully in one of the guest rooms on the first floor. "This can be your place. I'm happy to share my closet and all that in our bedroom, but this can be a space that's yours to retreat to when you need to be alone. The closet in here is empty. We can add other furniture if you like. A table, a desk. A different bed. Whatever. This is your home too."

All she saw when she closed her eyes was her front door with the big block of white paint over a slur.

"Did they fingerprint anything?" Hamish asked, taking her hand and leading her back out to the living room.

"They're not going to go to the trouble. The damage is a misdemeanor charge. The group knows how to go unnoticed too," she murmured trying to keep a moat around her feelings. She couldn't fall apart right then.

Pippa continued, "Maybe I'm paranoid, but that's a whole lot of things pointing at the group. Timothy called me a whore and a harlot the times he came here." She was so grateful they didn't know where Rebecca or Esther lived. "I should have moved before now, but it felt like running. I had the protection order. *Pride*."

She shot to her feet and started to pace. "I brought this whole thing on myself by not moving. I should have known they'd be back."

Xander growled at her. "Pippa, I'm not going to let you blame yourself for this. You have every right to be free of them. What did the police say? Will they question your family? Do they need to interview you?"

"No. They think it's just vandalism. My boyfriend is

famous. Plus I have *two* of them like a real floozy. They told Rebecca they had no reason to think it was anyone from the group. They'd rather not know. It's easier for everyone if we can just pin our hopes to it being a random act."

Xander said, "Everyone but you. Which is unacceptable. So, we engage some really excellent private investigators who'll do some looking. It just so happens I know several. My dads will be eager to help however they can."

Her hands flew up to cover her face a moment, and she had to fight every instinct to run off. "You can't tell them! *Oh my god.* They're going to think the worst of me. I come with all this drama. You need a normal person with a normal life."

Xander sighed and took her hands from her face. "Pippa, I know this is upsetting. I know you're afraid. And sad. Mad too. But *none of this is your fault.* No one believes that. *You* don't even, not really once you think about it. We'll figure out what your options are. You're safe here. We'll go and bring more of your things over before we head to Los Angeles next week with Hamish. We'll see about getting you out of your lease. You said you only had three months left anyway. Talk to Mick about it so he can be sure no one is just going to waltz into Twisted Steel."

"They're already on alert after that call." She was starting to doubt at the edges. Maybe it was a case of run-of-the-mill vandalism, and she was blowing it all out of proportion. "Your dads already found that Carl Brush guy was legit."

Xander shrugged. "They found there was a real person using that name who writes celebrity stories, yes. They also found his arrest record for drug dealing, so we certainly have reason to wonder if he'd get up to something dicey. The celebrity media thing he's been at for a few years, but he only gets work occasionally. We don't know what he does with the rest of his time when he's not writing about us. From what they uncovered, there's no way he could support himself on that alone, so there's more to find about this guy. He never answers his phone when they call, and he waits until late at night to call back and leaves a voicemail. That's dealer behavior. But also, celebrity follower behavior. Jumping to conclusions is dangerous and lazy, so they'll keep at it until they run him to ground. It's what they do."

She frowned at him. Xander had a way of taking the weight off her shoulders. Which she loved. It was lovely and made her feel safe. But he also just did whatever he wanted because he thought it was best. Oh, sure, he wouldn't say it in those exact words, but that's what he did nonetheless.

Case in point, Pippa hadn't known they were attempting to contact Brush to have a chat after they'd verified he was who he claimed to be.

"I'm sure they'll inform me before they go forward, once they do connect," she said. She had to push back with him, or he'd get too used to getting his own way all the time.

Xander made a noncommittal sound, and she narrowed her eyes at him.

He said, "Don't give me that face. This is serious. I'm not having you exposed to these people any more than necessary. Todd Keenan can get answers in ways sweet-faced, not-even-five-and-a-half-feet-tall Pippa Hall can't."

"That doesn't mean I don't need to be consulted about this stuff. This is *my* stuff. It's my life. You think I don't know it's serious? You can't go around me like I don't exist. I've been there, and I will never live that way again."

"You're right, of course," Hamish interjected. "I'm sure Xander will keep you informed. He's just worried about you right now. I am too. We can't punch anyone, so let us fuss a bit until we settle, aye?"

"Hmpf." She hadn't forgotten that *darlin'* from earlier.

"Hmpf? What have I done to get that sound?" he teased.

Well that pissed her off. She was going to let it go after she stewed a little more, but this *tee hee hee* bit was not the vibe she was aiming for. "Are you actually serious right now? *Darlin'*?"

"You know that wasn't anything."

Xander sucked in a breath.

"I know what it *felt* like." Pippa wasn't ready for the argument she just started over something totally stupid, so she kept glancing away.

"Stop looking at the fucking front door like you're keeping an exit in mind," Xander said. "It makes me feel like you're afraid of us."

If she thought about it too long, she'd cry. He was worried for her, that's what had him so wound up. So instead, she said, "I wouldn't want you to feel like that at all. Good night." She grabbed her purse and avoided being touched as she went into the room Xander had said was hers and closed it very quietly but firmly.

"What the fuck are you doing?" Hamish turned, anger on his features. "Of course she's afraid. Can't you see it written all over her?"

"She has no reason to be afraid of *us*! I don't appreciate

feeling like I've beaten her when all I've done is ask a question."

Hamish said, "Well, to be clear, you had some direction with this investigation your fathers are working on, and you haven't included her. And when she got prickly over it, I stepped in to protect you. But really? Bottom line is her behavior when it comes to looking for doors and ways out of a room has nothing to do with us. Your mother does the same thing, if I recall."

"Fucking ouch!"

"What? I'm right. You think Pippa can just toss away all that fear like a pair of jeans that doesn't fit anymore? Two of us, asking her questions at once. After she's spent the whole day first with my family and then with yours. Then her home is vandalized. Do you know how proud she was of that front door? She painted it herself. She's overwhelmed and grieving."

"I'm not minimizing what happened! I was there. I'm trying to help her not feel responsible for some shit someone else is doing. You're the one who had to go and flirt in front of her and then had the audacity to ask her what she was mad over."

Hamish looked at him like he had just said the most ridiculous thing in the universe. "Yes, dumbarse. And then we would have had a little tiff over something she absolutely knew was nothing. But we'd have been bickering about something not related to that ugly business at her townhouse. Then we could have made up, but she'd be less anxious. And it would have underlined that we can have our little bumps in the road but it's all really just fine."

Xander scrubbed his hands over his face.

.   .   .

Hamish took a deep breath. "I get it. People assume I'm all charming flirtation. And I am. It's a coping mechanism too, based on childhood trauma. In the future, I'll make more effort not to flirt the way I have in the past. Not because it means something. But because it makes you and Pippa uncomfortable. But I'm more than the outside, and I hope you'll figure that out at some point."

"I was wrong," Xander said, contrition clear in his tone and in his gaze. "I know you're more than the outside. I knew it when we were talking to Carrie. You did nothing wrong. I'm so sorry I underestimated you. I'm worried about her. I want to keep her safe. But that's no excuse."

"And what if I told you, Xander, that's *your* childhood trauma?" Hamish leaned forward and kissed him softly, feeling better after that apology. "We are all here today, who we are today, based on what we experienced along the way."

"I come from a great family who love me. I've never known want the way you two have. I've never, not once, doubted I was loved and valued."

"But just because you have this incredibly special and important connection to them doesn't mean you are without your scars. Your mother lost a child and then nearly her career. You lost the potential that comes with an older sister. Charlie is a delight to me. *Now.* But oh, when I was younger, she would torture us all to get us to do her chores. She used to roll her eyes so hard at the mere sight of us when she'd come home from school on the weekends." Hamish laughed. "I wouldn't trade it for all the world. You lost that. And part of your heart knew it even before you could understand the story. You are driven to protect, and that is part of why."

"I know you think I only saw the outside," Xander said. "And the outside is quite diverting. But your lyrics—if nothing else but your lyrics—are irrefutable proof that you have a way with emotion. And how that makes people do and feel the way they do. I saw it before we got together. I see it more every day now. But I have respected and been in true awe of it more than once."

They hugged, lingering a while to soak up that affection.

"I'm worried about her safety," Xander said quietly after looking at the—still—closed door she'd disappeared behind. "My dads did some research on his church. The Garrett Group, they call themselves. There's some main religious leader, Ralph Garrett, but he's not in Arizona, he's in Texas. Then there are churches in a few cities in other states. They described Garrett as being their conduit to God. He prepares all their study material and wrote their rules for daily living. Like what they can wear. Who can wear it based on gender, age, marital status. Everyone's appearance needs to be regimented. You remember her talking about her hair and how she had to keep it in braids. Anyway, they're still looking. Trying to get access but not through Pippa. They don't want to involve her any more than is absolutely necessary."

Hamish blew out a breath. "Good."

"By way of apology to Pippa, I'm going to show her the various panic buttons throughout the apartment. That might make her feel like she's got more control. I think you should move in here," Xander said. "Once you're finished with this album. My mother lived here before she was with my dads.

The security footprint has been updated multiple times as technology improves. Your house is safe, absolutely. This is far more difficult to get to simply because it's got limited access. There's a studio here already, though smaller than yours. So make it bigger. There's definitely room. Make it however you want to make it so you can be here with us."

Xander hadn't actually asked him personally to move in. It had been assumed by everyone, but the process had been interrupted with the tract on her car and getting her relocated had been the top priority. But something deep inside, some doubt Xander felt as deeply for him as he felt for Xander, eased at the request. At being wanted and being told outright.

"I can do that. But that means you'll come home to my sister being here a lot more often. I'll need a parking space just for her." Hamish thought about how important Jessi was in his life. How big a difference it made when she was around all the time to keep him grounded and honest with himself.

"All right. Three came with the apartment but others are available, though it may not be right next to ours. Tomorrow I can get more parking passes so you can give Jessi a few until we get that spot. Does that work?"

"You really don't mind?"

"Of course I don't. My family visits all the time. I assume Rebecca will do the same as she works not too far from here."

Hamish said, "That is, if Pippa doesn't move out tomorrow and take up residence in Rebecca's guest room. Her whole life she was told what ways it was acceptable to express a very narrow band of emotion. Trying to control that in any way is going to push her buttons. You were cranky because she was being threatened and it bled out into the conversation that was already fraught. So. Now go fix it."

"She's pissed, yes, but she's not going to run." Xander stood. "Doesn't mean I don't have to do some groveling though."

CHAPTER
TWENTY

Hamish pulled Pippa into his arms, laughing as he danced her in a grand circle right there in the lobby of the hotel. The meeting with Jet had gone amazingly well. He couldn't remember a time when he was this full of hope and excitement about the future.

"I take it you had a very fruitful appointment?" she asked him, a beautiful, wide smile on her lips. Her eyes shone with pleasure, and he soaked it in. The way she loved him made him feel ten feet tall.

"Most definitely. Yesterday's meeting was grand, but today? Jet gets me and my material." He'd felt so seen as an artist.

"I'm so happy to hear that." And she was. It seemed to radiate from her.

"I think we need a celebratory dinner," he told her and Xander. "They've got a table waiting at 3205 tonight. We can look out over the lights, drink champagne, and fortify ourselves for what I believe will be vigorous sexual activity when we get back to the condo."

"Should I skip dessert?" Pippa teased, and brought a laugh from his gut that seemed to change his entire life.

"I can restrain my vigor until we've digested our dessert. They've got a chocolate tart with berries and ice cream made in house I think you will enjoy."

Of course an hour later when they arrived at the restaurant he was sorry he'd made that declaration because she wore a snug minidress with a sweetheart neckline. The deep-blue color set off against her skin made her nearly glow like a pearl.

She'd gathered her hair up off her neck, but the curls seemed to rain down around her face she'd artfully done up. Far more than her day-to-day look with a smoky eye and sultry dark-pink lip. She was sexy as hell and a temptation to his hands and mouth.

"Bet you're regretting this reservation right about now. I sure am," Xander murmured in his ear, making them both laugh. Pippa, who'd wandered off to look out the windows facing the lights of the cities beyond, spread out like glittering jewels, gave them a look over her shoulder as she heard them.

"So give us details," Pippa urged once they'd been seated and their drinks had arrived.

"Both meetings were great. Leaving each I felt like I was on the right track. I believe in my songs more now than I did three days ago. But Jet, I don't know, they saw what I'd envisioned as harder, driving beats, as funkier. With a little bit of rock-and-roll drenched in R&B sprinkled throughout. Anachronistic but definite ribbons of 70s English rock. The material wouldn't just be highlighted to look its best—which it will be—but it was about that twist the right producer can add to raise the material above its origins and make it better. I think Jet can do that. So much so they put me on their schedule and will come to Seattle in a few weeks to start recording. I'll need to travel back here for studio work with other artists. They have connections to musicians I know *of* but not in person."

"That sounds fantastic. I'm excited to watch this whole process as it goes, baby," Xander said. "Feel free to stay at the condo whenever you need to. It'll be good for you to have a home base that's safe." He lifted a shoulder. "Avoid anything that's going to threaten your creativity unnecessarily." In other words, they wanted him to stay clean and healthy.

"I'm past the age when being high, operating on no sleep, stinking of sex with randoms, all while trying to finish an album is even remotely appealing." Frankly it had been exhausting.

"Always good to hear," Pippa said with a laugh.

"You never worry, do you? I know there was a time when I was skittish and stupid. But I would never do anything to break what we have. I love you. Period. There's no one else other than this one over here." Hamish jerked his head to indicate Xander.

She cocked her head, leaning in to kiss the corner of his mouth quickly. "I try not to worry about either of you. I'm only human, and sometimes the way you attract attention is difficult to deal with. I'm trying! But, no, of all the concerns I have, you going on a bender of drugs and randos isn't among them. As long as you don't call them pet names."

He drew an X over his heart. "No romantic or sexy pet

names for anyone but you and Xander. I have everything I've ever imagined, and a few things I didn't know enough about to even consider imagining," Hamish murmured before kissing her softly. "You're my personal miracle, aye?"

"Aye," she said. "I love you too."

Xander slowly petted the back of her neck with his fingertips, lulling, soothing. They were headed down to the bar in the lobby of the same building as the restaurant, and Pippa didn't bother to hide the way she stared at the picture the three of them presented in the mirrored walls of the elevator.

"You two look so absurdly delicious I'm a little lightheaded," Pippa said as she stood between them.

The two men couldn't have appeared more different. Hamish, long and lean in his very sharp navy-blue suit. A modern spin on a 1960's British feel with a narrow tie and a crisp white shirt.

He'd been to the barber right before they'd gotten on the plane, and he'd done some sort of tousled bit on top that made her think of the way he looked right after he made her come. The cuffs of his shirt contrasted with the ink on his hands. A mix of tough and elegant. So swoonworthy.

On the other side, Xander stood, wide shoulders draped in whisper-soft gray cashmere that picked up the pinstripe in his nearly black trousers. He wore one of his heavier gauge black clickers in his septum, and it gave her a shiver when he smiled at her, one corner of his mouth rising slowly. He was powerful and hard-edged, but the elegant touches, the sweater, the excellent shoes, did something to soften the sharpest parts of him. One of his arms was wrapped around her waist, his palm flat against her side and belly, and she saw he was wearing the watch she'd given him for his birthday.

He did his thing when they got off the elevator, walking at her side but also slightly ahead so no one could jostle her. It was not underrated.

Hamish had his hand at her back, protecting her other side as flashbulbs popped as they passed on their way inside the bar.

"Are you all right, love? I'm sorry about that," Hamish said in her ear. "I forgot this place tends to attract musicians, and so there'd be cameras outside."

"We just had security move them outside the lobby. They're not supposed to be in here. Our apologies," the handler who'd led them to a table said to Hamish.

"No worries." Hamish tipped her well, and she melted away only to be replaced by a server nearly immediately.

"You're not this famous in Seattle," Xander teased.

"It's why I live there instead of here. Imagine what a colossal dickhead I'd be." He snickered, and Pippa did too, leaning her head on his shoulder for a moment. "This place has an excellent brown liquor selection, and they try their best to keep cameras on the other side of those ropes."

Pippa got the feeling that the bar was where the old Hamish hung out. However, the music was great, Hamish was in celebratory spirits, and it appeared he was correct about the cameras, at least the ones belonging to the media outside.

Though she'd learned in the early days of their relationship that anyone with a cellphone could be a photographer. She'd been surprised to see photos of herself in Trader Joe's, wearing shop jeans, still in the beanie she used while working to keep her hair contained.

She was very glad she'd watched about three dozen makeup tutorials online before leaving on this trip because everyone in the place looked fantastic. When the inevitable photos came out, she'd hopefully keep up instead of coming off like a four-year-old playing in her big sister's makeup drawer.

The truth was, this sort of thing came with his life. And she had to find a way to celebrate it, so he never felt bad. He played Tri-Ominos with her sisters and Danny for hours and never complained a single time. She could dress up, put on her company manners, and play the part of adoring girlfriend. The latter wasn't hard at all because she certainly adored him.

"Do people always pay for your drinks like this?" she asked sometime later. Round after round had shown up at their table courtesy of this or that person who often would stop over and stay a drink or two. He introduced her to everyone as his love. She remembered telling him how it had made her feel when he'd introduced her as his friend, and it touched her how he seemed to go out of his way to indicate to everyone—including her—that he was in love and committed to her and Xander.

Pippa was pretty much a lightweight, so after her third drink, she ordered some appetizers and switched to lemon soda water. Xander did the same a few rounds after her. Hamish kept going. It was the most tipsy she'd ever seen him, but he remained genial, and he was clearly so happy his mood was infectious.

"I'm getting too old to drink this hard," he said with a smile. "But it's been a grand night all around. Thank you for your patience." Hamish took her hand and kissed her knuckles.

"I'm so glad I was here to share this moment with you."

"There's an excellent burger place around the corner from the condo," Xander said. "I vote we grab a bag of cheeseburgers and take it back to eat in our pajamas."

Hamish's gaze sharpened, and he sat straighter. "Yes. Let's."

"I can drive us back," Pippa said. "I haven't had a drink in a few hours."

"Will you guide us like a very stern governess?" Hamish asked, a whisper in her ear that sent shivers rioting over her skin.

"We already have a very stern headmaster. He doesn't seem to want to share power with a stern governess." Pippa and Hamish looked over to Xander, who sent them a rather roguish grin.

"Time to go." Xander stood. "I'm still headmaster," he said quietly to them both, "but I'm good with a beautiful woman driving us home. Maybe we can play naughty chauffeur afterward instead."

"She'll be the kind of chauffer who changes into sneakers once we get to the car."

Xander hugged her to his side and then kissed her. "That's my favorite kind of chauffeur."

"Seconded. Come on then, you two. It's time for burgers and naked times afterward." Hamish slung an arm around her waist, and they headed out for burgers and sexytimes.

. . .

The next morning, as she was up on the rooftop deck to get her steps in, Rebecca called to catch up. "This morning when I logged on to my email there were multiple hits on my automated search of your name. I like to keep an eye on you," Rebecca said, and Pippa snorted a laugh. "You three were very smartly dressed. I'll say your clothes have gotten cuter since you've been with them. For a tiny scrap of a girl, you have great legs."

"Covered in freckles and SPF eight thousand."

"Adorable like the rest of you. It'd be more annoying if you weren't so stinkin' sweet. In one you're outside a bar of some sort. Xander looks furious that you've been jostled. Hamish put himself between you and the camera on your other side. The better ones are of inside the club. I guess that because you're wearing the same clothes. Xander is kissing you in one and Hamish is kissing you in another. It's all rather sweet and glamorous too."

"It was a pretty swanky club, I must say. All sorts of famous people came over to hang out either because they knew Hamish or Xander via his mom or uncle. I danced some. Did a lot of people-watching. My feet hurt so bad by the end. I had a bag in the trunk from when we'd gone to the beach, so I put my sneakers on to drive home." Pippa laughed, trying hard not to overthink the situation. People liked to look at Hamish. He photographed well. He was always friendly and charming. At least she'd been cute last night.

"By the way. Vivi wanted you to know you can store any of your furniture that you can't take to Xander's but don't want to get rid of entirely."

"Tell her thank you." She didn't need her couch or her

dining table. But she had a trundle bed she was putting in the spare room she'd taken over at Xander's, along with her recliner chair and her bookcases. "I was going to see if anyone at work wanted anything I'm not taking, and then donate or get rid of the rest."

Rebecca said, "Look. I want this thing to work out for you and Xander and Hamish. But you're giving up your townhouse and moving in with them. First, keep your own bank account and make sure you have enough saved to get yourself a new start if you need one. A joint account is fine. Whatever. You three will figure all that out. But have something that is yours alone and add to it regularly. If something goes left and you break things off, you shouldn't have to buy all new stuff. Or if you decide you want a new car or other big purchase, you should have the ability to make that choice. I just think it can also be a way for you to feel steadier about all the change going on in your life. No matter what, you always have a place wherever I am if you need it. Choices mean freedom."

Having choices meant a great deal to Pippa and her well-being in general. No one knew that better than her sisters did. "I wanted to take more time. Talk about it. Set up some ground rules. But then the tract on my car followed by the vandalism at my place made it impossible to do anything but move. I don't want to be a thing on their to-do list. A damsel in distress."

"You know them better than I, obviously, but they've never given me any indication they feel anything like that about you. Regardless, you don't have to move in anywhere because you don't feel safe at the townhouse. There are two bedrooms here no one uses but you and Esther. Park yourself in one until you decide what you want.”

“If I truly had felt uneasy about moving in with Xander, I would have shown up at your door, bags packed. I promise. I love them both. So far, living together has been good. I’m finding ways to put my stamp here and there. Xander is easy with whatever it takes for me to be comfortable.”

She thought about her little room. Ha. *Little* was actually pretty large, with an attached bathroom and doors leading to the sheltered part of the outdoor terrace.

“Hamish will join us full-time after he’s done with this project. While we’re here, someone came by to look at the studio to create the plans to make it whatever Hamish says he needs. He’s using the same firm that did the studio at his house.”

“Things are good for you, Pippa. I’m so happy to hear it.”

“Me too. You and Vivi are getting married next year. Esther is going to make us the best aunts in the whole world in just six more months. Things are going well for all of us. It’s awesome.”

CHAPTER
TWENTY-ONE

"As much as I love it in the Northwest, I am not in love with snow on the ground for longer than a day, two max," Pippa muttered. "It's like the cold radiates up into my feet, legs, and the rest of me. It snowed for a week after Christmas. It's rather unseemly to do so again now that we're in January."

Xander picked her up, swinging her into his arms and cuddling her close. "Better? I can keep you warmer this way. And it'll keep you out of trouble. Let's spend the bail money on food instead."

"Well. I could complain, but then you'd put me down and you're very warm."

He chuckled, not putting her back on her feet until they got to the front entry of the restaurant where their friends were waiting.

"Did I just see him carry you in here?" Rennie asked, looking absolutely gorgeous in a bright red sweater, her hair up in a bun.

"You did. I was whining about the cold."

"She's not too far from the ground, you know. She gets cold faster than I do." Xander winked as they sat across from various cousins, as well as Jessi, Mick, and Adam, and PJ and Asa.

"Duke and Carmella ducked into his office right as we were leaving." Asa smirked. "Gonna guess they'll be along in a while."

Pippa looked up from the menu to see Hamish coming through, and she waved him over, patting the seat to her left.

Ah, there she was. Hamish gave in to her pull, bending to kiss her before sliding into his chair with liquid grace.

"How did it go?" she asked of his day with Jet and their team, and everything felt even better because he was there with her.

"My brain is numb. But for good reasons. Finished a track and we're on to the next. We're nearing the end." Hamish hummed as he read the menu.

"Already? Wow. Which one is it...can I ask?" Pippa bounced a little in her seat. Hamish found so much pleasure in the way she was interested in his work. It was a big boost to his ego that she was always so engaged and wanted to hear more.

"It was 'Backyard Chickens'."

Her entire face lit up with a smile. Despite the silly name, it was a song about the first night he'd kissed her. When he'd shown up at his parents' house for a welcome home barbecue and she'd been there. He'd managed to lure her away from the house, to get her all to himself, by showing her where the chickens roosted in the woods out back during the warmer months.

He'd kissed her right then, under a sky going purple as the sun was setting.

"I can't wait to hear it." Cheeks still flushed from pleasure, she looked down at the menu again. "We need to have a celebration when you finish. I know there'll be a listening party or what have you. But I want to hear it before everyone else."

"Yeah?"

She turned with a grin. "I don't make you buy me diamonds, so I think I can pull the girlfriend card to hear your new album before the public."

It was the idea of a lifetime of these little, wonderfully normal moments with her that had him leaning close to kiss her. "I promise you and Xander can hear it once it's done." He said in her ear, "You please me so much with the way you love me, my beautiful Pippa. Thank you."

She squeezed his arm, and they went back to their menus. Once they'd ordered, she said, "Now Xander can tell everyone who he's going to be tattooing in two weeks."

Ever their best cheerleader, Pippa got Xander to tell them all about Sam Flanigan, a very high-profile tattoo artist who'd seen and admired Xander's work and had called that day to say he wanted some ink.

"He and Raven worked together back when she was just starting out in Los Angeles. She sends him pictures of my stuff from time to time." Xander ducked his head. "Was stunned, no lie, when he asked when I could fit him in."

Martine said, "This guy, for those who may not know him, is like the Mick Jagger of the tattoo world. He does what he wants, where and when he wants. He's got a shop in Los Angeles and another in San Francisco and multiple product endorsement deals and television work. If Xander's name is on his lips, that's the sort of publicity that gets product deals and partnerships."

Xander gave up trying to look nonchalant. "Let's not get ahead of ourselves. I've got to design something good and then execute it well. If I fuck up, it's the opposite for my career."

Pippa put her hand on Xander's arm a moment. A reassuring touch. Hamish smiled at them both.

"I guess maybe he should get Raven to tattoo him? Or someone else in town?" Pippa asked, all innocent-like.

"What?!" Xander looked at her and then snorted before stealing a kiss. "Fine. I see what you're doing."

"You're amazing at what you do. He came to you based on the work you've already done. I have no doubts at all you'll do a fantastic job and Sam Flanigan will sing your praises all over the place." Pippa smiled up at the server who'd materialized to take their order.

In the two months since that trip to Los Angeles, Hamish had spent a great deal of time drawing together the right material and people to come together on the new album.

His usual band had rolled into town for the project. Everyone's energy was good. They worked together well and would go out with him for live shows. They were a big part of his success. He treated them fairly, paid them what they deserved, and as a result of that respect, they got on.

Hamish knew exactly what he wanted. And that wasn't to be in a band full of people writing songs with him. They were *his* songs. There was no need to be a prick about it, however.

"So, I heard part of that earlier," Jessi, who'd been seated to his immediate left, said. "Sounds like things are good with the new producer. Tell me more."

Hamish told her all about what was going on. What material he'd chosen and why. She was enthusiastic and pleased. Which only added to how he'd been feeling. Positive. Things were heading in a direction he'd worked toward for years. And to top that off, there was Pippa at the end of every day. And Xander. Their man who'd been such a steady presence.

Every time he walked into that apartment it felt a little more comfortable. When he opened a cabinet and found a mug Pippa had bought for him. Or that she'd moved some of his clothes over from his house, so he had things to wear if he drove to Xander's on autopilot after they'd wrapped for the day.

At first, he'd figured he'd sleep at his place and see them both around his schedule. And they'd stayed back, let him work. Though Pippa checked in on him daily. Sent texts and often, when they'd taken a break from recording and gone upstairs, it was to find she'd dropped off fruit or sandwiches or whatever. Just little signposts to mark his way. Keep him on the path.

And yet, when he'd finished up and crawled into his bed, it was too big and too cold. By the fourth time he'd given in and wound up at Xander's, Hamish had accepted the comfort that big apartment offered. At the end of his workday, whenever that was, he locked up and pointed himself toward downtown.

Even if she and Xander had gone to sleep, his place was there. And when he eased into bed, she snuggled into his side, Xander reached his arm across her pillow and over to Hamish's, tangling his fingers in Hamish's hair, and everything was exactly how it was supposed to be.

He went *home* every night. They were his light in the window.

"Will there be a tour?" Jessi asked.

"Yes. I've got some plans in the works." He gave her an overview. He might have been dreading that if he hadn't spent the last months working out a path to do live shows and keep healthy. He liked the stability of his life. Liked that he knew who the fuck he was.

After dinner, Hamish and Xander walked out to where she'd parked her truck when she'd driven straight from work. She halted, her mouth open in horror, as she took in what had happened.

"What the fuck?" she whispered. A word she rarely ever used. But the sight of Gretchen, her windshield caved in, tires slashed, deep gashes in the paint along the driver's side, made the F word necessary.

Xander, who'd been hanging back, chatting with Fox, swore. Loudly. He called Hamish's name, and both rushed to her, stepping in between her and the wreck of her truck. A truck she'd lovingly restored herself over the course of years.

She couldn't even cry about it. The shock had sucked away all emotions as she leaned around Xander to look again.

"Baby, let's get you to my car. Then we'll call the police."

Xander wrapped a gentle arm around her and turned her away, guiding her to the passenger side of his vehicle where she sat, blinking, trying to clear her head because this wasn't actually happening.

"Who is doing this?" Jessi demanded, very angry. "Honey, you're shivering. Let's start the engine so we can turn the heater on."

"I don't know." But she did.

"Pippa, once the police are done, I'll box up everything from inside the truck and get it to you. We'll have Gretchen brought to Twisted Steel. She can be brought back to glory. I promise you," Mick said.

Xander's adrenaline coursed through his system, driving him to fix anything that had upset Pippa so much she'd actually said *fuck*.

The sight of her truck having been so vandalized had gutted him; he knew it had to be a thousand times worse for her. Knew she'd done ninety percent of the restoration on her own, in downtime around her work schedule. When she'd gotten the money and/or the skills she'd needed to do the next part, she'd done so.

"One foot in front of the other," she'd described the process of restoration. What he'd heard over everything else was how proud she'd been of doing it on her own.

He told Hamish, "After we deal with the cops and insurance, we need to get her home."

Hamish nodded as they watched her.

Mick approached. "Tow company on the way. We'll have Gretchen brought to Twisted Steel so we can get her back to top shape. We aren't going to let Pippa go through this alone."

"Appreciate it," Xander said, glancing toward the car where she sat, surrounded by their friends and family. "Hamish, I think you should contact Rebecca. That way Pippa won't have to. Just let her know the basics. I'll tell Pippa we've done that, so she won't be pissed."

Hamish actually laughed. "*Mate.* She's going to be pissed either way. So, I suggest we let Pippa tell her sisters on her own. Getting in between them will make matters worse. It's after eleven. Rebecca will be asleep, and Esther is pregnant. Pippa isn't won't thank you for waking them up for something none of them can help with. Rebecca would be at the apartment in twenty minutes, and then what? They'll both get even more wound up. Let's wait until tomorrow and then include her in the conversation."

Xander frowned, scratching his chin. He wanted to spare Pippa the upset of having to retell the story to anyone else.

He looked over to Pippa, and a wash of red and blue lights hit as a cruiser slid into the lot. Her features were blank. She'd had enough for one day. Hamish was likely right. As much as it annoyed Xander.

"Too late for anything else anyway," he said, heading over, meeting Pippa halfway to take her hand. They'd deal with the authorities together. At the very least, he could protect her during that.

CHAPTER
TWENTY-TWO

"You're on my last nerve, Xander. Go to work," Pippa told him the following morning. He'd been lurking around since she woke up, checking in on her, barking orders at people—other people, not her—being overprotective and grumpy.

"I'm taking the day off."

"No, you aren't. Look." She took a deep breath. He was worrying because he loved her. "I know you're concerned. But I'm up here on planet Brown in my ultra-luxurious, super-high-security spaceship. Nothing is going to happen to me."

"What if you'd been alone? And that person had decided to hurt you instead of your car?" He flopped down next to her on the couch where she'd set up. If she wasn't going in to Twisted Steel, she could at least finish paperwork and feel useful.

"But I wasn't alone. I was with you and Hamish and no less than ten of our friends. In a restaurant." It wasn't as if she hadn't wondered that very thing herself. But that way lay madness, and she didn't want to freak herself out any more than she already had. "They hurt my car. Not me. They couldn't have hurt me because I was with you."

The police hadn't been dicks about it. Well, one of them had been. But overall, it was that there wasn't a whole lot to be done. Car prowling and vandalism were things they saw all the time.

They didn't seem that interested in requesting surveillance footage from the businesses around the parking lot. "We've got real crime to deal with," one of them had said. And Pippa wasn't ignorant to that. But what had happened to her and Gretchen had been a real crime. Even if it wasn't as serious as a murder or assault.

Xander, however, had been flat-out amazing. He'd pressed the point about the vandalism of the night before being the second such incident, reminding them of the damage at her townhouse. One of the guys on the scene had looked to Xander and then Hamish before his gaze landed back on Pippa.

And said, "Sometimes people need to keep a low profile instead of putting their whole lives out in public."

Xander was not a fan of that comment at all.

Pippa hadn't been either. But it did drive home the possibility it might be related to some disgruntled fan. An ex. Even someone who thought, as that officer clearly did, she was a thot who'd done something so wrong she deserved to have her possessions ruined for it.

She felt cornered. Dreading what might be next. Mostly it didn't matter when people who didn't know her judged her harshly. Her job and her personal life were safe and full of acceptance. But the worry that anyone was out there waiting for the opportunity to show her just how much they hated her was something she really didn't think she could bear. Okay. She could. But she didn't want to.

Xander had stepped closer to that cop who'd said it. Mick —thank goodness for Mick—had moved, putting a hand on Xander's shoulder, pulling him back from the edge.

"Sometimes, people would be better off understanding they don't know what they're talking about, I'd guess, about forty percent of the time," Xander ground out.

The cop who'd said all that earlier looked up, and then up some more. Whatever he saw on Xander's face was enough to send him away.

The other one, the person in charge, was a woman, whose delivery was about four thousand times better. But in the end, it was the same. Vandalism happened a lot. That part of downtown was having a wave of car prowls. They'd file a report to help with her insurance, but they weren't going to fingerprint anything or do an exhaustive investigation because they didn't have the time or inclination for a minor property crime.

Xander had been in a mood ever since. Not to her. Not about her. He'd gone out of his way to be sure she understood he placed blame where it belonged, which was not Pippa.

Hamish had been a sweetie, making her tea, bringing her favorite blanket from the couch to their bed. They'd snuggled her and made her feel very safe.

But it was the next day, and while Hamish had finally agreed to go to his house where his band and producer were going to show up within the hour, Xander was lurking. Overprotective and lovely. But still.

"You're being stalked. Don't you think I can see?" He clenched his jaw.

Her heart broke a little for him. The situation must be stirring up the heartache of losing a sister, and his mother losing a child. No matter that it happened long ago. Some things change you forever, even if you weren't there when they occurred.

"We don't know for sure. There was just a whole flurry of new items about us that hit the media last week." Pictures of her with Hamish. She'd been looking up at him, a smile on her face. His hand had been at her waist. They'd been at a listening party for Harlow's band, Above Me, for their new single. He'd been pleased for his friends. Pippa had been pleased she'd gotten along with everyone. Miles was Xander's closest cousin. The one he looked up to and went to for advice. It would have been awful if they hadn't liked her!

But the pictures—because Xander had been on Pippa's other side, holding her hand—had gone wide. Even the accounts of the sites that still had print magazines had posted them to their social media. Naturally, Carl Brush's name had been among the dozen or so others.

There was endless fascination with them being a threesome. Miles had even been asked about it in an interview, much to Xander's annoyance. Miles had said he really liked and respected Pippa and Hamish and that they were perfect for Xander, who was very happy.

But then the number of people who'd tried to walk in to Written On the Body skyrocketed that next week to the point they had to add someone at the front door to control access for a few days until it stopped.

Twisted Steel was already used to the tourists, as the shop

called those who seemed to be obsessed by the number of people in someone else's bed from when Mick had gotten together with Adam and Jessi. There had been someone with a camera leaning on a car just on the other side of the fence that opened to the employee parking lot. He'd taken her photograph, and a few weeks later it had shown up in a totally different story.

But at work, no one got into the lot who wasn't supposed to be there. The employee lot was fenced with keycard entry, along with the door leading from the lot into the shop portion of the business. During the daytime, someone took a walk through the area at least once an hour as people went out to get coffee or boba at the little shop nearby, or just to stretch their legs. The absolute stunner of a receptionist also happened to be a total badass. She knew a hundred ways to tell people to bug off and look good doing it. At night, the state-of-the-art security system kept the cars and motorcycles in the showroom protected as well as whatever they were working on in the shop.

Pippa was fine at work. And she was totally fine once she drove into the garage of their apartment building. When she visited Hamish's house to drop off something or just check in on him, she waited until that garage door closed behind her before she got out. Todd had gone over a basic safety plan with her. The Pippa she'd been a year before would have been so embarrassed, but the person she'd grown into appreciated that he'd helped her assert control. Especially for the whole world beyond those known safe harbors. Her life was wonderful. She was in love and loved in return. She had a close group of found family as well as her sisters. She'd struggled and fought fiercely to have her life, and though it was shrinking because of the chaos, the safety plan process had helped her.

She wasn't going to let this steal her happiness. But it was a lot. Had been so before her truck was vandalized.

"I don't want to leave you alone. I can see you're upset." Xander scratched his chin through his beard.

She said, "Can I be totally honest with you?"

"Always."

"I need to fall apart a little. I need to cry and be very sad and then very mad. If you're here, I'll edit myself. And I really just need to break. You can even come back in a few hours. But I need to be alone for a bit. I'm sorry if this is making you feel bad."

The line between his eyes eased as he leaned in and kissed her forehead. "I get it. How about this? I'll see my next client and check in when I'm done. I've already moved my last appointment of the day. It's Fox, and he told me last night to cancel it so I could be with you."

"He did? I like that dude."

"He likes you too." He gave her another kiss. "I'll be checking in via text. That way all you have to do is just send a K or whatever to let me know you're fine. If you don't, I'll worry and come home."

She knew it was pushing things to get him to leave, so she nodded. She'd want to know the same in his place.

And when he left, she took her things into the bathroom and allowed herself a cry long and hard enough at the end she had the hiccups and a need for a nap.

. . .

Xander looked up as he came into Written On the Body. Todd Keenan was fiercely proud of his son. He had the heart of a lion and a depth of honor and loyalty that humbled his parents.

And the way he'd grown and matured as he'd started this triad had only made them all the prouder. It wasn't the three-people part—they'd never seen it coming that he'd end up in a throuple—it was the way Xander handled himself. He wanted to be the best he could for Pippa and Hamish. He wanted to be a better person, and wasn't that the key to longevity in anything?

"Wasn't expecting to see you today. Everything okay, Pop?"

Todd hugged him and settled in the corner chair of Xander's station. "After your call last night, I wasn't sure you'd be here. Dad was though. Damn it. He loves to be right, and I'll have to admit he was. You have a few minutes?"

That morning he and Ben had listened to the detailed message their son had left, and he'd been the one delegated to seek Xander out and figure out what he needed most.

"I just finished up. Next client isn't due for twenty minutes or so. I was going to cancel it, but I promised Pippa I'd let her be for a few hours." Xander's annoyed expression told Todd what he thought of that.

"She needed some space to cry a little?"

Xander exhaled sharply. "How did you know?"

Every year on the day Adele had been killed, Erin broke in her own way, and though every year it was a difficult task for them both, Todd and Ben had to give her the space to fall apart, standing ready for when they could get close enough to comfort her through.

Instead of saying any of that, Todd settled on, "Everyone needs some privacy to break a little sometimes. Your Pippa seems so eminently capable all the time. In control. Must have been hard for you to let her be alone. But you love her, and you did what she needed."

"She's trying to keep a brave face. Until last night, I think she was willing herself to forget the vandalism at her old townhouse. Write it off as random. But now she knows different. She's fanciful in many ways, but none of them mean she's going to ignore reality." Xander looked out into the shop a bit and then took a deep breath and swung his gaze to Todd once more. "She's being stalked."

Todd certainly thought that was a very strong possibility. And looking at Xander just then, he knew his son had made an emotional connection to the loss of the sister he'd never met, and the way his life had been shaped was absolutely a response to that.

"Dad is contacting all the stores around that lot to see if we can get footage. The cop from the scene last night was correct. There's been a wave of car break-ins and vandalism. Quite often after a game lets out. Steady stream of people who've been drinking beer all night, maybe frustrated with the outcome, or even a smart group of criminals using the crowds for cover. One positive though is that when businesses start suffering, things get done. Cameras go up. Security sweeps are done more often. If we can get any footage of the vandalism as it was happening, we have some ability to identify the responsible parties. We can package it up with other footage from the same area. The news will sometimes do a crime-enders segment. That'll help with the authorities too. Every little bit."

Xander told him what one of the cops had said about Pippa. "She *doesn't* thirst for attention. She's a super private, low-key person, and being with Hamish, and me too, has brought a spotlight to her life. I'm used to it. Hamish is used to it. And yet neither of us is the target here. Which makes me think it's her family."

"I'm going back to work now. Cope and Dad are already on this. I'll add everything you gave me. We'll figure this out. If you need anything at all, you know where we are. Day or night. This is going to be fine. At this point, it's just property damage."

"Maybe legally. But they damaged the symbols of her independence. She found that truck—she *named* that truck Gretchen—in a garage in Oregon. I've seen pictures of it when it was towed to her old shop. Anyway, it took her three years to do all the restoration work, mostly herself, because some of it she had to learn first. The planters on her porch?" Xander smiled. "Saw the kit at the home improvement store. Declared it too expensive. But she's good with her hands. Quick to pick things up. After some planning, she bought the raw ingredients and built them herself. Painted them the same color as her front door. Her ceramic pots were ones she's spent years collecting from various yard sales wherever she goes. They destroyed things that mean something to her far beyond being possessions. *This is personal.* This is about attacking and destroying the things she uses to enjoy her freedom. How would they know about any of that stuff if they hadn't been watching closely in the years since she left?"

Todd blew out a breath. "You have good instincts. It does feel very personal. Meanwhile, you said yourself she's safe at work and home. You just be her man right now, okay? Let us handle the investigation. I'll update you soon. I just wanted to come down, well, Dad and I thought it would be good to give you a hug and tell you we love you. I know you're grown and can take care of yourself. But I'm your pop. We want you to know we've got your back."

CHAPTER
TWENTY-THREE

"Oh, for Pete's sake!"

"Who's Pete?" Hamish asked. They were driving to pick Xander up and then head over to SaltBranch for a Valentine's Day dinner party event type thing that seemed very modern and cool.

"A person I can use in a cuss that isn't holy," Pippa said as she scrolled through a bunch of pictures of Hamish, Pippa, and Xander from his wrap party. While they were in Whistler for a few days before New Year's Eve, Todd had told Pippa about the alert he'd created to keep an eye on media about the three of them. Rebecca's boss had advised her to do something similar, so after a few days of thinking about it, Pippa had gone ahead and set one up, hoping it would give her a feeling of some sort of...dominion when so much was out of her hands.

The pictures were of the usual type. Either a decent lens from outside a place where they had to enter or leave, or camera phone pictures from whoever had been inside the party or restaurant who needed the extra money they got for tips or pictures.

She was glad her butt wasn't hanging out or there hadn't been a visible booger. Hamish always looked better than she did. Pippa accepted that. He had a sense of style that was very much organic. Xander was handsome and protective, usually looking at her or Hamish. It made her smile even if the photograph itself still felt creepy.

Pippa had rules about this stuff. She rarely ever clicked because it made her more self-conscious. But sometimes she could see keywords in the thumbnail if there was a headline or article lede that led her to open it up for a cursory glance to make sure it wasn't too bad.

A Mother's Heartbreak. What the heck?

As she read, Hamish teased, "And why are we using cusses of a non-holy type?"

If she showed too much annoyance or concern about media attention, he took it as a personal attack, so she tended to choose her words carefully. Plus, this had to do with his biological mother, which was also a sensitive topic.

And that night was *hers*, darn it. Pippa had romantic plans with her men and time ahead with their friends and new people. Which always charged Hamish, who was extroverted and loved new people. Xander would be pleased because Miles and Harlow would be there, and he hadn't seen Miles in a month or so.

The things Carol had been quoted saying would only upset him. There was time for that later; Pippa wasn't going to let that woman steal another moment of Hamish's happiness. "Oh, just the usual. Pictures from your wrap party. We all look good though."

"Ah, well then. At least there's that."

Rather than a dress, Pippa chose a black-and-white jumpsuit with a boat neck and flowing legs. It made her feel so pretty, and it was definitely warmer than the dress she'd also considered. Plus, she could wear her tallest heels and not feel so totally short.

At her side, Xander wore suit trousers and a snowy-white button-down shirt with braces that made him look old-fashioned in contrast to the tattoos. "This whole look is incredibly sexy," she said in his ear as he pushed the door open for her.

"I'll wear it tonight when you and Hamish are wearing nothing at all. That works for me. You?" His lips hitched slightly at the right corner and had her lifting to her toes to kiss that very spot.

"That *always* works for me." When he got extra bossy and dominant, especially when he did it to her and Hamish at the same time, it made her giddy with delight.

At the restaurant, she got pulled into what felt like a dozen hugs, and people kept handing her things like chocolate and roses.

"Look at you, love," Hamish teased as she set all her presents down at her seat.

"I didn't realize we were giving things to anyone else. I feel bad."

He shook his head. "I think that part was organized by the restaurant. Mostly you don't give things to others who aren't your Valentine."

"We had our Galentine's dinner a few days ago with

nearly all the women here. There was a gift exchange then." That had been so much fun. She'd hung out, eaten well, spent time with amazing people who taught her things every day about being a badass.

The rest she'd figure out as they went. For *this* to be the first Valentine's Day she'd had while in a long-term committed relationship was pretty nifty. But also, a high bar for the future, she realized.

She confessed, "I've never been to anything like this. It's wonderful."

"You deserve this every day." Hamish kissed her softly and then once more. "God, you're delicious."

"That's what I hear," she teased back.

One armed, he pulled her to him again. "Seems to me, I've the best Valentine in this whole place."

"Who is this kissing up on our girl?" Xander arrived with drinks, and after he handed Pippa hers, he dropped his own kiss on her mouth and tasted Hamish too. Mmmm.

"Can we keep him?" she asked, amusement and affection in her tone.

"Definitely." Xander leaned to kiss Hamish.

"First course coming out in five," their host called out. "Please take your seats."

Xander had just settled next to Pippa when his phone buzzed with an incoming text from his pop.

"We've been keeping an eye on media about you three, and today a bunch turned up in various packages across the fan sites and a few other celebrity spots. Pictures from Hamish's

wrap party. I've attached a link to the relevant one. Call me when you want to talk about it."

Xander kept an eye on Pippa and Hamish as he opened the link and read Carol Wilson talking about Pippa Hall being so controlling, she forbade Hamish contact from his mother. Said Pippa had pushed her out of her son's life and then blamed "the cult she grew up in" for it all.

He wasn't going to ruin their night with this garbage. He texted back to let his father know he'd received the info and would contact him the next morning.

Naturally, it was all he thought of that whole dinner. Worrying about what sort of creeps this might draw from under various rocks.

"Do you want to talk about whatever is bothering you?" Rennie asked him quietly from his other side.

"Not right now," he said, appreciating that she'd noticed and cared to ask. Even if she had no idea why, she'd back off because he said he wasn't ready.

And soon enough, he'd put it from his mind as much as possible to pay more attention to Pippa, who seemed to take in every detail of the evening and place it in a special memory box.

Many times since she'd come into his life, he'd been able to reframe things from her perspective, and it had made so much difference. It wasn't that he was used to things like Valentine's dinners, because he wasn't. He'd avoided even dating in January because it was beyond uncomfortable to be newly dating someone near a holiday with so much importance placed on it.

But like with so many other things about Pippa, it felt

right to be there with her and Hamish. Not suffocating or held back. Held down, definitely. In the best way.

Hamish hummed his delight as they closed the apartment door at their backs and were alone at last. Even as social as he was, Hamish liked the time the three of them shared at the end of each day.

Since he'd wrapped his next album a week before, Hamish had moved in officially. He'd decide what to do with his house in a few months when they'd all gotten used to living with one another day to day. The apartment was gigantic, but they'd have to find a way to put their own stamp on the space or move elsewhere.

Pippa more than the others needed alone time. So when she wanted, she just tucked herself into her room, and they let her be until she was ready for company again. It pleased Hamish that she'd taken the shelves on one wall and filled them with her things. Books and photographs. Little knickknacks here and there, like a set of ceramic birds, fat and slightly grumpy, tucked around.

The space was so strongly imprinted with her that sometimes if he was home and missing her and she was out, he'd just take a quick walk through the room, and it was like a hug.

Hamish, too, had a spot all his own. The pre-existing home studio had all the great bones for upgrading it to what he needed. The contractor and his sound people had already started to move important bits from his house.

He'd also taken over the adjoining room as a workspace. He was up later or earlier than the others all the time, so being able to work or watch a movie in the media room without worrying over waking anyone was a huge plus.

Each day it felt less like Xander's place and more like theirs.

After he let himself enjoy the last fleeting glimpse of Pippa as she dashed off to remove her makeup and dress clothes, Hamish turned his attention to Xander.

"Want to tell me why you've been upset all night?"

Xander looked chagrined at first and then he shook his head with a smile. "I don't know why I thought I could hide it."

"You did, mostly. Enough that I figure you're not mad at me or Pippa. Something external? Share your troubles?"

Xander took a deep breath. "Your mother gave an interview about you. And blamed Pippa and her quote *bible thumping cult* for pushing her from your life."

Hamish was so taken aback he didn't have words for a bit. "Mother? You mean *Carol*? Why didn't you tell me earlier?"

Xander leaned in quick and pressed a kiss to his temple. "Baby. I didn't bring it up at dinner because I wanted us all to have a nice time. I wasn't going to lie if I was asked directly, but it wasn't necessary to ruin the evening. You aren't in contact with her at this point, are you?"

Having been settled by the sweetness of that kiss and the affectionate pet name, Hamish said, "I haven't had more than a three-minute conversation with my biological mother in about five years. She and my mom—Addie—got into what nearly turned into a brawl. Carol came to confront my parents. I got there midway through an argument, and to get me on her side, she offered me drugs."

Xander sucked in a breath. "In front of Addie?"

The slight thread of fear in Xander's tone made Hamish smile. "Exactly. My mom had been standing behind the counter out in the waiting area, and when she heard Carol… she fucking flew over a four-foot-high barrier like it was nothing. She was up and in Carol's face before I could say a word. Leif had to physically take our mom out of the room while my dad and I got Carol outside. I had a car service take her to the airport, gave her all the cash I had on me, and then told her she needed to be out of my life because we were bad for one another. I should have said she was the problem, but I just wanted her gone. I've sent her money a few times. Through my agency. I shouldn't. She doesn't care about me at all."

Xander shook his head. "The money is about you, not her. You should have done whatever you felt like you needed to do. You don't have to feel bad that you're a good person. So it sounds like maybe she saw those photos or some of the others that hit the media and got the urge to get some attention for herself via you."

Hamish leaned against the counter at his back. "Carol knows how to manipulate people better than most anyone else I've ever known. She can take a throwaway detail and build a whole story around it. Designed to hit all the high points and evoke a response. It's diabolical. And yet there are times when I wish she could have found a useful outlet for her talents. A job that needed this skill set. A hobby. Whatever. She's not stupid. She understands people in a way that's uncanny. She just uses it to fuck people over."

Xander gave him a hug. "We do all we can to keep her out of your life. And Pippa's. Carol brought up Pippa's background. If they connect with her, or if she connects with them? Christ, the potential for her getting caught up in some hurtful bullshit is high."

"If you're going to talk about me, at least either do it when I'm not at home or invite me into the conversation," Pippa said as she padded toward them.

"It's not like that," Xander said.

"Tell me what it is like then. Perhaps it's what you were distracted by at dinner?"

Xander snorted a laugh. "I thought no one would see, but apparently everyone did. Rennie noted it too."

"You pay attention when you love someone," Pippa said.

With no small amount of admiration, Hamish had watched Pippa grow into her role in their relationship. Celebrated as she used her voice in ways each man heard best. Both Hamish and Xander liked to be in charge, and she found herself frustrated, though touched, by the way they both protected and took care of her.

She was sweet and soft and definitely the one of the three who was the most even-keeled toward a constant state of happiness. But. Pippa bit back when it wasn't about sex.

It made Hamish proud she trusted them, and herself, enough to stand up to them when she felt they'd crossed a line. And relieved none of it seemed to push her away or hurt her.

Xander told her about the interview and the text from Todd. She rolled her eyes. "I saw another version right before we picked you up. Some garbage like *A Mother's Pain*. I'd planned to talk about it once we all got home. But the one I saw before dinner just had some quote in it like *oh pitiful me. I am such a great mother, and she is mean.* As I've never even met her, I figured it was maybe something she did because she got bored or needed the money. I know Hamish wouldn't have shared any private with her."

Relief hit, followed by gratitude that she trusted him the way she did.

There was nothing run-of-the-mill about Carol. She always had a reason for what she got up to when she decided to fuck with someone.

"So what's her endgame then?" Xander said in a very sexy growl. "Is it chaos? Or pointed at Pippa for a reason?"

"From the outside, Carol would see Pippa as pure, and by that, I mean she's with me for me. Not for money or fame or tables at great restaurants or whatever. It's sort of adorable how it's clearly a production for her to do those things rather than foaming at the mouth for it." He winked at Pippa because he wanted her to know he wasn't upset by that. "That would be off-putting for Carol. She doesn't know how to work that for her benefit because she doesn't have anything that would tempt Pippa away from loving me into serving Carol. Even though we've had no contact, she'll always be looking for ways to get to me should she want to."

"Then why not come for me?" Xander challenged, and it brightened Hamish's heart to hear it because their man was declaring his affection too.

"Because you have something she might want. You're famous in your own way. Your family certainly all are."

"That and you're scary," Pippa added.

"Yes, that too," Hamish said. "She'll see you as more work. Mistakenly assume Pippa's an easy mark. But she doesn't know our girl has the soul of a warrior."

Pippa, who'd been looking angry, softened at that and gave him a smile.

"Well, it seems to me at this point there's not much we can do that we aren't already doing. You promised sex, which I demand now, please and thank you." Pippa then turned herself around and sashayed from the room.

"You heard her," Xander said as he held his hand out for Hamish to take. "Let's get to work."

It was Pippa's absolute favorite thing to be loved by Xander and Hamish. The way they looked at her and spoke to her told her in a thousand ways how they saw her. Strong and smart, beautiful.

She'd been shaken a bit by all the things Carol said, but in the end, there was nothing to do about it right then. What had soothed her to the point where she could let it go as something out of her control, was the way they united— always—to defend or protect her in some way. They listened to her concerns, and that told the little girl she'd been, the one who'd never been believed or believed in, they were worthy of her love.

Satisfied she'd made several very good life choices that landed her in their bedroom, naked as the day she was born, waiting on the bed for two ridiculously gorgeous men to come in and worship her body until she came. Several times.

"My." Xander paused in the doorway, raising an arm to lean, and looking sexy as heck doing it. Breath gusted out of her at the way the fabric stretched over his biceps. "I suppose I should say part of our Valentine's gift is coming up."

Pippa's voice felt thick and rich as she said, "Orgasms are my present? I love that for us."

"Hamish, get naked and turn the fire on please. We don't want Pippa getting cold."

Xander stalked over to where she'd perched herself on the bed, pausing, his very obvious delight in her nakedness pressing against the front of his trousers at eye level.

"Is that my present? I like it."

He laughed, grabbing her under both arms, hauling her to her feet and against his body in one easy movement that left her dizzy.

The edge of his teeth closed against her bottom lip before he laid her flat. "I had some things put in." He took one of her wrists and brought her arm up to the ten o'clock position where he fastened a cuff around it. Snug. It sent goose bumps to riot over her skin. He did the same on the other side.

"How does that feel?"

"Good. So good," she whispered, confessing. Wanting more.

"See what your range of movement is then, baby," Xander invited.

Pippa pulled and realized the way the cuffs had been placed under the mattress meant she could struggle all she wanted but not get loose. The freedom of that was a drug, humming through her system.

He smiled, and everything was okay again.

"That's why we do things. Because we like them. But if you don't like something, you need to say so." Every once in a while he gave a reminder that his dominance was all the hotter because everyone liked it.

A reminder that being the dominant one in a relationship was a responsibility. A position one earned and then continued to be worthy of.

Her eyes drifted closed, just for a moment, as Xander ran covetous hands down her arms, her ribs, over her hips and to her ankles.

Over and over until she was so relaxed, she let go of all her background anxiety and embraced that moment with them.

Hamish finished undressing and got on the bed on the opposite side, facing Xander, who looked down at Pippa, concentration—and adoration—on his features as he stroked large hands over all that pretty skin.

He waited, watching, knowing Xander had a master plan in his head. There'd be a point when he'd be able to touch Pippa, and it was coming up shortly, so he let himself be contented with the way her breathing had deepened, a deep-pink blush staining her neck and chest. Her arms not quite above her head but secured just right.

The cuffs were a deep blue. Lined to keep their girl safe and comfortable so she could struggle all she pleased. He and Xander had chosen the color and type of bindings, both thinking of her safety and also what would feel best and look good against her skin.

Xander's gaze flicked up to Hamish's, and a roguish grin marked his face. "Go on then."

Hamish hummed at the sight of her unbound breasts as the firelight danced and made shadows over her skin.

Dipping his head, he dropped kisses along her collarbone, delighting in the way her flesh pebbled in his wake.

"This," he murmured, kissing down her ribs, across her belly and then mirrored on her opposite side. A dark thread of desire unfurled and rushed through him as he licked over the swell of her right breast before closing his teeth against it. Hard enough to leave a mark. Hard enough she made one of his favorite sounds. A surprised gasp of pain that melted into a purr of pleasure.

"There's something about marking all this pretty skin that drives me to distraction."

Xander chuckled. "I hear that."

"I love it," she said in a whisper. "Partly because of how much you get off on it. Like you need me so desperately you can't help yourself. It's sexy."

"I do need you desperately." She was in the center of his thoughts constantly. The idea of her being scared—worse, that his mother might be involved—only made need beat at him harder. He stretched up to take her mouth as he pinched and tugged her nipples until she sighed softly. He moved from her lips, back to her nipples and then down, pausing to nibble at her belly button before delivering a sharp nip that had her gasping.

Pippa remained breathless, knowing what was next as he licked his way over to her hipbone and then slightly down. He laved over his favorite spot, sending pleasure skittering through her system.

He opened his mouth, his beard tickling as he did. Time slowed like honey until the edge of his teeth slid over her flesh, teasing them both. And then he bit. Behind her closed eyelids, lights danced as the pain bled into something else. Something she'd stopped feeling guilty about liking so damned much.

"She's so very stressed out," Xander crooned, blowing over a nipple still wet from his mouth. "I think you should fuck her and then I'm going to eat her pussy. Don't pout, you can eat her pussy next time."

"We'll leave her ankles free. That's for me too. I do like it when she wraps her thighs around me when I'm deep inside," Hamish said as the crinkle of a condom wrapper was nearly a caress. He scored his nails over her ribs, making her body bend toward him, the cuffs holding her back. His hum of satisfaction echoed through her.

When she opened her eyes, ready to smile at him, it was to be struck absolutely silent by the picture he made there situated between her thighs, naked, a gleam of sweat on his chest, a look of concentration on his features.

His hair had been styled back away from his face, but now tumbled forward, down over his forehead and eyes.

There was a cold pressure against her nipple, and when she turned, it was to catch Xander settling a metallic clamp into place. When he let go with a smile that had her anticipating whatever was coming, it was a bolt of sharp pain that brought her struggling against the cuffs. At the same time, Hamish thrust up and into her pussy in one movement. Pleasure rushed through her, not erasing the pain, but coaxing it to bloom.

Xander's attention shifted from her tits up to her face, intent on what she was feeling. Waiting, she knew, for confirmation that she was either fine or not a fan of whatever he'd done.

"She likes that a whole lot," Hamish said, and bent his head to lick over the nipple being held in the clamp.

"Wait 'til I take it off."

She let her eyes drift closed as that fuzzy, otherworldly haze settled in. She floated then in all the things they did to her, working together. Talented fingers found her clit, circled it until she was nearly at climax, and then he pulled his hands back and within a breath, pressed his cock into her pussy in one deep thrust that would have moved her forward were he not holding her at her hip to keep her in place.

Hamish never did anything—at least nothing about her —halfway. When he settled in to fuck her, he never took shortcuts. She had zero complaints about that.

Especially when Xander's fingers found her clit and didn't pull away until climax hit fast and hard.

Hamish teased her until she writhed, shifting legs and hips so she tipped up slightly, taking him deeper. Loving the helpless little groan he gave in response.

She did it over and over until that groan turned into a snarl of her name as he sped his thrusts, which continually bounced her breasts, sending waves of pleasure/pain each time. Driving her wild.

One last utterance of her name and he pressed in so deep, pulling her hips toward him as he as he came.

Hamish dropped a kiss on her lips and darted off to deal with the condom.

.   .   .

Something just seemed to throb inside Xander's gut every time they were all together. Each time he watched Hamish sink his teeth into Pippa's skin in all his favorite places it sent a bolt of heat through him.

Maybe it was because they were both *his* in ways no one else ever had been. Maybe it was because yes, he was watching, but because of their relationship, he was also participating. He didn't know.

But he accepted it all the same. He cherished it for the miracle it was.

His best miracle turned her head to look at him, a smile on her lips, her eyes glazed with pleasure.

"Before I remove the clamp, let's get you situated." Xander loosened the straps at the head of the bed to pull her toward the end of the mattress, where he fastened two wider straps around each of her thighs, holding them open for him.

This was more intense than they'd done before, so he kept his attention on her reactions. Her eyes had widened as she stretched her neck to see what he was up to, but gooseflesh rose on her skin and her arousal scented the air.

Once he'd tightened her wrists again, he moved to the foot of the bed and still dressed, settled on his knees on the blanket chest there. He climbed up over her body to look down into her face. "Ready?"

She nodded slowly, and he pulled the clamp free. She made a sound from deep in her belly as all that sensation rushed into place.

He licked gently over the inflamed flesh and then blew over it, semen leaking from his cock at the way she gave a full-body shudder of pleasure.

"We definitely need to try this again," Hamish murmured.

Xander agreed.

He kissed her softly until she sighed his name into his mouth.

"I love you, Pippa," he said, moving to the foot of the bed.

She made a disappointed sound that had Hamish barking a laugh.

Back at her pussy, Xander leaned close. "All spread out for me like the best thing I've ever eaten," he told her, his lips brushing against her labia before he used his thumbs to open her to a nuzzle of his lips against her clit and then a lick.

He lost himself in her taste, in the fine tremor of her muscles the closer she got to orgasm until her demanding little sounds got more urgent and she rained honey all over his face.

Quickly, he managed to get his cock out of his trousers and rolled on the condom Hamish handed his way.

"Undo my legs, please," she said, and he complied, moving one of her thighs up before teasing around her entrance and then sliding inside.

He dragged it out as long as he could, her body stretched around him, so hot and slick it took all his concentration and control not to give in and fuck her hard and fast. He took his time, staying deep, fucking her in a series of short digs.

"You are the most beautiful fucking creature I've ever seen. I cannot imagine life without you in it," he said moments before she squeezed herself all around his cock and his vision grayed at the edges as orgasm grabbed him and wouldn't let him go.

He got rid of the rest of his clothes and came to join them both under the blankets.

"Best Valentine's Day presents a gal could ask for," she said sleepily.

"You knitted us sweaters. What's an orgasm compared to that?" Hamish asked, making her laugh.

She'd given them both a sweater that morning when they'd woken up. Xander's had been deep green, and Hamish's had been a wine color.

Then Pippa had told them she'd been making the sweaters for the last two months and that Rebecca had been helping.

"Well, in addition to the fuck me straps, I can't complain about a custom tattoo design and a pair of earrings," Pippa said. "Plus a really good dinner out with friends. Going to be hard to top next year."

Xander approved, very much, that she was thinking in those terms.

"Next year we can leave out anything to do with my birth mother ruining it," Hamish said ruefully. "Ouch! Offsides, Pippa!"

Hamish rubbed his side.

"I'm going to pinch you every time you try to blame yourself for something she does. It's like how people quit smoking and stuff. Negative reinforcement. Don't make me pinch you again. Mainly because I don't want to. But I will." Pippa had delivered all that in a prim manner that managed to get a few interested twitches from Xander's cock.

"I thought Xander was the one who liked to give a little pain."

Pippa giggled. "He likes it. I just do it because it's

necessary." She climbed over Hamish and set about putting on pajamas. Xander texted his pop that he'd be in contact the following morning and then followed Pippa and Hamish from the room toward the kitchen where he heard them getting water and snacks.

Best Valentine's Day ever was right.

CHAPTER
TWENTY-FOUR

Xander loved giving tattoos. It was what he'd wanted to do for as long as he could remember. He'd spent a lot of time perfecting his work. Learning new things. Striving for perfection because he was marking someone's skin forever.

And because he'd been taught by the best. Brody and his out-of-the-park color realism and American traditional styles, and Raven, the queen of black-and-gray work and portraits gave him the basics other artists could only dream of. Add to it that he was a nephew and nearly a son to his teachers, and they held him to a standard that'd honed his technical skills as well as his creative tools like drawing.

So, it had been a while since he'd been so nervous to do a thing he did at least five, more often, six days a week.

Sam Flanigan had been tattooing for three decades. He mainly did American traditional but liked to dip into geometric black and gray as well. He had his own shops in California but spent time doing guest spots as part of a podcast and an independent television show about tattoo culture across the United States.

He could do a lot of good for Xander, should he like the work he got. A roll of the dice. But Xander wasn't going to lose his job either way, and it was a chance to show off, so he'd spent the last two weeks coming up with a design Sam had only just approved a few hours before that.

Brody checked in, trying to stay back but also letting Xander know he had plenty of support and people who believed in him.

"You got a delivery," Martine said and brought back a basket.

The card said, *No one's day ever got worse after a cookie or a brownie. Since they were baked by me, you know they were made with love. Can't wait to hear how today went. I love you. P.*

There were chocolate chip, peanut butter, snickerdoodles, fudge and blonde brownies and another plate that had gluten free treats. The ones with nuts she'd put inside glass containers with locking lids.

"She made all those?" Brody asked, grabbing several of each.

"She bakes to relax. Who the hell am I to get in the way of that? I just say thank you and stay out of the kitchen unless she gives me tasks."

He'd lived in that penthouse for more of his life than he'd lived anywhere else. It had been his for the last six years, and in that time, Xander had put his stamp on it. Slowly buying the kind of art he liked and could afford. It helped that he knew so many artists.

But Pippa had created a beating heart in their home. She

was always baking or knitting, and plants began to pop up in nooks and hanging near sunny windows.

He and Hamish cooked several times a week, but there was something emotionally nourishing about the meals she put together. The way she thought about feeding them was a declaration of love.

"I'm a very lucky man," he admitted to Brody.

Raven came into the shop with Jonah on one side and Sam on the other, but after Jonah said hello and grabbed a brownie, he went up front to speak with Martine.

After some handshakes and chitchat, Xander got Sam's calf shaved and prepped and laid the stencil.

"I've been saving that skin for just the right tattoo," Sam said. He lay face-down on the tattoo bed as Xander stood next to him. "When you sent me the design, I knew exactly where it had to go. I've got ribs for another time."

"Can't say I'm disappointed in that choice." The curve of the calf was a good place for this one, a neo-traditional, art nouveau-styled female face. A tattoo that melded some aspects of a few different Celtic goddesses including Brigid and Áine with staghorns and a serpent wending its way through her hair with springs of heather here and there.

Ambitious with the level of detail he planned. But Sam was going to sit for six hours. Xander personally found his tolerance tapped out after five when he was getting ink, but everyone had different pain thresholds. Pippa was getting a new tattoo in May, and he was starting with four hours for a back piece. He had a feeling she'd be fine up to six and would come back for more the next day without a second thought.

He and Sam talked about new school tattoos, which was

Ca's specialty, sailor tattoos—as American traditional was sometimes called—and Los Angeles. Raven came up frequently as his had been the shop she'd gotten her first real break in with multiple artists willing to share their knowledge and Sam willing to let her be the apprentice.

"I knew the first time she showed me her drawings that if she could learn how to tattoo even moderately well, with her drawing talent, she'd do great. I was right," Sam said.

"Tasha tells me I'm *medium famous*," Raven called out from her station.

"Never thought I'd see the day when Raven was a wife and a mother, but here she is, and damned if it doesn't look perfect on her," Sam told Xander. "They have one of those play-set things in their yard and a soccer goal net set up."

"Like you didn't give me advice on which ones were best," Raven teased.

"Tell me about your girl, then," Sam said.

It was the easiest thing in the world to talk about Pippa and Hamish and their life, going quiet when Xander needed extra concentration. The other artists came by from time to time to steal cookies and look at Xander's work in progress.

When he had about twenty minutes to go to hit six hours, Xander made the last wipe and stood back.

"Xander, that's a fucking tight tattoo," Raven said.

She was right.

The color saturation was the best he'd done, with little pops of purple in the heather and the greens and browns of the horns and the snake. All the scales pointed in the right direction, the musculature was correct, and her face was gorgeous.

"She's pretty, but those staghorns and the snake give it

the right sort of edge so it doesn't look like it should be on someone else," Sam said as he looked at it in the mirror. "That little bit of amber around her pupil and the more oval shape instead of a circle, excellent choice, man. You've made her otherworldly in the right way."

Xander couldn't wait to share this news with Pippa and Hamish.

"Over dinner tonight, let's talk about the episode of my show I'm going to set here in Seattle and how you'll figure in it. I'd love to interview you for the podcast too," Sam told him.

"Okay then."

Just a few hours later, Pippa walked at his side, looking fresh and pretty in navy high-waisted pants and a white sweater with a navy collar. She'd left for work at seven that morning, and still, after a full day and a three-hour-long dinner full of big talking and big personalities, she radiated happiness.

"I'm still so blown away by that tattoo, Xander. I want that design. I mean I guess it's copying or whatever if I get exactly that. But I want something *like* that instead. But still on my back or shoulder. Maybe with soft greens and pinks instead of the deeper greens and browns though."

Flattered and pleased, he smiled and leaned down to kiss the top of her head. "Let me work through a few ideas for you, and we can talk later on next week, and you can look through whatever I come up with. We'll go from there." Xander moved to the outer side, between her and the street. Hamish was right behind them, chatting with Raven about the gala coming up in just two months.

Brody had collected Sam, and they'd gone out to some dive Xander's uncle and a bunch of other tattooists of his generation liked to hang out and tell stories in. But at dinner, they'd spent at least ninety minutes talking about the possibilities for Xander. Sam had influence in their community, and a number of emerging and established contacts with advertisers and media outside the tattoo world as well.

Xander's head spun with all the exciting potential the future held. Even if nothing more than Sam's tattoo came out of it, that was enough. His list would still be full, and he'd be great either way because of the woman at his side and the man at his back.

"That you were right there beside me when all of this went down means everything," he told her quietly.

She rested her head against his arm for a moment as they walked. "I'm so excited for you. So proud of how talented you are."

Which meant even more.

Pippa listened to the voicemail again.

When they'd gotten back to the apartment and she'd changed into her pajamas, she'd picked her phone up automatically and saw there was a voicemail in the unknown caller folder. Usually those were spam, though sometimes they were from new friends or business contacts. But when she saw the opening of the transcription of the message, she knew who it was from.

Epiphany, this is your father, and I'm telling you to stop shaming your family. Come home. Get married to a good man.

There are those here who'd have you. Give you a second chance. Have children. This is your path in life. Your calling is to be a mother, not...being a harlot with multiple men. Not doing it on camera for the whole world to see your downfall.

It's too late for your sisters. But you can still be saved from this sinful life surrounded by demons and blasphemers. You're keeping a son from his mother. Repent from this life, Epiphany, or burn for eternity.

He'd obviously seen one of the bits with Carol's quotes and thought he had a place to speak to her at all, much less attempting to use his parental authority over her after throwing her away all those years ago.

His opinion of her life didn't hurt her feelings. She'd moved past that some years ago. What did upset her was the meanness in his tone. Bringing it up was a threat. This is what will happen to you. To be branded a harlot was intended to break her spirit, shame her, and make her give up. Which she was never going to do.

Pippa needed to think about how to respond to the call—including not at all—for a while before she made a choice. The following day she'd tell Rebecca in person because Pippa knew if she didn't share this, her sister would kick her butt. Esther was in her last trimester, so she and Rebecca would decide whether or not to share. Neither sister wanted to cause any emotional upheaval that might affect the baby.

Someone was "willing" to marry her? So she could be an object lesson for the rest of her life about what happens to girls who leave? So her children could be hung with her imagined crimes and be punished as well? Because Pippa *would* be punished. They might be nice to her right after her return, lull her into complacency. But soon enough it would come. She'd have to be *reeducated,* and there'd be much public repentance.

A shiver broke out as she imagined that life.

"What's wrong?" Xander demanded.

Startled, Pippa looked up from her phone. She hadn't even heard him come into the living room. The next holiday that came up, she was going to buy him a bell so he'd stop sneaking up on her.

"Nothing." She smiled up at him.

He just raised one of his brows by way of calling her out.

"Let's talk about it in the morning. Everyone is tired and had a great time tonight. You've had an amazing day. Please don't make me ruin it," she said, giving him baby-animal eyes.

He had the audacity to snort at her and toss himself on the couch at her side. "Did you really think that was going to work?"

"Well." She firmed her lips a moment. "It was worth a try. I really think we can talk about it tomorrow. It's not an emergency, I promise. There's no danger or anything like that."

"I'll just think about it all night long, worrying. Do you think you can't tell me?"

"Now who gets to ask if you think that will work?" she asked.

"We both know it will," he told her with a confident air. Because he was right.

Hamish wandered out, looking for them, and after he caught an eyeful of what was going on, he sat across from her on the low table.

"She's about to tell us what's happening," Xander said.

"I swear, you two." She held her phone up and played the voicemail for them, and then said, "I wasn't hiding anything. I was just giving myself some time to think about how to deal with it. But Xander figured out I was chewing over something and here we are."

"Do you want to go back there?" Hamish asked carefully.

She physically recoiled at the very idea. "No. My world is here. With you two. There's nothing in Arizona I want."

Hamish visibly relaxed. "Okay. I wanted to be sure. We want to stand at your side, not in your way."

"Speak for yourself. I would *absolutely* stand in her way if she wanted to fuck off back to Arizona," Xander snarled. "I wouldn't hold her against her will, but I'd sure as hell make every freaking argument I could think of to keep her from doing it."

Pippa took a deep breath, relieved she'd shared what had happened, pleased they'd reacted the way they had.

"As it happens, it's not necessary. I'm here, with you both, because I choose to be. I like being able to choose. That's why I'd never return, even if there weren't three dozen other reasons not to go back. Let's talk about it in the morning as far as what I need to do. But for now? I'm tired, and I have a very full day tomorrow. Let's snuggle and go to sleep."

Xander stood and pulled them both to their feet. He cupped Pippa's cheeks briefly, kissing her. "You're a lot of things, but none of the things he said about you are true."

"I know. I promise."

"Come on then. Let's go to bed."

CHAPTER
TWENTY-FIVE

"'ve never been to a gala before," Pippa whispered. "But this whole thing seems to fit exactly with what I thought one would be."

All around the exquisitely decorated ballroom were exquisitely decorated people in conversational knots while others strolled past all the various auction items set up on long tables up against the walls.

In one of those knots of pretty people, Hamish stood, charming the society matrons and their spouses right out of their money. He rarely spoke in public about the details of his time on the street, but he was open and generous with how the Franklin family had given him love, safety, and a home. He wanted that for other kids who'd been cast out of their biological families for one reason or another.

And how could anyone argue with that while saying they loved children? Shouldn't they have stable lives full of love?

That was why she hadn't gone over and slapped all those hands people kept putting on him.

"I want to run them over with my car when they do that

to Jonah," Raven murmured as she handed Pippa a tall glass of champagne. "He says I can't because that would be assault. Imagine." She rolled her eyes. "He's an officer of the court and might have to report me, though he promises he'd represent me at the trial."

That made Pippa laugh, which she thought had been the intent all along.

"My first time at this event I nearly got into a fistfight in one of the bathrooms. A now-ex sister-in-law then tried to claim I'd started it. She's a distant memory, while I have presents under the tree at the Warner family home, and my children's stockings hang on the mantle. I love winning." Raven snickered.

The more time Pippa spent around Raven, the more she got a glimpse of the person behind that surly mask. The more she understood why Xander absolutely adored this person who was essentially his second mother.

"You lead a very exciting life. I've never nearly gotten into an altercation in a bathroom of a fancy gala ball."

"You're young yet. Give it time."

Xander, who'd just walked up and put an arm around Pippa's shoulder, made a skeptical sound. "God help us all if you're giving Pippa tips."

Raven rolled her eyes at him. "I wasn't at work the day he finished your recent ink. May I see it?" she asked Pippa.

Pleased, Pippa held out her right arm, turning it to showcase the design Xander had given her as a Christmas present. A custom design.

Apple blossoms done in mainly black and gray, but he'd added a pop of pale pink at the outer edges of the blossom, a bit of brown in the shadow of the blossom, near the stem, and here and there a little green. They flowed from the front of her biceps around toward her back, and she absolutely loved them.

"The blossoms are connected to a piece I'm going to do for her next. A similar flavor to Sam's but suited to Pippa and her coloring. They'll meet here." Xander brushed a spot on her back. "If she wants more, we can unite with others."

"Of course I'm going to want more. I wanted that piece you just described about thirty-five seconds after seeing it on him. And we'd already scheduled this one." It was very handy being in love with a tattoo artist when one liked getting tattooed.

"You want to meet my mother-in-law?" Raven asked as a silver-haired woman approached. "I hope so, because she's on her way over, and there's not much you can do to sway her once she's decided something. I really fucking love that woman."

"Hello, darling. Please introduce me to your friends," she said to Raven.

"Liesl Warner, you already know Xander. This is Pippa Hall. Pippa, Liesl is Jonah's mother, and she's responsible for about seventy percent of everything you see here," Raven said.

"It would be a waste of all the time I've put in over the years to get everyone nice and scared of me, if I didn't wheedle auction items and the like when necessary. Most of the people here have plenty of money to shower on something other than a mistress, a yacht, or a new fifty-thousand-dollar handbag they can't even carry."

Liesl wore her hair in a sleek, shoulder length bob. She wore a coral-toned close-fitting gown with a dramatic, asymmetrical neckline. Every bit of her outfit was eye-catching but also elegant.

She held out a hand to Pippa, who shook it. "It's very nice to meet you in person. Raven and Hamish have been telling us about the planning of this event for months. It's clearly the result of a lot of work."

"Hamish speaks of you quite frequently. I'm pleased you're as lovely as he claimed. Twisted Steel has donated a fantastic package."

Well, that was nice to hear. "Asa, Duke, and Mick are all connected to the community, so I'm not surprised. It's a great group of people to work with," Pippa said.

"And he's also Hamish's boyfriend." Raven jerked her head toward Xander.

Liesl's perfect lips hitched up ever so slightly at the right corner. "Hamish speaks of you a great deal as well. Your tattoo shop has given us several great items."

"We're community minded too. And also afraid of waking up to Raven standing over our beds with a frying pan, demanding we donate something," Xander said with charm.

Liesl laughed, and it was a lovely sound. A woman who knew her impact and her worth.

And she smelled so good. Spicy and a little sweet. Pippa wondered if it was perfume or just how very rich, elegant women were.

"When Jonah first brought Raven around, I wasn't sure how she'd fare. What with all that body and ink and hair."

If anyone else had said it, it might have been an insult. But Raven kept smiling, and there was clear affection in Liesl's tone.

"And then she took on my mother-in-law in my defense, and I realized a few things. One, I'd have to be made of stone to ignore the way my son looked at her. Two, I'd be mad to push this woman out when she had gotten in between me and my husband's mother—she's an absolute harridan. And three, I'd be a hypocritical bitch to be the same sort of mother-in-law as the one I'd been stuck with. I decided to keep Raven if for no other reason than to throw her between me and that old cow."

Pippa couldn't stop her delighted laugh.

"Jonah's first wife is a wet piece of tissue paper. Liesl is just happy I keep her son out of trouble," Raven teased.

"Well, you've certainly kept him busy and out of trouble, so there is that. And you're great with Carrie. My oldest grandchild," Liesl explained to Pippa like Pippa didn't know who Carrie was. "And you gave me two more grandchildren after that." She turned to Pippa again, "Have you met Leander and Tasha? Aren't they darling? All their soccer and other various activities that have me standing out in the cold on a Saturday morning takes me back to the same with my sons. It's nice to have the chance to do it again as a grandmother. I'm never responsible for bringing the snack, and I don't have to be social with the other parents."

Raven and Jonah had decided not to have any biological children. He had Carrie, who'd been about to turn eighteen when Raven had first come around. And Raven had, Xander had told her, worries about some of the genetic predispositions she might pass to offspring. But they'd had a home and a happy, stable marriage, and though Raven had her own struggles in the foster care system growing up, she hadn't forgotten there were plenty of kids who needed a family to love them. So they'd done some shorter term foster placements, but when Leander had come to them, they'd fallen for the eight-year-old and adopted him the following year. Tasha had followed a couple of years after that, and Raven had connected with the toddler who'd immediately latched herself on and never really let go. She'd been formally adopted two years later.

Leander was starting high school that fall, and Tasha was in the fourth grade. Though their family was complete, Raven and Jonah continued to open their home to short-term and emergency placements that came up from time to time.

Pippa wondered if it would ever be possible for them to do the same. Hamish would love that, she knew. On paper, regardless of what sort of love and care they'd be able to provide in the future, they were likely not to be chosen because there were three of them.

"Why do you look so sad?" Xander asked. Raven and Liesl had moved off to work the room, so it was just the two of them for the moment.

"I was thinking about how we can't be foster parents probably. I know Hamish would like to do it, but I don't know how to make it work with a harlot, a bisexual tattoo artist, and a former street kid turned musician, also bisexual."

Xander kissed her. "I know you're joking, but don't call yourself that. As for the rest? We support this cause because it's important to him. And because it's a good cause. But there are lots of ways to build a family if and when we decide we want kids. He'd rather have us. We'd rather have him. We can work on the rest because of that."

"That's very wise." And what she needed to hear. "I love you."

"Never get tired of hearing that," he said.

Hamish made his way over to them, clearly pleased with how everything was going. "Hello, loves."

"Hey. Congratulations. This event is perfection. Liesl was telling us you're already ahead of where you were last year at the end of the event. She said it was your work that brought in the big donations from the music industry."

He colored a little, and Pippa loved him for it. So pleased at how proud he was.

"I just cut through the shite and called them all directly. I give for their stuff. Turns out they give for mine."

"You should do a kiosk at all your shows," she told him. "Where your fans coming to see you can donate money or gift cards. Backpacks with school supplies? New socks and underwear. Whatever. I know it's easier said than done, but." It was her turn to blush. She didn't tell either of them how to do their jobs.

"That's a great idea. I've seen them for other types of community projects and charities other acts raise money for while on tour. I'll bring it up with Liesl to see what she thinks would be best, and then I'll bring it to my team to put it into action." He kissed her soundly. "Thank you."

"Well." She fanned herself. "I shall endeavor to keep coming up with good ideas, so I get kisses as a thank you."

A tease, yes, but also, she was ridiculously pleased that he liked her suggestion. Since they'd all come together, it had been a joy for Pippa to observe the monumental growth in Hamish. The confidence he carried himself with when it came to music had also settled into his personal life as he'd begun to accept he was worth the love he was given daily. He was a man who took care of her and Xander. He paid attention. He listened. He received their affection with ease and returned it with not just physical responses, but emotional ones.

Hamish's trust was very special to her.

"Come dance with me?" Hamish held his arm out, and she took it after Xander waved them away and said he was going to look at auction items and say hello to various friends.

CHAPTER
TWENTY-SIX

"Where's Pippa this afternoon?" Miles asked Xander. They were sitting poolside at some very exclusive rooftop club.

They'd spent the morning at fittings for the wedding party, and afterward some producer friend of Miles's had given them passes, so they'd headed up to spend the afternoon catching up while having lunch, some drinks, and getting a little sun.

"Pippa's sister had a baby last month, so I'm certain when I get back to the condo later on it'll be full of packages with storks and bunnies and a lot of baby koalas and frogs. Baby boutiques love baby frog logos, I've discovered. Anyway. She's traveling up there again in six weeks, and the amount of stuff she's packing for this kid..." Xander laughed, "...is astonishing. They're going to need another closet and dresser after her visit."

Miles lifted a brow. "A visit out of state? I'm surprised you let that happen. Will one of you be going with her?"

"Surprised? What the hell does that mean?" Xander

groaned. "Sorry. Sore spot, I guess. I know you didn't mean it like that."

"I'd be a fool to miss how protective you are. I recognize it because I feel it for Harlow too. You want her to be safe, and this vandalism stuff has to be difficult for her. And for you. And because there are echoes to your mom's past. And mine."

Xander knew that back when Gillian had first gotten together with Adrian, someone had used tabloid stories to cause trouble between them. It had nearly broken them up. Xander and Miles had grown up in a family unit that while ever larger, was incredibly tight-knit and protective. No surprise then that a distrust of outsiders came from the cradle.

"She's getting used to the background noise of celebrity. It's placed some hindrances on her movement, which is a hot button. But for the most part, Pippa rolls with it. The underlying problem is every time there's a spike in media coverage her family surfaces again."

That had created a sense of dread as she waited for the next thing. He hated his inability to protect her from it all.

"Have they tied the vandalism to them yet?" Miles asked.

"We were able to get camera footage from the night her truck was vandalized, but the angle didn't catch the passenger side of the cab and windshield. From what we do have, there were at least two people involved. They had on ski masks with dark sweatshirts and gloves. It was a cold night, so none of those things would have stood out. Her townhouse is a whole other matter. They didn't have any cameras in public spaces at all. Several others in her little complex had doorbell cameras and that sort of thing, but all we were able to get was three people running out to the main road beyond. It might not even be related, they told her."

"It's totally related," Miles said.

"Yep. But they let her out of her lease early and didn't charge her for any of the repairs. And she guilted the property managers into putting better lighting and surveillance in the common areas. At least there's that."

"She lives with you now, so you know home is way safer these days. It sucks when I have to be away from Harlow, so I know how that feels. Truthfully, we're thinking about moving. We want to stay in the Northwest, but even with the gates we added, we've had security issues from the water side of the property lately. My parents' land accommodates setting the house far enough back from the road and the water and at the right angles to encourage privacy in ways our lot doesn't. Even if we tore the house down and rebuilt, it's still a matter of the land. And the increased traffic since our mini-tour ended has made our formerly tolerant neighbors into very annoyed neighbors. We don't blame them. But that underlines the need to move on to a new place. Day after tomorrow we're headed back home to look at a few different places. Ben is coming along to give us all the security backup we need."

"Think about downtown. There are many buildings like ours. Some new construction so you can design your own space from the start."

Miles said, "We're looking at two condos in downtown Seattle and another two in Bellevue. Up where Harlow's aunt lives in Issaquah there's some land we could build something custom on, so an architect is meeting with us to discuss what's possible. It's not the exclusive thing I'm chasing. I just don't want to wake up to strangers in my yard or ringing the doorbell at all hours. I want to know she's safe when she's there alone and I'm out working."

"Fair enough. Like I said, I feel the same way. I'd have a moat if I could. Filled with alligators."

The server refilled their iced tea and brought over their lunch, and melted away again after adjusting the umbrella so the sun wasn't beating down on their heads.

Miles said, "Your mom told me she was glad social media wasn't a factor back when they first had you. It was bad enough as it was. Now people think they know you because another person you don't know has filmed you or written something that's half likely to be an outright fabrication. Sometimes it's nice—there are decent people out there writing about entertainment—but other times, it's too damned much. It sure doesn't help that Hamish's birth mother hasn't met an opportunity to talk about Pippa she wanted to decline. It's obvious she's never even met Pippa; to think anyone would believe her bullshit claims."

Xander sighed heavily. "She's a nightmare. He hasn't spoken to the woman in years. And before that it was fraught and there'd been long periods of estrangement. He doesn't want to address her directly, and I'm in support of that. She wants that attention. But Hamish's P.R. team managed some interviews to blunt whatever else she might try. Praised Addie and James and told the story of how they legally adopted him at twenty after being frustrated for years by his birth parent. It was so clever the way he handled it."

"He said it all without saying it to her directly," Miles said, as he nodded approvingly. "Also the coverage, by and large, is positive. Yes, there's this ugly little undercurrent with Pippa's family and this thing with Carol. But even the video of you in the bar confronting some chode hitting on Pippa made you look good."

"You saw that?" Xander sent an exasperated look Miles's way. "I didn't even know anything had been filmed until a week later. Nothing happened! I told them to fuck off, and we walked away. I drank beer and listened to Depeche Mode and Adam and the Ants while your sister taught Pippa how to play a drinking game."

His cousin shrugged, absolutely unrepentant. "What? It's the family business. We all keep track. Like I said, it looked good. Some dick hits on a sweet-faced woman, and her boyfriend comes to defend her honor. No fisticuffs, but you didn't need them given your expression. I've been with you in an impossibly broad variety of circumstances, and I've never seen you look at another person that way before."

"She's..." Xander searched for words. "She's so small and fierce, and she works really hard. She's good. And kind. The amount of time and energy she puts into loving me and Hamish is astonishing. She's the center of my world, you know?"

Miles nodded.

"So, she's this warm, welcoming, safe part of my life. I am *eager* to get home to her every night. Her satisfaction is important." Xander hadn't understood before her what it would feel like to truly love someone.

He continued, "More than that, it's *necessary.* For months, she's had to look over her shoulder. She just got her truck back a few days before we left to come down here. It's parked at Twisted Steel right now so some new this or that thing can be replaced while we're here. She told me she was so glad that everyone had lent a hand to help get Gretchen back in tiptop shape, but that sometimes when she drives, all she can do is wonder what's coming next. I hate that! I want to prowl around and punch everyone who makes her feel bad for even a second. She needs freedom. She grew up without it, you see. So, no matter how much I want to say how dangerous it could be for her to fly to Alaska when these people are bothering her, I can't. I can't limit her movements or make her choices. And I certainly cannot get between her and her sisters. Now that the baby has come, she'll want to travel up there more often, so I need to find a way to make sure it happens. Hamish is doing a show up there, just a one-night thing, and I'm certain he added it so he could be with her when she went. I'll go the time after that." He shrugged.

"You have to—all three of you—find a way to navigate this world, or she'll have to break things off. Hamish is only going to get more attention as he starts all these shows. Plenty of opportunities for video and pictures. They used telephoto lenses from a tree at the set to look into my trailer. After those shots of me changing clothes—*Miles Brown flaunts toned body,* like I was on vacation instead of having my privacy violated—I had to keep the blinds closed at all times. You'll figure it out and do what you can."

His dads were keeping an eye on everything they could. His pop had crafted a security plan with Pippa, and Xander really felt like her being part of the process helped give her some control. And, because it meant she was taking things seriously, Xander felt some measure of control as well.

• • •

It was a gorgeous June day, the sun was out, and the ocean glittered off in the distance as Hamish drove them down Wilshire.

She very rarely allowed him to spend a lot of money on her, but that afternoon as she was still on an endorphin high from buying what seemed like every single baby outfit the state had to offer, he coaxed her into letting him buy her some clothes and shoes to go with them. She'd been so pleased and pretty he'd been able to divert her from the numbers on the receipts.

They'd had lunch in Santa Monica, and then he'd dropped off some paperwork with his manager, whose offices were on Wilshire as well. It was surprisingly easy to do just about anything with her, even running errands.

"Oh!"

Pippa leaned forward and turned the satellite radio up as Hamish's single from his new album came over the speakers.

She sang along, and he was worried if he said anything at that moment he'd choke up with emotion. Pippa knew every pause and inflection, and it filled him with a deep and profound gratitude and joy that she saw the parts of him that mattered most and celebrated them.

The kid he'd been, even the happier one who'd lived with the Franklins, wouldn't have known to want this feeling he'd never experienced before in any context but with her.

"I'm glad you and Xander could be here for these shows," he said.

Instead of the world tour route—he was utterly sure he didn't want to be away from Pippa and Xander for months on end—he and his team had decided to do two-night stands in various cities. Not months or years. He could have breaks in between the shows, and between the three of them, either Xander or Pippa would be with him while he was away from home. Keeping the bad habits at bay and reminding him who he was.

"I'm glad too. And I'm very thankful to you for scheduling a show in Fairbanks."

He and Xander had known she wanted to visit her sister more often since the baby came along, so Hamish had found a venue—and they were thrilled to have him—and they set up a show that had sold out in less than an hour. That way he could be with her, and if he could attach a business reason, she'd be less annoyed they followed her around to keep her safe.

"It'll be fun. I've not been to Fairbanks, only Anchorage."

"Esther and Danny are more excited about you visiting than me," she teased.

He barked a laugh. "That is a bald-faced lie. Your sisters adore you, and I expect little Daniella already loves you with the same zeal. Danny just likes that I know how to play *Mario Kart*."

"He really does. It's very sweet of you to play with him."

Hamish scoffed. "I have fun every time I'm with your sisters and Danny. I like playing video games."

"You're really working it today," Pippa told him with a laugh. "Are you trying to get me to do butt stuff?"

"Goddamn I love you," he said through a gale of laughter.

She said in a singsong voice, "Because I let you do butt stuff?"

He was still recovering from the occasional snicker when Pippa angled her head to look in the side mirror. "How many white crossover SUVs are there in this city? I swear that's the tenth one I've seen today. Every time I look up there's another one."

"At the risk of sounding like a line from *The Matrix*, is it the *same* crossover SUV or different ones?"

Hamish had been followed by photographers more than once, and since she was with him, it made him extra wary. The three of them were a very hot topic. Pictures sold well, videos even better.

Hamish had rolled with it. Fame was a wild ride. He was grateful the attention, though intense, had been mainly positive. That fascination had sold even more units of his new release, and the tour people had tried to get him on board with scheduling shows in a three-night stand instead of two so they could work some tongue-in-cheek references to threesomes into their PR.

He'd shut that down so fast he left skid marks. Then he triple-underlined that such a thing was *never* to happen because it might endanger Pippa and Xander. She was uncomfortable enough, though she tried so hard to never let it show in front of him. She was always so mindful of his feelings; how could he be anything other than just as mindful of hers?

That and his private life was small enough as it was, given his chosen career. He needed to protect what he could.

"I don't know. Is that...should I be...?" Pippa seemed to freeze as it became clear to her. "Has this happened before?" she managed after a bit.

"I didn't want to alarm you. But yes, I've been trailed a time or two by paparazzi."

She sighed. "I don't know if it's the same one or not.

They've been the same make and model, but I've seen a dozen white cars of the same make and model other than an SUV today too. Did you know the most common car color in California is white? Washington too."

Hamish didn't question her accuracy on her facts or the specific SUV she saw. She worked around cars every day, so if she said they were the same make and model, they were.

She asked, "Well, what do we do? How do you handle this sort of thing? Obviously, we aren't going to tear through the streets of L.A. like we're in a movie. People could get hurt. But I don't want them to know where we're staying. Or where Xander and Miles are."

"I've been to the club they're lunching in. It's low key and high security. He'll be fine. As for what we do? This is why we pose for pictures outside an official event. There's a demand for this sort of stuff, so if I address it in an appropriate setting, it cuts down on ambushes and the like. Not entirely, but enough. I'm sorry. I know you hate this."

"I don't hate that your fans love you and want to see you. I accept this comes with the territory, and I'm doing my best to take it as it is."

"But for whatever reason, you're the target of the most upset. I wish I could fix that."

Her laughter was slightly bitter at the edges. "I wish you could fix the patriarchy too. I'm the target because I'm a woman who gets two men and I'm not coy. I don't apologize for it. I'm a slut. I'm a clout chaser. I'm a gold digger. I'm the symbol that you and Xander are taken. Two handsome and successful men to one woman no one knows? Unacceptable. To people like my family, I'm reveling in sin and modeling terrible behavior to all other women. I can't win, so I just try not to play."

He thought about that a lot through the next day, including at sound check, when she watched from the front row, Xander at her side. Where he stayed through the whole show. Hamish seeing her being protected tackled his concern for the time being. So he put all his other worries away and let himself fall into his music. And it fit him like a bespoke suit.

CHAPTER
TWENTY-SEVEN

Pippa had been feeling weird all day. She'd chalked it up to that thing with the SUV the afternoon before and finding out cars had trailed him in the past. Which meant without a doubt they'd trailed her too and she hadn't even noticed.

Granted, she did acknowledge how she felt each night when the gate at their building's parking garage closed behind her car, and when she pulled into the locked Twisted Steel lot every morning.

Maybe she'd been fooling herself that she'd gotten used to it. That the security she'd surrounded herself with because of the situation with her family also served her when it came to anyone trying to take photos of her. That, and truthfully, when she wasn't with Hamish or Xander, she was a far less interesting subject.

A small enough consolation, but a consolation nonetheless.

With Hamish having shows back-to-back in a place there were already a lot of celebrity media types, it meant everyone was looking when the three of them went anywhere, but especially near the venue when he was in full Hamish Wilson mode in his custom faux leather pants and sparkly, pointy-toed boots. His hair had been tousled, and he'd lined his eyes.

Pippa would want to take pictures of him for her job too. He looked like every bad boy wet dream come to life. And with Xander at her other side, especially when he wore the braces—or suspenders as he called them sometimes—with a pale blue or white shirt open to show part of the ink on his chest.

She did her best to keep up, but they were on a totally different level, so she didn't really begrudge anyone for looking twice.

"Everything okay?" Hamish asked. They'd just left the amphitheater he'd absolutely killed it in. Seeing live music outside was such a joy, and it'd been magic watching him own every single inch of the stage. He loved what he was doing as he melded the older material with the new, and it showed.

"Yep," she said and then squeezed his hand. "You were fantastic tonight. Three encores. They love the new stuff. I should also tell you I lifted one of these Hamish Wilson hoodies because it looked amazing. I figure I can wash dishes for you until I pay it off."

Hamish laughed. He was amped up and seemed to vibrate with energy. "I'm going to suggest we go back to the condo," he murmured into her ear. "Maybe you can wear the hoodie. And nothing else."

Xander chuckled in that sexy way she really liked, so he obviously knew what Hamish was suggesting.

Naturally, she knew those were the moments that would be photographed and would show up. It would look like they were double penetration-ing it all over town.

That made her laugh, and as she was explaining what she was giggling about to them, there was a hail of Hamish's name, and they all stopped and turned as Hamish stepped forward.

Then someone rammed into her, carrying her a few feet away before the breath whooshed from her when she was slammed against a waist-high wrought iron fence.

Bright shards of pain sliced through her hip and back as she hit the metal, and the force had her nearly doing a backbend across the top and the decorative finials that sent the breath from her.

There were several blows to her stomach and sides, and it felt like she'd slipped out of time somehow. It was so very slow but lightning fast all at once.

She pulled her arms up to protect her face and push her attacker off.

"You adulterous harlot! Repent now before I send you to hell," a voice said. *Timothy's* voice, she registered right before he clocked her in the side of her head and her vision went fuzzy.

She kicked and tried to evade him, and she experienced sharp pressure as his hold slid up her side while they grappled.

A sound came from deep in her gut, a scream that seemed to pour out every last bit of the rage she felt. How dare he hurt her!

Then she realized the roaring in her ears was actually Xander, who'd wrapped his arms around her brother's upper body and picked him up before slamming Timothy to the concrete.

Hamish stepped in between her and where her brother lay. Event security had arrived, and Pippa wiped a hand across her brow, feeling sweaty and nauseated.

She needed to lean against something to get her breath back. Maybe sit down. The ground didn't seem so far away, and maybe that was because she was actually on it.

Hamish's face lost all color as he dropped to his knees at her side. "Pippa?"

"What?" Her words slurred slightly at the end as he screamed out for an ambulance.

He grabbed her brand-new totally stolen sweatshirt and wadded it up. The warm day had cooled down. She didn't want him to be cold, and she tried to say so when he eased her back to lay down before pressing something on her chest.

The entire situation was very confusing.

"She's been stabbed!" Hamish yelled.

"I have?" She had?

"Do not close your eyes. Stay with me, Pippa," Hamish ordered.

If she took a nap, she could rest up for tomorrow when she'd have to deal with Timothy stabbing her. He better not have stabbed her anywhere she wanted to get tattooed because she read once that it was harder to tattoo over scars.

CHAPTER
TWENTY-EIGHT

At the hospital, no one would tell them anything because they weren't married, but Xander's father Todd had managed to connect with a cop he knew, and that in turn got them an update. She was in surgery because one of her arteries had been nicked. That's why she'd bled so much.

Someone took pity on them at about two thirty in the morning, and a nurse let them know Pippa was out of surgery and in serious but nearly stable condition. But they couldn't see her, and Hamish wanted to weep at the thought of her being all alone after being nearly killed.

What if she thought they'd left her? What if she didn't know what was happening? What if she was frightened? Of course she'd be frightened. Jesus.

He got to his feet again to pace and began a circuit that included the bathroom and his real destination, the nurses' station outside ICU.

"Her feet get really cold at night. Can you make sure her toes are covered since we can't check?"

It was clear the woman at the desk recognized him, but when he'd spoken, her eyes softened. Very quietly—not to be overheard sharing info, he figured—she said, "I just checked on her about ten minutes ago. The blankets were tucked in at the foot of the bed. Her vitals are improving. She's out. She wouldn't know if you were there or not."

"No one can get to her but staff?" What if another one of her crazed family members tried to get to her when he and Xander had been kept out?

"No one else is going to hurt her. I'm sorry this happened."

Hamish thanked her and went back to join Xander in the waiting room where Miles and Harlow had turned up.

Harlow held up a bag. "Change of clothes for you both. I tossed in a few notepads. Just in case you wanted to do something with your hands while you wait," she told Xander.

It wasn't until he was in the bathroom, changing, that Hamish noted he still had blood on his T-shirt. Pippa's life rushing from her body with beat after beat of her heart as he'd held a fucking sweatshirt with his face on it to her chest, willing her blood to stay the fuck in her veins where it was needed.

Trying not to think of that, he used some paper towels to clean up the best he could before heading back to them.

To Xander. God. Xander sat so straight, tension in every muscle. When he saw Hamish walking toward them, his features shifted from that tight, forced blankness into a smile that made him want to cry all over again.

"We brought blankets." Miles handed them over. "And some food and stuff to drink. I know better than to suggest you go back to the condo to sleep until her sister arrives. So you may as well be comfortable as you can here."

"I have to call my parents," Hamish murmured. It was nearly three in the morning, and he'd been putting it off. But...he needed them. And they'd want to know. They could tell Jessi, and she'd handle the Twisted Steel people.

"What's wrong?" his father demanded as he answered on the second ring.

"It's Pippa" was all he got out before the tears came so hard Miles came over and took the phone, finishing the explanation as Xander pulled Hamish close while they both lost their shit.

The sun had risen, but the area remained the sort of enforced quiet people tended to keep around the gravely wounded. Xander tucked the blanket around Hamish a little better before he got up to stretch.

The text from Rebecca saying her plane had just landed and she was on the way had roused him from that place between sleep and wakefulness he'd been in for hours. Every time he'd closed his eyes, he remembered that moment he'd turned and seen her on the ground, her skin alabaster except for the red smears of blood.

And Hamish, his face a mask of total control as he ordered Pippa to keep her eyes open. Xander'd gone to his knees and helped, pressing his weight over Hamish's hands, praying they could stanch the bleeding long enough for real medical intervention.

He wasn't even sure if he could remember how they got to the hospital once the ambulance had left. The rental car must look like a crime scene, he thought briefly as he stared out the large windows over miles of the city beyond.

The police would be by soon enough. There'd been a short interview at the scene, but they'd let Xander and Hamish go quickly so they could get to the hospital. He knew Timothy had been taken into custody and vowed that if he'd gotten out on bond, Xander'd show up at that fucking compound in Arizona and beat the shit out of not just Timothy, but the father too. All the calls and letters, the tracts on her windshield, the vandalism, it had started because of the father. The brother had been a tool.

He paced much as Hamish had, and about an hour later, Rebecca rushed in looking pale and exhausted.

When she saw them, Xander opened his arms, and she came to him, hugging him back.

"You're here," he assured her, knowing she was panicked. Vivi rushed in shortly, and he was very glad she'd come along for emotional support.

"I was parking. We're good. Let's talk with the doctors to get an update, and then we'll figure out what we need to do so Xander and Hamish can have access to her," Vivi said, taking over and handling them all. "Wait here, I'll be right back."

"She's amazing in a crisis," Rebecca told them of Vivi. "We were supposed to have a wedding, but we'd rather spend the money on travel. So we went to city hall and got married yesterday, and then we took the deposit money we'd gotten back from the venue and put it toward a trip to Costa Rica. We were going to have you all over and announce it. I should have at least texted Pippa to tell her. She'll be so happy for us. I told Esther but not her. Not yet. That was selfish. What if?"

"None of that *what if* stuff," Xander said. "That way lies madness. You're here, and the doctors will speak to you so we can have an idea of what's happening. We will all get through this, and you can tell her yourself."

He'd lost his shit at four a.m. or so in a bathroom stall. He'd cried and raged, and when it was over, he'd felt numb. But numb was better than helpless, and he didn't want to go back there. None of them needed that right then. It was time to put all their energy into Pippa.

Rebecca said, "I'll make sure you're allowed to have information from now on. You might think about creating a medical power of attorney for one another. Let's pray nothing like this ever happens again, but a broken toe, a car accident, whatever, can happen. Vivi and I did that. You know how hospitals can be sometimes about same-sex partners. I never wanted that to happen, and if Pippa had been gone, or Esther, I really didn't want our family to get contacted." She blinked several times. "I guess that happened. Timothy. Jesus. He broke my arm."

Xander's attention shot back to her. "What?"

"When they found out I was gay and that Pippa and Esther had known and hadn't told on me, they held a tribunal to decide if the community would allow us to stay or what. I had already decided to run, and I knew Esther would come with me. Danny was in love with Esther by that point, though no one at the group knew it. He would help. But we couldn't leave Pippa. I knew she wouldn't be safe if she stayed. Anyway, us three sisters were taken to the middle of the room. All the bishops and leaders from the church sat behind a long table—the same one we had summer meals on out in the yard—and they had all these *charges* to read off about how I was a strumpet lesbian out to make them all gay and practice witchcraft. All lies except for the lesbian part. I tried to defend myself, and Timothy, he grabbed me and pushed me, and then he picked up this metal dowel we used to open the high windows, and he raised it above his head and brought it down on my arm. Here."

She pointed to a place on her forearm.

"He said, as he was doing it, that physical pain needed to go hand in hand with true repentance or I'd go to hell. It was shocking. Even to the bishops. To this day, I think that's what made them decide to let us go and for them to sign over guardianship of Pippa to Esther. They could count on the authorities to ignore a lot, but what my brother had done was too much to overlook. It would have brought heat on them, and they didn't want that more than they wanted three uteruses for the cause."

Xander opened his mouth to speak several times, but in the end all he had was that he was sorry. Internally, though, he knew Timothy Hall was a threat until he was put on trial and sent to prison.

But if Timothy was that dangerous, what did it say about whoever pulled his strings?

The doctor and Pippa's surgeon came out to give an update. She continued to recover well. No signs of infection so far. The artery was repaired. They were going to keep her for the following few days, and they'd be able to visit with her in a few hours once the morning rotation went through.

"We're at a hotel about four blocks away." Vivi handed them a keycard envelope with the room number on it. "Take a shower and change. You'll both feel better. If you can't see Pippa for another ninety minutes, take the time. We'll be here, and if anything at all changes, I'll call you. I promise."

He didn't want to go, but his eyes had started to burn, and even though he'd washed his hands and forearms a dozen times, he felt her blood in every wrinkle, whether it was there truly or not.

Forty-five minutes later and Vivi had been totally correct. The shower and getting into clean clothes—thank goodness for Miles and Harlow—revived him and Hamish as well.

"You should sleep once we can see her," Xander told Hamish as they drove back to the hospital. They'd gotten a room for themselves at the same hotel. The condo wasn't too far, but four blocks was less than five minutes, and the condo could be twenty or an hour given traffic. Neither of them wanted to risk it.

"I'll sleep later." Hamish looked out the window, clearly thinking about forty other things.

"You need to work tonight, which will be tough enough, but on no sleep at all it'll be a nightmare. You'll end up in the hospital too. Come back here, eat, and nap for a few hours."

"Are you mad? I'm not performing tonight!" Hamish threw his hands up. "Once we're able to see Pippa, I'll contact my people. No one is going to be upset I'm cancelling. My girlfriend got stabbed right outside the venue. Jesus wept. Even if they were upset, they can kiss my ass if they don't like it."

Xander pulled into a parking spot and turned to Hamish.

"Baby." He caught Hamish's face in his hands and pressed a kiss to his forehead. "This is more than you. There are hundreds of people counting on you tonight."

Xander grew up in the business; he understood a tour was a giant undertaking that employed a lot of people from sound and tech to the set-up and pull-down roadies. Catering. The venue had staff that night that would take tickets, monitor the crowd to be sure they were in their correct spots, people who ran concessions and handled parking. Even the front office folks and Hamish's own tour team.

"Pippa will tell you the same thing." Totally true. In fact, she'd feel terribly guilty if Hamish canceled. But Xander didn't say that out loud because Hamish needed to make his own choice, and while it would be easy to manipulate him into choosing what Xander thought was best, it would be a shitty, selfish thing to do.

"How can I just prance around singing for two hours while she's here?" Hamish asked, obviously anguished.

"*It's your job.* You worked hard, really hard, to get here. You structured your show dates in a specific way to embrace the direction and speed you want your career to take for the next however long. Go to soundcheck, come back here, and return to the venue when you're due. Miles and Harlow will go with you." Xander knew without even asking they'd be pleased to do anything they could to help. This way, they'd help keep Hamish on track at the venue, and they'd be able to bring him back once everything was over.

"We'll be here when you finish. It's really only a few hours here and there. And then you'll have fulfilled your responsibilities and you're free until the Fairbanks show."

Though, he wasn't entirely sure if Pippa would be up to traveling up to Alaska in six weeks. They'd deal with that later because he was *not* going to get between Pippa and that baby, but he sure as hell wasn't going to let her endanger her health.

That was a discussion for another day, and if it came to that, he'd have no guilt whatsoever tossing Rebecca at Pippa and making her be the bad guy to say no to travel.

"You'll stay here with her the entire time?" Hamish asked.

"Of course. And I swear to you if anything changes, I'll text Jamey, and he'll get you out of there ASAP." Jamey was the tour manager, and he had a soft spot for Pippa. "He's a seasoned pro. If there's a real problem, he'll get you where you need to be. You need to do this, and I understand. Pippa understands. Miles and Harlow know how to get you in and out of there lightning quick. They'll work with Jamey. It's going to be okay."

"Promise me, Xander."

There was a taut urgency in Hamish's tone that echoed against the fear threatening to pound through Xander's chest.

"I promise you. We will get through this. Together. One of us needs to marry her." There, he'd said it. "We can protect her better. If Rebecca didn't like us, or didn't want to give us access, we'd have had no rights. We can do power of attorney for medical purposes, and that's what we need ASAP. But with these fucking assholes in Arizona lurking around, I want to pull her into the legal shelter marriage can be."

Xander wanted it to be him. He wondered if his dad felt this way before his mom and his pop had married.

"We can work out the details later. There's enough on the plate for today." He reached over and kissed Hamish before they headed back inside.

Vivi was in the waiting room when they got back. "Only one visitor at a time. They just let Rebecca go in. You're both looking a little better."

He handed the keycard over. "Thanks for the offer of the shower. I feel half human again."

"When you've both visited her, we're all going to breakfast. No arguments. He's going on stage in twelve hours, and you'll be holding down the fort. You need it. And Rebbie hasn't eaten since before you called. She's running on terror and the last bits of adrenaline she had. I need her to take care of herself too."

Because Vivi put it in those terms—and because she'd reinforced Hamish going to his show—they agreed and then flipped a coin to see who'd go next.

"Hey there, Pixie Stick," Rebecca said softly as she settled next to Pippa.

Pippa wasn't entirely sure what was going on, but it must be serious to have her sister using an ancient nickname.

She was in the hospital and had been hurt. She knew that because there was a strain and tightness in her chest and her arm had been strapped to her body.

She took a small sip of water and breathed carefully, as it wanted to come right back up. "What happened?" Pippa managed to croak out.

"The doctors said the anesthetic sometimes made it take a bit longer to get the memories of what happened back. They assured us it it'd return, though perhaps in bits and pieces. And the shock took a toll as well." Rebecca's voice wobbled at the end, but it firmed up again soon enough. "Timothy stabbed you."

The relevant bits did slowly start to form in her memory. Of the way he'd been screaming in her face as he kept punching her. The weird pressure on her side and chest. Hamish yelling for her to stay awake.

Tears clouded her vision as the chaos and terror came back in a rush.

"Don't cry. Oh, sweetheart, I'm sorry that happened to you. But you're going to be all right. Esther is trying to figure out how to get here, but I forbid it and Danny forbid it, so she's not talking to either of us. But she won't come. At least for now. Your boys are waiting to see you. I wasn't entirely sure when you first sprang on me that you were all three together. I figured you'd be crying in my guest room a few months later, but then I got to know them both. And see them with you and you with them. Don't let Timothy try to take that from you. You live to spite them, Pippa. You live so you can thrive and love whoever the hell you want. Fuck them."

"Is he in jail?"

"I spoke on the phone with the officer in charge of the case. Timothy is awaiting arraignment today. They're requesting he be held without bail because he's a flight risk. They're going to ask for a mental health evaluation. The defense certainly will."

"He was screaming at me that I had to repent, or he'd

send me to hell. Or maybe it was repent before I send you to hell. Both, I think? I had a no contact order. How can they let him go if he violated it by doing the same thing he got in trouble for the last time, only with a knife and murder on his mind?"

"I wasn't able to speak with the attorney, just the officer in charge. But I can't imagine they won't bring that up. Whether it moves the needle one way or another is going to depend on the judge. But nothing is going to happen to you. Period. I won't allow it. Vivi has wanted to run members of our family over with a car for a few years now. Maybe I'll let her."

Rebecca stayed another two minutes or so before Hamish came in.

"Hello, love." He gave her the gentlest of kisses, and she drew in the way he smelled.

It was going to be okay. They wouldn't let anything but that be the result.

"Are you all right?" she asked as she caught sight of the shadow of a bruise on his cheek and temple.

He laughed a moment. "You're lying in a hospital bed, hooked up to machines, and you're asking if *I'm* all right?"

"He hit you in the head."

"Massive fists, that fuckwit has. But I've a very hard head, I'm told. I'm tired and obviously worried because my heart is here in a hospital bed. But I'm fine. How are you? Aside from having a hole in your chest and a stitched-up artery?"

"I'm pretty high right now, so I'm not really in pain. Is Xander okay? Oh my goodness, Erin?" She worried this would echo through him to those memories tied to old wounds. His mother. His sister. As she lay on that pavement, both men pressing down on the wound, each alternating telling her to stay awake with their words of love and encouragement, she'd slipped away a little; it felt like she'd been washed out to sea and had gotten further and further from shore with each beat of her heart.

She wasn't going to let go, because she had a life with them. Because she had a future with them. And because she knew each man would react to her death in self-destructive and terrible ways.

"High isn't so bad if you're stuck in a hospital bed while your body heals. They said they'd be upgrading you from serious to stable later on today if you kept on this path. Flowers have been arriving for you since last night."

"Ooh, I'll get red flavor gelatin. Wait, flowers? For me? From who?" Probably his family or Xander's.

"Red flavor?"

She swallowed, and he helped her put her cup back after another tiny sip. "Could be cherry or berry of some general type. Red is generic for that combo of chemicals to indicate berry adjacent. You don't eat the strawberry popsicle, you eat the red one."

"I love you so fucking much. Up here in Intensive Care using words like adjacent just hours after major surgery." He brushed her hair back from her face. "Red flavor indeed. You are correct. As for the flowers. The usual suspects from friends and family, but dozens and dozens of arrangements are from my fans. Yours too as it turns out."

He smiled at her, and she wanted to smile back, but it hurt and tugged when she tried, and when she reached up to touch her lip, she found it swollen and stitched.

"He split your lip when he punched you," Hamish said darkly.

"Feels like it, yep. I love you, Hamish. I forgot to say it back. I'm very highly medicated. Did I mention that either?"

"I might have noticed. It'll be our secret." He sucked in a breath that made her think of diving into the lake. "I'm the reason your family has gotten all worked up. Without the attention on me, there wouldn't have been all those pictures that set them off."

"Pffft." At least that was what she was aiming for. She probably got the point across in the end. "I already had a no-contact order on him for assaulting me before. He likes to hurt people. Weaker than him usually. I have no doubt he has been looking all this time, just waiting for a reason to spring into action. I wasn't expecting the murder attempt, though. Surprise!"

He snorted a laugh and then groaned.

She remembered his eyes and the spittle that flew as he'd yelled.

"He's not going to be beating anyone up. He's in jail. Being arraigned later. Rebecca deals with the legal system all the time, so she's watching that. I've given my attorney a call, and someone at her firm is looking into this and will keep us updated on what happens at the arraignment later since the victim doesn't get their own representation."

He frowned.

"My stolen sweatshirt got ruined," she said sadly, her eyelids getting heavier.

"I don't know if I should tell you I had those brought in for you because I knew by the time we left the arena, the night would have gotten colder. Thank fuck you had it; that's what I held your blood in your body with as you bled out on the pavement. You had on the tiniest blouse. I remember. Little purple flowers and a perfect, tiny lilac bow between your breasts. Tonight you won't be there when I play. I shouldn't go," he whispered. "I need to be right here. What if something happens?"

Tears welled in his eyes, and he dashed them away with the back of his hand before the fight seemed to leave him and he dropped his head, resting it on the bed on her uninjured side. Long enough for her to bury her fingers in his hair, which centered her.

"Darn. I was so excited to have embarked on my life of crime. Though don't tell anyone but I left two twenties on the table. Probably cost a hundred bucks. That's the real crime."

She closed her eyes a moment and gathered her strength. "I remember you saving my life. Thank you."

He sat up. Silent as tears fell down his cheeks. "You are everything. I can't face the idea of a world without you in it."

"Good thing you don't have to. But you do have to play tonight. I'm certain Xander already told you all the reasons, and since I'm high and a little low on blood, I won't repeat him. I'll be right here. I promise."

A nurse chased Hamish out, and Xander appeared shortly after, worry all over his features, so she lifted the hand not bound to her side and beckoned him closer.

"Damn it, that black eye better be gone by your photo shoot," she said to tease, but he frowned as he sat.

"You cursed."

"Someone stabbed me. I get some leeway. And possibly red gelatin."

She loved him so much when he just gave her a raised brow but didn't even let that weird comment slow him down. "I kicked him in the face a few times. I probably knocked a few of his teeth out." He said this as a challenge. As if he expected her to be turned off. Or reject him.

They were all a darned mess of baggage.

"It hurts if I try to smile, so stop being so cute," she told him crossly. "Tell me you love me."

That made *him* smile. "I love you." He reached for her hand, but only left the barest touch as he drew back.

"If a stab wound didn't kill me, you can touch my hand. Not the other one, that one hurts because of all the tubes and junk. Do you think they will let me have pudding? I don't need any right this moment but later I might."

"You're sleepy and a little high." He gave her an affectionate look, and it made her feel so wonderfully normal it wrenched her back from the edge of tears.

"I might take a nap. I love you."

"Even after I couldn't protect you?"

"You and Hamish both have such a god complex. I was with you. I was in public. I had a no contact order already. I've made it clear repeatedly that I want nothing to do with the group and my family there. He jumped out of the shadows and started punching me like he was under a spell. How can you protect against that sort of thing? I thought he might try to beat me up, not stab me. That was very rude. Just popped up in a totally random place and shoved a knife into my chest. I can't think of a clever insult to call him on account of the high volume of pain medication. I hope every time he goes to grab his cereal box or a bag of chips, it's only crumb dust. And that his pillowcase is always hot."

"Even with three stitches in your lip you can stick it out in such a pretty little pout."

"There will probably be stories that I got lip injections and this attack is just a smokescreen." She giggled, and he lost his anguished expression. Once she sobered—sobered-ish—she continued, "Lots of work to do to recover so I can get out of here and go back to my life. I can't if I'm worried you two feel responsible for something you had nothing to do with. It's all very simple, Alexander. I already backed you up to get Hamish to the venue tonight. You two worked together to save my life. We will all work together and not only get through this, but thrive. Rebecca said I need to thrive just to spite them, and that's totally what I'm going to do."

She gave her permission, signing papers that allowed him and Hamish access to her medical information and her treatment plans and all that. It hadn't occurred to her that they'd be walled out the way they had been.

"You go tonight. Hamish needs support," she told Xander as he made to leave the room.

Xander snorted and then shook his head. "You're *definitely* high if you think that's what will happen. He only agreed if I stayed here with you. And, my beautiful redheaded warrior, I'm not leaving you. He and I are in total agreement on that. You can't win, so let's cry peace."

She growled.

"I already spoke to Miles while Hamish was in here with you. They're going to come over in a few hours and be his cheering section and support. Hamish promised once we got done with the breakfast Vivi is threatening us into eating, he'd sleep a few hours. That way he'll get some rest before performing. How's that?"

"Good work. They're very nice. *You* will sleep too. Then I can, and I won't feel bad."

He rolled his eyes. "We've worked out a schedule with Rebecca so someone will be here while we get some rest in shifts. If I don't rest, he won't. Then you won't. It's an avalanche of bad choices."

"Not an avalanche!" she gasped, but it turned into a yawn.

Xander stepped close one more time, kissed her cheek softly, made sure her feet were covered up, and then ducked out after telling her once more he loved her.

CHAPTER
TWENTY-NINE

Four days later, they let her leave the hospital, but she needed to remain in Los Angeles for two weeks, so she could do her follow-up appointments with her medical team. Any possible complications would be better dealt with by her existing doctors. Pippa was healing well, but they wanted to monitor her awhile longer. Once all that had been said in front of Xander, Hamish, Rebecca, and Vivi, there was no way she was going anywhere.

Pippa was adorably grumpy as they set her up on the couch in the living room. She wore pajamas emblazoned with cowgirl-style pinups from the fifties Hamish had gotten her for Valentine's Day.

Erin, Todd, and Ben had arrived the day after Pippa was attacked and had managed to borrow a vacant condo in that same building, so Pippa could stay where she was without having to worry. Hamish's parents had shown up right before he was about to go to soundcheck, and though his father had flown back home once Pippa had settled, his mother was in a spare room in the other condo.

Pippa had suffered a traumatic assault. She'd endured surgery and a number of other painful treatments of various injuries. Physically and emotionally, she'd taken a lot of blows, and it was totally normal that she might process it with more tears or dark humor, both of which seemed to be Pippa's outlet.

While it was good to know it wasn't a bad sign that she cried, something nearly came undone in his gut every time he saw her fall apart. But he didn't want her to have to think about anyone else's feelings as she processed the nightmare she'd endured, so he and Xander did all they could to never let her see their distress.

"When Rebecca comes down next week, she'll stay here," Pippa announced after they'd calmed some tears and worry that she'd chased Xander's parents out of their own apartment.

"Absolutely. I've already talked to her about it," Xander said.

"And when do you go back?" she asked Xander.

"When we all drive back in two weeks."

She still got tired easily, but the way they'd tucked pillows and a blanket around her, she could easily nap there if she wanted, or they could help her to bed.

Later on, Hamish wanted to take her on the balcony for just a few minutes. She'd been in a hospital room for days. Toward sunset the light would be gentler, and there'd been a slight breeze all day he thought she'd like.

The bruises on her face had settled into a sickly yellow-green, and she looked frightfully small for a moment until she frowned, shook her head, and reminded him she'd been healing well enough that there were glimpses of sassy Pippa.

"You have a job, Xander. Not just your scheduled tattoos, but you have a photo shoot. The ink you gave Sam Flanigan brought you this ad work. *You built this career.* For this exact moment. You can't just let it wither because the timing went sideways. And you don't need to. Hamish is here. Rebecca is coming. Your mom and Addie are going to be here all day long. You know there will be a revolving crew of people who will take me places, pick things up for me, all that. Will I miss you? Of course. But I don't want you to blow these things off. Your black eye should be healed by then, but if not, they can cover it up with makeup."

Xander growled as Pippa's and Hamish's gazes met briefly. It was such a relief to have that rhythm again, their little family of three.

Xander finally said, "You're recovering from being *stabbed.* You think I can go take pictures with fucking watches while you're down here?"

"You thought that's what I needed to do not even a full twenty-four hours after she got stabbed to start with," Hamish said with affection. "She's right. Come back when it's time to drive her home."

Things were beginning to happen in this next stage of Xander's career. He had commitments he needed to keep so his reputation didn't suffer. And the fact was, that ad campaign Xander was shooting for was one of those right place/right time things. Opportunities like that one didn't come every day.

Pippa said, "There's no reason I can't fly in two weeks, but I gave in because that's what was necessary to make you both feel comfortable. Go to work, Xander. Hamish and I know it's what you have to do. No one is mad or upset. We love you."

"I have the leave, damn it. Any client who would never use me again because I rescheduled due to my girlfriend being stabbed can fuck off a pier."

"Even if you didn't have the leave, Brody would give it to you. That's not the issue." Hamish lifted a shoulder. "It's only two weeks."

"I've never been away from her for more than four days."

Pippa started to cry.

Before he started in too, Hamish put a hand on her calf to calm them both and said, "You can FaceTime us every night when you get home from work. You're already taking time to drive back. This will all be over before we know it."

"I want to be at her doctor's appointments too."

"We can have you call in for it," Pippa said. "You've already had to reschedule several days' worth of clients. Every day you do that you're behind. And you're taking time for the wedding in September. I'll never forgive myself if you have to cut corners on that because you took time off to be here."

"I need to think about it," Xander said, rising. "I'm going to grab some smoothies. I'll be back shortly."

After a few kisses for them both, he grabbed his keys and headed out, locking up behind himself. Then he texted Hamish to tell him to throw the extra security latches.

"Do you think Timothy will get out and come here?" Pippa asked.

"No. He's in custody pending his mental evaluation. He's on lockdown. And he never came here. He attacked you at the venue. I don't think he knew where we'd been staying. This building is secure enough for Erin, so I feel pretty safe in saying even if he knew, he couldn't have gotten up here."

That did the trick. Pippa relaxed a little as Hamish put away his distress at how freaked out she'd been. Just a flash of panic, but it exposed the underlying fear for her safety.

"Xander will go back. We have to make sure he does," she told him. "He's worked too hard. You'll be here." She smiled, trusting him totally.

"I'll be here. Right here. I've got you. And we'll get Xander where he needs to be too. Rest a while. I love you."

After a bit, she drifted to sleep, and he rested nearby, listening to her breathe.

Hamish had wondered if he had it in him to be there for her when it counted the most. And as he'd fallen for Xander, he'd wondered the same. Here he'd just stepped up, he realized. Automatically, because of course he had it in him. She'd believed in him from the start.

His mother tapped on the door about twenty minutes later, and they went into the kitchen where he could watch Pippa, but they wouldn't disturb her by talking.

"Tea?" he asked, and his mom nodded.

"She looks better than she did yesterday."

"You can't see the bruising on her side, neck, and chest." He sighed, steadying himself, reminding himself she was okay.

"Xander popped over to see his folks, so I told him I'd let you know where he was. It gave me an opportunity to check on you. Have you eaten?"

"Not lately, no."

"Let me make you something. She'll wake up when she's hungry. The fridge here is stocked. Your father was stress cooking. Check the freezer too."

Hamish hadn't been at the condo for the last four days as they'd stayed at the hotel close to the hospital. Even when they'd brought her home, he hadn't looked in the kitchen for food.

There was something about a tuna sandwich and mushroom soup your mom makes you that was a particular sort of magic.

He let it wash over him.

"Everything is going to be all right," she murmured to him as they ate at the kitchen island, Pippa still in his line of sight. "Jessi is making plans with Rennie. One will come down one week and then they'll switch out. This wasn't presented as an option. They want to help. They love you both. Pippa is going to need the diversion as she heals, and you're going to need a break. You can't be on guard like this twenty-four hours a day. It'll wear you down. There's an open bedroom over there, so they'll take that one."

There was no arguing, so he didn't.

"There are paparazzi outside," she told him quietly after he'd finished his sandwich. "Todd says we need to coordinate when we leave and use the parking garage instead of walking out the lobby."

"I'm thinking of canceling the remaining dates for my shows," he said in a rush.

"Why would you do such a thing?"

"She isn't safe, and it's my fault. I've been trying to pause to let them take pictures of us. They don't hound us so much after that. But we went out to dinner, and it was known I was here doing shows. I was in full Hamish Wilson mode! I treated it like a game, and look what happened."

His mother rolled her eyes. "Sweetheart, you're a celebrity. Media attention comes with the job. Your persona and your ability to keep fans interested is part of your success. She might be uncomfortable with all the attention, but she understands that. She *accepts* that because it's part of you."

"The media coverage whips them up."

His mother made a face. "Those group people are unhinged. If it wasn't photos of you three, it'd be something else. And anyway, why are they nosing around doing social media searches for something they tossed out well over a decade ago? They're looking to be aggrieved. Live your life and concentrate on being happy. And that includes the shows you've very carefully planned. She would fight you on canceling anyway."

That was totally true.

Pippa moved a little and opened her eyes.

"I'm glad to see you're awake," Addie called out as they went into the living room. "James made a batch of chicken soup before he had to go back home. It's here in the fridge. Would you like some? I made mushroom soup for Hamish, and there's some left if you'd rather that."

Pippa smiled up at them and then winced slightly. "I would love some soup to start. Whichever is easiest. I'm a little cold."

"I'll get you some tea," Hamish said after he put a throw blanket over her feet.

"Three lumps please," she said, anticipating the question.

.   .   .

"When I walked out the front, they were there. Three of them yelling my name, asking me how Pippa was recovering," Xander told his parents. "You need to go home," he urged his mother. This was all triggering for her.

"I'm not doing that bad, to be honest with you. You'd be amazed how much good an edible can do." He made a face at her, but she shrugged and said, "I'm not kidding. This didn't happen to me. It happened to her. You can't be here. Not the whole time. She doesn't have a mom. But you do. She's yours. So she's ours too. You can figure out which one of your fathers you want to go back home with, but I'm staying here, and since I am, Dad or Pop will also insist on staying. Pick one and I'll keep the other. We'll take care of her when you can't." She winked at him.

"They want me to leave like she stubbed her toe or broke a bone." He couldn't stop hearing the surgeon telling them that a hairsbreadth more and she'd most likely have bled out by the time help arrived on scene. She'd meant it to sound comforting. How lucky they were.

And it did emphasize how lucky they'd been. Which had also emphasized how much of it had been out of their control.

Control gave him comfort. Not being able to make everything better for her made him jittery and uncomfortable in his skin.

Ben spoke, smoothly stepping over Xander's protests. "Okay, so your schedule. When is this photo shoot?"

"I cannot possibly fucking do this. She could have died."

"Alexander, I need you to pay attention," his dad—Ben—

said. "If you go down this road, it will spiral, and nothing will come of it but misery. *She did not die.* He did not stab to the right or left or up or down. He stabbed where he did, which was bad enough, but it is *over*. He's in jail. She is recovering from her injuries, and in two weeks she will be able to come home. Now. When is your photo shoot?"

"Assault? He tried to kill her!" Rebecca said, throwing her hands up and beginning to pace. She'd arrived that morning, too late to attend the meeting with the attorney who'd laid the situation out in blunt terms.

Hamish looked over to Pippa, who, at nearly two weeks post attack was feeling a lot better. Though she currently attempted to hold back tears because she was sick to death of crying.

"I know you're upset. I am too," Pippa told her sister. "Xander is on his way from the airport. Depending on traffic, he should be here in forty-five or so. We can talk more when he arrives."

If other people heard before he did, Pippa knew Xander would take it hard. It had been difficult enough for him to leave her in Southern California when he'd gone back to work.

Rebecca made a growling sound that told Pippa her big sister's patience was fraying.

"*Fine*. I'm going to make you some lunch."

Xander had left two weeks earlier to tend to pressing business. He'd returned the week prior for one day, and neither Pippa nor Hamish had protested that it was too much travel for such a short time. They'd welcomed him. Hamish had been relieved to have Xander around. It was the only time he'd truly relaxed over the whole time she'd been recovering.

The following day they had Pippa's last medical appointment before starting their trip home, so Xander had worked that morning and caught the next flight south.

Pippa said, "I'll let Erin know Xander is on the way. Though I'm sure Xander or Ben texted ahead. You text your mother."

"Tell them I'm making lunch," Rebecca called out.

The last two weeks had given Pippa and Hamish the opportunity to get to know Erin and Todd better, and it wasn't an exaggeration to say it had created an intimacy and sense of family that would have taken a lot longer in any other circumstance.

Erin knew what Pippa was dealing with in ways no one else could. Pippa could cry in front of her and know she didn't have to manage Erin's response. The weight of that was lifted. A gift.

They'd put together puzzles and read. When Rennie had come down, they'd allowed Pippa to go to the pool deck and get some light and air. From that perch she could see the ocean in the distance when the day was clear. Hamish had swum, checking in on her regularly, making sure she reapplied sunscreen and stayed out of the direct sunlight.

Every night they'd FaceTimed Xander, and they'd texted

regularly. But she missed him so much. And wished she wasn't going to have to relate everything that had happened that morning with the prosecutor.

If wishes were fishes.

Addie and Jessi appeared shortly.

It had felt like that time around a big holiday when people were off work and there were houseguests. She didn't know the date, much less the actual day of the week. It would be odd to be home again and have a work and life schedule to keep to.

Pippa looked forward to it. Yearned for a time when people weren't constantly at her to go slow and be careful. Hoped for a life when she didn't feel like she needed to nap during the day. At least it wasn't four naps a day, she reminded herself.

She was healing. She would recover and get better and go back to work.

Pippa clutched that to her heart. She needed to remind herself when things like a trial and criminal charges came up.

"You want to sit out on the balcony to eat?" Hamish asked her. "I've moved the umbrella, so you'll be cooler, and there's no direct line of sight."

"It will be nice to spend time on our deck when we get home. I miss the Sound and the ferry horns." She missed their apartment. Her bed. Her things. Privacy. She hadn't slept with the two of them since the night before the attack. Hamish was still so careful. He'd only agreed to sleep in the same bed with her a week ago. Even to that point he surrounded her with pillows and kept on the other side.

Hamish kissed her so gently the tears she'd chased back returned in force.

"I'm sorry about today. I'm so bloody angry, but I'm trying to hold it back because you've got enough to process. And like you, I think we need to wait for Xander. He'll feel better for that too. I just didn't want you thinking I didn't care."

"I'm sorry too. But I never thought you didn't care. I get why you're reining it in, and I appreciate it." She was trying not to fall apart, and if he did, she would too.

Hamish thumbed away a tear and kissed her cheek where it had fallen.

"I love you."

"I know. How wonderful that is. I love you too."

But she'd brought so much drama into their lives. So much energy spent on absolute garbage. Pippa hated it.

Before she could unpack how she was feeling too much, Xander arrived with bags of her favorite chili cheeseburgers and fries, along with the bright-pink concoction they called lemonade but probably hadn't seen a lemon in all its life.

He unloaded everything on the table and moved directly to her. She stood and met him halfway, melting into his embrace.

"You're here," Pippa said into the front of his shirt.

He loosened his hold and let go with one arm to wrap it around Hamish, who'd joined their hug.

"I'm here," Xander agreed. "And here you two are. Damn, I've missed you so much. I got you some food, but my mom told me Rebecca was making lunch, so protect me from her wrath?" he asked as he set her back gently, kissing her forehead. "Your color is good."

"Hamish likes to escort me places. When we're sure we aren't followed," she assured him. "Miles and Harlow took us out on a boat. God, that was so lovely. And we spend a lot of pool and balcony time."

Rebecca came out to hug Xander and then waved his apology away when he'd addressed all the burgers he'd brought.

"I made a pasta salad and was going to lay out the makings for sandwiches. Sit and eat. You've probably had a long day to this point." Rebecca pointed at the table. "Oooh, onion rings too?"

Before long they'd all filled plates.

"Dad didn't come with me. He's overseeing some security upgrades to the apartment and also at Twisted Steel," Xander said.

"Why Twisted Steel?" Pippa asked.

Xander grunted. "Can we eat first?"

Hamish startled them all with his laugh. "Love, it's been quite a day here too. I agree. Let's eat. Then we'll talk more about difficult stuff. For now, fill us in on what the photo shoot was like."

Over the last weeks, Hamish had settled into his place in her life. He'd claimed it was more accurate, she supposed. Though *she'd* chafed at the slow pace of healing and the way she had to be driven everywhere, and even then, they had to leave in a coordinated fashion that wore her out. He'd taken care of things with total focus and competency.

She'd found it deeply romantic. Soothing too. Despite having to depend on people, which wasn't really her strong point, it had never felt like it was too much. Or that he was panicked by the pressure.

It was steady. Gentle. Annoyingly bossy as he'd made sure she rested and ate well. He united with the matriarchs if she got pissy about it, and that was the end of that. When Erin and Addie stood together on something, they were supercharged, and all that maternal power increased exponentially. It was impossible enough to resist them one on one!

Now that Xander had returned, he'd stepped right into the place he'd always occupied, and that settled her nerves enough she could take pleasure in his presence.

Xander bided his time until they'd finished eating and had cleared away the food and plates. He'd told them about the shoot, pleased to be asked. Overjoyed to be with them again. He hadn't slept more than five hours a night since leaving two weeks prior. Even that night he'd spent the week before, he'd been afraid to hurt her and insisted on sleeping on the lounger he'd pulled next to the bed.

"Before we get back to difficult topics, let's go into the living room," Hamish urged. "That way she can rest."

"I'm fine," she said in a hiss that was so delightfully familiar it made Xander hurt.

Once everyone had gotten comfortable, Xander took her hand and said as gently as he could, "Gretchen was vandalized again." Vandalized was a kind word. The truck had been absolutely destroyed. "The cameras caught two people cutting through the chain link to get into the lot. They had on hoodies, sunglasses, and masks. They used a long pole to tip the camera away before they touched your truck, so we don't know how long they remained and who all did the destruction. We sent what we had to the Seattle police and to the ones on the case down here. The insurance company has been handled. Good thing we did all that power of attorney stuff, huh? Everything is in process now. Duke and Asa are working on sourcing all the various parts we'll need, and when that's all handled, they'll get Gretchen back into tiptop shape." Well, what they'd said was they thought it was totaled, but they wanted to try everything possible before giving up. "Another tract was left in the cab of your truck. Same as last time."

"When did this happen?" Pippa asked.

"The night of the bond hearing. When they held him over until the results of the mental health screen."

"When I was in the hospital still. Before you came down last week." If her brows rose any higher, he'd be worried.

"Yes. I know I should have told you. But we all decided it was best for you to focus all your energy on healing. There was nothing to be done that wasn't already being done, and you were stuck here for another ten days."

"*We all*?" Pippa looked around the room, noting guilty faces, including Hamish's.

Xander said, "When I came to see you last week, I didn't want to bring any negativity with me. I had thirty-two hours with you, and I wasn't going to waste it on making you even more upset. You can be mad at me for that. It was my call to wait."

"You all knew, and no one said anything. To me. About something that happened to me. Because *you* made a call. Oh. Okay then." Pippa blew out a breath, put her blanket aside, and left the room.

"Let her be," Rebecca said when he and Hamish both

made to go after her. "She'll get over you not telling her when it happened. It was the right decision. It just came after a day that's been a lot already. Give her a few minutes to get herself together so she can see it wasn't a lie, just a delay."

Hadn't she told him early on how being lied to was a button of hers? He hadn't wanted to lie, damn it. He couldn't bear to put more things on her shoulders when she was barely getting through. And yes, selfishly, he'd wanted some time with her when he didn't have to bring her yet more upset.

Jessi added, "She's sick of falling apart in front of people. She feels like she's brought all this drama into your lives, and she's feeling down about that."

"Which is bullshit, and we'll address that. Fill me in, then," Xander urged.

Rebecca told him, "First thing this morning, the prosecutor called and asked to meet with Pippa. I was on the way here from the airport, so couldn't get there in time to attend. When she arrived there with Hamish and her attorney, they were told our parents are in town. I stopped to pick Jessi up, and while they were in the meeting, we waited in a corner of the public lobby area. That's when our mother called and left a voicemail for me saying she wanted to speak to Pippa. She can blow a goat."

Hamish laughed, putting a hand on Xander's thigh and squeezing.

"I'm glad to be here with you both," Xander said as he kissed the top of Hamish's head.

"We wanted to wait until you arrived, so you could attend

as well, but they couldn't move it." Hamish sucked in a breath, as if he were getting ready to jump into water. "They're going to charge him with felony assault with a deadly weapon as part of a plea deal. Four years. Ten thousand dollar fine. He has to do anger management and get therapy for his whatever it was they called it in the capacity hearing. Essentially his obsession with Pippa and her soul. And there's a drug treatment mandate too. He was high on crystal meth the night he attacked her. Looks like it might have been an issue for some time. The family has hired some attorney the prosecutor says is pretty good. And very bloodthirsty."

Xander blinked a few times, trying to wrap his head around it all. "He tried to kill her. Why isn't this an attempted murder charge?"

"They don't think they can prove premeditation," Hamish said.

"Why give him a deal? They know what he did. There's video evidence. There are eyewitnesses."

"Four years is pretty much what they'd get in a trial anyway. A plea would save them the time and money. And, my family is floating stories to damage my reputation. The threat is if we push for a trial, those little tidbits will begin to go public," Pippa said, sounding tired as she came back into the room. "Sorry about that," she said to everyone but Xander and Hamish. "I just had to be by myself for a little while."

"Don't worry," Erin said. "Sit down, sweetie."

Addie jumped up to refill Pippa's water as she got settled in her little corner of the couch. She was pissed. It was in the lines next to her mouth. Xander felt bad to have made her so upset, but they'd work it out because he was always going to protect her when he had the option.

"What stories?" Xander asked.

"The worst kind of stories," Hamish said.

"The ones that insinuate maybe I asked for what came for me. After all, my awful lifestyle is all over the media, and Timothy is such a good boy, and he was so worried for my soul. But there I am. Slutty McSlutbag, and he was driven to it by my moral failures. Even if he did wrong, I made him do it. He gets to be earnest and wayward. I'm a hedonist who was kicked out for being a liar and a danger to my younger siblings. They even insinuate I'm the reason he started using crystal meth. To cope with the grief of his baby sister's depravity."

The bitterness in her voice broke his heart.

"So. If it goes to trial, even if they can't admit that salacious stuff into evidence, they flood the internet with these stories and people will see, and all it takes is one person to be swayed and I'll have testified and gone through all that for what? I can't, so don't ask me to."

Xander turned so he faced her better. "I would never ask you to. Neither of us would."

"This is what I told her more than once," Hamish agreed.

"She's right. Four years is the max usually and what he'd likely get at trial." Todd shrugged. "I don't like him thinking he's getting off easy by taking the prosecutor's offer. But this way we know for sure he'll do time. And Pippa won't have to go through the ordeal of a trial. And it *will* be an ordeal. This case has so many elements that fascinate people, and their attorney—we did some research—would definitely tear Pippa apart. These little media stories they're offering around have started on their attorney's go-ahead, we're being told. Pippa doesn't want to go through the spectacle of a trial. In her place, I'd feel the same."

His pop looked at Pippa and smiled. Her bottom lip wobbled, but she held it together.

"I want to make a statement. Not just in a letter. I want to say it to his face and in front of the judge."

CHAPTER
THIRTY-ONE

Pippa dumped her silverware into the gray tub and the little bowl from her tapioca pudding into a similar receptacle. They'd arrived at the courthouse early and suggested she eat. She wasn't hungry, but Hamish had managed to tempt her sweet tooth. For courthouse cafeteria tapioca pudding, it had been surprisingly good. Plus, it had taken up some time she hadn't spent obsessing about what she'd say.

Otherwise, she felt like she was empty inside. Like one of the cornhusk dolls they made to be sold at various fairs in the county. Brittle.

While her back was still to the room, she fought back tears and tried to pull herself together. If Xander or Hamish noted even more upset, they'd spring into action, and there wasn't a darned thing they could do to fix this. And heaven help her, she simply couldn't face crying in front of anyone else. Not right then.

"Epiphany."

Surprised to hear the familiar voice, Pippa jumped,

turning to see her eldest sister, Mercy, standing in an alcove where the water fountains were located.

Xander was on her in three breaths. "What's wrong?"

"I was startled, that's all. Over there by the water fountain? That's my sister, Mercy. Don't ask me right now. I'll tell you when I'm done," she said to Xander. *Told* him, because he'd take over otherwise.

He wanted to ask her. She could see it all over him. Instead, he scratched his chin and said, "If she even looks at you wrong, I'm coming over there. I'm going to stand right here pretending to look at pudding cups to keep an eye on you. I'll signal if any of your other family members comes around."

"Thank you." She meant it. She knew he wanted to keep her inside the apartment and bring the world to her where she'd be safest. Each time they left—she'd returned to work the week before after being out a month—he had to let go a little, and for a control freak like him, it was hard.

Which was why he'd insisted she be driven by him or Hamish. And why she agreed. Well, that and it was still a little difficult even as her chest and arm continued to heal. Gretchen had been declared a total loss by the insurance company. And Asa, who, if anyone had been able to resurrect her, it would have been her boss. The frame had been bent severely in three different places, and the engine had been beaten by a hammer and destroyed so badly it would have had to be replaced. Her father and uncle, along with some of her brothers and oldest male cousins, ran a windshield replacement business. They dealt with cars that had been in accidents all the time. They knew just where to damage that couldn't be fixed. And that's what they'd done.

She was going to have to start over with a new vehicle she was determined to christen Gretchen 2.0. In the meantime, she needed a replacement that would get her around. She was toying with using a teeny bit of guilt to wheedle them into letting her use one of their restomods—a classic car or truck they'd restored but also added modern safety and convenience to. The Caddy was too long to manage in the parking garage of their building; backing out would take a 14-point turn. But there was a '69 Camaro she'd helped on sitting in the showroom. Maybe…

Feeling tears threaten again, Pippa turned all her attention on a sister she didn't know if she should hug or punch.

Mercy looked around nervously. The memory of that particular fear pushed the urge to punch away. That terror and violence had put Pippa in the hospital, but at the end of the day, she went home to men who'd never use fear as a tool to manipulate her and gain her compliance. Mercy didn't have that.

"They're going to start looking for me soon," Mercy said in a rush. "Edgar Garrett's wife died ten months ago. Father promised him a new wife. Offered him Prosperity, but Edgar wants *you*. Same as he did before." Prosperity was only sixteen! She'd been a toddler when Pippa left.

"Timothy is still close with Edgar's oldest boy and Cyrus?" It was beginning to make a sick sort of sense. Cyrus was Mercy's husband. And more importantly, Edgar's nephew.

Mercy nodded as she continued to scan the room, looking for threats. "Yes. For years Father and Timothy have been obsessed with bringing you back. Making you a symbol of their faith and strength in the group. Timothy said you'd be upset at first, but after a while, you'd remember yourself. Then they'd marry you off. Edgar would get you pregnant right away, and father's position within the group would rise and Timothy's with his. Timothy and Cyrus travel up the coast, across to Montana and south again back to Arizona at least once every few months for Blue Sky. They've been watching your job for years. Just because Timothy is in jail—where I hope he rots—doesn't mean they're done with you. Cyrus is convinced you owe us now because they've lost Timothy. They have your address at your apartment, and they know you have a doctor's appointment in Seattle in four days. They have the date and time."

Years? "How do they know about my medical appointments?" The apartment thing wouldn't be hard to figure out. Erin lived there for many years and the building was in a few of those celebrity home maps.

Pippa reminded herself the building was secure. There was a security checkpoint in the lobby. All guests had to be cleared up from there by a resident. The garage was locked and monitored twenty-four hours a day with a fully staffed security post. And, though she wasn't going to say it out loud, their floor was ultra-high security, only accessible by an additional keycard and code.

Her medical stuff, though? *Not* public knowledge.

"There's a reporter friend of Timothy and Cyrus." Mercy's expression soured. "Something wrong with that man. He always makes Cyrus worse. He's related to someone you work with. Trevor. He's been in contact with Father and the group directly recently, Cyrus said. They're letting him think he can marry you. They'll let him join the group, but you'd be given to Edgar and they don't think he'll say boo." Marcy shuddered. "I have to go. I've been gone too long. I'll say I've got morning sickness."

Trevor? What the heck? Also sadness twisted in Pippa's gut knowing each baby Mercy had was another obstacle to getting out.

She only had seconds left with Mercy. "Why did you tell me all this? I mean, thank you. But why?"

"You may be a sinner, but so are the rest of us. And you're still my sister. Timothy has hurt enough people. He had no right." Mercy's lips softened. "I prayed for you when we learned what he'd done. I'm glad you're recovered. I couldn't sit by and not warn you. Watch out for Cyrus. He's using drugs too." Mercy paused and then blurted, "He was in Seattle six weeks ago."

With a quick look around, Mercy darted off and into the nearby restroom.

Xander was at Pippa's side, guiding her back to the table where it seemed half the world sat. Xander's parents, Rennie, Hamish's parents, Jessi, Mick, Adam, Harlow and Miles, Rebecca and Vivi. Esther had demanded to come, but Pippa and Rebecca continued to remain united, telling their sister to stay home with her baby and husband. A courthouse was no place for Daniella, and they'd be in Fairbanks shortly anyway for Hamish's show and a visit. Rebecca and Vivi were going to come along as well, which meant Pippa would have to brawl for all the baby time she could steal. That made her smile.

"I don't want to talk about it here. I can't risk being overheard. But there's some stuff I need to share," she told Xander quietly.

He sent Hamish, who'd been speaking to his mother, a tip of the chin toward the front of the building before wrapping an arm around her shoulders and guiding her from the room. When Hamish reached them, they went outside, heading across the street to a parking lot that was currently empty of anything but vehicles.

Hamish gave her a look and took her by the elbow down half a block to a spot under shade cast by the trees lining the lot.

"Thank you," she said and kissed him.

"Can't have you getting a sunburn," he murmured.

Then she told them about Edgar's wife dying and explained about the twelve-month mourning period that was about to end. Of Blue Skies, one of the vehicle salvage businesses the group operated, and of her brother-in-law, Cyrus, being in Seattle around the time Gretchen was totaled.

While they were still staring at her, dumbfounded, she revealed the rest about Trevor.

"Trevor from accounting, Trevor?" Xander asked, and his tone sent a shiver up her spine and not in the holy-cow-he's-so-gorgeous way. He was violently angry, though not at her.

She shrugged her un-injured shoulder. "I'm as confused as you are. Our address is one thing. That's public enough. But." She sucked in a breath, and there was a tiny twinge in her chest she was determined to ignore. "Twisted Steel has an internal calendar. It's where my billable hours are logged, so accounting can invoice on the final project. And so, when the partners are deciding to take on a new build, they can see which of us will be available. Anyway, what I mean is that it's not something just anyone can see. It's Duke, Mick, Asa,

Carmella because she's the office manager, and Trevor. I only added that appointment three days ago, so he must have gotten in contact with them right after. Even after I got stabbed, he kept helping them. They're making him think he can marry me and join the group. Like this is the fifteenth century. I'm not even that great. Jiminy Cricket! I don't fold laundry in time, so it's always wrinkled."

"I've been meaning to bring that up. That and the fact you can't wing your liner is a concern," Xander teased as he hugged her gently. Even six weeks after the attack both men treated her as if she were made of cotton candy. Which was, to steal a phrase from Hamish, bloody annoying. Hamish hadn't bitten her once! She had to seduce them into sex because they'd been so worried about hurting her, and it was so gentle and hesitant that even her orgasm was frustrating.

She was sick and tired of the entire situation as it was, but the Trevor news on top of that had really knocked her off her stride. A stride she had worked really hard to achieve as she'd recovered.

Hamish smoothed a hand over her hair. "We need to let Mick know. They have to cut off Trevor's access to all that stuff. They can deal with his employment after, but he's a danger to you where he's at right now. That little fucker. I bet he's why the people who destroyed Gretchen knew where to cut into the fence to keep from setting off the alarm. And they certainly knew exactly where to push that camera, so it wasn't pointed on your vehicle."

"Surely we have to tell the prosecutor all this," Xander said.

"What for?" Pippa asked. "I'm trying my best not to be bitter and to understand that sometimes even when something isn't exactly what you want, it's fine. So, he's going to do his four years, and I don't have to go through a trial. It's acceptable because the range of options included this as the best one."

Xander opened his mouth, but she shook her head. "Not done. My sister is *never* going to testify. Maybe if they subpoenaed her? Even then, she's going to claim she can't remember anything. She lives in that world still. Her husband is *mean*. He's Timothy's best friend, so you know the kind of person that makes him. You saw what he did to my truck? He's hurt *her* before with that level of violence. Our parents sent her back home to be *a better wife, so he won't need to hit you.* She risked a lot to tell me what she did. And she's pregnant again. I can't endanger her more. And it won't make a bit of difference anyway. Not to Timothy's case. So what if some widower wants to marry me? That's not illegal. And the guy who hared off on his own to kidnap or kill me is already going to jail. They'll pretend to be concerned while bringing up my personal life. In the end, it exposes Mercy to possible violence, and it changes nothing."

"I hate that you're this jaded." Xander briefly caressed her cheek and throat before he remembered himself and stood back.

"Me too. But what else is there? Naïve? I've been that before and it didn't protect me. It infantilized me and kept me in place. It took years of therapy and being away from the group to recover. No thanks to naïve. What I'm going to be right now is pleased I have concrete answers. It's been the group all along. We know why this all started up again around Halloween. We know why things escalated. It's a *relief* to know." The not understanding what was happening and why was the worst part. "This has been the group." Not crazed fans. Thank goodness.

"When we return to Seattle, I want you to speak to your attorney about getting protection orders based on this information. We know how much good a piece of paper did when your brother decided to ignore it," Xander added quickly, "but it's just another thing to protect yourself with."

"And to keep a paper trail of what is happening. It's harder to impeach my character when I keep receipts of what they do," Pippa agreed.

The portion of the proceedings where a victim impact statement was made was open to the public, so Xander, Hamish, and what felt like half the population of a large high school came in, settling on the long benches behind the counsel tables and facing the raised dais where the judge resided.

Rebecca sat, hand in hand with Vivi, as she stared right back at her father, who'd attempted to cow them with a glare.

Pippa tucked all her upset deep inside as they pointed her to the chair next to the bench. The witness box, Rebecca had called it when she was going over what Pippa could expect.

She'd be upset about what she'd learned from Mercy later. At that moment, she needed to be brave. So she looked Timothy in the face after reassuring herself the bailiff standing a few feet away would tackle him if he moved from his place at the defense table, and began to speak.

"My name is Epiphany Hall, and six weeks ago, my

oldest brother, Timothy Hall, attacked me as I was leaving a concert venue." She described the attack, the way he'd shoved her so hard against that low iron gate that one of the finials had left a bruise deep enough one of her kidneys had been affected. Of the infection she'd developed a few weeks after the surgery that she had only just gotten over before starting back to work. A schedule now curtailed at four days a week and five-hour slots because her stamina had been so impacted. Her doctor did clear her to start light exercise the following month, and Pippa had been assured that her endurance should return after six months or so.

So much of her life was packed into the next six months, it seemed unimaginable she'd have to wait until after Miles's and Harlow's wedding to start feeling like her old self again.

"Our household growing up was not a gentle one," she said, and the truth of it rang through that courtroom.

Her mother made a sound of despair, and her father began to speak. The judge sent him a look, her gavel raised, just waiting for him to interrupt. Timothy had broken her gaze, looking down at the hands he kept clasped in his lap.

"Continue, Ms. Hall," the judge said as a muscle on Timothy's jaw tightened. Trying to hold back public displays of temper.

"Timothy used to run at the littlest siblings, windmilling his arms. I know many big brothers do something similar. But Timothy balled his hands into fists, and he aimed for heads and faces of four- and five-year-olds. Even as he grew older, his victims stayed young and defenseless. Enough that my parents must have heard dozens and dozens of excuses for why bruises popped up. A shepherd's rod is used to guide the sheep, not hit the sheep in the head with a fist," Pippa said tartly. "That's what I wish I'd have said those years ago when I was told spare the rod, spoil the child. It's an exhortation to guide and discipline. It is not *anyone's* job to break bones, lock children in closets and basements where they'd be confined, on their knees and left in the dark for hours or days."

"Sir, you will be quiet, or I will have you removed from my courtroom. This is not your time to speak," the judge admonished Pippa's father when he started to interrupt.

Pippa shook herself from all those memories because she wasn't going to let her father steal these precious few minutes she had to address the court.

"I was going to beg the legal system to make sure Timothy served every single day and got *a lot* of therapy to deal with his violence. But the last time I begged was when I begged my brother to stop hitting me. I will not beg again. I *demand* this man does every single day of his sentence, which is far too light for what he did to me. *He should be in prison for life for trying to kill me.* I accept this proposed plea because Timothy was raised in that same environment. All my siblings and I are who we are because of that. He needs to understand when he gets out that it is unacceptable to act with his fists when things don't go the way he wants. Otherwise, he'll do this again, and as I've been his target, multiple times, I don't want that."

Xander swallowed back a lump of emotion. He and Hamish clutched hands so tight it probably hurt. But it kept him from stalking over, plucking Pippa's father to his feet and ramming his face through a wall.

"I've had to relearn how to hold a wrench, so my muscles don't ache and shake severely. The least he should do is serve his sentence. He needs help and punishment because I shouldn't have to look over my shoulder for the rest of my life waiting for him to jump out of the dark to try to kill again. It's not too much to demand. He's got a record of this. Hold him accountable."

Her brother curled his lip, but she didn't show one bit of the fear Xander knew she felt.

"Thank you, Ms. Hall. I am very sorry for the pain and suffering caused to you by Mr. Hall's actions, and it is my judgment that the plea be accepted by the court with Timothy Hall remanded for immediate transfer to state custody to begin his sentence."

Pippa returned to where the rest of them sat. He and Hamish sat to either side, protective. Watchful.

Timothy's attorney said, "Your honor, if Mr. Hall can be allowed to return to Arizona to get his affairs in order before he begins his sentence, that would be most helpful. He's got a wife and small children to provide for in his absence."

The prosecutor said, "We object to that. When he was first arrested after his assault on Ms. Hall, Timothy Hall was under the influence of crystal methamphetamine. During the mental capacity process, it was discovered he had been habitually using this drug for nearly two years. Not only is he a flight risk, he's at risk to begin using again, which would render him even less reliable to show up and turn himself in to begin his sentence. He has had plenty of opportunity until today to handle his business and personal affairs, as one of the dilatory tactics used by opposing counsel was to ask the court to give him time to do that very thing."

"Sustained. The court agrees with those points. Say your goodbyes, Mr. Hall. Ms. Hall," the judge said to Pippa. "The court appreciates the courage it took to stand up and speak about what you've endured. I'm relieved you're recovering from your attack and hope you continue to do so until you're even stronger than your old self. Somehow, I don't doubt you'll manage it."

Pippa went off to take a shower once they'd returned to their hotel. They made plans with everyone else to meet up in three hours to drive over for a meal together at Richie Martin's house. Harlow's dad wanted to offer a place they could all spend time in privacy while also getting to know each other better.

For the time being, it was just the three of them, something they all needed after the emotion of that day.

Xander sat across from him, stretched out on the chaise in the living room of their hotel suite. "We've talked about having one of us marry Pippa. Yes, to keep her safer against her family, but also because I believe, *I feel*, our relationship has deepened to this point. But I wanted to talk with you about who will marry her and why. And to make it clear that I love you, Hamish. We started out liking one another and having great sexual chemistry. But that's a shadow of how I feel for you now. If we could all three marry, I'd do that in a flash. These people want to try to control her. If she's married, regardless of how fair it is, they couldn't get between her and us. We'd have more leverage, even more than with power of attorney. Marriage comes with cultural weight that protects her more too."

Hamish drank his tea as he gathered himself, definitely pleased to hear that official declaration of love from Xander and finding himself in agreement about marriage. "My thoughts have turned in a similar direction. And today as we learned about this ridiculous idea of marrying her off to someone in the group, and I can't stop hearing it." He sucked in a breath. "Turns out, I love you too, Xander. I never expected this. You. Pippa. You and Pippa. But I treasure it. Let's work this through, then."

Pippa came out of the bedroom just a few minutes later after they'd talked more in depth and reached a decision. She gave them both a suspicious look. "What are you up to?"

"We were just talking about marriage," Hamish said. He agreed that it should be Xander who married her officially. So now they had to talk her into it and make sure she understood it wasn't just because they wanted to protect her from the group.

Her suspicion faded with a big smile. "I'm not going to lie, I'm so looking forward to going over there tonight. Harlow said there were pictures from her last fitting for her dress. I can't wait to see them."

"And Hamish and I were telling one another that we love each other," Xander said.

Pippa's features warmed as her smile changed, full of emotion as her bottom lip wobbled slightly. "Well, as obvious as that is, I love it anyway."

"But the marriage talk wasn't about Harlow and Miles," Hamish said.

"Pippa, will you marry me?" Xander asked.

At first her eyes lit with pleasure, and then distrust chased it away. "To protect me from the group? Like a duty?"

"It would certainly give us legal protection when it comes to anyone from the outside of our relationship, yes," Hamish agreed. "But that's not *why*. It's just a benefit."

"We love you. We all love one another. Which is special. And wonderful. Hamish and I want to protect that, and we know you do too. And when we're married, it'll help keep our family safe. That's what you, me, and Hamish are. A family. That'll continue. We build a life, the three of us, and each layer we can add to make ourselves and our relationship stronger, we're better off."

Pippa wrung her hands a moment. "But then I have to choose one of you over the other. You two could get married instead."

Xander pulled a ring box from the table where he'd put it after he'd shown it to Hamish earlier. "Since Valentine's Day, Hamish and I have been talking about marriage in some way or other." He opened the box and showed Pippa. "The center stone belonged to my great-grandmother. My grandmother had been saving it for when I got married. And the two stones sitting to either side are from Addie. The band is platinum from a piece of jewelry my mother had. Every bit of the ring is full of love and family. From Hamish and me too. A reminder that just because a license will say you and I are married legally, we're all married. We'll make sure whichever one of us isn't married has us both as power of attorney. Do all we can to protect our community of three. Lucky for us, we know some people who've made it work."

Hamish told her, "It isn't choosing Xander over me.

His family is, frankly, more powerful than mine. It's an advantage—" he avoided the word protection, "—I can't meet. Yes, my family has already taken you as one of their own. But I come with some potential problems if someone ever wanted to try to hurt you with my past. Including a birth mother who pops up now and again to cause mayhem. If she were to find out you and I got married, she'd rise from the deep like the kraken. She'd make it a point to track your family in Arizona down because she finds pleasure in making other people unhappy. She'll know I love you, which puts you at risk, but I can't help it now, can I? It's best for us all that we keep her out of our lives as much as we can." She would see Pippa's softness as weakness and as way to manipulate her or Hamish. If Pippa was married to Xander, she'd be a further step away from any business Carol Wilson tried to start.

Xander said, "My grandmother gave me another stone that belonged to her mother." He pulled something else out and passed it Hamish's way.

Hamish had agreed Xander was the best person to marry Pippa. But seeing the platinum band with an inset sapphire inside the ring box he'd just been handed made everything perfect.

"When I was having Pippa's ring made, I had one made for you too."

Grinning, Xander slid the ring on Hamish's finger before leaning in for a kiss.

"It's beautiful," Pippa said as she looked it over closely. "But you don't have one, Xander. Wait." She got up and left the room, returning in just a minute or two.

"We can go ring shopping. I know a few places," Hamish said as he admired his hand.

Xander held her ring out. "Will you marry me? But really in truth be married to *us*? I love you so much I'm stupid with it," Xander said.

"Ditto," Hamish said.

"I didn't think you were going to ask all official and everything." Pippa blinked back tears, but her smile told them her tears were happy ones for a change. "I'm so glad you did. Yes." She held out her hand, and Xander slid the ring on her finger before he kissed her long and slow.

It was her turn to pull out a velvet bag. "It's not as fancy as what you've done for me." She blushed furiously as she brought out a similar one but in another color. After handing one to each man, she said, "King's sister makes jewelry. She lives out in the high desert, but she made a trip all the way here to bring these to me. I was going to give them to you for Christmas. But this is better. This is meant to be."

Hamish stared at the gold band in his palm. The design curled around it looked like runes, but on closer inspection, they were trinity knots. In the center was a thistle flower.

Xander hadn't expected this.

He marveled at the triquetras along the band leading to the flower in the center.

She took the ring from him. "Will you marry me, Alexander?"

"Absolutely. All day every day." He held his hand out, and she slid the ring home.

"The flower on your ring is a forget-me-not. A symbol of

my love, fidelity, and devotion. The triple knot, three independent, unique things all connected to make one whole. While still remaining ourselves."

Hamish handed her his ring.

"Will you marry me, Hamish? When I said yes to Xander, I was also saying yes to all three of us being married. We don't need a paper to honor that as long as you understand —and feel—like an equal in our family."

"Love, until the three of us got together, I'd never allowed myself to consider marrying. I figured I'd be an aging rocker living the single life, drinking at ten in the morning type of guy. Yes, I'll marry you."

"Your ring has a thistle in the center. Prickly on the outside but soft and downy on the inside. Strong enough to resist everything life has thrown your way. I see you, Hamish. All of you to your very soul. I love you."

When they broke the kiss on Pippa's happy sigh, Hamish said, "Great. Now let's get moving. We have some shopping to do before we go to dinner. Even though we have rings, our love needs a dress, and we need suits. I'll tell everyone we'll meet them there. I know several places near Harlow's dad's house."

CHAPTER
THIRTY-THREE

They got up at four thirty the next morning.

"So many nights of my life I was just getting home at this time, and now, here I am starting something instead of ending it," Hamish said as he came into the bedroom where she was applying makeup. "Put that aside for the moment. I've got coffee and some pastries."

"You're the best," she said, and he danced her into the main room where Xander was stirring some sort of flavored sugar syrup into his cold brew.

She leaned down to kiss the top of his head, but he turned quick and caught her lips with a smile.

"There's a chocolate croissant for you," Hamish said, and while she was diverted by all those delicious, buttery layers and chocolate, he presented a pale-yellow box with a flourish.

"For me?" Pippa asked as she nudged the lid open and then lifted a crown of forget-me-nots and sunflowers from it.

"Because Xander will have one of your hands and I'll have the other, you can wear your bouquet as a crown like the queen you are. These flowers are a symbol of unity, of the three of us blooming together." He grabbed Xander's boutonniere and passed it over. "I have one too."

She blinked hard, looking up at the ceiling while fanning her face. "How did you manage this on such short notice?"

"You have your magic," Hamish said, "I have mine. When I saw the design on Xander's ring, I got the idea."

"I do agree you're magic." Pippa smiled at him.

"How do you always know?" he asked softly.

"Know what?"

He said, "Just exactly how to respond to something to make me feel like I'm ten feet tall."

She turned toward him, taking both his hands. "I love you, Hamish. You make me happy. It's never hard to show you that. You're my hero. You love me and see me for who I am, flaws and all, and you still make me feel beautiful and cared for. And? You saved my life. You and Xander risked your own lives to save me. How does that *not* make you ten feet tall to me?"

"You're getting her all sweet, and that's going to make me cry," Xander grumbled at Hamish. While wearing a grin.

"You're not nervous?" Pippa asked Xander as she sat at the table, sipping her coffee and looking at the flower crown.

"I'm about to get everything I've ever wanted," Xander told her. "What's to be nervous about? I'm the luckiest guy in the world to have you two."

Pippa pointed at him with her croissant. "I finished my eye makeup. Don't make *me* cry."

They ate and finished dressing, and then they met with a hastily gathered group of friends and family—with the promise to everyone else who couldn't arrange to get there on such short notice, they'd hold a proper party later in the year after Miles and Harlow's wedding—in the hotel lobby and boarded a commuter van that took them to the beach.

She wore a deep-blue dress that hugged her torso but flared out to mid-calf and swirled around her legs as she walked. Barefoot. Flowers in her hair. She was like a being from a fairy tale. Magic and light danced over her as the sun finished rising and turned everything a warm honey gold.

The officiant was Sam Flanigan's wife, Cat. She stood with the ocean at her back. Flowers, an explosion of forget-me-nots and sunflowers, had been set up, creating a makeshift altar. But when they reached Cat, Hamish tried to let go to step slightly to the side. Pippa shook her head, tugging him back to where he'd been.

She told him, "This is our marriage. *Yours too.* I asked Cat if we could bring you into the ceremony, making sure it was legal and stuff for me and Xander. We want you here, with us, as we do this."

"We know you would happily stand next to us as we said our vows. That you're willing to let me be the one who gets the legal position of spouse when you love her just as much as I do?" Xander leaned over and brushed a kiss over Hamish's mouth. "Means everything. I love you. Marry us today?"

"Stand with us and make the same vows." Pippa looked up at him, and love seemed to overflow from every single part of himself. There'd never been a substance he'd used to bring *this.*

He'd been so certain he'd be the one everyone else had to take the extra weight for.

"I never thought I'd be enough on my own," Hamish told

them. "At first having three people meant the pressure wasn't so overwhelming. Which is ironic, because it was being in a threesome that enabled me to understand I'm absolutely enough. Let's do this." Hamish gave them both a quick kiss, and they turned toward the officiant.

Cat smiled at them. "You ready to get married today?"

Hamish examined the rings on his left hand. One, like Pippa's, created with stones and metals given to them by the mothers in their lives. Handed down from grandmothers and great grandmothers. Given to him by his man, to bring them all together. The other, given to him by his woman, covered in symbols that celebrated their relationship and his place within it. Like the flowers. Like having Hamish be included in the ceremony. A grand gesture of love from each, done without the knowledge of the others, presented as a surprise. Like the ingredients of a magic spell.

The energy of it made Hamish's poet's heart sing. It made every bit of difference to the day. Hamish didn't feel closed out, even though the paperwork only had Pippa's and Xander's names on it. Because his name was on the symbolic paperwork that bound the three of them together. By the heart, where it counted most.

They'd left the beach and ended up at a nearby restaurant that showed them to a private dining room where breakfast had been laid out.

Pippa had been worried Harlow and Miles would feel bad, or upstaged somehow, but Xander had coaxed her around, saying Miles and Harlow were guests at breakfast, pleased to share their excitement. He'd added that they had to eat anyway, and if she were in their shoes, she wouldn't be upset at all.

The room hummed with conversation in happy tones. The vibe was fantastic, and the eggs alongside a bagel and pillowy, satiny lox had been an excellent way to celebrate their wedding.

Ben took the chair next to Hamish. "Beautiful morning, right?"

Hamish looked across the room to where Pippa stood with Rebecca, her big sister's arm linked through hers. They smiled over at Addie, who was showing them something on her phone. Probably a picture she'd unearthed of Hamish when he was younger.

"The best," Hamish agreed.

"You're my son-in-law now, so I hope you won't take offense at a fatherly conversation," Ben said.

"Are you going to ask what my intentions are?" Hamish teased and then sobered a little. "I always welcome input from people who I can learn from." He was undoubtedly pleased by being thought of as a son-in-law by Ben and Todd. Not just as Xander's fathers, but as men who managed to build a family in the same type of unconventional way Hamish, Pippa, and Xander wanted to.

"If we hadn't already seen what your intentions were toward our son and Pippa, we wouldn't be having a happy conversation." Ben lifted a shoulder briefly. "People *say* all sorts of things. Sometimes they're true. Sometimes they're only true for a short period of time after they get said. I prefer to watch what people do."

Hamish tended to agree. Words were easy. Making them sound good was easy. Hell, it was his job! What someone did when everyone wasn't looking or when there wasn't a crisis? That's what told you who they really were.

Ben flicked a fingertip against Hamish's boutonniere. "I bring this up because even though it was a *legal* marriage of two people, today absolutely felt like a marriage of three. The little touches each of you added to be mindful of that fact make me so proud of you. As a father, you hope your kids make good choices. You want them to find the depth of love and security that will serve them the whole of their lives. Of course, we love Pippa. But part of why we love her is how clear it is to us that she loves you. And is committed to you and your happiness. Xander... He's been so used to being loved and adored the whole of his life, you know? It's why he's such a strong individual. Confident. Overbearing and bossy and very grumpy when things don't go the way he thinks they should."

Hamish laughed because all those things were true. And all those things made up a person he loved deeply.

"He grew up in a family where he was adored, definitely. But he grew up in a family with a sibling who was a ghost. A memory. A series of photographs he would look at with Erin. He also grew up in a family torn to shreds by grief. Not just of the loss of his sister, but the loss of the mom Erin was before Adele's passing. He and his mom are super close. Xander watched her deal with anxiety attacks about going outside. Or sudden loud noises. Our life has been defined by always thinking of security so the woman we love—his mom —can feel safe.

"I was admittedly concerned as this stalking situation with Pippa continued to develop. As the interactions got more and more severe, he wanted to take over."

Hamish didn't stop his scoff. "He *did* take over. Many times. There were a lot of heated discussions. He took it hard that she'd been attacked so many times. That she couldn't do all the things she liked doing with the same freedom as before. He knows what's important to her, and he wants to give it to her."

"Freedom," Ben said.

Hamish nodded. "It is what it is. That's a saying I normally think is a cop out. But there are instances where it's true. We're working together and with you all to create a security plan where she's as safe as we can make her. But no matter what we do, given the options we have right now, we can't make it totally foolproof."

Ben nodded. "Her family is a wild card. Timothy may be going away for four years, but her truck was destroyed while he was in custody. Like the sister said, others are involved including Cyrus and his father who wants to order Pippa for a wife like she's in a catalog. As for how Trevor is connected? I've got some information on that. And, I think, perhaps a way to keep her family out of your lives for good."

CHAPTER
THIRTY-FOUR

Pippa loved their friends and family, but she was so glad when they all finally left the hotel suite and it was just her, Xander, and Hamish for the first time since they'd left that morning.

"How are you feeling, husband?" Pippa asked Xander as she climbed into his lap.

"Turns out, your wedding day is a pretty fun time. But I was about five minutes away from bodily throwing everyone out so we could be alone. And how you are, wife?" Xander kissed her, and when he settled back against the couch, she snuggled into his body, the heat of him always a comfort.

"I'm tired but in a good way." Not that she'd done anything taxing. After a very illuminating meeting with Ben and Todd, who'd filled in some of the blanks they'd been struggling with, the family had spent the rest of the afternoon out by the pool at Harlow's dad's house. There'd been a cookout and she'd been able to relax and just…be.

The whole day had been a conscious choice to turn her back on the drama and fear of yesterday and embrace her future. Anything else would have been capitulating to the group. They'd have their moment the following morning before they left for the airport, but until then, Pippa wanted to keep that night about the three of them. Celebrating now that they were finally alone.

"You should go to bed. You've had a really long few days," Xander said with a kiss to the top of her head.

She sat up to look him in the face. "What the heck?"

He cocked his head, and his hair fell down over his eyes, so she pushed it away. "What do you mean?"

"I have been throwing myself at you and Hamish for weeks. Before the attack, we had sex daily. You sprang on me every time I'd come into view. Don't you want me anymore?"

"I want you all day. Every day." He took her hand and kissed her fingertips. "It takes all my control not to leap on you every time you come into view. But you're recovering from being stabbed. I'm not an animal. I can wait. There are decades of jumping and leaping on you at any and all times ahead of us once your health has turned the corner."

"I asked the doctors, and I asked the surgeon, and they all said we could have sex. Weeks ago, we got the all-clear. *Weeks*. There's only so much masturbation I can handle, and it's really not a substitute for you two anyway."

"Sounds like this is an interesting conversation," Hamish said as he squeezed in next to Xander and took her legs, pulling them into his lap. "Please, do elaborate more about masturbation."

"I was asking if I'd suddenly turned into some sort of homunculus since the two of you used to be all over me, and now I have to shake my tits at you while yelling your names to get your attention."

Hamish laughed but noted Xander wasn't amused. "You can't be serious?"

"I've just finished reminding our rather sexy wife that she's recovering from a stab wound and we're letting her heal instead of setting on her like rabid beasts," Xander said dryly.

"And *I* was reminding him that my doctors said it was fine weeks ago. I miss you both." She pouted a little, feeling rather put out by the whole thing.

"We had sex three days ago. I remember it because I was there. Am I so forgettable?" Hamish teased her.

"You didn't bite me. Not a single time. Xander didn't cuff my throat or wrists. You were so gentle. Even the orgasm was gentle. Ugh. I'm not glass. I don't want that. I want all of you, or it feels different when I don't have it."

Xander fought a grin and finally gave over to it. "Not that!" He stole a kiss. "I'm not confident enough in your physical state to bind you. I don't want you twisting and pulling something. Once I get started with you, it's very hard to rein in my baser instincts."

She lost her consternation and rolled her eyes with a snicker.

Hamish encircled one of her ankles in his hand. "Sex hurt isn't the same as what it would do to reinjure you. It's not that we don't want you. It's the opposite. We want you constantly. We're greedy for you."

"However," Xander said, his hand coming to rest on her stomach, his palm hot against the slice of skin between her T-shirt and leggings, "we can't have a *gentle* orgasm on our record. Like a big red zero."

Pippa held her breath.

"What if it got out and the other wives heard of such a travesty?" Hamish said in a slow drawl.

"We certainly can't have her unsatisfied," Xander purred, and it sent gooseflesh racing over her.

She gulped, nodding. "You really can't. We didn't say those exact words in our wedding vows, but they were there, between the lines, so to speak."

"Mmm. Our wife needs taking care of at home." Hamish's hold left her ankle and moved slowly—tortuously slowly—upward, pausing at her knee with one fingertip sliding back and forth at the back.

When they teamed up like this against her—or more aptly, for her—it drove her wild. Her heart pounded so hard she wasn't going to mention it lest they stop. She wasn't stabbed in the heart!

Pippa stopped arguing with herself when Xander stood, still holding her.

"Let's take this into the bedroom and get you laid out," he said.

She clapped. "Yay! In anticipation of this momentous victory, I used that lotion you both seem to like the smell of so much. Also, I'm not wearing any underwear."

Xander groaned as he put her down gently. She grabbed his shirt in her fist and tugged him to her for a kiss.

"You don't have to hold back. You're not going to hurt me."

"What I want to do to you? It definitely might pull something." He kissed her again, hard, his teeth closing around her bottom lip sharp enough to sting and bring a gasp he eagerly sucked down.

"Well, okay, so don't hang me from a chandelier or

anything like that. Let's stay intermediate-type sexytime adventures until after my next checkup. I'm sure we can save the iron maiden or whatever until then."

Xander laughed, pulling off his shirt and then hers with a little more patience. She was so fucking pretty he just loved looking at her. No matter what she wore. But naked was a particular favorite.

Hamish managed to get himself naked before snatching her leggings and panties off. Then she knelt on the bed and waved a hand at them. "I'm naked and Hamish is naked, but your pants are still on, Xander."

Xander tried not to notice the—admittedly healing well—evidence of the stabbing. They'd recovered the knife at the scene. A hunting knife the authorities figured he'd brought with him from home. He recalled seeing photos of it and being grateful he hadn't even noticed it where it lay a few feet away from where Pippa had been. Big. A powerful blade that could have killed her.

He shivered.

"Don't look at it," she said.

Xander shook his head. "No." He gently touched the skin around it. "I don't avoid it because it's ugly. It's hard for me to think about what you went through. What we could have lost. I need to stop that because it's part of you like your eyes. Like the scar on your right ankle. Evidence not so much that someone hurt you, but that you survived. This is a mark that you fought for your life and won."

She paused, mulling over his words. "All right. Thinking on it like that helps. I remember at some point being so mad at Timothy because he stabbed a place I wanted to get tattooed."

Despite the seriousness of the subject, she still made him laugh. "I can work a tattoo around this easily. We can hide it or display it. Whatever you prefer." Raven had a sleeve Brody had inked, tucking away the scars that had been her way of feeling anything at all during a very dark time. Lots of people got ink as a way to achieve closure or healing from a traumatic event.

"Oh. I like that." Her gaze dropped down to his cock, now freed from his pants and shorts. "I like that too. So many choices." She looked to Hamish and fluttered her lashes.

"In our caution, we've given you reason to feel undesired. That couldn't be further from the truth." Xander reached out to pinch her left nipple, and she hissed, arching into his touch.

Hamish stepped to his side as they took her in, her hair in tousled curls around her face, her eyes wide and dark. She looked back with as much frank appreciation as they gave her.

Xander went to his knees, leaning close to wrap his arms around her waist, pressing his face into her body.

He'd been so focused on being careful—both of them had —and on getting her through the emotional upheaval of the victim impact statement that they'd gone too far the other way. Leave it to Pippa to let them know in her own manner.

His desire had roared back into his body until he felt like he'd burst. The scent of her pussy rose, and he sucked in a deep breath and got to his feet to help her to her back, Hamish on the other side of her.

Pippa looked up at them, her lip caught between her teeth, a flush spreading up her chest and neck. "My husbands," she said softly.

Xander kissed down her ribs, and she slid her fingers through his hair. Hamish echoed his movements as they licked across her belly, pausing to kiss as she drew in a breath in the background.

That she was affected watching them turned Xander on a great deal. It was one of the most scorchingly hot things about their relationship.

They slid her thighs up and then wide, opening her to them totally. Her breathing sped, and when Xander lowered his mouth, so did Hamish. They met at her pussy, kissing her and one another until she made those little breathy, demanding sounds as she got closer and closer to climax.

When Hamish's fist wrapped around his cock, Xander groaned, thrusting into his grip. *Not too far.* He needed to come inside Pippa and very fucking soon. But he didn't need to stop just yet.

When it was clear Hamish was jerking Xander's cock, a molten wave of lust blasted through her. The sight of the two of them together had always been dizzyingly sexy, but right then it was so beautiful it hurt a little.

This was theirs alone. So delicious and sexy and achingly intimate. All their attention on her after the day they'd had, after the emotion of the discussion had brought her to the edge, sharp and hard until need was an ache.

Throbbing until finally it washed over her, climax so intense her teeth tingled. Their hands on her legs, their weight as they leaned in toward her body, the slight sting of Xander's fingertips as they dug into her thighs with enough force to—delightfully—bruise, those things held her safe enough to let go and fly.

And when she opened her eyes, it was to find Xander kissing Hamish as he cuffed Hamish's throat. Similar to the way he held hers, but a notch rougher. From where she lay, she heard Hamish's intake of breath and the guttural moan to follow.

Xander said in a near growl that sent goosepimples racing over her skin, "I'm going to fuck her. And then while you fuck her, you can suck my cock."

Her strangled gasp of pleasure had them both turning while she gulped like a cartoon character. The stuff he said! Filthy and yet full of affection. The combination was a delicious, dark secret that never failed to make her hot all over.

"How does that sound to you?" Hamish asked her in slow, sexy drawl. His hair was the kind of messy it only got during sex. He approximated it on stage, but she knew the difference. This was the real Hamish. His lashes swept down a moment before sliding back, half-mast.

Absolutely beyond speech just then, she nodded enthusiastically.

Xander's chuckle tore her attention from Hamish, right in time to watch the way his forearms looked as he moved her, adjusting one knee up.

"Have I told you how sexy your forearms are?" she asked, dazzled by the ink and the taut skin over muscle honed by tattooing all the time.

"I'm always pleased to hear you find me sexy." He

paused, the head of his cock just brushing her pussy, making her squirm as she tried to get more. "Greedy."

"Yes! For goodness' sake, get in me!"

"Now who's bossy?" he said as he pressed into her body to the root in one stroke that had her arching her back.

"It worked, though," she said.

She made him want to preen, this woman he adored. Wanted to somehow brand himself into her so that she never wanted to forget what he meant to her. Or what she meant to him.

But he sort of lost his ability to think for longer than a few seconds as her cunt hugged him so tight he wheezed in a breath.

In a few moments their rhythm set, clicked into place. She had a way of always looking at him, whatever her emotion was at that moment shining through her eyes. It hit him that she never hid from him when it mattered. That she trusted him to receive the weight of her feelings made him ache, it was so good.

That he'd have it forever was still something he was accepting.

Xander curved himself around her, kissing first her mouth and then Hamish's. Loving her taste on his lips.

"Make her come, baby," Xander told Hamish, who slid a hand down her belly, between her body and Xander's until he got to her clit.

The contact seemed to buzz through her straight up Xander's dick as Hamish teased her, kissing down her neck to her nipple as he slowly worked circles around her clit in time with Xander's movements.

Even as she came all around him, Xander held on, dragging it out as long as he could before he couldn't hold back any longer.

Hamish had nearly climaxed twice between eating her pussy with Xander and then being next to them, making her come, listening to her little, urgent sounds, her sweet/salty taste, mixed with Xander's on his tongue.

It was that connection between them that made everything with them a million times hotter. And when Xander moved to the side, Hamish pulled her close again, and she draped herself over his body like a sensual blanket.

Her weight against him, sleepy and warm, was perfect. "There's my missus," he said, kissing her shoulder.

"Here I am," she agreed, swinging one leg over his waist and sitting up as she straddled his body.

"My absolute favorite view," he murmured as she rose above him. Her hips fit in his palms just as they'd been made for him.

Xander ran his hands down Pippa's arms and then her legs before he moved to Hamish, delivering the same firm strokes until he was simultaneously relaxed and wildly turned on.

She undulated her hips, keeping him deep, the way he liked it best. Ripples of pleasure rolled through him.

His future. The person who fit like a puzzle piece and made everything better for him and Xander.

Then Xander's cock tapped his lips, and his gaze locked on Hamish's. "Open," he said, low and a little dangerous.

Eager to obey, he parted hips lips and took, first the head

and then slowly the rest of Xander in, both working to adjust so their timing was synched as Pippa continued to fuck herself onto Hamish's cock. Xander ran a tender hand over his head and then gathered Hamish's hair in a fist tight enough to bring tears to his eyes.

It was hard and sticky and so mind-blowingly hot, Hamish groaned, awash with desire so thick there was nothing to do but ride it out, let it sweep him up until he thrust up one last time and held her down on him as he came in wave after dizzying wave.

On the heels of Hamish's orgasm, Xander found his own climax, and in the aftermath, Pippa collapsed to her uninjured side, her fingers tangled with Hamish's as they all caught their breath.

"Aren't you glad I made you service me?" she asked, sleepy.

Xander slapped her ass, sending the sound bouncing around the room.

"I need to shower," she said lazily, making no movement to do so. "I'm a mess."

"My favorite," Hamish said, nuzzling her neck.

"Everything's your favorite."

"Everything about you."

Xander snorted. "Come on then. I'll scrub your back."

It was her turn to laugh then. "Perfect. I can't reach my back. So handy."

She scampered off the bed, and they followed.

Xander waited, leaning against the wall in the doorway that led into the lobby of the hotel the Hall family was staying at. The Halls were staying until the following day, but the women, led by Pippa's mother, had taken the small group of children who'd come along to the play area adjacent to the hotel.

Across the street, standing near the corner, Xander's dad raised his left hand, flashed two fingers, and jerked his head to the left slightly.

Showtime.

Cyrus Kelso strolled up, his attention on the ass of the woman walking in front of him, but before he could get inside, Xander stepped in his path, causing Cyrus to bounce off him and back a few steps.

His expression went ugly very fast, but the man with him, Kenton Hall, Pippa's father, had more control. He put a hand on Cyrus's shoulder.

Hamish approached to stand with Xander. Kenton's lip curled.

"We have nothing to say to you," Kenton said.

As if Xander was *asking* to have a conversation?

"Good. Be quiet then, and listen closely," Pippa said as she moved from her place behind Xander.

Neither man had wanted her to be part of this confrontation, but she'd refused, telling them she had to be the one to slay this particular demon or worry over it for the rest of her days.

"Don't interrupt and don't make me repeat myself," she told them quietly. "I'm not coming back. I made that choice fourteen years ago, and I've made it every day since. I'm not marrying Edgar. Least of all because I'm already married."

Cyrus said, "I don't know what you're talking about. You need to get yourself right with God. I'm protecting my family from demons like you."

Xander didn't so much as raise an eyebrow. Instead, he bristled, and it made him even bigger. "Does that mean you'd like to become more acquainted with my displeasure at the way you and your family have harmed my wife?"

"Wife?" Kenton sneered. "Don't use words you can't define, son."

"I'm not your son. My fathers are decent men. And yes. Wife."

"Beautiful ceremony as the sun rose," Hamish said. "The bride was absolutely gorgeous."

"Here's what's going to happen," Pippa said before her father diverted them into an argument over the wedding. His opinion on that didn't matter. "You and everyone connected to you are going to leave me, Rebecca, and Esther alone. For good. There will be no more vandalism. No more calls and letters. No more tracts. You have other children who still live with you. Be satisfied with that."

"You can't tell me what to do," Cyrus scoffed.

"Mary Fairweather." Pippa dropped the name of her father's long-time mistress and watched Kenton's expression change. Surprise. Shock. Then he tried to construct a way out.

She knew her father, knew he was about to talk his way around it, so she landed the blow that would keep everyone out of her face from then on.

"Blue Skies. Which I think is a great name. So many other businesses named Blue Skies, and I'm certain nearly all of them are law-abiding and pay the appropriate taxes, keep a clean payroll, and source their materials from legitimate dealers of safe products." She blinked at her father slowly, watching him go pasty.

"Watch what you say, girl," her father warned.

"I know exactly what I'm saying. And so do you." Pippa looked to Cyrus. "Not only are you part of the Blue Skies *problem*, you—you specifically, Cyrus—filed false statements to the IRS. Every year for the last nine, looks like. Maybe Carl Brush can help you research the possible penalties for that. We had a chat with him not too long ago. Very illuminating."

Hamish's laugh at Cyrus's expression at the mention of his meth dealer was mean, and Pippa went more than a tiny bit tingly at the sound.

Todd had staked out the address they had for Brush in Bellflower, and he'd finally come home. To a very important conversation that had filled in even more blanks in this whole saga.

They'd wondered how Carl Brush had paid his bills when he didn't seem to sell a lot of celebrity media that wasn't about Pippa, Hamish, and Xander. Dealing drugs, including crystal methamphetamine was how he'd managed to keep a roof over his head.

Carl had first met with Cyrus and Timothy in Southern California while the latter were there working for Blue Skies. But over the following eighteen months, Carl expanded his business to a few dozen other members of the group at jobsites in several Western states.

Brush had been in the midst of a multiple-day binge with the others when the stories about Pippa had first come out. In a drug-addled scene, her brother and Cyrus had raged about her. Carl, still trying to make his career as the next host of *Entertainers This Week* happen, saw a way to get a unique angle on the story and make some money while he was at it.

Because when he did a little looking, he saw where Pippa worked. The same custom car and bike shop his second-cousin Trevor did the accounts receivable for. Carl claimed when he first contacted him, Trevor eagerly sold information about her for a hundred and fifty bucks a pop. So he, the drug dealer working with her abuser of a brother incited his cousin who had delusions about some supposed future together into feeding Brush information then used to harm her.

They had answers. Even if they were stupid. And those answers were the ammunition she needed to keep them away from her.

"Here's what will happen. You and the rest of the group will leave me, Rebecca and Esther alone. There will be no further contact. There will be no further attacks on me personally, or anything and anyone connected to me. If this does not happen, all this information will fall into the hands that can best handle it. Move on with your lives like you should have fourteen years ago, or lots of folks will be getting an education about who their husbands, fathers, and business partners are."

Kenton stared at Pippa, who would turn into dust on that spot before she'd break this little staring contest.

"And," Hamish added, "if Brush does another story or is involved in any way with a story about us or Pippa, that would be disastrous. We've spoken to him about that too. Just so you understand."

"Who is Carl Brush?" Kenton demanded of Cyrus.

"Who is Mary Fairweather?" Cyrus demanded back.

"Are we clear? Do we understand one another?" Xander said to them. "There's a zero-tolerance policy here. I will burn you to the ground and salt the earth afterward to protect her. I don't give a shit about you or your cult. Stay the fuck away."

"Fine," Kenton snarled.

Cyrus nodded. "Okay."

Xander slung his arm around Pippa's shoulders and walked past them.

Xander drove them toward Twisted Steel. Their plane had only landed about an hour prior, and they'd wanted her to go home and rest for a few hours. But Pippa wanted to get this part over with, so she said she'd let them take her to lunch and then take a nap *after* they dealt with Trevor.

"I'm thinking on an appropriate gift for your dads and Uncle Cope for getting us all that information. Without it, the shadow of the group would always be lurking."

"My dads were positively gleeful after you finished with your father and Cyrus, and they slunk off. You can bake them something. Or take over that lemon curd you made a while back. You should make extra though. You know, so we'd have some at the apartment."

Happy, Pippa grinned. "I'll make some this week. Several baked goods to thank your mother and also your parents, Hamish."

Hamish leaned forward to touch her shoulder a moment. "I know this is how you show your affection, so I'm all in support. Just also know they did it because they love you, and if you give a present for it, do it so they know you understand it's not obligation, but love in return."

Oh. That was lovely and so insightful. "All right. I...that's a very important distinction. Thank you." She swallowed back her emotion. "Well, my father will never risk his position as bishop. He could survive a single mistress. Probably. If she was within the group. But Mary isn't the first. Nor is she within the group. She's an outsider. She's twice divorced and lives in town. He can't recover from that."

"Fuck that guy," Xander said as they got off the freeway.

"As for Cyrus. He and my brother have not only done drugs habitually, their dealer has been meddling in their internal business for juicy stories. He's a...what was that word, Xander? Chonk? No, that's the fat cat at your parents' house. Chode! That's the one."

"What are you teaching our girl?" Hamish teased.

"Anyway," Pippa continued, "between the tax fraud, the drug charges, and the mistresses, they'll stay away. Carl Brush can blow a goat. Don't blame Xander for that one, I heard Rebecca use it."

Xander chuckled as they turned into the drive that led to the employee lot and the gate that opened for them once she'd tapped her employee ID card to the pad.

"This is our insurance policy," Xander said as he parked. "This keeps them out of our lives even when Timothy's sentence is done."

"Okay. Thank you both for working with Todd, Ben, and Cope to put this grand plan into action," Pippa said. "And now you're going to hate what I'm about to say, but I need to speak to Trevor on my own. You can wait outside, just a few feet away. But I need to talk to him first."

They both made sounds she knew were the opening salvo in denials of that statement.

Hamish said, "He helped them hurt you."

"We know how the pieces all fit and we've handled everyone else. But I..." she chewed on her bottom lip, "...I need to understand why he did it. It's absurd. You want to protect me. And just so you understand, I do feel protected. Despite all the chaos out there in the universe, I know that when I'm with you two, I'm going to be okay. This is nearly finished. Let's see it through and go get pasta afterward."

He and Hamish glanced at one another and then sighed.

Once inside, they headed up to Carmella's area. Duke was there already, waiting for them. He'd texted that as soon as

Pippa was finished speaking with Trevor, the partners were going to fire him and have him escorted from the building. Carmella had cut his final check. There would be no recommendation. There'd been a scuffle because Mick wanted to underline that with his fists, and while Duke and Asa agreed with the sentiment, they also knew it would complicate things and end up upsetting Pippa more.

After she went over what she wanted to do a few more times in her head, she stepped to Trevor's door, tapping on the jamb. They took a chance he hadn't been contacted by anyone about that bit of delightful blackmail from earlier that morning, and given his reaction when she stepped into his office, they'd been right. His cousin had given him up rather easily, and the threat Todd had made was sufficiently scary, so he hadn't bothered. Good.

"Pippa. When did you get back?" he asked.

She sat in a chair near the open doorway. "An hour ago. Did you hear? The insurance company declared my truck a total loss." He'd been looking at her, but at that his gaze skittered away. "The damage done when you gave your cousin Carl the information to pass to his friends in Arizona? Like how to get into the lot, and where the camera pointing at Gretchen was so they could push it out of focus? Remember that? It was when I was still in the hospital recovering from emergency surgery to repair a damaged artery from a stab wound. Anyway. They said it looked like the vandals knew exactly how to damage a vehicle to render it unsalvageable."

She cocked her head as he realized she'd said that bit about his friends in Arizona.

"What are you talking about?" he wheezed.

Pippa curled her lip. "Here's what we're going to do. I know you're the one who gave personal information about me to Carl Brush. I know you also have been in contact with my father in the delusion that somehow you and I would go live in Arizona in a church compound, and they'd give me to you like I was luggage you won on a game show. I can't be traded like a baseball player."

The rage of it still burned low in her belly. All these men she didn't even have a relationship with had decided what her future would be.

Trevor opened his mouth, and she shook her head and wagged her finger to shut him up.

"I know about Carl and the drugs. I know he paid you for info on me. I know so many *completely ridiculous* things, but I don't know what exactly motivated you to do any of this. To me. Someone who has never done anything to hurt you. You're going to tell me. And then you'll lose your job."

She sat back. If she pretended she was on a soap opera, it was easier to fake being confident.

"And if I don't tell you? What are you going to do? The cops aren't going to care. You have nothing."

Well, that made it easier to be mean to him to get him to do what she needed him to. "You're so right that the cops probably won't care. But what I do know, is that I can—and will—let every single workplace you apply to that I find out about—don't think for a second I won't, this world is small and unlike you, I'm well liked—and let them know what you did to me while I was in the ICU. I will show up in your neighborhood. At your favorite coffee shop. I will chitchat with every woman unfortunate enough to get your romantic attention. I will pay to put the footage of my attack in movie theaters and local television, complete with the information that you helped that happen."

He gaped at her, the color draining from his face.

Channeling her inner diva, she leaned forward and said, "*You're* weak. Soft. You think I'm nothing more than someone you put your dick in and clean your house? They never would have let you marry me anyway, you absolute bag of concrete. You wanted to ruin my life? I'm happy to educate you on why *I'm* anything but weak. I'm feeling very mean, so I almost hope you punk out and take the coward's way. It's up to you. What's it going to be? Shall I be your shadow for the next however long? Let everyone in your orbit know exactly what you are?"

"I didn't know how far they'd go," he said.

"You're a liar. Tick-tock, Trevor. Time's up."

"You sold yourself away for cheap! It was bad enough when it was just the musician. Then there was the tattooist. And worst of all, *both* of them. I had no chance against that. I'm the nice guy. No one wants the nice guy. After those two burned through all your beauty, they'd move on to the next skank, and you'd be used up. Like all the rest. So when my cousin contacted me and offered me fifty bucks a pop to give him information about you, he told me you had family back home who only wanted you safe with them. You had a life where you would be respected instead of debasing yourself with Xander and Hamish. I even contacted your father directly to talk to him because Carl was writing disrespectful things about you. Your father told me the truth. Offered me a place there because I can give you what you need. Not those two perverts!"

He yelled the last, and she knew she only had a short

time left before those two perverts in the hall came in and started swinging.

"Get yourself under control, Trevor," she said as icily as she could, channeling a character she'd seen in a movie recently. The super-bitchy mother-in-law.

"Your brother went over the edge. He wasn't supposed to hurt you like that. It was the damned drugs. Stupid fucking Carl He was always this way. I only saw him once every few years when we were kids and even that was enough to know he was a loser. But your father and me? We just wanted to get rid of all the things you used to stay out here in the world instead of returning home. You'd realize your mistake and accept what you were meant for. We could be so happy. We can still make this a reality."

Not even mixed concrete. Just a bag. No water. "Did Carl sell you meth too? Is that why you're so hopelessly clueless? By the way, he told me it was a hundred and fifty bucks a pop for information about me, so you're lying, or you got played." There were so many very bad words she wanted to say. "You asked me out years ago. I said no. And from that you have built this fantasy you have done me violence to protect. Knowing what they were capable of, you continued to help them."

Pippa took a deep breath and stood. He opened his mouth, and she held a hand up.

"You're not a nice guy. Being nice is like being rich or powerful. If you have to tell everyone you are, you really aren't."

A blush of shame marked his cheeks. Good.

"You come near me or mine or cause trouble for any of us at any point in the future and I'll start my little campaign, and as a bonus I'll let Hamish and Xander do what they begged me to on the way over here. Whatever job you do next, it better not have any access to private employee files, or you might have to disclose your inability to obey workplace rules about them. Have the day you deserve."

She went to the doorway and moved to the side as Asa, Duke, and Mick went into the office and shut the door at their back.

There they were. Having waited because she asked them to. Because they understood she had to deal with this herself to get real closure.

Love swamped her as she held both her hands out. "Come on then. Take your wife to lunch."

They took hold, both pulling her toward them. "You've got a deal," Xander said.

"Dessert's on me," Hamish added.

ACKNOWLEDGMENTS

No author does this alone. I am so blessed to have support in my life!

I want to thank my wonderful readers. Without you all, I'd just be talking to myself in weird voices all day.

Thanks always go to my spouse, who through the chaos of being married to a creative person (some might say dramatic, I say, entertaining), remains steadfast, hands me snacks, listens to all my ideas is my best cheerleader.

Sasha Knight – your edits were amazing. It's so hard to manage the start of a new author/editor relationship and you were fantastic all the way through. You worked me to the point I may have muttered some unkind things I never really meant (I promise). Thank you for helping me whip this book into shape.

Frauke at Croco Designs – from pretty much the start of my writing career, you've created amazing covers, graphics, websites and have helped me countless times with myriad aspects of publishing. Thank you.

Tony Mauro – The covers for the Brown and Delicious books are some of my all time favorites and I'm thrilled you've done such amazing jobs with Reckless and Ignition. I can't wait to see what else you've got in store for these characters.

SIGN UP FOR LAUREN'S NEWSLETTER

Don't want to miss Lauren Dane's latest book?
Sign up for Lauren's newsletter and get notified when she
has a new one out.

www.laurendane.com/newsletter

COMING UNDONE

INSIDE OUT

NEVER ENOUGH

LAID OPEN

DRAWN TOGETHER

————

CASCADIA WOLVES

Paranormal Romance

RELUCTANT MATE (formerly *Reluctant*)

PACK ENFORCER (formerly *Enforcer*)

WOLVES' TRIAD (formerly *Tri Mates*)

WOLF UNBOUND

ALPHA'S CHALLENGE (formerly Standoff)

BONDED PAIR (formerly *Fated*)

TWICE BITTEN (formerly *Unconditional*)

————

CHASE BROTHERS

Contemporary Romance

GIVING CHASE

TAKING CHASE

CHASED

MAKING CHASE

CHASE BROTHERS: COMPLETE COLLECTION

———

CHERCHEZ WOLF PACK

Paranormal Romance

WOLF'S ASCENSION

SWORN TO THE WOLF

———

CO-WRITTEN WITH MEGAN HART

Contemporary Romance

TAKING CARE OF BUSINESS

NO RESERVATIONS

———

DE LA VEGA CATS

Paranormal Romance

TRINITY

REVELATION

BENEATH THE SKIN

DELICIOUS

Contemporary Romance

SWAY

TART

LUSH

DIABLO LAKE

Paranormal Romance

MOONSTRUCK

PROTECTED

AWAKENED

FEDERATION CHRONICLES / PHANTOM CORPS

Sci-Fi/Futuristic Romance

UNDERCOVER

RELENTLESS

Phantom Corps:

INSATIABLE

MESMERIZED

CAPTIVATED

————

GODDESS WITH A BLADE

Urban Fantasy

GODDESS WITH A BLADE

BLADE TO THE KEEP

BLADE ON THE HUNT

AT BLADE'S EDGE

WRATH OF THE GODDESS

BLOOD AND BLADE

BAD BLOOD

GODDESS WITH A BLADE VOL.1

GODDESS WITH A BLADE VOL.2

————

HURLEY BOYS

Contemporary Romance

THE BEST KIND OF TROUBLE

BROKEN OPEN

BACK TO YOU

————

INK AND CHROME

Contemporary Romance

OPENING UP

FALLING UNDER

COMING BACK

RECKLESS

IGNITION

———

METAMORPHOSIS SERIES

Sci-Fi/Futuristic Dystopian Romance

ALL THAT REMAINS

ALL THE LITTLE PIECES (*coming soon*)

———

PETAL, GEORGIA

Contemporary Romance

ONCE AND AGAIN

LOST IN YOU

COUNT ON ME

———

WHISKEY SHARP

Contemporary Romance

UNRAVELED

JAGGED

TORN

SUGAR

———

SINGLE TITLES

BELIEVE

CAKE

LAND'S END

SECOND CHANCES

SENSUAL MAGIC

STRIPPED

———

ANTHOLOGIES

THREE TO TANGO

(including *Dirty/Bad/Wrong*)

ABOUT LAUREN DANE

The story goes like this: While on pregnancy bed rest, Lauren Dane had plenty of down time so her husband took her comments about "giving that writing thing a serious go" to heart and brought home a secondhand laptop. She wrote her first book on it before it gave up the ghost. Even better, she sold that book and never looked back.

Today Lauren is a *New York Times* and *USA Today* bestselling author of over sixty novels and novellas across several genres.

For more information:
www.laurendane.com

www.ingramcontent.com/pod-product-compliance
Lightning Source LLC
Chambersburg PA
CBHW060514160726
47991CB00001B/31